Praise for SMOKE AND MIRRORS

". . . a master of urban fantasy."   —*Library Journal*

"Huff is one of the best writers we have at contemporary
fantasy, particularly with a supernatural twist, and her
characters are almost always the kind we remember later."
           —*Chronicle*

"This latest offering is just as gothic and horror-filled as its
prequel. The conversational writing is a pleasure, fitting the
occasional quip into the mounting tension with ease. Huff
continues to add many details of filming and life on the set
of a television show while maintaining suspense."
           —*VOYA*

Praise for SMOKE AND SHADOWS

"Huff's long-awaited addition to her popular Henry Fitzroy
series. . . . The author's delightfully light touch lends a
sense of timeliness to this effortlessly told fantasy mystery."
           —*Library Journal*

"Lots of action and amusing show-biz detail keep things
moving for a fun dark-fantasy adventure."   —*Locus*

"The Henry Fitzroy vampire detective novels have always
been my favorite from Tanya Huff . . . has the feel of those
earlier books . . . suspenseful and well written."
           —*Chronicle*

D0958774

SMOKE
AND
MIRRORS

♠ ♣ ♦ ♥

TANYA HUFF

DAW BOOKS, INC.

DONALD A. WOLLHEIM, FOUNDER

375 Hudson Street, New York, NY 10014

ELIZABETH R. WOLLHEIM
SHEILA E. GILBERT
PUBLISHERS

http://www.dawbooks.com

First Paperback Printing, June 2006
1 2 3 4 5 6 7 8 9 10

DAW TRADEMARK REGISTERED
U.S. PAT. OFF. AND FOREIGN COUNTRIES
—MARCA REGISTRADA
HECHO EN U.S.A.

PRINTED IN THE U.S.A.

For Judith and Dave
who opened the door
and then gently shoved
me through it.

One

ABOUT A THIRD of the way down the massive wooden staircase the older of the two tuxedo-clad men paused, head up, nostrils flaring as though he were testing a scent on the air. "We're not . . . alone."

"Well, there's at least another twenty invited guests," his companion began lightly.

"Not what I meant." Red-gold hair gleamed as he turned first one way then the other. "There's something . . . else."

"Something *else?*" the younger man repeated, suspiciously studying the portrait of the elderly gentleman in turn-of-the-century clothing hanging beside him. The portrait, contrary to expectations, continued to mind its own business.

"Something . . . evil."

"Don't you think you're overreacting just a . . ." The husky voice trailed off as he stared over the banister, down into the wide entrance hall. His fingers tightened on the polished wood of the railing as green eyes widened. "Raymond, I think you'd better have a look at this."

Raymond Dark turned—slowly—and snarled, the extended points of his canine teeth clearly visible.

"And cut!" Down by the front door, Peter Hudson pushed his headphones back around his neck, peered around the bank of monitors, and up at the stars of *Darkest Night.* "Two things, gentlemen. First, Mason; what's with the pausing before the last word in every line?"

Mason Reed, aka Raymond Dark, vampire detective and currently syndicated television's sexiest representative of the bloodsucking undead, glared down at the director. "I was attempting to make banal dialogue sound profound."

"Yeah? Nice try. Unfortunately, it sounded like you were doing a bad Shatner, which—while I'm in no way dissing the good Captain Kirk—is not quite the effect we want here. And Lee," he continued without giving Mason a chance to argue, "what's on your shoulder? Your right shoulder," he added as Lee Nicholas aka James Taylor Grant tried to look at both shoulders at once. "Actually, more the upper sleeve."

A streak of white, about half an inch wide, ran from just under the shoulder seam diagonally four inches down the sleeve of Lee's tux.

He frowned. "It looks like paint."

Mason touched it with a fingertip and then pointed at the incriminating white smudge down at the entrance hall and the director. "It *is* paint. He must've brushed up against the wall in the second-floor bathroom."

Two of the episode's pivotal scenes were to be shot in the huge bathroom and one of the painters had spent the morning giving ceiling and walls a quick coat of white semi-gloss.

"That's impossible," Lee protested. "I wasn't even *in* the second-floor bathroom and besides, this wasn't there when Brenda delinted us."

"Brenda delinted us fifteen minutes before Peter called action," Mason reminded him. "Lots of time for you to wander off and take a tinkle."

"Oh, no." Lee checked to make sure that the boom

was gone, then dropped his voice below eavesdropping range. "*You* wandered off to suck on a cancer stick, I didn't go anywhere."

"So you say, but this says different."

"I wasn't in that bathroom!"

"Look, Lee, just admit you screwed up and let's move on."

"I didn't screw up!"

"All right then, it was a subconscious—and I'd have to say somewhat pathetic—attempt to draw attention to yourself."

"Don't even . . ."

"Gentlemen!" Peter's voice dragged their attention back down to the foyer. "I don't care where the paint came from, but it's visible in that last bit where Lee turns and as I'd like him to keep turning—Tony, run Lee's tux jacket out to Brenda so she can get that paint off before it dries. Everett, if you could take the shine off Mason's forehead before we have to adjust the light levels, I'd appreciate it. And somebody, get me a coffee and two aspirin."

Tony froze halfway to the stairs. As the only production assistant on location—as the only production assistant who'd ever remained with CB Productions and *Darkest Night* for any length of time—he was generally the "somebody" Peter'd just referred to.

"*I'll get him the co . . . shkeeffee, Tony.*" The voice of Adam Paelous, the show's first assistant director sounded in Tony's ear, pushing through the omnipresent static. "*You get the tux . . .*"

One finger against his ear jack, Tony strained to hear over the interference. The walkie-talkies had been acting up since they'd arrived at the location shoot. It was impossible to get a clear signal and the batteries were draining at about five times the normal speed.

"*. . . out to wardrobe. The exci . . . shsquit of watching paint dry might kill us all.*"

Waving an acknowledgment to Adam across the

entrance hall, Tony jogged up the stairs. It had definitely been a less than exciting morning—even given the hurry-up-and-wait nature of television production. *And there's not a damned thing wrong with boring,* Tony reminded himself. Especially when "not boring" involved gates to other worlds, evil wizards, and sentient shadows that weren't so much homicidal as . . . actually, homicidal pretty much covered it.

Everyone else at CB Productions—with the exception of CB himself—had no memory of the metaphysical experience that had very nearly turned the soundstage into ground zero for an otherworld/evil wizard/homicidal shadow invasion. Everyone else probably slept with the lights out. After almost two months, Tony was finally able to manage it four nights out of five.

Lee was out of the tux and frowning down at the paint by the time Tony reached him.

"I didn't go into the upstairs bathroom," he reiterated as he handed it over.

"I believe you." Fully aware that he was smiling stupidly up at an explicitly defined straight boy—or as explicit as the pictures the tabloids could get with an extended telephoto lens—Tony folded the jacket carefully so the paint wouldn't smear and headed back down the stairs thinking, in quick succession, *It's still warm.* And: *You're pathetic.*

He slid over against the banister to give Everett and his makeup case room to get up the stairs, wondering why Mason—who was a good twenty years younger and thirty kilos lighter—couldn't have come down to the entrance hall instead. *Oh, wait, it's Mason. What the hell am I thinking?* Mason Reed was fully aware of every perk star billing entitled him to and had no intention of compromising on any of them.

"That man sweats more than any actor I've ever met," Everett muttered as Tony passed. "But don't quote me on that."

Just what, exactly, Everett had once been misquoted

on was a mystery. And likely to remain that way as even a liberal application of peach schnapps had failed to free up the story although Tony had learned more about butt waxing than he'd ever wanted to know.

Jacket draped across his hands and held out like he was delivering an organ for transplant, Tony raced across the entrance hall, out the air-lock entry—its stained glass covered with black fabric to keep out the daylight—sped across the wide porch, and pounded down the half dozen broad stone steps to the flagstone path that led through the overgrown gardens and eventually to the narrow drive. *Time is money* was one of the three big truisms of the television industry. No one seemed to be able to agree on just what exactly number two was, but Tony suspected that number three involved the ease with which production assistants could be replaced.

The wardrobe makeup trailer had been parked just behind the craft services truck which had, in turn, been snugged up tight against the generator.

Brenda, who'd been sitting on the steps having a coffee, stood as Tony approached, dumping an indignant black cat off her lap. "What happened?"

"There's paint on Lee's jacket."

"Paint?" She hurried out to meet him, hands outstretched. "How did that happen?"

"Lee doesn't know." Given that Tony believed Lee, Mason's theory didn't bear repeating. Handing the jacket over, he followed her up into the trailer. The cat snorted at her or him or both of them and stalked away.

"Was he in the second-floor bathroom?"

"No." It was a common theory apparently.

"Weird." Her hand in the sleeve, she held the paint out for inspection. "It looks like someone stroked it on with a fingertip."

It did. The white was oval at the top and darker—fading down to a smudge of gray at the bottom of the four-inch streak.

"Probably just someone being an asshole."

"Mason?" she wondered, picking up a spray bottle and bending over the sleeve.

Tony stared at her back in disbelief. There was no way Mason would do anything to make Lee the center of attention. Not generally, and especially not now, not when at last count Lee's fan mail had risen to equal that of the older actor. And Mason'd always been particularly sensitive to anything he perceived as a threat to his position as the star of *Darkest Night*. That wasn't an opinion Tony'd actually express out loud, however— not to Brenda. The wardrobe assistant was one of those rare people in the business who, in spite of exposure, continued to buy into the celebrity thing. For most, the "Oh, my God, it's . . ." faded after a couple of artistic hissy fits extended the workday past the fifteen-hour mark.

Also, she was a bit of a suck-up, and the last thing he wanted was her currying favor by telling Mason what he thought. Well, maybe not the last thing he wanted—a repeat of the homicidal shadow experience currently topped his never again list, but having Mason Reed pissed off at him was definitely in the top ten since Mason Reed sufficiently pissed off meant Tony Foster unemployed.

Realizing she was still waiting for an answer, he said, "No, I don't think it was Mason."

"Of course not."

Hey, you brought it up. He picked up a scrap of trim . . .

"Don't touch that."

. . . and put it back down again. "Sorry."

"Are you taking the jacket back or is Lee coming out to get it? Or I could take it back and make sure it looks all right under the lights."

"You could, but since I'm here . . ."

"And as it happens, so am I."

They turned together, pulled around by an unmistakable rough velvet voice to see Lee coming into the trailer.

"There's another mark on the pants." He turned as he spoke.

It looked as if someone had pressed a finger against the bottom of Lee's right cheek and stroked up. Tony thought very hard about cold showers, police holding cells, and Homer Simpson.

Lee continued around until he faced them again, toed off the black patent leather shoes, and unzipped his fly. "I swear it wasn't there earlier."

"The jacket would have covered most of it," Brenda reminded him in a breathy tone Tony found extremely annoying. He held on to that annoyance—it was a handy shield against a potentially embarrassing reaction to Lee stepping out of his pants and passing them over.

Clad from the waist down in gray boxer briefs and black socks, Lee wandered over to the empty makeup chair and sat. The chair squealed a protest. "I have no idea how it happened. I swear I wasn't anywhere near wet paint."

"Of course you weren't," Brenda purred. Lifting the jacket off the ironing board she handed it to Tony, her heated gaze never leaving Lee's face until she had to lay out the pants. She made up for the loss of eye contact by taking her time caressing the fabric smooth.

Rumor insisted that Brenda and Lee had recently shared a heated moment on the floor of the wardrobe department while Alison Larkin—the head of wardrobe— was off rummaging through charity sales for costumes her budget would cover. Given the intimate way Brenda spread her hand and pressed it down next to the paint to hold the fabric still, Tony had to admit it looked like gossip had gotten it right. Standing there, while she spritzed and then rubbed slow circles over the ass of Lee's pants, he felt like a voyeur.

And he was definitely odd man out.

"Listen, Tony, as long as Lee's here, there's no need for you to stay." Apparently, Brenda thought so, too.

"Yeah, I should go."

"Yes, you should." *Because the moment you're out the door and we're finally alone, I'm going to show that man what a real woman can give him.*

He had to admire the amount of bad fifties subtext she could layer under three words.

"I'll tell Peter you'll be back when Brenda's finished with you," he said handing Lee the jacket. The expression on the actor's face was interesting—and a little desperate. Desperate for him to leave? Desperate about him leaving? Desperately seeking Susan? What? Tony was getting nothing.

"Are you still here?" *What part of we want to be alone don't you understand?*

Well, nothing from Lee. Plenty from Brenda.

"Tony!" Adam's voice rose out of the background noise. *"The minute that paint's . . ."* A couple of words got lost in static. *". . . get Lee back here. We've got a shitload of stuff to cover today."*

He dropped his mouth toward the microphone clipped to his collar. "Roger that, Adam."

"The point ishsput to make sure no one's getting rogered."

"Yeah, I got that." Most of it, anyway.

Adam had obviously heard the rumor, too, although his choice of euphemism was interesting. Rogered?

"How much longer?"

"Jacket's done, pants are . . ." Tony glanced over at Brenda and shrugged apologetically when she glared. ". . . pants are finished now. Lee's dressing . . ." The pants slid quickly up over long, muscular, tanned legs. Feet shoved into shoes and Lee was at the door, mouthing *Sorry, gotta run* back toward the wardrobe assistant. "And we're moving."

"You're shoving?"

"Moving!"

"Glad to finally friggin' hear it. Out."

They were almost to the path before Lee spoke. "Yes, we did."

Tony shrugged. "I didn't ask."

"And it was a stupid thing to do."

"I didn't say." Brenda was standing in the doorway watching them leave. He knew it without turning. Feeling the impact of metaphorical scissors between his shoulder blades, he increased the space between them to the maximum the path would allow.

"It was just . . . I mean, we were both . . . And she was . . ."

"Hey." Tony raised a hand before details started emerging. "Two consenting adults. Not my business."

"Right." As the path finally lined up with the front door, Lee stopped. "It's a great house, isn't it?"

"Yeah, it's cool." Tony had been ready for the change of subject—guys, especially guys who weren't exactly friends, had a low level of TMI. Actually, since Lee wasn't the kind of guy to brag about his conquests, Tony was a little surprised he'd even brought it up.

"I asked Mr. Brummel if he thought the owners might sell."

"What did he say?"

"This isn't your average house, boy. You don't own a house like this. It owns you."

Lee's impression of the caretaker's weirdly rhythmic delivery was bang on. Tony snickered. A middle-aged man in rumpled clothes, scuffed work boots, and an obvious comb over, Mr. Brummel—no first name offered—had taken the caretaker clichés to heart, embracing them with all the fervor of someone about to shout, "And I'd have gotten away with it, too, if not for you meddling kids."

But he was right; Caulfield House was anything but average.

Built around the turn of the last century by Creighton

Caulfield, who'd made a fortune in both mining and timber, the house rested on huge blocks of pale granite with massive beams of western red cedar holding up the porch roof. Three stories high with eight bedrooms, a ballroom, a conservatory, and servants' quarters on the third floor, it sat tucked away in Deer Lake Park at the end of a long rutted path too overgrown to be called a road. Matt, the freelance location finder CB Productions generally employed, had driven down Deer Lake Drive to have a look at Edgar House—which turned out to be far too small to accommodate the script. Following what he called a hunch, although Tony suspected he'd gotten lost—it wouldn't be the first time—he spotted a set of ruts and followed them. Chester Bane, the CB of CB Productions, had taken one look at the digital images Matt had shot of the house he'd stumbled on at the end of the ruts, and decided it was perfect for *Darkest Night*.

Although well within the boundaries of the park, Caulfield House remained privately owned and all but forgotten. Tony had no idea how CB had gotten permission to use the building, but shouting had figured prominently—shouting into the phone, shouting behind the closed door of his office, shouting into his cell as he crossed the parking lot ignoring the cars pulling out and causing two fender benders as his staff tried to avoid hitting him. Evidence suggested that CB felt volume could succeed when reason failed, and his track record seemed to support his belief.

But the house *was* perfect in spite of the profanely expressed opinions of the drivers who'd had to maneuver the generator, the craft services truck, two equipment trucks, the wardrobe/makeup trailer, and the honey wagon down the rutted road close enough to be of any use. Fortunately, as CB had rented the entire house for the week, he had no compunction about having dressing rooms set up in a couple of the bedrooms. He'd only brought in the honey wagon when Mr. Brummel had informed him what it would cost to replace the elderly septic system if it broke down under the additional input.

The huge second-floor bathroom had therefore been painted but was off-limits as far as actually using it. The painters had left the window open to help clear the fumes and Tony glanced up to see the bottom third of the sheer white curtain blowing out over the sill.

He frowned. "Did you see that?"

"The curtain?"

"No, beyond the curtain, in the room. I thought I saw someone looking down at us."

Lee snorted and started walking again, stepping over a sprawling mass of plants that had spilled out of the garden onto the path. "Probably Mason sneaking a smoke by the window. He likely figures the smell of the paint'll cover the stink."

It made sense, except . . .

"Mason's in black," Tony argued, hurrying to catch up. "Whoever this was, they were wearing something light."

"Maybe he took the jacket off so he wouldn't get paint on it. Maybe that's where he went for his earlier smoke and maybe he did a little finger painting on my ass when he got back." One foot raised above the top step, Lee paused and shook his head. "No, I'm pretty sure I'd remember that." Half turning, he grinned down at Tony on the step below. "It seems I have a secret admirer."

Before Tony could decide if he was supposed to read more into that than could possibly be there, Lee was inside and Adam's voice was telling him to "*. . . get your ass in gefffst, Tony. We don't have all fissssking day.*"

Fissssking had enough static involved it almost hurt. Fiddling with the frequency on his walkie-talkie as he followed Lee into the house, Tony had a feeling that the communication difficulties were going to get old fast.

♠

"He peeped you. Not the actor, the other one."

"Don't be ridiculous, Stephen."

"Well, he looked like he saw you."

"He saw the curtain blowing out the window, that's all. I'm very good at staying out of sight." Her tone sharpened. "*I'm* not the one that people keep spotting, am I?"

"Those were accidents." His voice hovered between sulky and miserable. "I didn't even know those hikers were there and I don't care what Graham says, I hate hiding."

Comforting now. "I know."

"And besides, I never take the kind of chances you do. Truth, Cassie, what were you thinking, marking him a second time?"

She smiled and glanced down at the smudge of paint on one finger. "I was thinking that since I'd gotten him to take off his jacket, maybe I could get him to take off his pants. Come on." Taking his hand, she pulled him toward the door. "I want to see what they're doing now."

♠

"Raymond, I think you'd better have a look at this."

"Cut and print! That was excellent work, gentlemen." Tossing his headphones onto the shelf under the monitor, Peter turned to his director of photography. "How much time do you need to reset for scene eight?"

Sorge popped a throat lozenge into his mouth and shrugged. "Shooting from down here . . . fifteen minutes, maybe twenty. No more. When we move to the top of the stairs . . ."

"Don't borrow trouble." He raised his voice enough to attract the attention of his 1AD . . . "Adam, tell them they've got twenty minutes to kill." . . . and lowered it again as he pivoted a hundred and eighty degrees to face his script supervisor. "Tina, let's you and I go over that next scene. There'll be a bitch of a continuity problem if we're not careful and I don't need a repeat of episode twelve."

"At least we know there's ninety-one people watching the show," she pointed out as she stood.

Peter snorted. "I still think it was one geek with ninety-one e-mail addresses."

As they moved off into the dining room and the techs moved in to shove the video village out into the actual entryway where it wouldn't be in the shot, Adam stepped out into the middle of the foyer and looked up at the two actors. "You've got fifteen, guys."

"I'll be in my dressing room." Turning on one heel, Mason headed back up the stairs.

"If anyone needs me, I'll be in my dressing room as well." Lee grimaced, reached back, and yanked at his pants. "These may dry faster off my ass."

Mouse, his gray hair more a rattail down his back and physically the complete opposite of his namesake—no one had ever referred to him as meek and lived to speak of it—stepped out from behind his camera and whistled. "You want to drop trou, don't let us stop you."

Someone giggled.

Tony missed Lee's response as he realized the highly unlikely sound could only have come from Kate, Mouse's camera assistant. He wouldn't have bet money on Kate knowing *how* to giggle. He wasn't entirely certain she knew how to laugh.

"Tony," Adam's hand closed over his shoulder as Lee followed Mason up the stairs and both actors disappeared down the second-floor hall. "I saw Mason talking with Karen from craft services earlier. Go make sure she didn't add any bagels to his muffin basket."

"And if she did?"

"Haul ass upstairs and make sure he doesn't eat one."

"You want me to wrestle the bagel out of Mason's hand?"

"If that's where it is." Adam grinned and patted him manfully on the shoulder—where manfully could be defined as *better you than me, buddy.* "If he's actually taken a bite, I want you to wrestle it out of his mouth."

Mason loved bagels, but the dental adhesive attaching Raymond Dark's fangs to his teeth just wasn't up to the required chewing. After a couple of forty-minute delays while Everett replaced the teeth, and one significantly longer delay after the right fang had been accidentally swallowed, CB had instituted the no-bagels-in-Mason's-dressing-room rule. Since Mason hadn't had to ultimately retrieve the tooth—that job had fallen to Jennifer, his personal assistant who, in Tony's opinion, couldn't possibly be paid enough—he'd chosen to see it as a suggestion rather than a rule and did what he could to get around it.

As a result Karen from craft services found herself under a determined assault by a man who combined good looks and charm with all the ethical consideration of a cat. No one blamed her on those rare occasions she'd been unable to resist.

Today, no one knew where she was.

She wasn't at the table or the truck and there wasn't time enough to search further. Grabbing a pot of black currant jam off the table, Tony headed up the stairs two steps at a time, hoping Mason's midmorning nosh hadn't already brought the day to a complete stop.

As the star of *Darkest Night,* Mason had taken the master suite as his dressing room. Renovated in the fifties, it took up half the front of the second floor and included a bedroom, a closet/dressing room, and a small bathroom. Provided he kept flushing to a minimum, Mr. Brummel had cleared this bathroom for Mason's personal use. Lee had to use the honey wagon like every one else.

All the doors that led off the second-floor hall were made of the same Douglas fir that dominated the rest of the house, but they—and the trim surrounding them—had been stained to look like mahogany. Tony, who in a pinch could tell the difference between plywood and MDF, had been forced to endure a long lecture on the fir-as-mahogany issue from the gaffer who carved themed chess sets in his spare time. The half finished knight in WWF regalia that he'd pulled from his pocket *had* been impressive.

Hand raised to knock on the door to Mason's room, Tony noticed that both the upper panels had been patched. In the dim light of the second-floor hall, the patches were all but invisible, but up close he could see the faint difference in the color of the stain. There was something familiar about their shape, but he couldn't . . .

Hand still raised, he jumped back as the door jerked open.

Mason stared out at him, wide-eyed. "There's something in my bathroom!"

"Something?" Tony asked, trying to see if both fangs were still in place.

"Something!"

"Okay." About to suggest plumbing problems were way outside his job description and that he should go get Mr. Brummel, Tony changed his mind at Mason's next words.

"It was crouched down between the shower and the toilet."

"It?"

"I couldn't see exactly, it was all shadows . . ."

Oh, crap. "Maybe I'd better go have a look." Before Mason could protest—before he could change his mind and run screaming, he was crossing the bedroom, crossing the dressing room, and opening the bathroom door. The sunlight through the windows did nothing to improve the color scheme, but it did chase away any and all shadows. Tony turned toward the toilet and the corner shower unit and frowned. He couldn't figure out what the actor might have seen since there wasn't room enough between them for . . .

Something.

Rocking in place.

Forward.

Back.

Hands clasped around knees, tear-stained face lifted to the light.

And nothing.

Just a space far too small for the bulky body that hadn't quite been there.

Skin prickling between his shoulder blades, jar of black currant jam held in front of him like a shield, Tony took a step into the room. Shadows flickered across the rear wall, filling the six inches between toilet and shower with writhing shades of gray. Had that been all he'd seen?

Stupid question.

No.

So what now? Was he supposed to do something about it?

Whatever it was, the rocking and crying didn't seem actively dangerous.

"Well, Foster?"

"Fuck!" He leaped forward and spun around. With his heart pounding so loudly he could hardly hear himself think, he gestured out the window at the cedar branches blowing across the glass and lied through his teeth. "There's your shadow."

Then the wind dropped again and the shadows disappeared.

Mason ran a hand up through his hair and glanced around the room. "Of course. Now you see them, now you don't." *I wasn't frightened,* his tone added, as his chin rose. *Don't think for a moment I was.* "You're a little jumpy, aren't you?"

"I didn't hear you behind me." Which was the truth because he hadn't—although the admiring way he said it was pure actor manipulation. Working in Television 101—keep the talent placated.

As expected, Mason preened. "Well, yes, I can move cat quiet when I want to."

In Tony's admittedly limited experience, the noise cats made thudding through apartments was completely disproportionate to their size, but Mason clearly liked the line, so he nodded a vague agreement.

"It's fucking freezing in here . . ."

Maybe not freezing but damned cold.

"Is that jam for me?"

Jam? He followed Mason's line of sight to his hand. "Oh, yeah."

"Put it by the basket. And then I'm sure you have things to do." The actor's lip curled. Both fangs were still in place. "Important production assistant things."

As it happened, in spite of sarcasm, he did.

There were no bagels in the basket but there was a scattering of poppy seeds on the tray next to a dirty knife. Setting down the jam, Tony turned and spotted a plate half hidden behind the plant that dominated the small table next to the big armchair by the window. *Bagel at twelve o'clock.*

Mason had made himself a snack, set it down, then gone to the bathroom and . . .

One thing at a time. Bagel now. Bathroom later.

He reached inside himself for calm, muttered the seven words under his breath, and the first half of the bagel hit his hand with a greasy-slash-sticky impact that suggested Mason had been generous with both the butter and the honey.

"Foster?"

"Just leaving."

All things considered, the sudden sound of someone crying in the bathroom was not entirely unexpected.

As Mason turned to glare at the sound, Tony snagged the other half of the bagel. "Air in the pipes," he said, heading for the door. "Old plumbing."

The actor shot a scathing expression across the room at him. "I knew that."

"Right." Except old plumbing seldom sounded either that unhappy or that articulate. The new noises were almost words. Tony found a lot of comfort in that *almost*.

Safely outside the door, he restacked the bagel butter/honey sides together and headed toward the garbage can at the other end of the hall, rehearsing what he'd say when Mason discovered the bagel was gone. *"I wasn't anywhere near it!"*

No nearer than about six feet and Mason knew it.

Although *near* had become relative. These days he could manage to move unbreakable objects almost ten feet. Breakables still had a tendency to explode. Arra's notes hadn't mentioned explosions, but until the shadows, she'd handled FX for CB Productions, so maybe she considered bits of beer bottle flying around the room a minor effect. Fortunately, Zev had shown up early for their date and had been more than willing to drive him to the hospital to get the largest piece of bottle removed from his arm. His opinion of juggling beer bottles had been scathing. Tony hadn't had the guts to find out what his opinion of wizardry would have been.

The phrase special effects wizard had become a cliché in the industry. Arra Pelindrake, who'd been blowing things up and animating corpses for the last seven years, had been the real thing. Given the effects the new guy was coming up with, it turned out she hadn't been that great at the subtleties of twenty-first century FX but she *was* a real wizard. The shadows and the evil that controlled them had followed her through a gate she'd created between their world and this. The battle had gone down to the wire, but Tony had finally convinced her to stand and fight, and when it was all over, she'd been able to go home—but not before dropping the "you could be a wizard, too" bombshell. He'd refused to go with her, so she'd left him her laptop, six gummed-up games of spider solitaire that were supposed to give him insight into the future, and what he'd come to call Wizardshit 101; point form and remarkably obscure instructions on becoming a wizard.

He wasn't a wizard; he was a production assistant, working his way up in the industry until the time when it was his vision on the screen, his vision pulling in the viewers in the prime 19–29 male demographic. He'd had no intention of ever using the laptop.

And there'd been times over the last few months where he'd been able to stay away from it for weeks. Well, one time. For three weeks. Right after he'd had the jagged hunk of beer bottle removed from his arm.

Wizardry, like television, was all about manipulating energy.

And occasionally bread products.

Mason's door jerked open and without thinking much beyond *Oh, crap.* Tony opened the door he was standing by, dashed into the room, and closed the door quietly behind him. He had a feeling *I wasn't anywhere near your bagel* would play better when he didn't have butter, honey, and poppy seeds all over his hands.

The smell of wet paint told him where he was even before he turned.

The second-floor bathroom.

There were no shadows in this bathroom. On the wrong side of the house for direct sunlight there was still enough daylight spilling in through the open window to make the fresh coat of white semigloss gleam. Although the plumbing had been updated in the fifties, the actual fixtures were original—which was why they were shooting the flashback in this room.

Weirdly, although thirty years older, it made Mason's bathroom look dated and . . . haunted.

It was just the flickering shadows from the cedar tree and air in the pipes, he told himself.

Whatever gets you through your day, his self snorted. *Bite me.*

The heavy door cut off all sound from the hall. He had no idea if Mason was still prowling around looking for him, hunting his missing bagel.

At least if the taps work, I can wash my hands.

Using the only nonsticky square inch on his right palm, Tony pushed against the old lever faucet and turned on the cold water. And waited. Just as he was about to turn it off again, figuring they hadn't hooked up the water yet, liquid gushed from the faucet, thick and reddish brown, smelling of iron and rot.

Heart in his throat, he jumped back.

Blood!

No wait, rust.

By the time he had his breathing under control, the water was running clear. Feeling foolish, he rinsed off his palms, dried them on his jeans, and closed the tap. Checking out his reflection in the big, somewhat spotty mirror over the sink, he frowned.

Behind him, on the wall . . . it looked as if someone had drawn a finger through the wet paint. When he turned, changing the angle of the light, the mark disappeared. Mirror—finger mark. No mirror—no mark.

And now we know where the paint on Lee's tux came from. Next question: who put it there? Brenda seemed like the prime suspect. She'd been upstairs delinting both actors before the scene, she'd have noticed the marks had they already been laid down, and the result had been Lee bare-assed in her trailer. . . . *and let's not forget that she's already familiar with his ass.* He probably hadn't even noticed her stroking him on the way by.

Opportunity and motive pointed directly to Brenda.

Time . . .

Tony glanced at his watch.

"Crap!" Twenty-three minutes since Adam had called a twenty-minute break. Bright side, Mason wouldn't be able to bug him about a rule-breaking snack in front of the others. Slipping out into the hall, Tony ran for the back stairs figuring he could circle around from the kitchen. With any luck no one had missed him yet—one of the benefits of being low man on the totem pole.

As he ran, he realized Mason had been right about one thing. *It's fucking freezing up here.*

♠

"Why was he in the bathroom? Graham said we'd be safe in there, that they wouldn't be using it until tomorrow."

"Be quiet, Stephen!" Cassie pinched her brother's arm. "Do you want him to hear you?"

"Ow. He can't hear us from way over here!"

"I'm not so sure." She frowned thoughtfully as the young man disappeared through the door leading to the stairs between the servants' rooms and the kitchen. "I get the feeling he doesn't miss much."

Stephen snorted and patted a strand of dark blond hair back into the pomaded dip over his forehead. "Good thing we weren't *in* the bathroom then."

"Yes . . . good thing."

♠

Sunset was at 8:54 PM. It was one of those things that Tony couldn't not remember. He checked the paper every morning, he noted the time, and, as the afternoon became evening, he kept an eye on his watch.

Wanda, the new office PA, showed up at seven with the next day's sides—the half size sheets with all the background information as well as the necessary script pages. Tony helped her pick them up off the porch.

"This is so totally embarrassing!"

He handed her a messy stack of paper. "Don't worry about it, everyone trips. Earlier, I did a little 'falling with style' down the back stairs." The risers were uneven and he'd missed his step, very nearly pitching headfirst down the narrow incline.

"Falling with style is better than falling with skinned knee," Wanda muttered, shoving the retrieved sides under one arm and dabbing at the congealing blood with a grubby tissue. "And how many people saw you?"

"No one, but . . ."

"You saw me." She pointed at him. "And Brenda did." She pointed back toward the trailer. "Because I heard that distinctive snicker of hers. And the Sikh with the potted plant."

"Dalal. The prop guy."

"Whatever. My point, three people saw me. No one saw you and *I'm* bleeding."

"Yeah, well, don't bleed on the weather report. What would we do if we didn't know there was a seventy percent chance of rain tomorrow?"

She snapped erect and glared at him, nostrils pinched so tightly he wondered how she could breathe and talk at the same time. "That's not very supportive!"

"What?"

"That comment was not very supportive!"

"Kidding." Tony tapped the corners of his mouth. "Smiling, see?"

"It's not funny!"

"But I wasn't . . ."

"I'm taking these inside now!"

"Whatever." He wasn't quite mocking her. Quite. Okay, maybe a little. "I'll just be out here cleaning your blood off the stone."

"Fine." Spinning on one air-cushioned heel, she stomped in through the front doors.

"Someone needs to switch to decaf," he sighed. He'd been standing not three feet from the steps when she fell, close enough to hear her knee make that soft/hard definite tissue damage sound, and he had a pretty good idea of where she'd impacted with the porch. Weirdly, while there'd been lines of red dribbling down her shin, he couldn't find any blood on the stones. As embarrassed as she was, she'd probably just bounced up before the blood actually started to flow.

Probably.

The show packed up around 8:30 PM.

"Nice short day, people. Good work. Eleven and a

half hours," he added to Sorge as he moved out of an electrician's way. "No way we'll make that tomorrow, not with all those extras."

Tony's grasp of French profanity wasn't quite good enough to understand the specifics of the DP's reply.

Two

"HEY, HENRY, it's Tony." He shifted the phone to his other hand and reached into the back of the fridge. "It's highly likely that we're going to run late tomorrow night..." How long had that Chinese takeout been in there? "...so I was thinking that I'd better..." Opening the container, he stared at the uniform greenish-gray surface of the food. He had no idea what he'd ordered way back when but he had a strong suspicion it hadn't looked like that. "... meet you at the ..." The click of a receiver being lifted cut him off. "Henry?"

"Tony? Sorry, I was in the shower."

"Going out to eat?"

He could hear the smile in the other man's voice. "Is that any of your business?"

"Nope. Just curious." The bologna still looked edible. Well, most of it. He tossed it on the counter and closed the refrigerator door. "We've got extras working tomorrow, so I'll likely be late."

"You say *extras* like you're thinking of calling in pest control to deal with them."

"I'm not, but Sorge and Peter are. They hate working with extras." Tony grabbed a little plastic packet of mustard from a cup filled with identical plastic packets, ripped off the top with his teeth, and squirted the contents out onto a slice of bread. "It might be best if I meet you at the theater. The show starts at ten, so if I'm not there by quarter to, just go in and sit down. I'll find you."

"We can call it off."

"Not a chance. How often do you get to go to the theater in the summer?" Friends of Tony's from film school were taping the play and the high-profile television stars playing the leads for the local cable channel. Opening curtain was at ten because they couldn't get the camera equipment until after their day jobs finished with it. Tony had no idea how they'd convinced the theater or the actors to go along with their schedule but that wasn't his problem. When he'd heard about it, he'd realized it was a perfect show for Henry. Given late sunsets and early sunrises, Henry didn't get out much in the summer. Ripping the slightly green edges off the half dozen slices of bologna, he stacked them on the bread and mustard. "You know where the Vogue is, right?"

"It's on Granville, Tony, practically around the corner. I think I can find it."

"Hey, I'm just checking." He applied mustard to the second slice of bread.

"Did you know that the Vogue Theater was haunted?"

"Really haunted or haunted for publicity's sake?"

"Bit of both, I suspect."

Tony took a bite of his sandwich. "Think we'll see anything tomorrow night?"

"I think we'll have to wait until tomorrow night to find out."

"I'm just asking because our last experience with ghosts wasn't much fun." Several innocents had died and, until the whole shadows-from-another-world incident, the experience had provided fodder for the bulk of Tony's nightmares. Well, that and the undead ancient Egyptian wizard.

"Apparently this guy is a lot less interactive," Henry told him dryly. "What are you eating?"

"Bologna sandwich."

"I was thinking I'd have Italian."

"Good night, Henry!" Shaking his head, Tony thumbed the phone off and tossed it into the tangle of blankets on the pull-out couch. "Over four hundred and sixty years old," he commented to the apartment at large. "You'd think he'd learn another joke."

Vampires: not big on the whole contemporary humor thing.

"Seventy percent chance of rain, my ass," Tony muttered as he drove out to the end of Deer Lake Drive and parked behind Sorge's minivan. The rain sheeted down his windshield with such volume and intensity the wipers were barely able to keep up. He turned off the engine, grabbed his backpack off the passenger seat, and flicked the hood up on his green plastic rain cape. Sure, it looked geeky, but it kept him and his backpack mostly dry. Besides, it wasn't quite seven-thirty in the freaking AM—ACTRA rules stipulated a twelve-hour break for the talent but only ten for the crew—he was in the middle of a park, about to head down an overgrown path to a forgotten house—who the hell was going to see him?

Stephen turned from the window smiling broadly. "Listen to the water roar in the gutters, Cass! This'll fill the cistern for sure. Graham's going to be on cloud nine."

"And it's all about Graham being happy, isn't it?" she muttered, rubbing bare arms.

"That's not what I meant." He frowned. "What's the matter with you?"

"I don't know." When she looked up, her eyes were unfocused. "Something feels . . ."

"Different?"

She shook her head. "Familiar."

The trees cut the rain back to a bearable deluge. Carefully avoiding new, water-filled ruts and the occasional opening where rain poured through the covering branches, Tony plodded toward the house. Half a kilometer later, as he came out into the open, and saw the building squatting massive and dark at the end of the drive, thunder cracked loud enough to vibrate his fillings and a jagged diagonal of lightning backlit the house.

"Well, isn't that a cliché," he sighed, kicked a ten-kilo hunk of mud off his shoe, and kept walking.

Finally standing just inside the kitchen door, he shook the excess water off his rain cape out onto the huge flagstone slab that floored the small porch, added his shoes to the pile of wet footwear, and pulled a pair of moccasins out of his pack. Stopping by the big prep table, he snagged a cup of coffee—more practical than most in the television industry, craft services had set up in the kitchen—and headed for the butler's pantry where the AD's office had been set. He shoved his backpack into one of the lower cabinets, signed in, and grabbed a radio. So far, channel one, the AD's channel was quiet. Adam might not be in yet or he just might not be talking—impossible to tell. On channel eight, the genny op and the rest of his transport crew had a few things to say about keeping things running in the rain. Impressed by the way the profanities seemed to make it through the interference intact, Tony set his unit back on channel one, and headed for the conservatory at the back of the house.

Extras' holding.

Tony could already hear them; a low hum as two dozen voices all complained about their agents at the same time.

Passing by the bottom of the back stairs, the servants'

stairs, another sound caught his attention. A distant, rhythmic creak. *Er er. Er er.* Like something . . . swinging. Someone had probably left the door open on the second floor. He thought about heading up and closing it, then spotted the black cat sitting at the three-quarter mark and changed his mind. Uneven, narrow, and steep, the stairs had tried to kill him once already and that was without the added fun of something to trip over. A sudden draft of cold air flowing down from the second floor raised the hair on the back of his neck and consolidated his decision. Damp clothes, cold air—not a great combination. Besides, he was already running late.

Sucking back his coffee, he hurried along a narrow hall and finally down the three stone steps into the conservatory.

The house had been deserted of everyone but hired caretakers for almost thirty years and it seemed as though none of those caretakers had cared to do any indoor gardening. The conservatory was empty of even the dried husks of plant life. The raised beds were empty. The small pond was empty. The big stone urns were empty. The actual floor space, on the other hand, was a little crowded.

Over on the other side of the pond, several men and women were changing into their own modern evening dress with the nonchalance of people for whom the novelty of seeing others in their underwear had long since worn off. Ditto the self-consciousness of being seen. Crammed between the raised beds and the stone urns, still more men and women—already dressed—sat on plastic folding chairs, drank coffee, read newspapers, and waited for their turn in makeup.

The two makeup stations were up against the stone wall the conservatory shared with the house. Some shows had the supporting actors do their own face and hair, but Everett had refused to allow it and CB, usually so tight he could get six cents change from a nickel, had let him have his way. Sharyl, Everett's assistant who worked part-time for CB Productions and part-time at a local funeral parlor, handled the second chair. Curling irons, hair spray, and a multitude of brushes were all flung about with dazzling speed and when Everett yelled, "Time!" Tony realized they'd been racing.

"Not fair!" Sharyl complained as she flicked the big powder brush over the high arc of male pattern baldness. "I had more surface to cover."

"I had a more delicate application."

"Yeah, well, I'm faster when they're lying down." She stepped back and tossed the big brush onto the tray. "You're lovely."

Tony didn't think the man—*white, thirty to forty, must provide own evening dress*—looked convinced. Or particularly happy to hear it.

"Next two!" Everett bellowed over the drumming of the rain on the glass. He waved the completed extras out of the chairs, adding, "Don't touch your face!" Tony couldn't hear the woman's reply, but Everett's response made it fairly clear. "So itch for your art."

Waving at a couple of people he knew from other episodes and a guy he'd met a couple of times at the Gandydancer, Tony made his way over to the card table set up beside the coffee urn. He pulled the clipboard out from under a spill of cardboard cups and checked the sign-in page. It seemed a little short of names.

"Hey! Everybody!" The rain threatened to drown him out, so he yelled louder. "If you haven't signed the sheet, please do it now. I have to check your name against our master list."

No one moved.

"If your names aren't on both lists, you won't get paid!"

Half a dozen people hurried toward him.

Other shows would have hired a daily PA or TAD—trainee assistant director—to ride herd on the extras. CB figured they were all adults and were therefore fully capable of walking from the holding area to the set without him having to pay to see that they managed it. Human nature being what it was, and with two thirds of the season in the can, Tony could pretty much guarantee that someone—or some two or three—would wander off and need to be brought back to the herd while he did his best border collie impression. Snarling permitted; biting frowned on.

It took a moment for him to realize that the scream was not a rehearsal. Extras generally did a lot of screaming on shows staring vampires. Some of them, disdaining the more spontaneous terror of their contemporaries, liked to practice.

On the other side of the conservatory, a half dressed woman clutching a pair of panty hose to her chest, backed away from one of the raised beds and continued to scream. By the time Tony reached her, the screams had become whimpers, barely audible over the sound of the rain.

"What?" he demanded. "What's wrong?"

Conditioned to respond to anyone with a radio and a clipboard, she pointed a trembling finger toward the garden. "I sat down, on the edge, to put on . . ." Taupe streamers waved from her other hand. ". . . and I sort of fell. Back." Glancing around, she suddenly realized she had an audience and, in spite of her fear, began to play to it. "I put my hand down on the dirt. It sank in just a little. The next thing I knew, something *grabbed* it."

"Something?"

"Fingers. I felt fingers close around mine. Cold fingers." A half turn toward her listeners. "Like fingers from a *grave*."

Tony had to admit that the raised beds did look rather remarkably like graves. *Yeah, and so does any dirt pile longer than it is wide.* He stepped forward, noticed where the dirt had been disturbed, and poked it with the clipboard. He didn't believe the bit about the fingers, of course, but there was no point in taking unnecessary chances. Over the last few years he'd learned that belief had absolutely nothing to do with reality.

The clipboard sank about a centimeter into the dirt and stopped with a clunk.

Clunk sounded safe enough.

In Tony's experience, the metaphysical seldom went clunk.

A moment's digging later, he pulled out a rusted, handleless garden claw.

"Was this what you felt?"

"No." She shuddered, dramatically. "I felt fingers."

"Cold fingers." Tony held the claw toward her and she touched it tentatively.

"Okay, maybe."

"Maybe?"

"Fine." Her snort was impressive. "Probably. Okay? It felt like fingers, it's barely dawn, and it's kind of spooky in here, and I haven't had any coffee yet!"

Show over, the other extras began to drift away and the woman who'd done the screaming pointedly continued dressing. Tony tossed the claw back onto the garden bed and headed for the door. Drawing level with Everett, he asked for a time check.

"They'll be ready when they're needed," Everett told him, layering on scarlet lipstick with a lavish hand. "But don't quote me on that."

"I kind of have to quote you on that, Everett. Adam's going to ask."

"Fine." He pointedly capped the lipstick and drew a mascara wand from its tube with a flourish. "But don't say I didn't warn you. Oh, calm down," he added as the middle-aged woman in the chair recoiled from the waving black bristles. "Thirty years in this business and I've yet to put an eye out."

"I put one in once," Sharyl announced and Tony figured that was his cue to leave. Sharyl's mortuary stories were usually a hoot, but somehow he just wasn't in the mood for fun and frolic with the dead. Pausing on the threshold, he glanced back over the room to do a final head count. Party guests and cater-waiters clumped with their own kind, making his job a little easier.

Twenty-five.

Only twenty-four signatures.

A second count gave him the right number of heads and a third confirmed it. He must've miscounted the first time—it wasn't easy getting an accurate fix on the crowd of guests around the central urn. About to turn, he stopped and squinted toward the back garden, a flurry of movement having caught his eye. It had almost looked as if the claw had stood on its broken handle and waved its little claw-fingers at him. Except that the claw was nowhere in sight.

Wondering what he actually might have seen—given the absence of the claw—got lost in a sudden realization. If the claw was missing, someone had taken it. *Great. We've got a souvenir hunter.*

Every now and then cattle calls would spit up a background player who liked to have a little something to help him remember the job. With a souvenir hunter on the set, small, easily portable items had a tendency to disappear. During episode seven, they'd lost the inkwell from Raymond Dark's desk. After CB expressed his thoughts about the incident—"No one from that group works again until I get my property back!"—they'd had four inkwells returned. Unfortunately, most of the small, easily portable items from this set belonged to the current owners of Caulfield House not CB Productions and the odds were good the crew wouldn't immediately realize it if something went missing.

I'd better let Keisha know.

He grabbed a cinnamon bun on his way through the kitchen, dropped the signed sheet in the AD's office, and headed for the drawing room. The original script had called for a ball and the presence of a ballroom was one of the reasons CB had jumped at using the house.

Problem was, the ballroom was huge and the number of people it would have taken to fill it—even given the tricks of the trade—would have emptied the extras budget. With episode twenty-two and its howling mob of peasants with torches and pitchforks still in the pipeline, the ball became a smaller gathering and the venue moved to the drawing room.

A huge fieldstone fireplace dominated one end of a room paneled in Douglas fir. Above it, mounted right on the stone, was a massive gold-framed mirror. Six tall, multipaned windows divided the outside wall and glass-fronted built-in bookcases faced them along the inside. The curtains were burgundy with deep gold tassels and tiebacks—the two colors carried into the furniture upholstery. The room seemed essentially untouched by almost a hundred years of renovation and redecoration. Standing in the midst of this understated luxury were Peter, Sorge, the gaffer, the key grip, and Keisha, the set decorator, all looking up.

"The ceilings are high enough. We can shoot under them," Peter said as Tony joined them.

"We are keeping the cameras low," Sorge agreed. "Keeping the shots filled with the people."

Still staring at the ceiling, the gaffer frowned. "A diffuser under each of them might help."

"Couldn't hurt," the key grip allowed.

Keisha made a noncommittal albeit dubious sound.

So Tony looked up.

"Holy fuck." Those were three of the most hideous looking chandeliers Tony had ever seen. In fact, he wasn't entirely certain they could even be called chandeliers except for the dangly bits. Although what the dangly bits were actually made of he had no idea. A certain *Leave it to Beaver*ness about them suggested the same 1950's vision that had been responsible for the redecorated parts of the master suite, the bathroom in particular.

Something.

Rocking in place.
Forward.
Back.
Not that particular.

"I think Mr. Foster has succinctly summed up the situation," Peter sighed and Tony looked down to find all four looking at him. "Did you want one of us for something?"

"Uh, yeah, Keisha mostly, but you should probably all know. We've got a souvenir hunter. There's already a piece of crap missing from the conservatory."

"Crap?"

"Broken end of a garden claw."

"Crap," Keisha acknowledged. "But not our crap either. All right, I'll make sure Chris keeps an eye out and we'll do a double count when we pack up. In the meantime, someone's going to have to get pictures of everything in those cabinets."

"Tony . . ."

Yeah, he knew it. He was usually "someone."

". . . get Tina's digital," Peter continued, "and get those shots while we finish setup. We all know how much CB loves unexpected bills."

Only the center cabinet was actually a bookcase. The others were too shallow for books and instead displayed cups and saucers, grimy bowls of china flowers, and the little plastic toys from inside Kinder Eggs—Tony suspected the three-part water buffalo and the working lime-green windmill were the most recent additions to the decor. Behind the water buffalo, he found a yellowed card buffed down to the same color as the shelf by a thick layer of dust. Theoretically, he wasn't supposed to touch.

When he flipped the card over, the black handwriting was still dark and legible.

Finger of a Franciscan monk killed by the Papal Inquisition, 1651. Acquired August 17, 1887.

There was no sign of the finger although on the next

shelf he did find half a dozen of the tiny china figurines that used to come in boxes of tea and were required inventory in every cheesy antique store in the country.

He finished up just as his radio sent a spike of pure static into his head.

"Adam, this is Brenda. Lee and Mazzzzzzzzzit are in wardrobe."

"Roger that. Everett's on his . . ." The last word was lost under another burst of static and some rather impressive profanity from the other end of the room. "Tony!"

He closed the last cabinet and turned toward the 1AD.

"Send Everett out to the trailer and start moving the extras up here."

"Why does it have to be extras?" Peter muttered as Tony dropped the camera back off at Tina's station. "I hear the Hall of Presidents is closed down for renovations; why can't we borrow their animatronics? Toss 'em in a tux, stick a martini glass in their hands . . . Washington would look very feminine in a high collar and some ruffles; he's already in a wig. Who'd notice? But no, we have to use real people. Real people who don't listen, who never know their right from their left, who all want their fifteen minutes, who make *suggestions* . . ."

The director's continuing diatribe faded as Tony moved out into the hall heading for the conservatory. Everett, who'd known the talent should be in the trailer at nine, was on the move when he arrived. Sharyl was packing up her case, ready for on-set touch-ups. All that was left was moving the extras.

Humming the theme from *Rawhide* was optional.

With most of the crowd on the correct heading, Tony raced across the kitchen to prevent an unauthorized side trip.

"Hey, where are you going?" Hand flat against the wood, he shoved the door closed before it actually opened.

The actress shrugged. "I was just wondering what was down there."

"Probably the basement." The door felt like ice under his palm. "Just keep moving."

Leaning in closer, she drew her tongue slowly across a full and already moist lower lip. "You're *so* serious . . . No hard feelings?" Her voice dripped single entendre.

"Give it up, love." One of the waiters took her arm, winked at Tony, and started her moving again. "I'd have better luck."

"What?" She shot Tony a frustrated look he answered with a shrug, and then allowed herself to be towed away. "Are there no straight men left in television?"

"You're asking the wrong fag, puss. Besides, he's only the production assistant."

"I know that! I was starting at the bottom."

"An admirable sentiment."

As they followed the rest of the extras down the hall, Tony lifted his hand from the door and stared down at the red mark on his palm. It looked a bit like a letter—a Russian letter maybe, or Greek, or Hebrew. Before he could decide which, it had disappeared. When he touched the door again, it was no colder than any other surface.

"You don't want to be going down there."

He spun around so quickly he had to catch his balance on the door handle. "Jesus!" Snatching his hand off the metal, he sucked at what felt like a burn on the skin between finger and thumb. "Why don't I want to go down there?" he demanded, the question a little muffled by his hand.

"Weather like this, the basement floods. Probably six inches of water down there now." Mr. Brummel's red-rimmed eyes narrowed. "Nasty things in the water. You just be keeping your pretty ladies and gentlemen away from the nasty things."

"What?"

The caretaker snorted and shifted his grip on the black cat in his arms. "Look, kid, we got the original knob-and-tube wiring down there. Damned stuff gets wet and every piece of metal in the place is conducting power. Now, I personally don't give a crap if nosy parkers fry, but I don't like doing the paperwork the insurance companies want, so stay out. You already picked up a spark off the door, didn't you?"

It could have been a spark. "Yeah."

"Well, there, then."

"Isn't all that free-floating electricity dangerous?"

"Yep. And that . . ." He enunciated each word carefully. ". . . is why you don't want to be going down to the basement. Let me see your hand."

Cat tucked under one arm, his fingers closed around Tony's wrist before Tony'd decided how he intended to respond.

The caretaker's second snort was dismissive as he peered at the dark pink splotch. "This is nothing. You aren't even bleeding." His grip tightened to the edge of pain, his fingers unnaturally warm. He leaned in closer, his eyes narrowed, his nose flared—he looked like a poster boy for dire warnings. "You don't want to be bleeding, not in this house."

"Why not?"

"Because we're miles from anywhere." He didn't so much release Tony's wrist as toss him his arm back. "For pity's sake, kid, use your head. These cinnamon buns for anyone?"

"Sure. Help yourself. The uh, cat . . . is it yours?"

"No. I just like carrying it around."

The cat yawned, the inside of its mouth very pink and white against the ebony fur.

Rubbing his wrist, Tony backed slowly out of the kitchen. He didn't turn until he was halfway through the butler's pantry and Adam's voice filled his earjack.

♣

"Graham's not going to like this, Cass. This isn't what I'd call staying out of sight."

She smoothed down the heavy velvet folds of her skirt and smiled. "It's hiding in plain sight. Like the purloined letter."

"What about that feeling you had? The familiar feeling?"

"What about it?" Rising up on her toes, she peered over the heads of the people milling about the drawing room. "It felt familiar."

"Cassie! You just want to meet that actor."

"Well, why not? He's cute. And you're the one who was complaining you were bored." She settled back on her heels, tucked her hand into the crook of his arm, and smiled up at him through her lashes. "This isn't boring."

"It's dangerous," Stephen insisted, but his hand closed over hers and he didn't sound as convinced as he had.

"With all those people and all those lights crammed into one room, there's energy to spare."

"It's not the amount of energy." He glanced around and shook his head. "They're all older than us."

"So frown. It makes you look older."

"They're going to notice . . ."

"They won't." Her smile was triumphant as she waved a hand at the bank of lights. "It's hot enough in here that in a worst case scenario all we'll do is drop the temperature down to a more bearable level. Seriously, they'd thank us if they knew. Come on, he's over by the door."

No one noticed them as they crossed the room. The waiters practiced holding their trays and offering drinks in ways most likely to get them asked back for a larger part, maybe even a part with a name, later in the season. The guests did much the same with bright, animated, but-not-upstaging-the-stars, background chatter.

"Cassie, this isn't going to work."

"Well, it won't if you're going to be so negative. Just think 'party guest.'"

"But . . ."

"Concentrate, Stephen!" As they neared the door,

she licked her lower lip and dragged her brother around to face her. "Is my face still on?"

He frowned. "I guess. But you overdid it with the eye shadow."

♣

Lee was standing by the door talking to a couple of the extras. It was one of the things Tony liked about him—he didn't have the whole, *I've got my name and face in the opening credits and you don't* thing going on. He was smiling down at the girl now, saying something she had to lean closer to hear, and Tony felt an irrational stab of jealousy. Irrational and idiotic and yes, still pathetic.

"Places, everyone!"

Interesting that Lee seemed to be telling them where they should stand. More interesting that they were standing almost entirely out of the shot.

"All right, people, listen up. This is what's going to happen!" Peter moved out into the center of the room and raised both hands as though he was conducting a symphony instead of episode seventeen of a straight to syndication show about a vampire detective—not so much a symphony as three kids with kazoos. "Mason and Lee are going to come in from the hall and cross the room to the fireplace as you all go through the usual party shtick. You'll all ignore them until Lee calls for your attention, which you will give to him. Mason will then say his piece, you'll listen attentively, reacting silently as you see fit—just remember that reaction because odds are good you'll be repeating it all morning. Do not drop your glass. The glasses are rented. Mason'll finish, and Ms. Sinclair . . ."

A distinguished looking silver-haired bit player Tony had last seen playing Dumpster diver number two in a CBC Movie of the Week, raised her martini glass in acknowledgment.

". . . you'll say your line: 'If you're trying to frighten us, Mr. Dark, you're not succeeding.' Then Mason will reply, 'I'm not trying. Not yet.' And we'll cut. Let's run through once for cameras."

The run-through necessitated a few adjustments in the crowd and their reactions.

"What the hell was that?"

"Astonishment?" the party-goer offered, cheeks flushed.

"Are you asking me?" Peter sighed. "Because if you are, I'd have to say it looked more like indigestion. Gear it down."

The girl divided her attention between the room in general and Lee, smiling in his direction like she knew a secret.

"Let's roll tape on this one." Peter disappeared behind the monitor and Adam moved out onto the floor.

"Quiet, please! Let's settle, people!" He glanced over the crowd and, when he was satisfied, yelled, "Rolling!"

Tony, along with nearly everyone else in a headset, repeated the word. It sounded in the hall outside the drawing room, at the craft services table in the kitchen, maybe even out at the trailers. Then Kate—because CB's budgets never quite extended as far as *second* assistant camera—stepped forward and called the slate.

"Scene three, take one! Mark!"

The boy standing next to the girl who'd been talking to Lee jumped at the crack.

Tony frowned. And he *was* a boy, too. Although his evening clothes fit him like they'd been made for him, he had to be at least ten years younger than anyone else in the room. Well, it wouldn't be the first time someone on the crew had snuck a relative or two in. As long as they behaved themselves, CB was all in favor of extras he didn't have to pay. It wasn't that these two weren't behaving themselves, it was just . . . Actually, Tony had no idea what it was about them that kept drawing his attention. Except maybe that Lee had been paying attention to them.

How often do I have to say this is pathetic before it finally sinks in?

Lee and Mason had barely reached the fireplace when Peter broke off a quiet discussion with Sorge and yelled cut.

"It's no good." Coming out from behind the monitors, he pulled off his headset. "The mirror over the fireplace is flaring out. Sharyl!"

"Yeah?"

"We're going to need to use some hair spray. Tony, take care of it. Meanwhile, Mason, as you come in ..."

The end of the suggestion was lost as Tony moved away from the director. He reached Sharyl just ahead of a mascara failure and a lipstick problem.

"I swear it's so hot under those lights, it's melting right off my lashes."

"It's actually comfortable where I am, but I can't help chewing my lips while we wait."

Lipstick Problem had been standing near the girl-who'd-been-talking-to-Lee and the boy-who-was-younger.

And why do I care? Tony wondered as he took the offered hair spray with a nod of thanks. He could reach the bottom half of the mirror from the hearth, but the whole area was so supersized he'd need a little help for the rest. The ladders that had been used to set the lights were out in the hall, but maneuvering one through a crowded drawing room would be time consuming. Figuring Peter would appreciate him thinking of and then saving production time, he snagged the director's chair on the way past and set it on the hearth.

The trick was to spray on a nice even coat. Enough to cut the glare but not so much that the audience wondered what the hell was on the glass. And he should probably move the chair in order to safely reach the other end of the mirror.

Yeah, but who wants to live forever?

Plastic bottle of hair spray in his right hand, thumb on the pump, left hand gripping the mantel, he leaned way out and just for an instant dropped his gaze below the line of application.

There.

In the reflection of the far side of the room.

The boy-who-was-younger was in a loose white shirt. Well, white except for the splashes of what had to be blood—had to be because a huge triangular cut in the right side of his neck looked as though it just missed decapitating him. The girl-who'd-been-talking-to-Lee was wearing a summer dress, one strap torn free, the whole fitted bodice as well as her bare shoulders stained a deep crimson. She was also short the top left quarter of her head—her face missing along the nose and out one cheekbone, her left eye completely gone.

He twisted around.

Now that he'd seen them, the glamour—or whatever the nonwizard, dead-people equivalent was called—no longer worked.

Nearly headless. Chunk of face missing.

Their eyes—all three of them—widened as they somehow realized he could see them as they were, not as they appeared. Actually, he kind of suspected his expression was giving the whole thing away.

The vanishing . . . not entirely unexpected.

The chair tipping sideways, as gravity won out and he headed for the floor . . . he had to admit he'd been kind of expecting that, too.

Then a strong hand closed around his arm and yanked him back onto his feet. He fought to find his balance, won the fight, and turned to look down into a pair of concerned green eyes.

"Are you all right, Tony?" Lee asked, one hand still loosely clasped around Tony's bicep. "You look like you've seen a ghost."

Three

"TONY! THE mirror!"

Right, the mirror. The mirror where he'd just seen the dead up and animate—or as animate as any extras ever were between shots. Oh, fuck ... the extras! If that feeling wasn't his blood actually running cold, it was pretty damned close—kind of a sick feeling in his stomach that moved out to his extremities so quickly he thought he might hurl. Traditionally, the presence of extras right before disaster meant a high body count and dead people in the drawing room certainly seemed like an accurate harbinger of disaster to Tony.

He stared at their reflections in the small part of the mirror still clear of hair spray. They all seemed oblivious to their fate. *Might as well dress them in red shirts now and get it over with!*

"Tony!"

He twisted around to see the first assistant director staring up at him in annoyance.

"Finish spraying the damned mirror!"

It might be damned, he supposed. Damned could explain why it showed dead people. ...

"Tony?"

Tony looked down into Lee's concerned face and

forced his brain to start working again. It wasn't as if these were the first ghosts he'd ever seen. Okay, technically, he hadn't seen the last set—he'd only heard them screaming—but he *was* used to metaphysical pop-ups. Hell, he used to sleep with one. "Can I talk to you for a minute? I mean ..." A gesture took in the chair, the mirror, and the plastic bottle of hair spray. ". . . when I'm done."

Dark brows drew in, and Lee glanced back at Peter still talking to Mason. "Sure."

Directing Mason—or rather, Mason's ego—took time.

A moment later, Tony was back on the floor. "Those two kids you were talking to . . ." At Lee's suddenly closed expression, he paused. "It's okay, I'm not going to get them into trouble. I know they weren't supposed to be in the scene." Hello, understatement. "I just wondered who they were."

Lee considered it—considered Tony—for a moment then he shrugged. "They're Mr. Brummell's niece and nephew. Cassie, short for Cassandra, which she informed me was a stupid, old-fashioned name, and Stephen. They were ... well, *she* was just so thrilled at being here that I didn't have the heart to turn them in. I warned them that they had to stay in the background, though."

"Yeah, I saw you positioning them. You didn't notice anything strange?"

"Strange?"

"About the way they looked."

"Only that they were younger than everyone else in the room. I'd say mid-to-late teens, no older."

And not going to get any older either. *All right. We're shooting an episode* about *a haunted house in a haunted house and that sort of thing never ends well. Real dead people not so big on the happy ending. So what do I do? I get everyone* out *of the haunted house. And how do I do that?*

Production assistants had about as much power as ...

well, bottom line, they didn't have any power. None. Nada. Zip. And zilch.

He had to call the boss. Since CB remembered the shadows and the Shadowlord, CB would believe him. Announcing to anyone else that he'd seen a ghost—two ghosts—would result in ridicule at best. *"A ghost?"* He could hear the broad sarcasm in Peter's voice. *"Why don't you go see if they'll work for scale; I'm sure CB would appreciate the savings."*

Come to think of it, CB *would* appreciate the savings. And he wouldn't be too happy about losing his chance to shoot in a house he'd already paid a week's rent on. Maybe he could get CB to agree to put the ghosts in the show. They clearly wanted to be involved; maybe official ghost status would be enough to placate them.

"You're going to exhaust the hamster."

"What?"

Lee grinned. "The hamster running around on that wheel in your head. You're trying to figure out how to keep those kids out of trouble, aren't you?"

Close enough. "Yeah."

"Don't worry about it. I'll put in a good word for them. *Darkest Night* isn't quite a solo act no matter what Mason seems to think." They turned together to look at the clump of people grouped around the actor who was standing, arms crossed, glaring at Peter. "You might tell them to keep out of his way, though."

Sure, I'll hold a séance and get right on that. Even if he got hold of CB, how was he supposed to get hold of the ghosts? Glancing around the room, he doubted there was a medium among all the size twos.

"Want to share the joke?" Lee asked as Tony snickered.

He did. And as bad a joke as it was, he even thought that Lee would appreciate it—right up until the back story killed the laughs. As he hesitated, Lee's expression changed; closing in on itself until the open, curious, friendly expression was gone and all that remained was the same polite interest he showed the rest of the world.

"Never mind. I should get back to work before we end up keeping the extras over their four-hour minimum."

Tony couldn't think of a thing to say as Lee flashed him the same smile he'd flashed a thousand cameras and walked away. An opportunity missed . . . An opportunity for what, he had no idea—but he couldn't shake the notion that he'd just dropped the ball in a big way.

A sudden soft pressure against his shins drew his gaze off Lee's tuxedo-clad back and toward the floor. The caretaker's black cat made another pass across his legs.

"Tony!" Ear jack dangling against his shoulder, Adam approached the fireplace. "You get that mirror done?"

He held up the plastic bottle. "It's covered."

"Good. Clean your grubby footprints off Peter's chair, put it back behind the monitors, and . . ." His head dropped forward and he stared at the cat now rubbing against his jeans. "Where the hell did this animal come from?"

"I think it belongs to Mr. Brummel, the caretaker; he was holding it earlier."

"Then grab it and get it back to him. The last thing we need is an unattended animal running around."

One of the extras shrieked with laughter. Both men turned in time to see Mason moving his mouth away from her throat.

"*Another* unattended animal," Adam added wearily, shoving the ear jack back where it belonged. "He's got a bed in his dressing room, doesn't he?"

"It's a bedroom."

"Right. Let's move it with the cat, then; we've got to do what we can to get these people out of here before he talks her into a nooner."

Given that it was the woman who'd put the moves on him in the kitchen, Tony suspected "You want to?" would probably be conversation enough. He bent and wrapped his hands tentatively around the cat. It squeezed through his grip, skittered about six feet away, sat down, and licked its butt.

"Adam . . . ?" Peter's voice.

"Tony's got it." Adam's answer.

A fine sentiment but less than truthful—every time he got close enough for another grab, the cat moved. Once or twice, his fingertips ghosted over soft fur, but that was it. As amber eyes glanced back mockingly and four legs performed a diagonal maneuver impossible on two, he had no doubt the cat was playing to its snickering audience. At least it seemed to be moving toward the small door in the back corner of the drawing room.

The library, he thought, as the cat slipped through the half-open door and disappeared. *I'll just close the door and the cat'll be out of our hair.* A sudden burst of static clamped his left hand to his head. *Son of a bitch!*

"Tony! We've got sfffft stored in there. I don't want the cat pissssssssstnk on it."

Yeah, well, nothing harder to get out than cat pisstnk on sffft. He sighed and kept going.

In spite of the rain, the two long windows to his left let in enough daylight for him to see the cat moving purposefully across the room toward the other door. He could understand why it didn't want to linger. The empty shelves didn't feel empty. They felt as though the books they'd held had left a dark imprint that lingered long after the books themselves were gone. The only piece of furniture in the room was a huge desk and a chair in the same red-brown wood. Tony had overheard Chris telling Adam that it had belonged to Creighton Caulfield himself. The fireplace shared a chimney with the drawing room and over the dark slab of mantel was a small, rectangular mirror framed in the same dark wood. Tony made a point of not looking in it. If there were ghosts in the library, he didn't want to know.

Moving out and around a stack of cables and half a dozen extra lights, he picked up the pace.

The cat slipped out the library's main door, Tony following it out into the main hall. His reaching hand touched tail. The cat picked up the pace, streaking toward the front doors, then turning at the last minute and heading up the stairs. Tony made the turn with considerably less grace and charged up the stairs after it. Three steps at a time slowed to two to one and at the three-quarter mark, as an ebony tail disappeared to the right, he realized there was no way in hell he was going to catch up.

He reached the second floor as the cat reached the far end of the hall. It paused outside the door to the back stairs, turned, and looked at him in what could only be considered a superior way—no mistaking the expression even given the distance—and then disappeared into the stairwell.

Just for an instant, he considered calling the cat to his hand, but the memory of the exploding beer bottle stopped him. While blowing up the caretaker's cat would certainly keep it off the set, it seemed like a bit of an extreme solution. *Not to mention hard on the cat.* Besides, from what he knew about cats, it'd probably head straight for the food in the kitchen where it would be Karen's problem.

Nice to have his suspicions about that creaking sound he'd heard earlier proved right—the upper door to the back stairs *had* been left open.

Mind you, that doesn't explain the baby crying.

The faint unhappy sound was coming from his left. He turned slowly. They weren't using that end of the hall, so he had no idea what was down there. *Gee, you think it could be the nursery?* And the million-dollar question now became: Was it a new ghost or were the two teenage ghosts he'd already seen just screwing around trying to freak him out?

"Tony!"

For half a heartbeat, he thought it was the baby calling his name. Apparently, the freaking-him-out part was working fine.

"Haul asssssssssssstkta wardrobe and pick up Maffff-fffffffffffffk other tie from Brenda."

"I'm on it, Adam." He thumbed off his microphone

and started back down the stairs. Investigating phantom babies would have to wait. *And I'm so broken up about that. . . .*

Crossing the porch, he felt someone watching him.

The caretaker's black cat sat staring at him from one of the deep stone sills that footed the dining room window.

"Good," he told it. "Stay out here."

Maybe a cat could make it from the second floor and through half of a very large house in the time it took him to cover a tenth of the distance. Maybe it was really motoring. Maybe he didn't much care. Cat weirdness was pretty low on his list at the moment.

♦

As Lee and Mason entered the drawing room for the fourth time, Tony headed for the kitchen and the side door. Tucked into the narrow breezeway linking the main house with the four-car garage added in the thirties, he thumbed CB's very private number into his cell phone. This was the number he'd been given when they'd thought a dark wizard's army from another reality was about to invade. This was the number he'd been told never to use except in the case of a similar emergency. Ghosts weren't exactly on the same level, but the bar *had* been set pretty damned high first time out.

"We're sorry, the number you have dialed is not in service. Please hang up and try your call again."

Great. His direct-to-CB number was worthless. One of the producer's ex-wives had probably gotten hold of it. No chance of getting to him through the regular office number either—not through Ruth the office manager, not by telling the truth anyway. Lying, on the other hand . . .

"Peter wants me to give CB a message."

"Give it to me and I'll pass it on."

"Uh, he said I was to give it directly to CB."

"Tough."

Something more complex, perhaps . . .

"There's been some of the usual trouble with Mason. Peter wants the boss to talk to him. I'm to hand Mason the phone the moment CB picks up."

That might work. When Mason was in one of his moods, CB was the court of last resort.

♦

"Sorry, Tony. CB's in a meeting."

"But . . ."

"Look, Peter'll just have to handle whatever it is on his own. Call back in about an hour."

"But . . ."

"It's a money meeting."

Crap.

Rumor was the police had called during a money meeting when they'd arrested CB's third wife for torching his Caddie after a matinee viewing of *Waiting to Exhale.* CB dealt with it when the meeting was over.

"How long's this meeting supposed to last?"

"How should I know?" He could almost hear Ruth roll her eyes over the phone. "All morning definitely."

"I guess I'll call when we break for lunch, then."

"Why don't you do that."

"Yeah, why don't I." Switching off his phone, Tony stared out at the rain pocking the puddles. "Nothing'll happen before lunch."

He just wished that sounded less like famous last words.

Nothing happened before lunch.

The ghosts stayed out of sight. The baby stopped crying. Flies didn't gather, the walls didn't bleed, and there were no spectral voices telling them to get out. The traditional high body count never happened. Peter finished with the extras, completed the close-ups on the one bit player, and sent everybody home before they legally had to feed them. Although not feeding them was a relative term since craft services looked as though a swarm of locusts had passed through as they exited by way of the kitchen. Their souvenir hunter didn't snatch anything else, but neither was the broken garden claw returned to the conservatory.

"I'm sure I can find a broken claw somewhere to bring in," Keisha sighed, standing over the kitchen sink washing makeup off cocktail glasses. "I'm just glad those tea bag figurines are still there. I could replace them off eBay, but we both know I'd never see my thirteen dollars again."

"Thirteen bucks?" Tony was amazed. Or appalled. He wasn't sure which. "No shit?"

"Shit was up to $72.86 last time I checked. Sure, they call it coprolites, but we know what it is. Are you going to let the cat in?"

The cat was sitting outside the kitchen window languidly tearing at the screen with the claws of one front paw.

"No." He threw the denial as much at the cat as at Keisha. "It lives with the caretaker, so it can just go home. It's not like it's homeless and starving."

And speaking of starving—the caterers had set up lunch in the dining room.

Tony crossed the kitchen toward the butler's pantry, passed the back stairs, glanced up and thought he saw a black tail disappear around the second-floor landing heading for the third floor. He turned back toward the window. The cat was gone. *Next time don't look up the stairs,* he told himself heading through the butler's pantry. *If you don't want to know, don't look.*

He'd barely settled down with a plate of ginger sesame chicken, noodles, and a Caesar salad when he felt a cold hand close over his shoulder.

"Geez, you're a little jumpy."

Considering he'd just dumped his lunch, not really much he could say to that.

"Listen, finish up quick . . ." Adam paused and grinned as Tony scooped another handful of chicken and lettuce off his lap. ". . . and head back to the studio.

CB wants you to pick up the two kids playing the ghosts
and bring them here." The 1AD cut off Tony's nascent
protest. "You did drive today, didn't you?"

"Yeah, but . . ."

"So that look's just because you've got ginger sauce
seeping into your crotch?"

"No . . . well, yeah." Setting his plate back on the table,
Tony applied a napkin to the warm, wet, fabric and
prayed that warm, wet and pressure wouldn't be enough
to evoke a physical reaction. *Oh, yeah, because that sort
of thing never causes wood.* He looked up in time to see
Lee glance away and realized the actor had seen him
spill his food. Tony's brain immediately threw discretion
to the wind and added Lee Nicholas to warm, wet, and
pressure. "Someone spoke to CB?"

"Peter called him about ten minutes ago." If Adam
noticed the strain in Tony's voice, he ignored it. "Why?"

"No reason." It was just going to make getting through
Ruth to the boss a lot harder. Hang on; he was going to
the studio. Problem solved. While CB had what could
charitably be referred to as a slammed door policy, it was
always easier to speak to him in person. Where *easier* was
generously defined as *taking your life in your hands*.

"Finish eating first."

"Right. Thanks." Might as well since standing up
wasn't currently an option.

♦

"CB's not here right now."

"And the kids I'm supposed to pick up?"

Amy glanced around the crowded production office
as though the pair of child actors might be hiding in and
among the gray laminate desks or the stacks of office
supplies. "No sign of them."

"Great. Why doesn't Wanda drive them over when
they get here?"

"Because the collate function on the photocopier's

broken again and Wanda's helping Ruth with some re-
medial stapling in the kitchen."

Tony half turned following Amy's gesture and realized that the background thudding was not in fact the
sound of a hammer falling but instead the distinctive
slam-crunch of a staple forced through one too many
sheets of paper. If he'd been paying more attention, the
intermittent profanity would have given it away. "So I'm
supposed to just hang around here," he sighed. Caught
sight of Amy's expression. "No offense."

"Taken anyway." Artificially dark brows drew in as
she scowled up at him. "I've half a mind not to tell you
what I've discovered."

"If it's about Brenda and Lee; Lee already confirmed it."

"No. Knew it. You should see the graffiti in the
women's can. What is it about wardrobe assistants anyway? Didn't Mason boing the last one?"

"Yeah. And *boing?*"

She snorted. "Perfectly valid euphemism. The house
is haunted."

It took him a moment to separate the sentences.

"Caulfield House?"

"Yes."

"Is haunted?"

"Yes!" Eyes gleaming under magenta bangs, she all
but bounced in place. "Isn't that totally cool?"

*The boy-who-was-younger was in a loose white shirt.
Well, white except for the splashes of what had to be
blood—had to be because a huge triangular cut in the
right side of his neck looked as though it just missed decapitating him. The girl-who'd-been-talking-to-Lee was
wearing a summer dress, one strap torn free, the whole
fitted bodice as well as her bare shoulders stained a deep
crimson. She was also short the top left quarter of her
head—her face missing along the nose and out one
cheekbone, her left eye completely gone.*

"Not really, no."

She snorted. "You know what your problem is? You have no imagination! No connection to a world beyond the day-to-day." This time she did bounce. "These are real ghosts, Tony!"

About to argue that there were no such things as real ghosts, Tony suddenly realized that this conversation had nothing to do with him. That he didn't have to be careful about being involved with the weird lest someone trace that weirdness back to Henry, who was helpless and stakeable during the day. Old habits died hard. And weird was Amy's middle name. "How do you know Caulfield House is haunted, then?" He propped one thigh on the corner of Amy's desk.

"Duh, how do you think? I did a Web search. There's been sightings by hikers. Well, sighting," she amended reluctantly. "A young man dressed in white standing in one of the second-floor windows."

And there was that blood-running-cold feeling again. "The bathroom window?"

Heavily kohled eyes widened. "How did you know?"

"Lucky guess. Most movies, the bathroom's haunted," he continued when Amy fixed him with a suspicious glare. "You know, the whole body-in-the-bathtub thing."

"Well, these bodies aren't in the bathtub," she snapped. "Back in 1957, September twenty-sixth to be exact, Stephen and Cassandra Mills' father freaked and attacked them with an ax. They died in the second-floor bathroom. Then he killed himself!"

"How?"

Mollified by his interest, she leaned closer. "With the same ax." She mimed embedding an ax into her own forehead.

So it was entirely possible there was a third ghost.

Or a fourth . . .

"Was there a baby, too?"

"You mean . . . ?" More mimed chopping. When he

nodded, she sat back and shrugged. "It didn't mention a baby on the Web site. Why?"

"No reason."

"Yeah, right. Like I tell you about a double murder/suicide and you ask about a baby for no reason. Spill."

"I don't . . ."

Leaning forward again, she dropped her voice below eavesdropping levels. "Spill or I tell everyone in the office what you told me about you and Zev on Wreck Beach."

He glanced over his shoulder at the door leading to post production, half expecting the music director to walk through on cue. When he didn't, Tony locked eyes with Amy and matched her volume. "You wouldn't do that because you wouldn't want to upset Zev."

"Hey, as I recall our Zev comes off pretty good in this story. You're the one who stars as the hormonally challenged geek."

Vowing, not for the first time, never to go drinking with Amy again, Tony sighed. Unfortunately, hormonally challenged geek was a fairly accurate description and he didn't doubt for a moment that Amy would follow through on the threat. "All right, you win. I was standing at the top of the main stairs and I thought I heard a baby cry."

"Too cool."

"Not really."

"Really." Throwing her weight back in her chair, she steepled black-and-magenta-tipped fingers together and beamed. The beaming was freaking Tony out just a bit. Amy wasn't usually the beaming type. Scowling, frowning, glowering, yes. Beaming, no. "It's possible that the baby is Cassandra, that she isn't able to manifest the way Stephen does and this throwback to her infancy is all she can manage."

"What the hell are you talking about?"

"Ectoplasmic manifestations. Ghosts, you moron!"

She took a long, almost triumphant swallow from her coffee mug and exchanged it for the receiver as the phone rang. "CB Productions. What? Hang on a sec." Swiveling her chair around, she bellowed toward the closed bull pen door: "Billy, it's your mother. Something about water getting into your comic collection!" There was a faint scream from one of the writers. Amy listened for a few seconds, then hung up the phone. "Apparently, his room in the basement flooded. Anyway, the ghosts . . . Stephen was a year younger, so he'll be stronger. You get points for hearing the baby—provided you heard what you thought you heard—but I suppose it's too much to ask if you've seen the young man in white?"

"You suppose right." Which, technically, wasn't even a lie. "*I* don't suppose you'd be willing to do a little more research on the house? You know, just in case."

"In case of what? The kind of 'oh, no, ghosts are dangerous' crap that shows up in bad scripts? Ghosts are unhappy spirits caught between this life and the next. They can't hurt you, you big wuss."

Someone had scooped a finger of wet paint off the wall of the second-floor bathroom and applied it to Lee's ass. Granted, no one had gotten hurt, but that did prove they could manifest physically. And physical manifestation wasn't good.

"I mean, it's not like they're poltergeists," Amy continued. "They're not throwing things or damaging anything or you'd know about them by now. They're lost and confused and probably lonely. They might not even know they're dead."

They knew. Their reaction to him seeing past the glamour had proved that.

"We're shooting in the second-floor bathroom this afternoon."

"So?" Amy snorted. "It's not like they'll show up on film, and I very much doubt that anyone who works here is sensitive enough to . . . CB Productions, can I help you?"

If they didn't show up on film and he was the only one who could see them . . . No wait, Lee had seen them. Except, Lee hadn't seen them as they were. Did that matter? No. None of this mattered. Bottom line; haunted houses were not a good thing, and he was only a PA; he had to talk to the . . .

"Daddy! Ashley shoved me!"

For the second time that day, Tony felt his blood run cold. He matched Amy's terrified gaze with one of his own, she hung up the phone, and together they turned toward the outside door.

"I did not, you little liar!"

"Did! You just want to get to Mason!"

"He's not even here, Cheese!"

"Zitface!"

"Girls, try to remember this is a place of business."

"And Zitface wants to do business with Mason!" Making kissing noises, a girl of about eight backed into the office both hands raised to ward off the attack of a slightly older girl.

Following them was Chester Bane. The six-foot-four, ex-offensive tackle, who ran every aspect of CB Productions with an iron fist and a bellicose nature to back it up, looked a little desperate. Tony didn't blame him. Ashley and Brianna's mother, CB's second wife, had convinced the girls that Daddy owed them big time for the divorce and they, in turn, had convinced CB. As a result, the man who had once made an opposing quarterback wet himself in fear could deny his daughters nothing. On the rare days they came to the studio, production went right down the toilet. Once or twice other, less easily recovered things went down the toilet as well.

They must be here because we're on location.

Wait a minute.

He was supposed to be picking up the two kids playing the ghosts.

God, no.

As Ashley chased a screaming Brianna through the

door leading to the dressing rooms, CB lifted his massive head and met Tony's eyes. "You're driving them to the house, are you? Good."

So much for the power of prayer. "Uh, Boss . . ."

"I promised them they could be on the show. They're thrilled about it." His expression lightened slightly. "Unfortunately, I have paperwork to catch up on." The sound of distant crashes propelled him toward his office. "You'll be the supervising adult of record. Amy has the paperwork. See that they have a good time."

"Boss, I have to talk to you! About the house!"

CB paused in the doorway and considered him for a long moment while Tony tried to make the words metaphysical emergency appear somewhere in his expression. Finally, as the office lights flickered and faint shrieks of girlish laughter lifted the hair on the back of Tony's neck, he sighed, "Keep it short," before disappearing into his office.

Amy snagged Tony's arm as he moved to follow. "You're not going to tell him about the ghosts, are you? He'll think you're nuts and you'll still have to drive the girls to the set!"

He pulled his arm free. Ghosts on Web sites were one thing. Ghosts in the drawing room talking to the actors were something else again. Hopefully. "You just don't want the terror twins to stay here."

"Well, duh!" They winced in tandem at the distinctive sound of a clothes rack hitting the floor. "I should never have told you about the ghosts."

◆

It wouldn't have mattered, but Amy had no way of knowing that. Although given what was at stake, even if he hadn't seen Stephen and Cassandra large as life and twice as dead, he'd have used Amy's information and tried to convince CB they were real.

CB's office matched him in size and, like him, was functional rather than ornate. The single fish in the salt-water tank glared out at Tony as he passed. The fish had been a recent present from CB's lawyer and the day it was put into the tank it ate the three smaller fish still struggling to live in the murky water—an omen of biblical proportions as far as Tony was concerned. He paused about a meter from the desk, took a deep breath, and decided to get right to the point.

"Caulfield House is haunted."

"So Amy informed me first thing this morning. You're wasting my time, Mr. Foster."

"Yeah, Amy told me, too, but she didn't need to. I saw them—the ghosts."

"You saw them?" When Tony nodded, CB laid both massive hands on his desk and leaned forward. "Is this because of . . . what you could be?"

"The wizard thing? No. Maybe. I don't know." On second thought. "Probably. Point is," he added hurriedly as CB's eyes began to narrow, "I saw them. Stephen and Cassandra, murdered back in '57 standing in the drawing room talking to Lee."

"Mr. Nicholas saw them as well?"

"Yeah, but he didn't know they were dead."

"How did you . . . ?"

"Bits of them were missing."

"And Mr. Nicholas didn't notice this?"

"He wasn't seeing them the way I was. And I saw Stephen standing in the second-floor bathroom window."

"*In* the window?"

"Well, you know, behind the window. I saw him from the front lawn."

"So the house *is* haunted?"

"Yes."

"Well. Thank you for keeping me in the loop, Mr. Foster." He glanced down at the Rolex surrounding one huge wrist. "I'd like both scenes the girls are in shot this afternoon, so you'd best get moving. You may tell Peter I won't be available to take his calls."

Given that Peter had been in a good mood when

Tony'd left the shoot, Peter didn't know about the girls. He'd be calling, that was a certainty. And beside the point. "Boss, I don't think you understand. Haunted houses are dangerous."

"In what way?"

He was kidding, right? "In the dead-people-walking-around way! People die in them."

"No, people *have* died in them. Not the same thing. Have you any reason for your fear or are you basing your theory on bad movies and the world according to Stephen King? Have these ghosts done anything that might be considered threatening?"

"They put paint on Lee's tux."

"Annoying, Mr. Foster, not threatening. Anything else?"

"Ghosts stay around for a reason. Usually because they're pissed off about something."

"Like being murdered?"

"Yeah, like being murdered. And they want vengeance."

"So they put paint on Mr. Nicholas' tux?"

"Yes! No. That wasn't vengeance, that was . . . I don't know what that was, but the point is we can't keep shooting in a haunted house."

"Because something *might* happen?"

"Yes."

"You might get hit every time you cross the street. Do you spend the rest of your life standing on the sidewalk?"

"Well, no, but . . .

"I've paid for the use of this house until the end of the week. If you have nothing substantial to base your fears on . . ." CB waited pointedly until Tony shook his head. ". . . I will not disrupt my shooting schedule because you have a bad feeling and dead people are hanging about the set."

Was the man listening to himself? "Having dead people hanging about the set isn't normal!"

"Normal?" His lip curled. "Being beaten in the ratings by half a dozen so-called real people eating earthworms isn't normal, Mr. Foster. And dead people have got to be less trouble than one of Mason's ridiculous fan clubs."

Tony had to admit that was valid. One last card to play. "Your daughters . . ."

"Are looking forward to this and I will not disappoint them. They've spoken of nothing else for the last ten days."

"But . . ."

"I will *not* disappoint them. Do I make myself clear?"

"Crystal." He'd rather risk his daughters' lives than their wrath. Or at least he'd rather risk his daughters being stroked with paint than their wrath and Tony had to admit he could understand where the boss was coming from with that. Maybe he had overreacted.

Once you turn to the weird side, forever will it dominate your destiny.

So the house is haunted. If I'm the only one who knows, does it matter?

"Is there anything else, Mr. Foster?"

Apparently not. "No, sir. I'll just get the girls."

The girls were standing by the front door, eyes wide and locked on Amy. Who was on the phone. Nothing unusual about that.

"Why don't you two wait for me by my car; I'll be right out."

They nodded and ran.

"What did you do to them?" he demanded as Amy hung up. "And can you teach it to me?"

"I merely looked at them like this . . ."

"That's pretty damned scary on its own."

". . . and told them if they didn't get their grubby hands off my phone I'd put a spell on them so that they'd wet the bed at every sleepover they went on for the rest of their lives."

Checking for eavesdroppers, Tony leaned closer. "Can you really do that?"

Amy sighed. "I'm not surprised Zev dumped you. You are such a geek sometimes."

Right. Of course she couldn't. He couldn't and he was the wizard. In training. In a not-very-enthusiastic-about-the-whole-thing kind of way. Although if it meant easier handling of CB's daughters, it might not hurt to check the more advanced lessons on the laptop.

"Tony?"

"Sorry. Ghosts, girls, I'm just a little freaked. Can you call Peter and give him a heads up?"

"Oh. My. God. He doesn't know?"

Before Tony could answer, a familiar horn sounded in the parking lot. And kept sounding. Throwing a terse, "He doesn't know!" over his shoulder, Tony started to run. How the hell were they hitting the horn? His car had been locked.

Four

WITH THE PRETEEN flavor of the month pounding out of his speakers, and a vaguely familiar blue sedan in his parking spot, Tony pulled in at the end of the line of cars and shut off the engine. "All right, we're walking from here."

Ashley, who'd grabbed the front seat by ignoring screams of wrath and shoving her younger and smaller sister into the back, opened her door, stared down at the ground, and closed her door again. "It's muddy."

"Yeah, so?" Hands braced on either side of the doorframe, Tony leaned back into the car reminding himself that these were his boss' daughters and the level of profanity had to stay low. Given the delay at the office and an unavoidable side trip for ice cream on the way back to the location—unavoidable if he'd wanted to retain even minimal hearing—they were running embarrassingly late. "It's stopped raining."

"You can't make me walk in the mud. I'll tell my dad. Drive me right to the house."

"I can't."

"Ashes is afraid she'll get all dirty and then Mason'll see she's really a pig," Brianna scoffed from the back. "Oink, oink, oink, oink, oink."

"Drop dead, Cheese!"

"Make me, Zitface!"

"Look, walk in the mud, then blame me when you get dirty," Tony broke in before the insults could escalate. Again. "Mason doesn't much like me anyway, and it'll give you two something to talk about."

Ashley stared at him for a long moment, brown eyes narrowed. "Fine."

"Fine," Brianna echoed mockingly.

With the dignity of eleven years, Ashley ignored her, scooped up her backpack, and got out of the car.

As Tony locked up, Brianna bounded down the road to the path.

"Are you just going to let her do that?" Ashley demanded. "She could get lost!"

"The ruts to the house are a foot deep. I doubt it."

"You have a stupid car." He shortened his stride as she fell into step beside him. "My mom has a better car. My mom's new boyfriend has three better cars. Your car looks like something puked on it."

"Something did." When she turned a disbelieving face toward him, he added, "Old drunk guy outside my building last night. Most of it washed off in the rain."

"Eww! That is like totally the grossest thing I've ever heard."

Tony felt kind of smug about that until he remembered he wasn't twelve. "Hey, I hate to ask, but why do you call your sister Cheese?"

"Duh. Brianna. Bri. Cheese." She shot him a disapproving glare that made her look disconcertingly like her father. "I thought gay guys knew all about cheese."

"I must've missed that part in the manual."

"You got a manual?"

A shriek from Brianna kept him from having to answer. *Memo to self: facetious comments bad idea.* He jogged ahead to find the younger girl balanced on one foot, her other foot bare, the sandal nowhere to be seen.

"The stupid mud ate my shoe!" she announced, grabbing a handful of his T-shirt. "You've got to carry me."

He grabbed her backpack before it could hit the ground and settled it back onto her shoulder. "Walk barefoot."

"Mom says you catch stuff when you walk barefoot."

"Yeah, on sidewalks. Not here. This is a park."

"It's a driveway!" For an eight-year-old, she excelled at implying *you moron* with tone of voice.

"We don't have time for this!" Unfortunately, Amy's expression didn't seem to work when it wasn't on Amy's face. "Fine. I'll carry you." If CB wanted the girls to finish up in one afternoon—and given his personal feelings on the matter, Tony was willing to bet that everyone else involved wanted the same thing—they had to haul ass. He moved around in front of her and squatted slightly. "Climb on my back."

For a skinny kid, she wasn't light. He hooked his hands under her bare knees and straightened.

"You better find my sandal. My dad will fire you if you lose my sandal."

"No, he won't."

"Wanna bet?"

Not really. "Ashley, could you . . ."

"Bite me. I'm so not digging in mud for . . . oh, here it is." To his surprise, she shoved one finger under the strap and dragged it out of the thick, black dirt. "You owe me. You owe me big."

"Fine. I owe you." Hiding a shudder at the thought of what she might demand to even the odds, he jerked his head toward the house. "Now can we walk?"

With Brianna bouncing on his kidneys and Ashley keeping up a running commentary of his shortcomings, the lane into the house seemed a lot longer than it had at 7:30. As they finally drew even with the last of the trucks, two familiar figures stepped out into their path.

"Well, well, Mr. Foster." RCMP Constable Jack Elson

smiled and waved a set of sides in a sarcastic salute. "Small world, isn't it?"

Elson and his partner, RCMP Special Constable Geetha Danvers, had been the investigating officers during the series of suspicious deaths that had occurred at CB Productions back in the spring. Although natural causes with a heavy subtext of unlucky coincidence made up the official conclusion, Jack Elson had been convinced there was something else going on and he'd been determined to get to the bottom of things. Unfortunately, since the something else had involved homicidal shadows from another reality, he'd been destined to disappointment.

Because Tony had been instrumental in defeating the Shadowlord, he'd been at the center of the RCMP's investigation. With no one to blame for the nagging sense of justice not quite done, Constable Elson had made his presence felt at CB Productions whenever time allowed—with Tony at the top of his shit list closely followed by CB himself, and then the rest of his employees in no particular order.

Constable Danvers, who'd been considerably more sanguine about the case from the beginning, accompanied her partner to the studio wearing an expression that clearly said, "I'm only indulging you in this because hanging around a television show is kind of cool."

"So we saw the cars out on the road and wandered down to see if the paperwork was in order." During his too jovial explanation, Elson didn't do anything as obvious as block Tony's path but he stood in such a way that it would be difficult to get around him. Especially carrying an eight-year-old. Tony waited silently. First rule of dealing with a suspicious cop—give them nothing new to work with. "And who are these young ladies?"

Second rule—answer questions promptly and politely. And the corollary—lie if necessary. "They're the boss' daughters."

"Visiting the set?" Danvers asked, looking honestly interested.

"We're not visiting," Ashley informed her disdainfully. "We're ghosts."

"Really?" Elson smiled down at Tony in a way that made him think of handcuffs. And not in a fun way either. "You wouldn't be contravening child labor laws would you?"

Before Tony could answer, Brianna lifted her chin out of the indentation she'd dug in his right shoulder, pointed a skinny arm toward Burnaby's finest, and declared, "I can see a booger in your nose."

"Why don't you two go find Peter?" Tony suggested easing Brianna to the ground.

Shrieking "Peter! Peter! Peter!" she shoved her foot into her muddy sandal and raced after her sister who'd gotten a three Peter head start.

As the director's name died down in the distance, Tony had a strong suspicion it was a suggestion that would come back to haunt him. And speaking of haunting . . .

The police had access to information the general public did not. Information—finding it, having it, passing it along in the way that would do him the most good—had always been Tony's preferred coin. Given that he'd survived everything an increasingly skewed world had thrown at him . . .

"Brianna! No!" Tina's distant protest had a hint of homicide in it.

. . . so far, maybe it wouldn't hurt to do a bit of digging now.

"Great house, eh?" He fixed both officers with his best *"fine, you want to stand there, then I'm going to talk"* expression. "I guess you guys are on top of that whole double murder suicide thing."

"In the house? This house?"

He let himself look smug as he repeated what Amy had told him.

Constable Elson rolled his eyes. "A little before our time."

Memory took him to the top of the stairs and a baby crying. "So nothing more recent?" He snapped back to himself in time to see them both staring.

Constable Danvers raised a questioning brow. "Recent?"

"Maybe he's been hearing things." When Tony scowled, Elson broke out laughing. "Maybe he thinks it's haunted." Waving his hands in the accepted gesture for *ooooooo, spooky* he headed for the road. "Come on, Dee. I'm so scared. Let's get out of here in case Raymond what's-his-fang has called up more of his dark brethren."

Rolling her eyes not entirely unsympathetically in Tony's direction, Danvers stepped onto the grass at the edge of the drive and followed her partner.

Although he would rather have had an answer to his question, Tony had to admit that giving Constable Elson an exit line he couldn't resist using worked, too. "Probably has all four seasons of *Due South* on DVD," he muttered as he rounded the trailer and nearly slammed into Brenda. She looked terrified.

And it begins . . .

"Ashley and Brianna?" Eyes wide, she grabbed a handful of his T-shirt. "Please tell me the ghosts aren't being played by Ashley and Brianna?"

Okay, not what he'd expected but valid terror nevertheless. "Wish I could."

"Have you ever tried to dress those two? I'd rather put pantyhose on a monkey!"

"And thank you for that image."

"Tony, this is serious. Does Peter know?"

They winced in unison at the crash from inside. "Well, Amy was going to call him." A second, louder crash. "He does now."

♥

"She's staring at me again."

"I think the word you're looking for isn't again, it's still," Lee pointed out, shifting to the right so that Ashley could have a clearer line of sight. "The only time she's stopped staring at you since she arrived was when she was in wardrobe."

Mason shuffled left, putting his costar's tuxedo-clad shoulders between him and the girl. "She's starting to creep me out. I mean, I know what to do when older girls stare at me like that, but she's eleven!"

"So ignore her."

"Easy to say."

Ashley, wearing her turn-of-the-century costume, sat in Peter's chair, stroking the caretaker's cat—allowed back on the set when the girls had screamed down the possibility of its exclusion—her eyes locked on Mason, her bare feet swinging in an inexplicably ominous rhythm. When he moved, she moved. Or she moved whatever currently blocked her line of sight.

In the interest of not having his crew ordered around and his schedule completely disrupted, Peter had told Mason to remain visible.

"Why can't I just lock myself in my dressing room?" Mason had demanded.

"Do you seriously think that would stop her?" Peter'd asked him. "You can suit yourself, but if I were you, I'd stay out where there are witnesses."

In all the time he'd been working on *Darkest Night*, Tony had never seen Mason at a loss for words. Even during an incident with the wardrobe assistant, he'd managed a fairly articulate, *"Get the hell out and tell Peter I'll be there in twenty minutes."* This time, however, he'd opened his mouth, closed it again, and latched on to Lee like the other actor was his new best friend.

Lee clearly found the whole thing amusing.

"Brianna!"

Everyone, cast and crew, turned toward the door as Brenda ran into the foyer.

Sliding to a stop just over the threshold, she swept a wild gaze over the assembled men and women. "Have you seen Brianna?"

Peter paled. "Don't tell me you've lost her!"

Brenda waved the apron she held like a calico flag of surrender. "I only took my eyes off her for a second! When I turned around, she was gone! I thought I saw her running toward the house!"

"Tony!"

Tony felt his heart skip a beat as the director and everyone else turned to stare at him. Had the house claimed its first victim? *At least I warned CB. He can't blame me for this.* Right. Just like no one blamed Bennifer when *Gigli* tanked.

"You brought them," Peter continued grimly. "You find her."

He brought them? Like he had a choice?

"I think we should divide up into search parties," Ashley announced before Tony managed to think of something to say. She stood, crossed to Mason's side, and took hold of his sleeve. "Groups of two, I think. I'll go with Mason."

"No." Mason managed half a step back before he realized Ashley was moving right along with him. "You heard Peter, Tony brought them! Brought you. He's responsible. Adult guardian of record, isn't he? Let Tony do his job. Let Tony find her."

"Tony's a dork," Ashley scoffed.

Tony caught the words, "Am not!" behind his teeth. *Because that would be mature.* "I wouldn't know where to start," he pointed out in what he thought was a fairly calm voice given the circumstances.

From the back of the house came the unmistakable scream of an angry cat.

"Start in the kitchen," Peter suggested dryly.

♥

"I didn't mean to hurt it," Brianna protested, filling her mouth with cheese puffs and wiping her hand on her dress. "It got right in my way and I stepped on its stupid tail! Do you think it hates me now?"

Picking up the bowl of cheese puffs to use as a lure, Tony backed away from the craft services table. "I doubt it. Cats don't have very long memories." Considering how fast it had to have been motoring to get from the front hall to the kitchen, the odds of impact between cat and kid had to have been astronomical. Although considering this particular kid . . . As she reached for the bowl, he took another two steps. And another.

"I just wanted to look behind the door!"

"What door?" Almost out of the kitchen . . .

"That door!"

His hand throbbed. "That's just the basement," he said, trying his best to make it sound like the most boring place on Earth. "And besides, the door's locked. Your father doesn't want us to go down there."

She snorted, spraying bits of damp cheese puff and turned toward the forbidden. "My father lets me go anywhere I want."

Oh, yeah. That went well. In another minute she'd be knee-deep in floodwater and old wiring.

"Tony? Have you ffffffffffffst her?"

Depended. Define ffffffffffffst. If it meant *wanted to strangle,* then that would be a big "God, yes."

"That was Adam," he said as Brianna stared up at him through narrowed eyes. "He says since you've been gone so long, Ashley says she'll be the only ghost."

"Oh, no, she won't!"

Wow. If he'd thought the cat could motor . . .

Ashley dealt with the resulting tantrum by knocking her sister down and sitting on her until she cried uncle. Tony suspected he wasn't the only jealous adult in the room. Unfortunately, when it was over, the girls backed him into a corner while everyone else was suddenly busy setting up the shot. Since when did it take seven people to check a light meter?

"I *never* said I wanted to be the only ghost!"

"You told me she said that!"

"I'm *so* telling my father on you!"

"Ashley . . ." Struck by inspiration, Tony bent forward and lowered his voice. ". . . Mason's watching. He'll think you're acting like a little girl."

Ashley's eyes widened, her mouth snapped shut, and gathering her dignity around her, she stalked back to Peter's chair.

Tony found Brianna staring up at him with reluctant admiration. "You're such a liar," she said. "Gimme the cheese puffs."

He hadn't realized he was still holding the bowl.

Fortunately, the apron covered the accumulated orange stains on the dress.

"Why cheese puffs?" Brenda asked as Peter placed the girls where he needed them. "Why do they even have cheese puffs anyway?"

"In general?"

"No, specifically. Specifically here. Specifically where those two could get at them. Cheese puffs do not make historic stains!"

Tony patted her shoulder in a comforting way. "It's not like we're usually that big on historical accuracy."

Spinning out from under his hand, she glared at him. "I do my best!"

"I just meant it's not that important because the stains can be deleted in post."

"That's not what you said."

"I know."

"They wouldn't wear the shoes and stockings."

"Barefoot works."

"You think?"

"Sure." Why not. It was summer and it wasn't like they had an option. Suddenly certain he was being watched, Tony turned in time to see Lee look away. *Figures. Not watching me. Watching Brenda.*

"My lipstick's all gone!" Had there been a second balcony, Ashley's voice would have carried beyond it. She'd clearly inherited her father's vocal abilities. "I can't act without new lipstick!"

"Tony!"

Ears ringing, he headed out to the trailer to retrieve Everett.

Thing was, when the girls actually settled down to work, they weren't bad.

"Look up at Mason and Lee on the stairs and smile. A little less teeth, please Brianna. Good girl. Now look sad. Good, hold it. Try not to move your bodies, just change your expressions. Can you give me angry? Good work. Now thoughtful. Yes . . . up through the lashes is good, Ashley. Okay, girls, smile again . . ."

The crew held its collective breath as Peter banked as many expressions as possible, shooting cover shots and then close-ups. Tony wiped sweating palms on his jeans and scanned the entrance hall for ghosts. Were he an actual ghost and a television show was in his haunted house filming *fake* ghosts, he'd be showing up in the shot. He'd fade in slowly, so slowly, so subtly that he'd be nearly opaque by the time they noticed him, and then when they did, at the inevitable screams greeting his gruesome appearance, he'd disappear. Poof. A lot more effective than just popping in to say boo.

"Why can't I just appear behind the kids, say boo, and then disappear?"

Cassie rolled her remaining eye at her brother. "Because we're not supposed to be seen."

"But we've been seen."

"Not on purpose."

"Excuse me? Dressing up and pretending to be alive wasn't being seen on purpose?"

"That was different; we were being seen as people." One finger picking at a bit of frayed wallpaper, she peered down the stairs at the television crew. "Something feels . . ."

"Wrong. So you said already." Stephen wrapped his arms around her waist and rested his head on her shoulder.

She reached up and absently set it back in place on his neck. "Wrong. Familiar. I wish Graham was in the house, I need to talk to someone."

"I'm someone."

"I know, love." But her gaze locked on the young man who'd known what they were.

♥

Brianna screamed and dropped to the floor when the light blew, but Ashley stood her ground as bits of hot glass rained down from above, glaring at the smoking piece of equipment like she couldn't believe it was attempting to upstage her.

"Cut!" Peter's voice rose above the chaos. "Is anyone hurt?"

No one was.

"Good. That's all right, then; no one's hurt and I've got what I need down here." He glanced around as though looking for a union steward or a representative from the government's workplace safety committee who might suggest he have a larger reaction. When neither presented themselves, the set of his shoulders visibly relaxed. "If you're not needed in the bathroom, you can help clean this mess while the rest of us head to the second floor. Everett, Brenda, stay close. Tony, until Adam lets you know we're ready for the girls, keep an eye on them."

An eye? Oh, yeah, like that would be enough. Tony made his way over cables and through the sudden throng of arguing grips and electricians standing by the blown light to where CB's daughters were respectively drumming bare heels against the hardwood and staring at Mason. Before either of them could take off for parts unknown or declare they didn't want to go upstairs or announce they were telling their father about the light, he said, "You two are good."

"No shit?" Brianna asked from the floor.

He crossed his heart. "No shit."

"You don't have to sound so surprised about it," Ashley snorted, actually looking away from Mason long enough to roll her eyes in a disturbingly mature way at Tony. "Our mom is an actress, you know."

"I know." She'd been a minor but reocurring character in CB's first moderately successful series *Ghost Town.*

"And she says our dad promised he'd make her a star and then ruined her career so she made sure that that bitch Lydia Turrent got caught doing dope and that flushed the show down the toilet."

Didn't know that, Tony thought as Ashley paused for breath.

"Did you like the way I fell?" A small foot drove into his calf with considerable force. "I'm going to always do *all* my own stunts." Brianna held out her hand and allowed him to haul her upright. "I'm not afraid of nothing. The light going bang—that didn't really scare me."

"You probably made it blow up," her sister snorted.

"Didn't. And I didn't do that neither," she added as a cable box slid off the lower shelf of the video village and bounced back down the stairs.

A passing electrician jerked to a stop, the transformer he was carrying nearly yanked out of his arms.

Brianna stepped off the dangling cable. "What?"

The second-floor bathroom had already been lit and a second camera was in place and ready to go. Although

Peter hadn't been prepared for CB's children, he *had* been prepared for children. Given that CB had made it quite clear they were to be used only this one afternoon, it was imperative to work as quickly as possible while they were on the set. Considering how long it often took between shots, the half-hour break between the front hall and the bathroom was up to pit standards at any NASCAR track in North America.

As the camera feed was hooked up to the video village out in the hall, the director went over the scene with all four of his actors—Mason standing as far from Ashley as close quarters allowed. "All right, we're going to do the girls' taunting dance once with Mason and Lee in the shot and then the exact same thing with just the two of you pretending that Mason and Lee are in the shot. Then we're going to do it again from the top with each of you individually so we can get close-ups, then we'll do it again from the top with the blood." And then remembering the age of his actors, he added heartily, "But it's not real blood."

"Oh, please," Ashley drawled, "we know it's not real. We're not stupid. Well, I'm not stupid. The Cheese is a moron."

Head cocked to one side, a stubby braid sticking straight up into the air, Brianna ignored her.

Peter took a concerned step toward the younger girl. "Brianna?"

She snorted and frowned up at him. "There's a baby crying."

The silence that followed her announcement was so complete Tony could hear a car passing by on Deer Lake Road way out at the end of the lane. He could also hear a baby crying.

"I don't hear a baby." Peter glanced around at his crew, his gaze moving too fast to actually see any of them. "No one else hears a baby." Statement, not question. They didn't have time for babies.

"I hear a baby!" Her brows drew down into a familiar obstinate expression. In spite of a two-hundred-pound difference she looked frighteningly like her father. "I'm going to find it!" Head down, she darted toward the door.

Fortunately, maneuvering around the camera and Mouse and Kate slowed her down. Tony caught up at the door as she circled around Mouse and under the camera assistant's outstretched arms and managed to keep her from getting out into the hall. "Why don't I find it for you? Where's the noise coming from?"

Her lower lip went out. "It's not noise; it's crying!"

"Fine. Where's the crying coming from?"

She stared up at him suspiciously. Tony could feel the rest of the crew holding their collective breath. Few things held up a shooting schedule like chasing an eight-year-old around a house the size of some third world countries. Finally, she raised one skinny arm and pointed toward the far end of the hall. "That way."

Yeah, that was where he heard it coming from, too.

"All right. You let Peter set the shot and check your levels. I'll go look and be back before the camera's rolling."

"Yeah, but you're a liar."

"Yeah, but you know I'm a liar, so why would I lie to you?"

He held her gaze as she worked that out—a trick Henry'd taught him.

"The dominant personality maintains eye contact—it's one of the easiest ways to differentiate the hunter from the hunted."

"You mean when you don't have that whole teeth, biting, feeding thing to fall back on?"

"I mean, I am not the only predator in the city."

"Uh, Earth to Henry; how the hell do you think I survived this lo . . . OW!"

After a long moment, Brianna nodded. "You check. Then you don't lie."

"Deal."

♥

Reaching for the door handle, Tony realized that the door at the end of the hall had been divided in half—like the doors of fake farmhouse kitchens in margarine commercials. He could no longer hear the baby crying and since he couldn't hear it, he doubted that Brianna could. Given that she was safely back inside the huge bathroom being fussed over by both Brenda and Everett, he briefly considered lying about having checked.

Except that he'd more or less given her a promise and, staring at the door with the hair lifting off the back of his neck and a chill stroking icy fingers down his spine, he realized that this was neither the time nor place to break his word—although he didn't know *why* and that was definitely freaking him out.

The brass door handle was very cold.

With any luck, the room would be locked.

Nope. No luck today.

He expected a dramatic creak as he pushed it open, but the well-oiled hinges merely whispered something he didn't quite catch as he stepped over the threshold. The sky had grown overcast again, replacing the afternoon light with the soft drumming of rain against the windows. His right hand went back to the light switch, found it where it always was, and flicked the first little plastic tab up.

Nothing happened.

They weren't actually using this space, so no one had replaced the thirty-year-old bulbs.

Tony really wished he believed that.

The air was colder than the air in the rest of the house and, considering the rest of the house had been comfortably cool in spite of television lighting, that was saying something. He could smell . . . pork chops?

There was ambient light enough to see the wide border of primary colored racing cars just under the edge of the crown molding. Light enough to see the hammock strung across one corner and filled with stuffed animals so covered in dust they all appeared to be the same shade of gray. Light enough to see the crib. And the changing table. And that the safety grate had been removed from the fireplace in the far wall.

Light enough to see the baby burning on the hearth. The border suggested it was a boy, but things had gotten too crispy to be certain. His stomach twisted and he'd have puked except there were close to a dozen adults, two kids, and a camera between him and the nearest toilet.

Besides, this was just a recording of something that had happened in the past. He wasn't watching *this* baby die and that helped. A little.

Man, you'd think I'd be used to this kind of shit by now.

He could hear it screaming again.

Or he could hear something screaming.

The room grew suddenly darker.

Tony stepped back and slammed the door. Realized it had separated and he'd only brought the bottom with him, realized the darkness had almost filled the room, spat out the necessary seven words in one long string of panicked syllables, and *reached*. The upper part of the door slammed shut.

The half-dozen people standing around the video village were watching him as he turned.

"What the hell was that?" Peter demanded sticking his head out of the bathroom.

Wishing that the skin between his shoulder blades would just fucking stop creeping back and forth and up and down, Tony hurried away from the nursery. "Air pressure," he explained, hands out and away from his sides, fingers spread in the classic 'not my fault' gesture. "It slammed before I could stop it."

"If we'd been rolling . . ."

"We weren't," Tina broke in pointedly from behind

the monitors, holding up her arm and tapping one finger on her watch.

Peter's eyes widened. "Right. Well, don't just stand there. Haul ass and tell Brianna you didn't see a baby." CB's "one afternoon only" trumped doors slamming, production assistants making lame excuses, and mysterious crying.

Lying in this house might be a bad idea, but—in this case—telling an eight-year-old the truth would be a worse one. Hurrying back to the bathroom, Tony really hoped that whatever weirdness was involved here would take that into account.

♥

"He saw Karl."

"That's unlikely, Cass, no one's ever seen Karl. They just hear Karl. Even Graham hasn't seen Karl."

"*And* he wasn't touching the upper part of the door when he closed it."

Stephen stared at his sister and sighed deeply. "You've never missed that part of your brain before."

"What?"

He waved a hand toward the place the ax had hacked through her head. "The living need to touch things to move them; he's alive, therefore he had to have touched the door. Q.E.D. And where are you going?" he added hurrying to catch up.

"I need to see what's happening in the bathroom," she told him without turning.

She was wafting, not walking, and that was never a good sign. Cassie was usually militant about them maintaining a semblance of physicality lest they forget how flesh worked—he hadn't seen her so distracted for years. Memories drifted around him. They had no form and less substance, but he didn't like the way they made him feel, so he hung on to what he knew for certain. "Graham told us to stay out of the bathroom while these people are using it."

"It's *our* room."

"Well, yeah, but Graham said . . ."

"Graham doesn't know what's going on in here."

"Of course not, he's just the caretaker, he couldn't possibly . . . Cass!" He sighed again, slipped through a bit of the camera operator, and followed her in under the lights.

♥

"But I want Mason to stay!" Ashley's protest carried easily over the ambient noise of Mason and Lee pushing past various crew members to emerge out into the hall. "He's my motivation!"

"There isn't room." Peter's voice had reached the preternaturally calm stage that seemed to suggest an imminent nervous breakdown—its tonal range so limited it sounded as though it had been Botoxed. "Besides, he's just out in the hall, watching you on the monitors."

To Tony's surprise, Mason, who'd been heading to his dressing room, stopped, sighed, and returned. Since the words "team player" and Mason Reed had never appeared together previously, the crew and his costar stared at him in some confusion.

"If we don't finish today," he muttered, "they'll be back."

Eyes widened and several heads nodded sagely, reassured that Mason's motivations remained vested self-interest.

Lee clapped him on the shoulder and murmured, "Greater love. I'll go get you a coffee."

"She is *not* in love with me," Mason growled, looking a little panicked.

"It's a quote, big guy. I'll be back in a minute," he added to Adam as he turned. "Peter won't even know I'm gone."

The 1AD shrugged. "Just be back when he needs you."

"I need you . . ." Peter's direction drifted out into the

hall. ". . . to dance around in that circle a few more times pretending that Mason and Lee are still . . . Ashley, don't turn on the water. Brianna! Don't touch . . ."

All things considered, the soft *phzt* was vaguely anti-climactic.

Standing behind Sorge's left shoulder where he'd have a good view of both monitors, the gaffer frowned. "Sounded like a halo lamp going. I'm starting to think the lines in this house are seriously fucked. We should bring in a second generator."

"And getting CB to agree?" Sorge snorted. *"Bon chance."*

Tony opened his mouth to say it wasn't the lines it was the house and then closed it again. His day was already crap; he didn't need to add the ridicule that would follow any explanation of ax-murdered extras or rotisserie babies. No, better just to stay quiet and right where he was, surrounded by people who wouldn't know a metaphysical phenomenon if it bit them on the ass. Almost literally in Tina's case although the specific piece of anatomy had been higher up.

"Malcolm! Adam!"

The gaffer and the 1AD headed for the bathroom.

"Everett!"

"It's starting to be like a fraternity prank in there," Tina snickered as the makeup artist forced his way through the crowd in the doorway using his case like a battering ram. "How many people can you fit in one bathroom?"

"Tony!"

Hopefully one more.

He squeezed past the camera—extra careful while squeezing past Mouse. Mouse had been shadow-held back in the spring and while under the influence had first locked lips and then worked him over with fists the size of small hams. Theoretically, Mouse—like the other shadow-held—remembered none of his time possessed, but once or twice Tony had noticed him staring and the possibility that some lingering memories remained had made him fanatical about giving the much larger man his space.

With any luck he remembered the beating and not the tonsil hockey; given Mouse's background the beating, at least, had been in character.

Fortunately, although Kate had also been shadow-held, their interaction during that time had been minimal. If she muttered something rude under her breath as he shuffled by her, it had nothing to do with the metaphysical and everything to do with Tony being one of the few people around who had less influence on the show than she did.

The bathroom was definitely crowded. The girls were sitting on the edge of the tub being powdered although they didn't seem to need it. Actually, given the number of bodies and amount of equipment, it was strangely cool.

The nursery had been cool.

Oh fucking great . . .

The girls, Everett, Peter, Adam, Malcolm, Mouse, Kate, one of the electricians—Tony wasn't sure of his name. Nothing and no one in the room who shouldn't be there. Then he glanced in the mirror and saw the two half-dressed, bloody teenagers flickering in and out of focus.

He didn't quite gasp when Adam grabbed his arm. "Tony, the battery in my radio's gone tits-up again. Go drop it in the charger and bring me a new one."

"Sure." Not a problem. Happy to get the hell off the second floor.

Clutching the battery, he pushed his way out into the hall and headed for the back stairs. The main stairs were just a little too close to the nursery. Of course, the back stairs were right across the hall from Mason's bathroom and the crying shadow crouched by the shower stall, but at this point, ghosts that merely rocked and cried were definitely the lesser of two or three or even four evils.

No. Don't even think evil. Don't give anything ideas.

He opened the stairwell door to be greeted by the same soft *er er er er* he'd heard earlier from the kitchen. From here, he could tell that it was actually coming from the third floor. *Oh, yeah, like I'm stupid enough to look up.*

An icy draft pushed him down the first few steps. The light started to dim. He moved a little faster. Missed his footing on the steep, uneven stairs. Started to fall. His feet sliding off every second or third step, his hands desperately grabbing for a guardrail that didn't exist, he plunged toward the kitchen, crashing against the bottom door which flew open. The impact slowed him a little but not enough for him to catch his balance and his out-of-control descent continued until he slammed into a warm and yielding barrier.

Unfortunately, yielding enough he took it with him to the floor.

Heart pounding, fighting to get enough air into his lungs, his body said *familiar* before his brain caught up. No mistaking the flesh sprawled beneath him. Man. Young man. Good shape. Then his brain reengaged. Young man in good shape wearing a tuxedo . . . he lifted his head off the snowy white expanse of dress shirt to see the bottom of Lee's chin. Then the rest of Lee's face as the actor lifted his head and shook it once as though to settle his brain back into place. The green eyes focused.

"Tony?"

"Yeah." One of his legs was down between the actor's thighs, their position a parody of intimacy. He was a little too shaken up to move, muscles doing a fairly accurate imitation of cooked spaghetti as the adrenaline left his system. No way Lee could know that, though, and he half expected the other man to heave him across the room. Didn't happen. *He's probably winded, too.* "You okay?"

"I think so." Lee shifted slightly and Tony thanked

any gods who might be listening for that whole cooked spaghetti muscle thing. "You?"

Him what? A half frown up at him and he abruptly remembered. "Yeah. I'm good. Not *good* good," he added hurriedly in case Lee started thinking he was enjoying this too much. "Just not hurt good." He had a strong suspicion he was making less than no sense.

"What happened?"

"I fell. Down the stairs."

From this angle, Lee's smile was nearly blinding. A warm hand closed around Tony's bicep. "No shit."

"Am I interrupting?"

And there was the expected, albeit delayed, heave. Both men were on their feet fast enough to reassure any onlooker that neither had been damaged by the collision. Except that the only onlooker had arrived after the collision.

"Zev!" Tony ran a hand back through his hair, and flashed a smile he knew was too wide, too hearty, and too guilty at CB Productions' music director and his most recent ex. "I uh, fell down the stairs and Lee was there at the bottom and I slammed right into him. He was just . . . I mean, he cushioned my fall."

"So I saw." A white crescent flashed for an instant in the shadows of Zev's dark beard although his expression remained no more than neutrally concerned. "You guys all right?"

"Yeah. Lucky, eh?"

"Very. Nice catch, Lee."

"Sure." His face flushed—although that could have been from either sudden change in position, going down or coming up—Lee picked two large yellow melmac mugs of coffee off the kitchen table. "You guys probably want to . . . uh, you know, talk and I've got to get one of these up to Mason."

Tony took a step toward him, hand outstretched, and stopped as the flush deepened. "You've got dust on the back of your tux."

"No problem. Brenda's dancing attendance on the girls. She can get it." He turned toward the stairs, paused, and visibly changed his mind. "Seems safer to use the other set."

As Lee left the kitchen, Tony spotted Adam's battery—flung out of his hand on impact—over by the sink. When he straightened, battery back in hand, he found Zev staring at him, dark brows almost to his hairline. "What?"

"You fell down the stairs?"

"Yeah . . ."

"And Lee just happened to be there to catch you?"

"Yeah."

"And having saved you, he sank to the floor with you cradled tenderly in his arms."

"It wasn't like that!"

Zev snickered. "Looked like that."

Tony rolled his eyes and pushed past the other man, heading for the butler's pantry and the battery chargers. On the bright side, of all the people who could have walked in on him and Lee in a vaguely compromising position, Zev was the least likely to blow it out of proportion. On the other hand, given their history, Zev was the most likely to tease him unmercifully about it, so he'd just nip that in the bud right now. "I hit him pretty hard, so it wasn't so much sinking to the floor as being slammed into the floor and he wasn't cradling me tenderly or any other way—bits of me were imbedded in his ribs."

"Looked like you were happy there."

Not much he could say to that.

"Looked like he was happy to have you there."

"You're delusional." Since he was there, he changed his own battery and tossed the rest of the fully charged into a box.

Hand shoved in the front pockets of his black jeans, Zev shrugged, the backpack slung over one shoulder riding up and down with the motion. "I'm just saying he looked like a man ready for a six-pack."

"What?"

"What's the difference between a straight man and a bi . . ."

Tony sighed and held up a hand. "Okay. I remember the joke. I should never have mentioned that whole crush thing."

"Since we were together at the time, it did seem a bit unnecessary." When Tony turned a worried face toward him, Zev grinned. "Because you know, I'm blind and stupid and would never have noticed on my own even if Amy hadn't discussed it at length."

"Bite me."

"Sorry. You gave that option up."

"You dumped me!"

"Oh, yeah. Nevertheless, biting remains off the agenda."

Back in the kitchen, Tony glanced up the back stairs and, much like Lee had, turned and headed for the main hall, Zev falling into step beside him. "So, unless you dropped by to taunt me with my relationship mistakes, why *are* you here?"

"Ambient noise."

"What?"

"I'm going to play some Tchaikovsky in the foyer and record it, then figure out how the dimensions of the space change the sound. I may be able to use the minor distortions when I score the episode."

"Tchaikovsky?"

"Onegin."

"Who?"

"Ballet based on a novel by Pushkin."

"Hobbit?"

"Russian."

"CB's idea?"

"Your lack of confidence in my ability to make musical choices is why we're no longer together."

"I thought it was my lack of being Jewish?"

"Minor reason."

"Or my inability to understand what you see in Richard Dean Anderson."

"Much larger reason." Grinning, Zev slid the back-pack off his shoulder and set it on the floor by the light-ing rig in the entrance hall. "Don't you have production assisting to do?"

He did. Adam was still without a battery, although given the radio reception and the fact that most of the crew was standing about six feet away from him, it wasn't likely he could be feeling the loss. "You want to go for a beer after work?"

The music director glanced at his watch. "It's just past six. Technically, I'm after work so it depends on what time you finish up."

"CB said he'd be by to pick the girls up at eight."

Zev winced at the reminder of the episode's guest stars. "They're safely upstairs, right?"

A crash from the second floor answered before Tony could.

"Why are they eating?"

"What?"

"They're eating soup in cups. Why are they eating and not leaving? I want my room back. This is *our* space." Stephen watched his sister pacing, flickering even to his sight as she moved through people and equipment and he added, more to himself than to her, "You'll be fine once they're gone. You'll see."

"So, I just spoke to your father and he says he can't pick you up for a while, so you can stay and finish the scene if that's what you want to do. Or Tony can drive you back to the studio."

Ashley, her gaze locked on Mason, nodded.

"You want to stay?"

Brianna spread her arms and whirled up and down the hall, crashing into people and equipment. "I like being a ghost."

♥

The red splatters were very bright against the hard gloss of the bathroom walls. Cassie touched one finger to the wall and then to the slightly darker splatter on the shoulder of one of the little girls. Faces, clothes, hair, both children were dripping with red. One of them kept licking it off her hand.

Red.

Some kind of syrup.

Red as . . .

She looked down at the crimson moisture on her fingertip. "Stephen, I remember. It's about the blood . . ."

Five

BRENDA HAD DONE more than remove the dust from Lee's tux; when Tony found them tucked behind an open door, she seemed to be taking a good shot at removing his fillings with her tongue. There was enough visible movement happening in his cheeks, he looked like he had a pair of gerbils making out in his mouth.

Back in the butler's pantry, Tony jammed dead batteries into the chargers with more force than was strictly necessary. Hey, Lee could play tonsil hockey with whoever he wanted. He was an adult, Brenda was an adult; they had history and so what if Lee had told him earlier that history had been a mistake—nothing like an accidental cuddle with another man to make a straight boy run off and prove his heterosexuality.

He just wished Lee hadn't been so stereotypical.

Oh, no! Gay cooties! Must wash them away with girl spit!

Fuck it.

"Man, what's that battery ever done to you?" Ink-stained fingers with black-and-magenta-tipped nails yanked the battery from his hand and slid it effortlessly into the space. "Aren't men supposed to be better at the whole insert tab A into slot B thing?" Amy demanded as Tony ignored her and moved on to the second charger. "I mean, it's a skill set that comes with the equipment, right? Unless you're having trouble with this because you're having man trouble and we're talking a classic case of displacement."

He glared at her over the final battery. "What the hell are you doing here?"

"Oh, my God, I'm right!" When he took a step toward her, she held up both hands and grinned. "Okay, okay, it's not like my inbox isn't already full of stories of erectile dysfunction."

Tony sighed, determined not to get involved in an argument he couldn't win. "I got you a spam filter."

"What'd be the fun in that? Anyway, I'm here with tomorrow's sides."

"Where's Wanda?"

"Who?"

"Office PA."

"I know who, I was being sarcastic. Bitch sold a movie-of-the-week script to an American network and quit this afternoon. She's moving to LA to become a rich-and-famous writer." Amy's snort carried the wisdom of six years in Canadian television. "Yeah, like that ever happens." She held up her hands again, this time so that Tony could note the black streaks across both palms. "Left me to deal with a printer jam in the photocopier and this crap doesn't wash off. I'd have asked the boss if he minded dropping the sides off when he picked up the girls," she added lowering her hands and looking around, "but I wanted to see the inside of the house. It doesn't look haunted."

Ethereal music drifted in from the front hall.

"Sounds haunted."

"That's Zev. He's distorting Tchaikovsky."

"Kinky. So, how long have I got to look around?"

Tony glanced at his watch. "Not long. It's 8:40 now, and when I came downstairs at 8:30, they were almost finished. You go take a quick look; I'd better call CB and find out if he wants me to drive the girls back to the studio."

"Suck-up."

"Adult of record."

"Responsible suck-up."

Cell phone reception in the house still stank and the signal he'd managed to pick up earlier in the breezeway had disappeared. Given the crap radio reception, he didn't think he'd better move too far away from the building in case Adam needed him. *Maybe the front porch.* It was raining again, so he came back into the kitchen, closed the door behind him, and . . .

Was that three quarters of someone's head?

No.

A flash of bloodstained shirt sleeve?

He was imagining things.

That's my story and I'm sticking to it.

He grabbed a handful of marshmallow strawberries out of the bowl on the kitchen table as he passed. Karen had started to move most of the food back out to the craft services truck, but the marshmallows remained. He wasn't having any problems a hit of sugar couldn't cure.

"Why can't he see us? He saw us before."

"There's more happening now; we can't get enough energy to break through his denial."

"What denial?" Stephen snorted, waving his hand back and forth to no effect. "He already saw us twice, once in the drawing room and once in the bathroom."

"He saw us in mirrors!"

"Okay, but then he just saw us."

"After the mirrors." Cassie closed her fingers around their quarry's arm, but he merely shivered and continued walking. "We need a mirror!"

"There's one on the wall by the kitchen door."

"Stephen! He's walking away from the kitchen door!"

"Hey, no need to get frosted; I'm just trying to help."

"The glass doors in the butler's pantry; you can see yourself in them!" She sped past their quarry and grabbed the pull on the last cabinet by the dining room door. "Help me get this open! It won't do us any good if he doesn't actually look."

"It's not going to make any difference to us."

"Fine. It won't do *him* any good. Now get over here!"

♠

The glass door on one of the upper cabinets flew open with enough force that the glass rattled as it slammed back on its hinges. Tony jumped, recovered, and instinctively reached out to close it. His brain came on-line about half a second behind his hand, but by then it was too late. He could see himself reflected in the glass and, standing behind him, he could see the dead teenagers as clearly as he had in the drawing room. Okay, *not* his imagination. It was suddenly very, very cold in the butler's pantry.

He tossed the last marshmallow strawberry into his mouth, chewed slowly, and sighed. "What?"

The girl—What had Lee called her? Cassie?—made a spinning motion with one finger.

"You want me to turn around?" They were standing behind him. If he turned around . . .

Her motion became a little more frantic.

If he turned around, he'd be able to see it coming. Whatever it was. Which wasn't particularly comforting.

What the hell.

And with any luck, he thought as he turned, *not literally hell.* After all, Lee had spoken to them earlier and nothing metaphysical had happened to him.

They were standing right where their reflections had suggested they would be. Large as life and twice as dead. Or dead twice anyway.

"So?" His voice sounded remarkably steady; given that his feelings about his current situation ranged between terror and barely suppressed annoyance, he was impressed. "Why'd I need to turn around?"

"Reflections have no voice."

"As a general rule—just FYI—neither do dead people."

Cassie rolled her eye, looking remarkably like Amy considering she was missing a quarter of her face. "Look, I don't make the rules."

"Hey!" He raised a placating hand. "I hear you. You wouldn't believe . . ." A moment's pause. "Actually, *you* might."

"It doesn't matter. You've got to get out of here!"

"What?"

"You've got to get everyone out of the house by sunset!"

Sunset? It was 8:47. Sunset was at 8:53. All those years with Henry had made sunset a hard habit to break. Six minutes. *Oh, crap . . .*

The ghosts kept up as he sprinted through the dining room, fumbling for his radio.

"You believe us?" the boy demanded. "Just like that?"

"I've had some experience with sunsets and things going bump in the dark." And speaking of bump, his battery was dead. *And one more time, oh, crap . . .*

"I'd worry more about splat than bump."

"You're not helping, Stephen!"

"Can anyone else see you?" he asked as he skidded into the foyer.

Zev looked up from his mini disk recorder and frowned. "Pretty much everyone, why?"

Cassie shook her head. "No, just you."

"Great." And to Zev: "We've got to get out of here."

"Well, *I'm* almost done, but you can't just bail on the job."

"Hey, job's almost done." He grabbed the music director's arm and gave him a little shove toward the door. "Why don't I meet you outside?"

"Why don't you switch to decaf?" Zev suggested, twisting free. "It's raining, I'll wait here."

"That ballroom is incredible," Amy announced emerging from the hall that led past the library and toward the back of the house. "It's bigger than my whole Goddamned apartment!"

"You shouldn't go into the ballroom," Stephen muttered. "There's too many of them in the ballroom."

"Too many what?" Tony demanded. Amy and Zev turned to stare at him. "Never mind. You guys get out of here, I'll get the others."

He'd gone up only half a dozen steps when the girls started down from the second floor dragging Everett behind them.

"We're going to get a facial in the trailer!" Ashley announced when she saw Tony.

"No, no!" Everett protested, struggling to keep up. "I said you needed to wash your faces!"

"Facials!" Brianna shrieked.

Tony got out of their way. If nothing else, the girls would be out by sunset. The girls and Everett. And Zev and Amy. Except Zev and Amy were still standing in the hall! He made a shooing motion toward the door and continued upstairs, pushing past the grinning grip carrying Everett's makeup case.

How many people were still up there? Peter, Tina, Adam, Mouse, Kate, Sorge, Mason, Lee—and Brenda. Given the problems with the lamps, at least one electrician. Chris, the gaffer, had gone out to the truck to check his extra lights and Tony hadn't seen him come back in. One grip following the girls and Everett. Maybe one or two still up there. Hartley Skenski, the boom operator, and a sound tech—there'd been more of the sound crew around before lunch when they'd been dealing with the extras, but Tony could only remember seeing the one by the bathroom. Thirteen, maybe fourteen. Under the circumstances, he'd rather it wasn't thirteen. He really didn't need anything that could be interpreted as an omen.

"I'm not going out there! It's raining and I'll get wet!"

Ashley's voice pulled Tony around. Both girls, Everett, and the grip were standing just inside the closed outer door staring out through the beveled glass into the twilight. Zev and Amy were standing just inside the open inner doors. It was dark enough outside that Tony could see all six reflections. At least there were only six. That was good, right?

Except they were supposed to be outside by now!

"You're running out of time."

"You know, Stephen, your sister's right." Shoulders against the wallpaper, he slid past the ghost and started back downstairs. "You're not fucking helping!"

He'd just stepped off the bottom step when he felt a sudden chill. The air grew heavy and still. The sounds of talking and laughter and cables being dragged along the upstairs hall became distant—wrapped in cotton. No. Given the way the temperature had plunged, wrapped in ice.

"You're too late," Stephen murmured.

Tony snorted. "*Quel* surprise."

A door slammed.

And then another.

And another.

And another.

The sound of the front door slamming echoed through the foyer and as the echoes died, the world snapped back into place.

"The front door was already closed," Tony said to Cassie as he charged past.

She shrugged. "So were all the others."

The girls, actually looking a little scared, had backed into the hall with the grip.

Everett reached for the door handle.

Tony couldn't see his reflection in the glass. Nor could

he see the porch, or the rain, or anything at all. It was as if the world had gone from dusk to dark in a heartbeat.

"Everett! Don't . . . !"

Too late. The makeup artist grabbed the handle, turned it, shook it, kicked the base of the door, and then turned back toward his audience. "It's locked. Or jammed."

The inner doors slammed shut, the blackout curtain billowing out into the foyer like a cliché villain's cloak.

It turned out the inner doors were also locked. Or jammed. Or held closed by the evil within the house grown more powerful with the setting of the sun—but Tony figured now was not the time to mention that.

Trapped between the inner and outer doors, Everett pushed while Tony pulled. Nothing.

"What the hell is going on down here?" Peter's voice drew everyone's attention around to the stairs. Tony started to do a quick head count. . . . *eleven, twelve, thirteen . . .*

Which was when the lights went out.

"I guess I should have mentioned that was likely to happen," Cassie murmured under the high-pitched screams of the boss' daughters.

The caretaker's hand stopped about ten centimeters from the kitchen door, his fingers stubbing up against an invisible barrier.

"That's not good." He glanced down at the black cat. "Yep, you were right. I'm sorry I doubted you."

Fortunately, Tina had a small flashlight in her purse and Hartley remembered seeing candles in a drawer in the kitchen.

"What the hell were you doing going through the drawers? Never mind," Peter continued before Hartley could answer. "I don't really care. Go with Tina and bring the candles back here. Everyone else, stay right where you are. We don't need to spend the rest of the night searching for someone who's wandered off in the dark."

The dark seemed a lot, well, darker after the small cone of light from the flashlight disappeared through the dining room.

"My cell phone isn't working." Amy's voice.

"Neither is mine." And Zev's.

After the incident in episode five, CB's announcement about cell phones on set had been succinct. *"Next one I find, I implant."* Afraid to find out just *where*, the entire crew had stopped carrying their phones although Tony was willing to bet that every backpack or bag in the AD's office held one. And that none of them would work.

He jumped about two feet straight up when a small hand grabbed his T-shirt.

"I don't like this!"

"Don't worry." Trying not to hyperventilate, he pried the fabric out of Brianna's grip and wrapped her fingers in his. "It'll be all right."

"No, it won't." Stephen drifted into his line of sight, looking for the first time translucent and traditionally ghostlike. "It'll be bad. And then it'll get worse."

"It's probably just a shift in air pressure." Adam's voice came from about halfway up the stairs. "One of the back doors blew shut."

"The back doors have been shut all day." That had to be Kate, Mouse's second, because it wasn't Tina or Amy or Brenda, the only other women in the house. *Other* live *women,* he corrected silently, wishing he'd taken the time to learn the Wizard's Lamp spell instead of the showier Come to Me.

"Then one of them blew open and the storm took the power out."

"Power in this house sucks." Given content, probably the electrician.

"The power in this house is ga ... Ow! Zev! What was

that for?" Definitely Amy. "All I was going to say was that the power is gathering!"

"She's right." Cassie joined her brother. "She's guessing, but she's right."

Zev's voice sounded like it was coming through clenched teeth. "Let's try not to scare the G. I. R. L. S."

"We're not deaf." Ashley. No mistaking the nearly teenage snort.

"And we can spell." Brianna sounded better than she had, but her hand remained in Tony's. "And our father's not going to like this!"

No one argued.

"And," she declared triumphantly, "I can hear that baby again."

So could Tony; not screaming this time, but crying. A thin, sad, barely audible sound that drifted down from the upper hall.

Both ghosts turned toward the stairs.

"Karl," said Cassie.

"He's just getting warmed up," Stephen added. Then he glanced at Tony and grinned. "Get it? Warmed up?"

Impossible not to snicker.

"Something funny, Mr. Foster?"

Peter knows my snicker? Now that was disturbing. "Uh, no."

"Too bad, I'm sure we could all use a chuckle. Adam, try to raise Hartley."

"Can't. My battery's dead."

"I thought you just changed it."

"I did."

"They'll be all right," Cassie murmured reassuringly. "As long as they go straight to the kitchen and straight back. It's still early."

"And later?" Tony asked, pitching his voice under the argument going on at the stairs.

"Later . . ."

She paused for long enough that her brother answered. "Later, no one's going to be all right."

"Well, thanks a whole fucking lot for that observation."

Brianna's fingers tightened around Tony's hand, and her small body bumped hard against his hip. "Thanks a whole fucking lot for what observation?"

"Brianna!" Ashley's protest gave Tony a short reprieve. "I'm telling Mom you said fucking!"

"So did you!"

"Did not!"

"Just did, Zitface!"

Other conversations were beginning to quiet as the girls' volume rose. Any minute now Peter was going to demand to know what was going on and Brianna would tell him and then Tony would have to explain why he'd said what he'd said and to who. To whom? *Oh, yeah, grammar and the dead. Let's make sure we get* that *right. . . .* He could almost hear Peter gathering up his authority. And then he saw salvation: "There's a light in the dinning room!"

Tina's flashlight.

Hartley emerged out of the darkness carrying a full box of white emergency candles. "I got no way to light them," he said as he reached the hall. "I stopped smoking five years ago now."

Kate hadn't smoked for two, Mouse for almost seven, and Adam for going on six months.

"Oh, for crying out loud." Mason's distinctive tones. He came the rest of the way down the stairs and thrust his hand, holding his lighter, into the narrow cone of illumination. His fingers gripped the blue translucent plastic in a way that dared his audience to comment. No one took the dare. Right at the moment, no one cared if Mason smoked and lied about it. Right at the moment, no one would have cared if Mason set fire to bus shelters and lied about that.

They lit six of the twenty-four candles. Six created a large enough circle of light for comfort but not enough flame to be a fire hazard.

"A fire hazard?" Mason snorted. "It's a twenty-foot ceiling, Peter. What the hell are we going to ignite?"

"This place is rented, and we're going to be careful." The director shut the box on the remaining candles and tucked it under one arm, so pointedly not mentioning the possibility of needing the other eighteen later that everyone heard it.

"Be careful, girls." Brenda motioned Ashley back as she moved in toward a candle. "Keep your clothes away from the flame; we can't afford to replace them."

"Not to mention," Sorge pointed out dryly, "it is a bad thing to have children catch on fire."

Brenda shot him a look that might have done damage given enough light for him to catch the full impact. "That's what I meant."

"I never doubted it."

The baby, Karl, continued crying. Tony glanced up the stairs, wondering if the sound had gotten louder, and realized that Lee was watching him, frowning slightly. Their eyes met and just for an instant, Tony thought he saw . . .

"Everett's lying down!"

And whatever it was, it was gone.

He spun around. Brianna pulled down the blackout curtain and was shining Tina's flashlight between the doors. The beam showed Everett lying on his back, head canted up against the baseboard on the west wall, left arm stretched out, right hand clutching his golf shirt right over the little polo player. "Oh, great! He's had a fucking heart attack!"

"You said fucking."

The door was still jammed shut. "Yeah, get over it."

"Stay back; none of you can help!" Peter's voice stopped the rush. "Tony, is he dead?"

"No," Cassie answered before Tony could.

He turned and gave a little shriek to see her three quarters of a profile also peering through the door about four inches from his shoulder.

"Tony?" Zev. And he sounded concerned.

Face flushed with embarrassment—it had been a distinctly girly shriek—Tony kept his eyes locked on the makeup artist and waved a hand in the general direction of the people behind him. "He's unconscious, but he's not dead."

"How can you tell?"

"I can see him breathing."

"His lips are kind of blue." Brianna flicked the flashlight beam down the length of Everett's prone body. "I like his sandals."

Tony was just beginning to consider stepping away and trying to call the door to him when Mouse's large hand closed over his shoulder and pulled him back. "Move. You too, kid."

She shone the flashlight at the cameraman. The beam gleamed along the length of the light stand he was holding. "Are you gonna break the glass?"

"Yes."

"Cool."

"I wouldn't," Stephen muttered.

Great. With no time to be subtle, Tony grabbed Mouse's wrist. The big man glared down at him. "What about broken glass? You know, shards of it sticking into Everett?"

"Risk," Mouse acknowledged. "But he needs help." He shook off Tony's grip and swung the stand, the heavy base slamming down toward the inner window.

From where he was standing, Tony wasn't even sure it hit the glass although the sound of an impact echoed through the hall. There was a flash of red and another impact as Mouse landed on his ass six feet from the door, the stand bouncing across the hardwood to clang up against the far wall.

"The house won't let you damage it," Stephen told him under the rising babble of voices.

"You couldn't have said that?"

"Would they have believed you?"

Point to the dead guy.

"All right, all right! Just calm down." With everyone used to following Peter's direction, the noise level dropped. "I'm sure we'll be able to get to Everett in a couple of minutes. The guys outside at the trucks are probably working on getting the doors open right now."

The silence that fell was so complete the soft *pad pad* of Ashley shifting her weight from one bare foot to the other was the only sound in the hall.

Then Tina took her flashlight back and snapped it off. "Shouldn't we be able to hear them?" she asked.

♠

"All right; on three."

Chris and Ujjal, the genny op, shifted their grips on four-foot lengths of steel scaffolding pipe.

"One." Karen wiped rain off her face and moved a little to the right where she had a better line of sight on the kitchen door. "Two. Three."

Impact. A flare of red light and both men were flung away from the house. Karen ducked as a pipe cartwheeled over her head to crash against the side of the truck.

"Told you it wouldn't work." Graham Brummel's voice sounded over the fading reverberation of steel on steel. "House is closed up tight. Won't be opening till dawn and there's nothing you can do from out here to change that. You might as well just do what I said and head home like the rest of the crew."

"Fuck you," Chris snarled as he got to his feet. "I'm not listening to you; you're in on this. I'm calling the cops."

"And why would you need to call the police, Mr. Robinson?"

Chris, Karen, and Ujjal turned. Graham Brummel stepped back into the shadows as Chester Bane moved out into the spill of light falling from the spotlight mounted on the side of the truck. He stood, dry under the circle of his umbrella, and listened impassively as his three employees, growing wetter and wetter, attempted to explain. Finally, he raised a massive hand. "You can't get into the house."

It wasn't a question, but Chris answered it anyway. "No, sir."

"You can't even touch the house."

"No, sir."

"You can't contact the people inside the house, but you believe that they are unable to leave."

"No, sir." He frowned as Karen drove her elbow into his side. "Yes, sir?"

"My daughters are still in there."

Propelled by a hindbrain response to danger, all three of them took an involuntary step back. Karen elbowed Chris again, and he coughed out another, "Yes, sir."

"And the caretaker knows what's going on."

"Yes, sir." In unison this time, powered by relief.

"Where is he?"

"He's . . ." Chris turned, realized Graham Brummel was no longer standing by the front of the truck and frowned. Before he could continue, the sound of a door slamming over by the garage answered the question.

CB made a sound, half speculation, half growl. His employees parted as he strode forward, walked around the truck, and crossed the small courtyard to the garage, the wet gravel grinding under each deliberate step. At the door leading to the caretaker's apartment, he furled his umbrella and handed it back, fully confident there'd be someone there to take it. The door was locked.

He rattled the brass knob for a moment, noting the amount of play in the movement of the door. Then he took four long steps back into the courtyard. Ujjal scrambled to get out of his way.

"Should I call the police?" Karen asked him as he stood, staring at the door.

"Not yet." A sledgehammer wrapped in an eight-hundred-and-fifty-dollar London Fog trench coat would have made much the same sound as his shoulder did hitting the painted wood.

Wood cracked.

"A lock," he said, forcing the brass tongue through the splintered casing and opening the door, "is only as good as the wood around it. Find someplace dry to wait where you can see the house. Come and get me if anything changes."

"Shouldn't we . . ." Chris began and stopped as CB paused, one foot over the threshold. "Never mind. We'll find someplace dry to wait and watch the house."

Two more steps inside, and CB paused again. "Is Tony Foster trapped inside?" he asked without turning.

"Uh . . . yeah."

"Good."

There was a black cat sitting at the top of the stairs. He ignored it. The door behind the cat was also locked.

"You have to the count of three, Mr. Brummel."

The door opened on two. Mr. Brummel didn't look happy, but he was smart enough to move well back out of the way.

"Tell me," CB commanded as he stepped into the apartment.

Graham Brummel snorted. "Or you'll what? Call the cops?"

"No."

The single word carried threat disproportionate to its size.

♠

"You guys know what's going on?"

Brother and sister exchanged a look as identical as injuries allowed.

"Sort of," Cassie allowed at last.

Tony sighed and slid a few steps farther into the dining room. There were about half a dozen arguments going on in the front hall, and so far he hadn't been missed. " 'Sort of' isn't good enough."

"It's mostly Graham's theory."

"Graham?"

"Graham Brummel, the caretaker. He's kind of a distant cousin," Cassie explained. "When he got the job as caretaker about six years ago, he began using the blood tie to pull us more into the world. That's why we're aware and the rest aren't."

The rest. Oh, yeah, that sounded good. Tony sank down on one of the folding chairs the caterers had provided and resisted the urge to beat his head against the table. "Start at the beginning."

"The beginning?" She took a deep breath—or seemed to take a deep breath since she wasn't actually breathing. "All right. The house is . . ."

"Or holds," Stephen interrupted.

"Right; it is or holds a malevolence."

"A malevolent *what?*" Tony demanded impatiently.

Cassie frowned. "There's no need to be rude. You know, we don't have to help you."

"You're right." Not that they'd been a lot of help so far—a little late with the warning. "I apologize."

Mollified, she gave the folds of her skirt a bit of a fluff before continuing. "Graham says it's just a malevolence."

"A piece of bad stuff?"

"Very bad," Cassie agreed. "And it collects tormented spirits. Graham thinks it got the idea from Creighton Caulfield who collected some very weird stuff. He thinks Mr. Caulfield was the template for its personality."

Tony held up a hand. "So, cutting to the chase—the malevolence, the evil thing in the house wants to collect us?"

"Probably. It hasn't added anything since Karl and his mother and that was almost thirty years ago."

"I didn't see his mother."

Stephen snorted. "Of course, you didn't. Karl's like a night-light, he's on all the time."

That seemed to jibe with Amy's theory of the youngest being the strongest. "And *Mr.* Brummel knew this when CB rented the house?"

"Yes and no. He knew the background of the house, but he also believed that because the house had been empty for so long, the malevolence was dormant."

"Sleeping," Stephen offered as Tony frowned.

"Yeah, I know what dormant means. Looks like he was wrong."

"No, he was right. We can feel it now, like we could before, but the feeling only just started up again."

Great. Somehow, they'd screwed themselves. "So shooting here woke it?"

Stephen shrugged and adjusted his head. "Graham says only blood can wake it."

He leaned in closer, his eyes narrowed, his nose flared—he looked like a poster boy for dire warnings. "You don't want to be bleeding, not in this house."

"Yeah, but all the blood we used is fake!"

He'd been standing not three feet from the steps when she fell, close enough to hear her knee make that soft hard definite tissue damage sound, and he had a pretty good idea of where she'd impacted with the porch. Weirdly, while there'd been lines of red dribbling down her shin, he couldn't find any blood on the stones.

"Oh, crap."

"Tony?" Holding one of the candles carefully out in front of him, Zev peered into the dining room. "What are you doing sitting all alone in the dark?"

He wasn't alone and the two ghosts shed enough light for conversation. Probably not a good idea to mention that though. "I'm . . . uh, just thinking."

"Well, think in the foyer. Peter wants us all to stay together."

"In the foyer?"

"He doesn't think we should leave Everett."

As they left the dining room together, Amy's voice rose to meet them. "Look, what we're involved in here is clearly beyond the usual and a séance is a perfectly valid way to contact the restless spirits holding us in this house."

"Restless spirits," Mason scoffed from the stairs. "That's the most ridiculous thing I ever heard."

But he almost sounded as though he was trying to convince himself.

"Do you have a better explanation, then?" Amy asked him. "Does anyone?"

No one did.

"So why *not* hold a séance?"

Tony turned just enough to raise an eyebrow at Cassie.

The ghost shrugged. "Well, the one with the purple hair would be perfectly safe, but make sure the younger girl isn't involved. If she can hear Karl, she could easily get possessed. That's what happened to Karl's mother."

"Not our fault," Stephen muttered. "We were minding our own business and she saw us in the bathroom mirror."

"So she tried to contact us and got grabbed by something else."

"The evil thing?"

"You saw what she did to Karl, what do you think?"

"I think . . ." Which was when Tony realized that the hall had gone quiet. And everyone was staring at him. "I . . . um . . . I think a séance is a bad idea. I mean, if we are being held by restless spirits, by the kind of spirits who'd trap us in the house and keep us away from Everett, do we even want to talk to them?"

Amy rolled her eyes. "Well, duh, Tony. They can tell us why we're here and what we have to do in order to get out!"

"Survive until morning?" Stephen suggested. "And we're not restless, we're just bored."

Karl's crying had gotten louder.

"We're not having a séance." There was a definitive tone in Tina's voice that said this was the final word on the subject. "This is not the time to start playing about with things no one truly understands. Not when we're in the middle of a situation *we* don't understand. And we are most certainly not involving the children in that sort of potentially dangerous nonsense."

"They wouldn't be involved," Amy protested.

"You couldn't get the little one far enough away," Cassie said quietly.

A little too quietly.

Tony turned. He could barely see her.

Stephen glanced down at his nearly transparent hands and grimaced. "Showtime."

The sound lingered a moment after he vanished. It was the only sound. Karl had stopped crying.

A door slammed upstairs.

"I know what you're doing!" A man. Not so much shouting as shrieking in rage. He sounded . . .

Like he's gone totally bugfuck. Tony jumped at the hollow *thunk* of something heavy and sharp impacting with one of the second-floor doors.

Heavy and sharp.

"Back in 1957, September twenty-sixth to be exact, Stephen and Cassandra Mills' father freaked and attacked them with an ax."

Showtime.

"Oh, no . . ." He was halfway up the stairs before he realized he'd started moving. A hand grabbed at his leg, but he shook it off. Voices called his name, he ignored them.

The man—Mr. Mills—yanked the blade of the ax out of the door to Mason's dressing room. Except it wasn't the door to Mason's dressing room; the hall had reverted to pre-seventies renovation carpeting and wallpaper. The small part of Tony's mind not anticipating terror took a moment to note it was an improvement. *And I guess that explains why the lights are back on.*

Mr. Mills staggered sideways as the ax came free and screamed, "You can't hide from me!"

White showed all around his eyes. The skin of his face was nearly gray except for a dark spot of color high on each cheek. Blood oozed out of the cut where he'd driven his teeth through his lip, mixed with saliva, and dribbled down his chin.

Bugfuck seemed a fairly accurate diagnosis.

The door opened across the hall and Cassie stepped out, pulling it nearly closed behind her. Her face was flushed, her hair messy, but her head was intact. "Daddy, what are you . . . ?"

Mr. Mills roared and charged toward her swinging wildly.

Cassie stared at him in astonishment, lips slightly parted, frozen in place.

At the last possible instant, the door behind her opened and Stephen dove out into the hall, one arm around his sister's waist, taking them both out from under the blade of the ax.

Which came out of the plaster and lath a lot faster than it had out of the wood.

Holding hands, Cassie and Stephen ran down the hall and into the bathroom, slamming the door.

"No!" Tony stepped out into the hall. "You'll be trapped!"

Mr. Mills seemed to realize the same thing because he started to laugh maniacally.

"Hey! Crazy guy!"

No response. The ax chopped into the bathroom door.

"Goddamn it, you can't do this! They're your kids!"

Another chop and a kick and the door was open.

Cassie screamed.

He couldn't let this happen. It didn't matter that they were already dead. That this had happened almost forty freaking years ago. He couldn't stand by and do nothing. He raced down the hall and threw his arms around Mr. Mills, hoping to pin the ax to his side.

Mr. Mills walked into the bathroom, swinging the ax, like he wasn't even there.

"Filth!"

The first blow took Stephen in the side of the neck, the force of it driving him to his knees. Cassie screamed again and tried to drag her brother with her into the bathtub. Her father reached past his dying son, grabbed the strap of her dress and yanked her forward. She stumbled and slipped on Stephen's blood. The strap tore. As the pressure released, she spun around just as the ax came down, chopping the chunk out of her head.

Tony really hoped that she wasn't the one moaning as she crumpled to lie beside her brother. He really hoped it was him.

Splattered with the blood of his children, Mr. Mills turned and walked out of the bathroom, Tony backing hurriedly out of his way. Once in the hall, he looked down at the bloody ax as though he'd never seen it before, as though he had no idea whose brains and hair were stuck along its length, then he adjusted his grip and slammed the blade down between his own eyes.

Tony skipped back as the body fell and realized the light was disappearing. "No . . ." He wasn't going to be stuck up here with . . . with . . .

"Tony!"

A light in the growing darkness.

A circle of light.

A hand grabbed his arm and a familiar voice said, "Are you okay?"

"Lee?"

"Yeah, it's me. Come on. Let's get you back to the others, okay?"

He was talking slowly, calmingly. Like he expected Tony to go off the deep end at any moment. As the last of the light disappeared and there was nothing in the upstairs hall but him and Lee and Tina's flashlight, as Karl started crying again, Tony had to admit that the deep end had its attractions.

Lee took his arm as he stumbled and got him to the stairs where other hands helped steady him as he descended. Once in the hall, he swayed and sank slowly to his knees.

"Amy, get the wastebasket out of the drawing room." Tina's voice.

"But . . ."

"Quickly."

Just quickly enough.

Tony puked until his stomach emptied, then took a swallow of water and puked again. Finally, when even the dry heaves stopped, he wiped his mouth and sat back on his heels.

Wordlessly, Zev handed him a tissue.

He wiped his mouth and dropped it in the bucket. "Thanks."

The music director shrugged. "Hey, not the first time I've seen you toss your cookies."

"Man, you two had a seriously twisted relationship!"

"He had the flu," Zev explained shortly, accepting a water bottle from Amy and passing it over. "You okay now?"

"I think so." Physically anyway.

"What happened?"

Polite "let's pretend Tony's not puking" conversations stopped. Tony glanced around the hall and found all attention directed at him. Not surprising, really—they must've thought he'd gone insane. He sighed. He'd been afraid he was going to have to say this at some point; he'd just hoped to put it off as long as possible.

I could still lie.

Except that he'd figured out what the house—the malevolent thing was up to—and if he couldn't save Cassie and Stephen, there were another eighteen people in danger. Coworkers. Friends. Kids. Lying wouldn't help them.

Another deep breath.

"I see dead people."

Someone snickered. Kate found her voice first. "Bullshit."

"No." Lee came slowly down the stairs, eyes locked on Tony's face. "I believe him."

Six

"SO, ALL THE TIME I'm growing up, I heard about my mum's cousin who married a rich guy, had two kids, a big house, and the perfect life except that her husband went nuts and killed the kids and himself. End of perfect life. She dies in the loony bin fifteen years later." Graham took another pull on his beer. "You sure you don't want one?"

"I'm sure." CB leaned forward, the chair creaking under his weight. "Get on with it."

"Yeah, okay. Maybe that story's why it's always been about dead people for me. Maybe not. Who knows? Point is, I never forgot it and a few years back, when I was at loose ends, I decided to go looking for the house. You know; the house where the perfect life ended." He jerked his head toward the window. "That house. I showed up right about the time the last caretaker took a walk out to the highway and stepped in front of an eighteen wheeler. It seemed like a sign—the timing and all—and, next thing I know, I'm employed. A month later, I'm in that second-floor bathroom—the bathroom where it happened, where my mum's cousin's kids got whacked—and I look in the mirror and there's these two dead kids standing behind me. I turn around and there's nothing there. I keep going back to the bathroom and I keep seeing them and I work at it . . ."

"You *work* at it?"

"Yeah, you know, I open up to it. I reach out to the other realm," he added when CB clearly didn't understand. "Never mind, it's not important. Soon I can see them even outside the mirror and soon after that we start talking. They're a little vague at first, after all they've been trapped at the moment of their deaths for years, but the longer we talk the more they remember who they were."

"What does this have to do with my daughters?"

"I'm getting there; you're not going to get what's happening without the background stuff. So while I'm talking to the family—that's the two dead kids in case you lost track—I'm scoping out the rest of the house and spiritually, that's one crowded piece of real estate." A long drink, then he set the bottle down on the table and leaned forward, mirroring CB's position. "Bad stuff leaves its mark, okay? I'm guessing with all the weird crap Creighton Caulfield brought into the house, he got his hands on a piece that wasn't just weird—it was out-and-out evil. Just to be on the safe side, though, I checked to make sure they didn't build the house on some kind of off-limits Indian burial site and they didn't. The First Nations out here, they're on top of that stuff."

"Get. On. With. It." CB growled. Had one of his writers pitched him a plot so heavily weighted with cliché, that writer would be back working the Tim Horton's drive-through before he got to the second act. Cliché applied to his daughters, however, that made a compelling story.

"Right. Now, Creighton Caulfield, he was a piece of work. Nobody liked him and the stuff he liked, well, you don't want to know a guy who likes that kind of stuff, see? And, fed by Caulfield, the bit of bad keeps getting bigger. After a while, it's no longer a mark left by bad stuff, it's reached a critical mass and it's now a bad thing all on its own. By the time Caulfield dies, it's a full-sized malevolence."

He paused, waiting for comment, but CB only nodded, so he went on. "Trouble is nothing's feeding it anymore. Caulfield's gone and nothing's making it any bigger. So it starts working on the new people in the house and a lot more proactively than just lying around and waiting for them to slip on it like some kind of evil banana peel. It finds the weakest link." Snickering, he sat back. "You are . . ."

"I wouldn't." Not a suggestion.

Graham's mouth snapped shut and he sighed. "You know, you should really keep a sense of humor about this or it's going to be a long night."

"A short night for you if you don't *finish* the story."

"What?" Then he found the threat. "Uh, right. So the malevolence finds the person most open to it and kicks him round the bend, but this person doesn't get to go bye-bye until he's offed someone else. The whole damned place, and I use the word damned in its literal sense, is full of murders and suicides and every death feeds the malevolence and makes it stronger, more realized."

"Again, and for the last time—what does this have to do with my daughters?"

"I'm getting there. In the mid-seventies, a woman named Eva Kranby tossed her baby in a lit fireplace and then killed herself. Her husband—another seriously rich guy . . ."

"The Kranby of Kranby Groceries?"

"No idea. Wherever this guy got his money, losing his wife and baby just crushed him, but he wouldn't sell the house. He's living in New Zealand now, but he still won't sell. The house has been empty ever since except for the caretakers. The first guy, he's a total stoner and when the house makes a move he thinks he's having a bad acid trip and takes off. No food for the house. Next guy, he's a religious nut who spends a lot of time praying and finally snaps, goes babbling to his minister about exorcisms and the like and he's gone. Still no food for the house. Next guy, the guy I replace, actually does kill himself, but he does it away from the property. So there's been nothing new coming in for a number of years and hardly anyone to work on, so by the time I get here, in order to keep from just bleeding away energy, the house goes dormant and as long as you're careful not to wake it up, it's perfectly safe. Okay, some parts of it, like the ballroom, can be freak shows in their own right—we're talking a lot of trapped dead in there and you spend any time in with them, next thing you know, you're going to be joining the dance. There was this electrician, back during the first caretaker, got brought in to fix some wiring or something and they found him dead in the ballroom. They called it a heart attack, but it was exhaustion."

"So the house *has* killed after the Kranbys."

"In technical post mortem talk, he wasn't killed, he died—I got the feeling that was the ballroom acting on its own." He frowned. "Mind you, the malevolence was still awake then, so who knows. Not something I'd want to risk anyway. The dead, one at a time, not so big a problem, but you get them in groups and they're like teenagers. Could get up to anything."

"We were going to use the ballroom."

"Yeah, I heard. Good thing you changed your mind." A quick glance at the window and the dark shadow of the house against the night sky. "Or a moot point. Hard to say."

"And, I note, you didn't say. Anything."

"Well, you didn't use the ballroom, did you? I figured as long as the malevolence was asleep, no problem. You got anyone that's too sensitive on staff, and I've seen your show so I'm thinking that's not likely, and they might be getting the whole cold chills and bad feeling about things, but that's all. There's only one thing that can wake the house."

CB waited out the caretaker's pause for effect with barely concealed impatience. It was, as a result, a short pause.

"Blood. One of your people got blood on the house. I warned them not to, so it's nothing to do with me. The house woke up. The malevolence is starving—the energy from the trapped dead is enough to keep it from fading, but that's all—and it doesn't have time to be subtle, so when the sun set, it locked everything down. It'll use what energy it has stored to score big, to get it enough juice to keep it going for years and years. Your guy outside says there's nineteen people in there. It'll use what's in the house already to drive the weak ones mad and they'll do the rest."

"The weak will murder the strong and then commit suicide?"

A long swallow finished the beer. "Yeah."

"How do we stop this?"

"Just like that? How do we stop this?" Brows drawn in, Graham stared across the empty bottle at his audience. "This is the part where you tell me that I'm crazy and that's the most preposterous story you've ever heard."

"I'm in television, syndicated television at that. Your story is derivative but hardly preposterous." Although belief came more from the gate to another world that opened into his soundstage. "Also, my own people have informed me that they cannot get into the house. Now then . . ." His hands closed slowly into fists. ". . . how do we stop this?"

Pale cheeks paled further as Graham Brummel suddenly realized he was also in a certain amount of danger. "We can't. We can only wait until morning and see who survives."

"That's not good enough."

"Look . . ." All flippancy had left his voice. ". . . I understand. It's your people in there, your kids, but you can't even touch the house right now, so it's a fair assumption we can't get inside."

"Is there a way for the people inside to get out?"

Graham shrugged. "You got me. I'm not inside."

"Theorize."

"Okay. Well, I guess that if someone took on the malevolence and won, then the house'd open up."

Given the plot thus far, that seemed to follow. "Good."

"But that's not going to happen. Your people are sitting ducks. They won't have a clue what's going on and the house is going to work them like the barker works the rubes at a carny. It'll twist them and terrify them and they'll stop thinking for themselves."

"Don't count on it."

"What, because they're television people and they're used to weird?"

"That, too." CB heaved himself up out of the chair and reached into his pocket for his cell phone.

"You can't call in. I thought your people told you that. It's sucking all the power out of . . ." He stopped as CB raised a massive hand, shrugged, and wove his way around the stacks of old newspapers and books to the kitchen for another beer.

His people *had* told him that, which was why he hadn't spent the last twenty minutes on the phone. What he needed now was a second opinion. "Mr. Fitzroy? It's Chester Bane. Mr. Foster seems to have gotten himself into a situation and we could use your insight. No, we're on location . . . Yes, that's right. I'll be waiting for you in the driveway. Thank you."

"If that's a cop you called," Graham muttered, twisting the lid off another bottle as he came out of the kitchen. "They can't help. And *The X-Files* left Vancouver years ago."

"He's not a cop. Now, you . . ."

"Me?"

"What are you? A wizard?" CB stared down at the beer sprayed nearly to the tips of his highly polished Italian loafers. "Not a wizard. What then?"

"I thought I told you. It's all about dead people for me—I'm a medium."

"Ah."

"You believe that, too?"

"Yes."

"Jesus." Dropping back into his chair, Graham took a long drink. "You're either the most open-minded guy I've ever met or the most gullible."

"Do I *look* gullible?"

"Uh, no. Sorry." He rubbed the shadow of stubble on his chin with one hand and under the weight of CB's gaze, began to talk again. "I used to work the carnival circuit till that kind of thing pretty much shut down. Then I did a bit of freelance, but I just don't got John Edward's touch, you know? Say, you're a producer. When this is over, do you think you could . . . ?"

"No."

"Yeah, fine, whatever. I guess you got a right to be cranky; after all, the house has got your kids."

CB walked over to the window and stared at the roofline barely visible through the rain. "The house may have bitten off more than it can chew."

"So . . ." Brianna glared up at Tony through narrowed eyes. ". . . you lied about the baby."

"Yes."

"Was it, like, way gross?"

"Yes."

"Cool."

"All right, just hold on for a minute. You lot . . ." Peter's gesture took in Lee, Hartley, Mouse, and Kate. ". . . can hear Brianna's baby crying. You . . ." A considerably more truncated gesture at Tony. ". . . can actually see it. Saw it. The ghost of it?"

"Yes."

"And other ghosts?"

"Yes."

"And a reenactment of them dying?"

"Yes."

Peter ran both hands back through his hair and sighed. "And we're locked in here because the house is trying to collect us. As ghosts?"

"Probably."

"So it wants us dead, and is planning on driving some of us mad . . ."

"Short drive for some of you," Mason muttered.

". . . and having them kill the rest?"

"That's what it's done in the past," Tony told him, suddenly needing to break the string of one-word answers.

"This is so unfair," Amy muttered, arms folded and chin tucked in tight against her chest. "I should be seeing ghosts. Why do you get to see ghosts? You don't give a crap about other realms. If anyone's going to be a medium, it should be me, not you."

"So you're what?" his mouth asked before his brain could kick in. "A large?"

"Bite me, ghost boy. And," she continued indignation levels rising, "why do they . . ." Her gesture verged on rude. ". . . get to hear ghosts and I don't!"

It was a rhetorical question, but Tony thought he actually knew the answer. Back in the spring, Lee, Mouse, and Kate had all been shadow-held—not once, but twice. First they'd been ridden by individual shadows sent out to seek information, and then, as the shit really started to hit the fan, they'd been controlled by shadows along with the rest of the crew. Hartley and Mason had also been individually controlled, but Hartley hadn't been at work the day the Shadowlord had come calling and Mason had still been under the influence of his original shadow. Because Hartley was an alcoholic of long standing, his synapses were probably already a little fried before the whole shadow incident so no surprise it had only taken a single to open him up. Mason . . . Tony shot a speculative look at the actor and received a clear, nonverbal *Fuck you* in return. Although Mason *said* he couldn't hear the baby, he had been shadow-held for longer than anyone else.

None of which he was going to mention to Amy.

As for Brianna . . .

He had no idea.

"I mean, Brianna makes sense," Amy went on. "She's a kid and certain energies are attracted to kids."

Oh.

"It's like the baby. The younger the energy the more power it has, that's why you can hear it."

Heads nodded. Tony wondered if it was the purple hair. *You got purple hair and suddenly you're an expert on the weird.*

"So what do we do now?" Zev asked over the sound of Karl crying.

Finally, an easy question. "We get out of this house."

"And how do we do that?" Mason drawled. "Given that we can't get the door open."

"Uh . . ." They all actually seemed to be waiting for an answer. From a production assistant. Which was weird. Granted, a production assistant who could see dead people, so maybe they thought the two weirds canceled each other out. Tony had no idea. "Why don't we try tossing a chair through one of those tall windows in the drawing room?"

"Oh, no, wait just one minute, Tony." Peter's hands rose into "soothing egos" position. "We should see if *all* the doors and windows are locked before we start breaking things. Windows cost money, and CB'll have my hide if this shoot goes over budget."

"I never think I'd say this," Sorge murmured, placing his hand on Peter's shoulder, "but if Tony is right and we are locked in with a crazy bad house, CB is the least of our worries."

"If Tony is right," Mason repeated. "Big 'if.' He's a production assistant, for Christ's sake."

"I'm not." Lee stepped forward until he stood by Tony's side. "Neither is Mouse. Neither is Kate. Neither is Hartley." They stirred as Lee named them, but they didn't step forward. "And you know what? It doesn't matter. Getting the hell out of here as soon as possible sounds like a good idea, and since it seems obvious that the guys outside can't get in—or they would have by now," he added pointedly, "—it's up to us." Pivoting on a heel, he headed out of the hall, throwing, "CB can bill me for the window," back over his shoulder. He paused at the edge of the candle-light. "Tina?"

Tina snapped on her flashlight and followed.

"No fair! I want to throw something through the window!" Brianna raced after the script supervisor, Ashley ran after her sister, and the moment after that, the hall began to empty.

"Baaa! Bunch of sheep," Amy muttered. "One person moves and the rest follow." But Tony noticed she picked up a candle and came into the drawing room with the rest.

With the curtains open, the glass in the windows looked like black velvet. Completely opaque and completely nonreflective. When Tina swept the flashlight beam across them, they seemed to absorb the light.

Mouse took the captain's chair from Lee's hand. "I throw harder."

A heavy glass candy dish flew past him and shattered against the window, the pieces skittering across the hardwood floor.

"Brianna!" Brenda's voice sounded a lot like the candy dish looked.

"It wasn't me!"

"I play baseball," Ashley explained as all eyes turned to her. "Third base. It didn't go through the window."

"I throw harder than you," Mouse pointed out. He

tested the weight of the chair, then took two long steps away from the window. "Give me room."

"All right, listen up; if you're holding a candle, step back to the far wall, we don't want them blowing out." Moving up next to the cameraman and waving Lee off to one side, Peter indicated where he wanted the candleholders. "Ashley, Brianna—Brianna, don't play with the lamp, it's an antique—you two stay with Brenda."

She jumped at the sound of her name. "I thought Tony was in charge of them."

"Well, right now, you're standing next to them. When that window breaks, I want them to be the first ones out."

Tony couldn't help but notice that final bit of information made Brenda a lot happier about babysitting.

"Everyone else," Peter continued, "make sure Mouse has room to swing. Are we ready?"

"Let's settle down people. Action in . . ." Adam's voice trailed off as he realized what he was doing. "Peter started it."

"I'm the . . ." Peter twisted around to see Mouse frowning down at him from about four inches away. "Right." During half a dozen quick steps to one side, he regained his composure. "What are you waiting for, then?"

The chair had the same effect on the window the candy dish had—none at all. The window had the same effect on the chair except that the pieces were larger and flew farther from the point of impact.

"Son of a fucking bitch!" Mouse yanked the splinter from his arm and tossed it to one side.

Tony watched it tumble through the air, saw the blood glistening on the wood, and knew he wouldn't reach it in time. Call him paranoid, but giving more blood to the house seemed like a very bad idea. Panic spat out the seven words in one long string of sibilants and vowels and the splinter smacked into his hand. He shoved it in his pocket, wiped his hand on his jeans, and realized that everyone had been too concerned with Mouse and/or the impregnability of the window to notice.

"What was that you just said?"

Fuck! Almost everyone! Heart in his throat, he spun around to find Lee staring at him speculatively. There were days he'd give his right nut to have Lee stare at him speculatively. This was not one of them.

"Just, you know, swearing."

"Yeah?" A dark brow rose. "In what language?"

He didn't know. Arra had written the words of the spells out phonetically. She hadn't mentioned the name of the language. Which, as it happened, wasn't the point. And Lee was waiting for an answer.

And waiting.

And . . .

"This is nuts!"

And Tony was saved by the breakdown. As half a dozen other conversations went quiet, Tony turned to see Tom, the electrician standing alone, his chest rising and falling in a jerky, staccato rhythm.

"This is totally fucking CRAZY!"

"Calm down, Tom." Adam moved toward him, one hand outstretched. "We'll get through this."

"No, we won't! We'll die!" Tom batted Adam's hand away and turned wild eyes toward Tony. "He says we're all going to die!"

Heads pivoted to follow the accusation.

Great. "I said the house was going to try and kill us. Not the same thing."

The same heads pivoted back again to catch the electrician's response.

"Damn right it's not. Because it's not going to kill me." Tom slammed his fist against his sternum. The room had gone so quiet that the hollow thud of impact sounded unnaturally loud. "Me, I'm leaving!" Before anyone could remind him they'd been locked in, he ran for the window.

"Stop him!" Rubber soles squealing against the polished wood, Tony raced to intercept knowing even as he moved he didn't have a hope in hell of getting there in time.

Easily avoiding Adam's grab, Tom shoved Kate hard into Mouse rather than go around her. He was running full out when he hit the window.

He didn't thud at the moment of impact.

He crunched.

Tony skidded to a stop beside the body.

"But . . . I thought I heard the window break," said Amy's voice in the background as he dropped to one knee and felt for a pulse.

"It wasn't the window." Zev's voice.

No pulse. No surprise considering the weird angles and the places the bones had come through the skin . . .

Fuck!

"Mouse! Lift him off the floor!"

"Wha . . ."

"Do it!" When Peter added his support, Tony started breathing again. Peter would remember about the blood. Directors saw the big picture. "Tina! Sorge! Get that drop sheet off the gear in the library!"

Then Peter's hand was around his arm, pulling him to his feet and out of the way as Tina and Sorge raced back with the drop sheet and Mouse laid the body on the plastic tarp and folded the edges up over it.

Then they all stared as the smudges of blood disappeared into the floor.

"Is that bad?" Peter murmured.

"Probably not good," Tony acknowledged.

"Still, the whatever is *already* awake."

"Yeah, but I don't think we should encourage it."

Brianna poked the side of the tarp with one bare foot. "Is he dead?"

"Yes, honey." Brenda dropped to her knees and put her arms around the girl, forcing comfort out past what looked to be imminent hysterics. "He's dead."

"Really dead?"

"Really most sincerely dead," Mason told her with exaggerated cheer. "He's the inconsequential character who dies in the first act so we all know the situation is serious."

"That's not funny," snarled one of the grips. Tony thought his name was Saleen but he wasn't sure; the man had only been with CB Productions a few weeks.

Mason snorted. His candle flame flickered. "I wasn't joking."

"And it's not even original!"

Fangs showed below Mason's curled lip.

Brianna poked the body again. "So he's not going to get up?"

"No, honey. He's ..." Brenda paused. Frowned. Paled. Looked up at Tony.

Who didn't understand the question. "What?"

"The g ... h ... o ... s ... t ... s."

Brianna rolled her eyes and ducked out of the circle of Brenda's arms. "I got an A in spelling. She wants to know if he's gonna come back as a ghost."

Good question. "I don't know."

"But you knew he was going to die!" Brenda's eyes showed white all the way around and, without Brianna to hold onto, she seemed to be having difficulty holding onto herself.

"I didn't ..."

The finger she pointed at him was shaking. "You tried to stop him!"

"Yeah, because everything else that hit that window broke." It had seemed like a logical assumption. Well, maybe under the circumstances *logical* was the wrong word, but experience had taught him that the metaphysical followed rules just like everything else.

"All right. Fine. What do we do now?"

She looked a bit maniacal in the candlelight. At least Tony hoped it was the candlelight. Before he could come up with a less inflammatory way of saying *I have no fucking idea,* Amy said, "Silver."

"Hi ho," Mason muttered.

"On his eyes!" Amy handed her candle to Zev and pulled off one of her rings. "We lay silver on Tom's eyes," she announced, twirling it so that it caught the light, "and his spirit won't rise."

Were the shadows gathering around the circle of candlelight growing darker?

"What a crock."

Amy's chin rose and pointed belligerently toward Mason. "So let's hear your plan?"

Had Karl's crying grown louder? Shriller?

"You mean something I didn't learn watching DVDs of *The X-Files*?"

"Bite me! Chris Carter was a surfer boy with delusions and this is valid old world ritual." She removed a second ring and knelt beside the tarp. "Right, Tony?"

Were those footsteps in the library?

"Tony?"

He jumped as Lee touched his arm. *Shouldn't he be back behind me a few more feet?*

He moved, you idiot.

And everyone was looking at him again. Great.

Across the body, Zev frowned. "You okay?"

"Yeah. Just . . ." Just never mind. Things were bad enough without him adding another two cents' worth. "I think it's a good idea. The silver. Amy knows about shit like this. That. You know."

Mason's turn to roll his eyes. "How articulate."

"You're not helping," Peter told him quietly. "Amy, go ahead."

"You know what would be cool?" Ashley said as Amy's hand closed around the edge of the tarp. "If, when she opened that up, if Tom opened his eyes. Really wide."

Amy froze. Everyone in the room considered it.

The silence grew weighted with the possibility.

The hair on the back of Tony's neck lifted as the build of emotion began to escalate into something else. Something they probably wouldn't want to spend the night locked in with. Or more accurately, something *else* they wouldn't want to spend the night locked in with.

"Didn't we do the eyes thing in episode six?" he asked, his voice awkwardly loud. "And again in episode eleven?"

"Cliché," Sorge agreed. "I say so then."

"It was a perfectly valid way to up the emotional stakes," Peter protested in the weary tone of one who had protested before.

The cinematographer dug his thumbnail into the soft wax at the top of his candle. "Maybe the first time."

"The second time, it didn't really happen," Peter reminded him. "It was all in Lee's head. In James Taylor Grant's head, anyway."

"And we were there—why?"

"We were where—why?" And in the same breath. "Brianna, stop poking the body!"

"Why in James Taylor Grant's head?"

"You know why; because he was imagining things!"

"No." Sorge shook his head. "Still doesn't work for me."

"It was six episodes ago!"

"Also eleven episodes ago."

"So you've had time to get over it."

"Still . . ."

"Oh, for crying out loud." Amy flipped back a corner of the tarp and quickly laid a ring on each of Tom's closed eyes.

Tony released a breath he couldn't remember holding as she covered the body again. A small sound by his right side. He turned his head just far enough to see Lee give him a quick thumbs-up, understanding that nothing defused tensions like rehashing creative differences for the seven thousandth time.

Then Lee's gesture continued until both his hands were clapped over his ears. Mouse grunted. Kate swore. Tony fought the urge to do all three and settled on gritting his teeth as every muscle in his body tensed. The lights came up and Karl's screams—which he realized now had stopped for a few moments, leaving the background under Sorge and Peter's argument empty of sound—became shrieks of panic and pain.

Fortunately, it had been a large fire and a small baby.

The faint, distant sound of a woman's voice singing nursery rhymes grew more distinct as the shrieking stopped, but he seemed to be the only one who could hear her and even he lost the thread of the song under Brianna's shrill demands to be let go.

"I want to go see the baby!"

She fought against Zev's grip, driving her fists into his shoulders, but he had her held too closely for her to put much force behind the blows. And too closely for her to use her feet, Tony noted. Smart guy, given that he was on his knees. Tony doubted he had a cup on under his jeans. At least he never had while they were dating.

"Let go! Let go! Let go!"

Zev murmured something against her hair that Tony didn't catch.

" 'Cause Tony said it was way gross and I want to see!"

Both brows rose, but he quickly schooled his expression and brought her face around until he could stare deep into her eyes, his tone calm and reassuring. "It's not real, you know. It's just bits left over from a long time ago."

She sniffed and stopped fighting him. "Like television?"

"Just like television. The house recorded what happened and now it's playing it back."

"Trying to fool us and make us think it's real?"

"That's right."

"But we know it's not real."

"Yes, we do."

Shoulders squared and chins lifted among the listening adults. Out of the mouths of babes—they *knew* it wasn't real.

"Stupid house."

"No argument from me." When she answered his smile with one of her own, Zev stood, scooping her up and settling her weight on one hip. "Let's get out of here." For the benefit of the others in the room, his gaze flicked down to the body and back up again.

Tony's heart stopped at the sight of a red-brown streak across Zev's cheek and then started beating again when he realized it had been left by some of the fake blood still in Brianna's hair. *No way. We don't lose Zev. Or Amy. Or . . . fuck. Who says I get to choose?* And even thinking about choosing put him in a Meryl Streep space he'd just as soon not have visited.

"Leaving is a good idea." Amy, now holding her candle and Zev's, started for the foyer.

How had the foyer become their safe place? Because they'd spent more time shooting in it and it had become familiar? Because it was a big empty space with fewer nooks and crannies for the weird to hide out in? Maybe because it was the last place things had been normal. Or what passed for normal during the long, overcaffeinated hours of television production.

"Mason?" Ashley tugged on the actor's tuxedo jacket. "Are you okay?"

"Fine. I'm fine. Just a headache."

It had to be one hell of a headache, Tony conceded, because when Ashley took hold of his hand, Mason's fingers closed around hers almost gratefully.

"Our contract says no smoking in the house," Peter told him as he followed the actor and the little girl out of the drawing room. "So if you feel the need to light up . . ."

"That's not it!"

It was something, though. Mason wasn't a good enough actor to entirely smooth out the ragged edges in his voice.

"Are we just going to leave him here?" Lee asked, pausing by the tarp and Tom's body.

Tony shrugged. "If he wants to join us, he knows the way."

"That's . . . ghoulish." One corner of Lee's mouth curled up. "This is me not laughing. Do you think he will?"

"No. If Amy's rings don't work, and if I actually understand what the fuck is going on, he should just keep running into the window over and over."

"One show and then immediately into reruns."

"Yeah, doesn't take much to go into syndication around here."

"Still not laughing." Although he sounded close.

"Me either." It felt so strangely right, standing there, together, staring down at the first casualty, making the kind of bad jokes that guys made when things got dangerously whacked, that Tony began to get just a little freaked. Fortunately, he had an easy out. "Brenda's waiting for you."

Brenda was standing by the door, doing a Lady Macbeth with her hands. Next to her stood Saleen who had the only candle still in the drawing room and was clearly waiting for the three stragglers to leave. Just as clearly as Brenda was waiting for Lee.

Lee said nothing for a long moment although Tony had the feeling things were being said just beyond the range of his hearing. Like Lee was talking at a level only dogs could hear. Or something. Then he snorted, sounding almost amused, and crossed to tuck Brenda up against his side. While she didn't exactly relax, the time frame extended on her obvious air of "I'm five minutes from a total breakdown."

"Move your ass," Saleen snarled at Tony standing alone by the corpse.

Was it his imagination or had Karl's crying picked up a mocking undertone?

With half a dozen candles burning and light reflecting off the polished floor and the high gloss on the wood paneling, the hall was almost welcoming—where *almost* referred to it as good as it got while trapped inside a homicidal house.

Tina stood by the inside door, shining her flashlight beam down into the entry. "Everett's still breathing, but he doesn't look good."

"He's never looked that good to me," Mason muttered. "Oh, come off it," he continued over half a dozen protests. "It was the perfect straight line; everyone was thinking it."

Most of the men, and Amy, nodded.

"I don't like that he's been in there so long." Tina brought her left wrist up closer to her face and frowned. "Damn, my watch isn't working. What time is it?"

No one's watch was working—although the hands and numbers on Amy's were still glowing in the dark.

"What difference does that make if it's not telling time?" Adam asked her.

She shrugged. "It's comforting."

"So what do we do now, eh?" Hartley asked, shifting his weight from heel to toe, arms wrapped around his torso.

"We survive until morning," Peter announced in the same no-nonsense tone he'd use to call for quiet on the set. "All of us."

"All the rest of us," someone said. Tony thought it might have been Pavin, the sound tech, but he wasn't sure.

"Yeah, and we stop listening to *him!*" That was definitely Kate. Arms folded in the more aggressive version of Hartley's position, she glared at Tony. "If it wasn't for his stupid idea of throwing stuff through those windows, Tom would still be alive!"

A little stunned by the accusation, it took Tony a moment to find the words. "I never said he should throw *himself* through!"

"Your idea to go into that room, so you put him in there. Your idea to throw stuff, so you planted the seed in a desperate man."

"Seed? What seed? And he didn't seem desperate to me."

"You're not denying it, then!"

"What?" Oh, crap. He hadn't. He hadn't thought he needed to, but from all the creased brows and narrowed eyes, it looked like Kate wasn't the only one who thought he was responsible for Tom's death. *Some of us will go crazy and kill the rest. Great. And guess which list I'm on.* As Kate stepped forward, he took an involuntary step back. *So I'm thinking it's too late for us to become friends.* As Mouse joined her, he stepped back again. And once more for luck.

"Leave him be, Kate."

Mouse was on his side?

"Can't blame Tony for Tom's death. Might as well blame Lee for going into the room first."

The narrowed eyes and creased brows fixed on Lee.

"Or Ashley for throwing the dish."

Creases began smoothing out. No one in the crew could blame a little girl. Or more specifically, they'd learned there was no percentage in blaming CB's daughter—even for things she was guilty of.

"Or me for throwing the chair."

And that killed the accusation cold. Tony was relieved to see that no one was suicidal enough yet to throw accusations at a man capable of bench-pressing a Buick.

In the awkward silence that followed, Tina picked up Everett's makeup case and carried it over to where Brenda and Lee were standing. "Brenda, why don't we get the girls' makeup off?"

"I'm wardrobe."

"So you're saying you can't do it?"

"No, I just . . . I mean . . . Fine." She pulled away from Lee so reluctantly Tony almost heard duct tape releasing. "Brianna, you're messier, so you should . . . Brianna?"

"Cheese!" Ashley reached past Zev and grabbed her sister's shoulder, shaking animation back into her face.

Zev gently but firmly separated them and then knelt. "What is it, Bri?"

"The baby's stopped crying."

"But that's good, right?"

She frowned. "I don't think so."

Neither did Tony. Previously, when Karl stopped crying, it signaled the beginning of a flashback. Cassie and Stephen, Karl's own death . . .

The lights in the hall came on. There was furniture—a couple of high-back chairs, a half-moon table with a vase of white tulips, an Oriental rug.

And Tony was alone.

Except for whoever was screaming, "Charles, don't!" up on the second floor.

The second floor still seemed to be in darkness, so whatever was going to happen was going to happen out here.

And there they were.

Ladies and gentlemen, if I could direct your attention to the top of the stairs. Charles was wearing a uniform. The woman with him wore a gray suit—snug, tailored, and obviously expensive. Tony didn't know much about women's fashions, but it looked like the one Madonna wore in *Evita*. Charles had his hands wrapped around her upper arms and was moving her slowly backward. She was crying, begging him to stop, but he almost seemed not to hear her, his face terrifyingly blank.

That's great. I can hear her and he can't?

Crap. He's going to throw her down the stairs. Knowing it was futile, Tony ran for the stairs anyway.

But they descended two, three, four steps down the long staircase and still no push.

Charles stepped down so they were both standing on the fifth step. "You want to hang around with your *friends* while I'm gone," he said quietly, emphasis making the gender of the friends clear, "you go right ahead." Then he lifted her and slammed her onto one half of the rack of antlers hanging on the wall. Fabric tore and the longest prong emerged out through the front of the gray suit.

"Okay, I'll believe that madness gave him strength," Tony protested, to the house, to the ghosts, to keep from screaming, "but there's no way those antlers would stay on the wall with a full-grown woman—even a short one—hanging off them!"

Which was when the antlers came off the wall and bounced down the stairs, the gurgling, thrashing woman still attached. Tony glanced down as Charles did to see that she'd come to a twitching stop halfway through his legs.

"Fuck, fuck, FUCK!" He danced back.

Stopped dancing in time to see the big finish to Charles' dive over the banister. Heads really did sound like melons splitting. The Foley guys would be pleased.

The lights went out. Became candlelight again.

And he was no longer alone.

"Stop staring at me," he muttered trying to catch his breath.

"They think you've gone crazy."

"Jesus fucking Christ!" He jumped back as Stephen and Cassie appeared suddenly in front of him.

"And that's not helping," Stephen pointed out.

"Thanks. No shit. Where the hell have you two been?"

"It took us a while to manifest again after we died and then we're stuck in the bathroom while the others take their turn."

The siblings were just translucent enough for Tony to see that no one had, in fact, stopped staring.

Some of them would go crazy and kill the rest.

Lunatic.

Or victim.

Now, he might be reading too much into expressions he could barely see—given the ghosts and the candle-light and all—but it seemed as though everyone had changed their mind about which description best suited him.

Seven

"I'M NOT CRAZY."

"You're reacting to things that only you can see, and you're talking to nobody."

"I'm reacting to old murders being replayed, and I'm talking to Stephen and Cassie." Tony jerked his head toward the brother and sister. Stephen was watching the exchange with some interest, but Cassie's gaze flicked all around the hall—her single eye working overtime to cover the whole area while both her hands clutched at the translucent fabric of her skirt. Given that she'd been brutally murdered years before and had apparently relived the incident numerous times since, he wondered just what remained for her to be uneasy about. "What's the matter?"

"She's listening for the music," Stephen answered when his sister didn't. "The ballroom creeps her out."

"You're talking to ghosts," Zev sighed.

"Yeah."

"And that doesn't sound crazy to you?"

"Zev . . ."

"I'm not saying it's not all true—my personal beliefs to the contrary, weird shit is definitely happening here tonight—but you have to admit it sounds crazy."

"He's right."

"Shut up, Stephen!" Tony turned to glare at the ghost as Zev's reassuring smile tightened.

"Case in point."

Tony ran a hand through his hair. He hadn't exactly been ostracized since his reaction to the last reenactment, but everyone seemed uncomfortable having him too close, forcing him out toward the edges of the light.

"In situations like this . . ."

And that was certainly using the phrase "like this" in its loosest sense.

". . . people look for someone to blame. You're setting yourself up to be that someone." Zev closed his hand around Tony's arm and squeezed gently. "You know you are."

"Yeah, and I also know I can't not tell you guys what's going on. In a situation *like this* . . ." Okay, maybe Zev was trying to help and maybe the sarcastic emphasis wasn't entirely called for. So what. ". . . I can't be the one who decides what's important information and what's not. Not when nineteen . . . eighteen lives are at stake."

"Seventeen."

"Everett's still alive." Suddenly unsure, he glanced over at Cassie who nodded. "Yeah, still alive. Eighteen."

"I'm not disagreeing with you, Tony, I'm just . . ." He paused and sighed again, his grip on Tony's arm tightening. "I'm just saying you should be careful. Emotions are fraying."

"He's right."

"Cassie agrees with you."

Zev nodded at the space to Tony's right. "Thank you."

Tony pointed left. "She's over there."

"Stop it! Stop it now!" Brianna's protest rose up and over and temporarily obliterated Karl's crying. As Tony turned, he noticed everyone's attention locking on CB's younger daughter, grateful for the distraction. "You're pulling!"

"Fine." Brenda stepped back, lip curling. "Then we'll just leave your hair like it is."

"No! I want it braided!"

"Then you have to hold still."

"I won't! Not for you! You suck!"

"No . . ." The pause went on just long enough that everyone leaned forward slightly, waiting for Brenda's response. ". . . you suck!"

Brianna's chin lifted and her eyes narrowed. "No, you! And I'm telling my father you didn't take care of me!"

"Don't tempt me!" The wardrobe supervisor held up her right hand, finger and thumb barely apart. "I'm this close to taking care of you!"

Zev released Tony's arm. "I think I'd better get over there before Brianna gets strangled."

"Don't hurry."

"Give the kid a break, she's just scared and acting out."

"I guess." Although it didn't look like any definition of scared Tony'd ever seen. Not unless she'd been scared eighty percent of the time she'd ever been at the studio. "I never knew you were so good with kids."

"Yeah, well . . ." He turned back just far enough for Tony to see a dark brow rise. ". . . we weren't together long enough for you to find out."

"Zing and ouch!" Amy stepped into the space Zev had vacated and they watched him cross to Brianna's side, taking the blue plastic comb from Brenda's hand as he passed. "This is why you should never date someone from work."

No surprise that she conveniently ignored having encouraged them both. "Should you be standing here? Aren't you afraid I'll finish going crazy and kill you?"

"Because you're seeing ectoplasmic manifestations?" She snorted. "Man, I'd love to see a ghost. What do they look like?"

"I don't know . . ." He shrugged and took another look. ". . . dead. Cassie's missing a chunk of her head, and Stephen's neck has been hacked into. Their clothes are covered in blood and . . ."

"And what?"

"Nothing." He'd just realized that Stephen wasn't wearing pants under the bloodstained shirt—with all the blood and them being ax murdered and, well, dead, he'd never noticed it before. They were both watching him when he lifted his eyes off Stephen's bare legs. "Hey." He spread his hands. "None of my business."

Amy looked in the same direction and frowned. "What?" she demanded, repeating the question again, significantly louder, when Tony didn't immediately respond.

With Brianna happily submitting to Zev's hairdressing, everyone now snapped their attention around to Amy.

"We're just talking," she sighed. "Get a collective life."

"Not entirely a bad idea." Peter pushed himself away from the wall under the stairs and walked out to the center of the hall, visibly becoming "the director" as he moved. "Listen up, people, it's going to be a long night if we just sit here, so let's try and come up with something a little more proactive."

No one spoke.

"You could kill yourselves now. Then you wouldn't have to wait for bad stuff to happen."

No one except Stephen. Tony decided not to pass his observation on.

"Anyone?" Peter pivoted on one heel. "Adam? Tina? Sorge?" With two shrugs and a nontranslatable mumble as a response, he threw up his arms. "Oh, for God's sake, we create this kind of crap. If this was an episode of *Darkest Night,* how would we resolve it?"

"If this was an episode of *Darkest Night,*" Amy snorted, "we'd all be red-shirts. Well, except for Mason and Lee—because they've got to be back next week and probably the kids since the last one of us standing sacrificed him or herself to save them. The only sure thing about this many people trapped in a haunted house is that the body count is going to be high." She swept a disdainful gaze around at her silent audience. "What? You know that's the way it would go down."

"All right, fine. Maybe," Peter snapped, over the chorus of muttered acknowledgments. "And now you've made your point, let's rewrite the script in such a way that we all survive."

"Oh, a *rewrite*. You should've said. I think . . ." Black-and-magenta-tipped fingers tapped her chest somewhere around Hello Kitty's left ear. ". . . that if there's a thing in the house attempting to collect us, we should destroy it, thus freeing the ghosts and ourselves."

New silence. Speculative this time. Tony was amazed that no one said anything about the *thus*. He, personally, was standing too close to comment safely.

"That sounds . . . simple enough," Adam admitted after a long moment.

"Too simple," Saleen scoffed.

"What? It can't be simple?"

The grip pointedly folded muscular arms. "If it's been around since before the house was built, how do we destroy it? And how do we even find it?"

"It's in the basement," Tony and Stephen said simultaneously. "The caretaker warned me away from the stairs," Tony continued on his own as Stephen made "fine, go ahead if you're so smart" faces. "And when I touched the doorknob, it gave me a shock."

"Oooo, a shock." Saleen recoiled in mock horror.

Tony ignored him; so far there'd been plenty of real horror to pay attention to. "The shock made a weird mark on my hand."

"So let's see it," Amy demanded, grabbing his wrist.

"Other hand. And it's gone now."

"Convenient." Saleen again. He was rapidly working through the goodwill he'd built up by waiting in the drawing room with the candle. Not that it much mattered, given he was almost as big as Mouse.

"What kind of mark, Tony?" Peter asked, brow furrowed.

"I don't know."

"Big surprise." And a change in the chorus as Saleen handed off to Kate.

"So." Ashley moved out of Mason's shadow, stepped to Peter's side and folded her arms, sweeping the group with an expression eerily reminiscent of her father. "Let's go to the basement and kick ass!"

Adam joined her. "Works for me."

"No." Kate shook her head as she stood. "Do you really want to go face-to-face . . ."

"It has a face?" Amy asked him. Tony shrugged.

". . . with something that makes people kill each other from a distance? You don't know what it's capable of up close!"

Saleen moved to stand by Adam. "Only one way to find out."

"Fine." Tina took Ashley's hand and pulled her away from the two men. "But the girls aren't going."

Ashley's struggles only proved what almost everyone else in the room already knew. When Tina made up her mind, she couldn't be moved. Figuratively. Physically. "But it was my idea!"

"I don't care." Tina's tone challenged and went unopposed. "The girls and I are staying here. I don't want to leave Everett alone again."

Brianna seemed to be considering making a run for it but settled as Zev's hand closed on her shoulder. "Okay, fine, but if I have to stay with Ashes, Zev has to stay with me."

"Then Mason's staying with me." Still held securely by Tina's side, Ashley reached out her other hand and grabbed Mason's jacket.

"Mason's . . ."

"No, that's all right." Mason twitched his jacket free

but moved close enough so that Ashley could tuck her hand in his elbow. "If she needs me, I'll stay."

Tony could almost hear responses to that considered and discarded.

"All right, then," Adam declared, squaring his shoulders. "Who else is coming?"

"I'm not going near the basement." Brenda's hands were back to performing a full-out Lady Macbeth as Sorge joined the other two men.

"Too obvious," Mouse muttered.

"He's right." Kate moved closer to her cameraman. "Why would it let us know where it is?"

"Why would it care?" Saleen demanded.

"Maybe it doesn't care if we know where it is because it wants us to face it," Pavin said, getting to his feet. Tony wondered if the sound tech had always had that slight twitch. Was it endemic to the sound department? Although Hartley's twitch wasn't exactly slight . . . "It wants us down there in the wet with the wires," Pavin continued. "Old, frayed, cloth-wrapped wires. And then, when we're all standing knee-deep in the flood, it'll turn the power back on and drop a wire in the water because if it can close the doors it can surely do that, and we'll all be electrocuted. Or one of us'll snap and pull the wire into the water, and we'll all be electrocuted. You know how you die when that happens? Soup."

And that pretty much killed the charge to the basement.

"Okay," Amy said after a long moment of soup-filled silence. "Then we protect ourselves here."

"Wouldn't moving into an actual room make more sense?" Tony asked.

"In there with Tom?" Kate snapped, glaring at him.

Tina's glare was less personal but more potent for all that. "I'm *not* leaving Everett."

Guess not.

"We need salt. Lots of salt." Amy drew a vaguely circular shape in the air. "We draw a circle of salt around us and the evil can't get in."

Tony was about to point out that, first of all, he didn't think the evil wanted in and, secondly, if it was permeating the house, it was kind of a moot point since inside the circle would be as much a part of the house as outside the circle when he realized the salt might calm a few fears and calm was a good thing. He'd be willing to bet that very few people went crazy calmly. "I saw some salt in the kitchen."

He was starting to get used to the staring.

"You want me to go get it, don't you?"

"Not alone," Kate muttered, brows drawn into a deep vee. "I don't trust you alone."

"No one goes anywhere alone," Peter amended pointedly. "It's not safe. Someone has to go with you."

And a whole new silence descended.

"Me!"

"Me, too!"

"Neither of you," Tina informed the sisters, who shuffled and muttered but obeyed.

"Oh, for . . ." Amy rolled her eyes with enough emphasis the gesture was visible even in the candlelight. "I'll go."

"No." Peter was as adamant as Tina had been. "You know what's happening . . ."

Hang on. Tony frowned. *He* knew what was happening. Amy just spent a lot of time on Web sites called creepycrap.com.

". . . you have to stay here."

He didn't much like the implication they could afford to lose him but not Amy. Not that he wanted to lose Amy, but he didn't much like the idea of losing *him* either.

"I'll go with him."

Lee. It was the first thing he'd said since they'd left the drawing room, and Tony turned to stare at him in surprise.

"Lee, no . . ."

The expected protest from Brenda, but why the hell were Zev's eyebrows up?

"Look, someone's got to go and if Lee's willing, fine." Peter waved down further protests. "We'll get nothing accomplished if we stand around arguing all night. Tina, lend Lee your flashlight."

And what? I can see in the dark?

"I don't know." She pulled it from her pocket and peered down at the purple plastic. "It's looking dimmer . . ."

"That doesn't matter. They can't walk and keep a candle lit."

A valid point, but if the flashlight's batteries died, they'd be screwed, and given the way other batteries had been lasting . . . or not lasting . . . "Maybe we should take a candle anyway, just in case."

"NO!"

Multiple voices, all unthrilled about the prospect of a night spent trapped in the dark.

◆

The kitchen seemed farther away than it had been barely hours earlier. The flashlight was definitely dimmer, the circle of light Lee kept pointed at the floor in front of them almost a brownish yellow—like a dirty headlight. They were walking close together—for comfort, for security, Tony had no idea why—and the sleeve of Lee's tuxedo jacket kept brushing against his bare arm, lifting the hair on the back of his neck, then taking a direct route to his groin.

His whole body remembered the feel of the other man sprawled beneath him in the kitchen.

Here's a thought, you pathetic geek, try to act like a mature adult in a dangerous situation instead of a horny fifteen-year-old.

"This reminds me of a job I had in high school," Lee said quietly, sweeping the flashlight beam up one wall, across the ceiling, and down the other. "I worked with the animal control guy clearing raccoons out of cottages in the spring."

Tony glanced at the actor and snickered. "You worked in tuxedos?"

"Only if we had a formal complaint."

That got the groan it deserved.

Back behind them, he could hear another argument starting up in the hall, but although he could tell it was an argument from the volume, he couldn't make out any actual words. They hadn't gone that far. He should have been able to hear words.

Their footsteps sounded strangely muffled, like the hardwood was absorbing the sound.

Yeah. Strangely—like that should come as a shock.

He felt like he should say something, discuss the situation, maybe bat around a few ideas for getting them the hell out of there, but he couldn't think of a thing to say that hadn't already been said.

"So, you and Zev aren't seeing each other anymore?"

Okay. That was unexpected. "Uh, no. We . . . uh . . . aren't."

"But you're still friends."

"Sure." Not a question, but he answered it anyway.

"How do you guys do that; stay friends? I mean, if a man breaks up with a woman, they don't slide immediately back into friendship afterward."

Tony snorted. "Are they usually friends before?"

"Not usually, no." Lee sounded a bit rueful. "But you and Zev; I see you guys together and . . ."

"Is that a problem?" Tony asked when the sentence continued to dangle.

"What? No, of course not. Like you said: two consenting adults, none of my business."

Had he said that? Oh, right, about Brenda. Who was not Lee's friend.

And you are?

Ah, but I'm not fucking him.

He was still trying to figure out just what he meant by that and whether his answer had any relevance at all to his question when the light went out.

The jacket sleeve stopped stroking his arm as they froze in place.

The muted clicking was less than comforting as Lee turned the flashlight on and off. Finally: "I think the battery's dead."

The darkness was so complete it had weight and wrapped around them like a heavy blanket. Eyes open, eyes closed, it made no difference.

"This could be a problem."

"You think?"

"There's a couple of lanterns and some matches in the cupboard in the conservatory."

A third voice.

"Jesus fucking Christ!" Heart in his throat, Tony whirled around, stumbling into Lee who reached out blindly, caught his arm, and steadied him. Cassie looked as sheepish as possible, given she was barely a pale gray sketch on the air. Stephen, equally translucent, shrugged not at all apologetically. "You followed us!"

"We came with you," Stephen amended.

"There's no point in staying with the others," Cassie said reasonably. "They can't see or hear us and they're boring."

Which was when Tony realized she wasn't looking at him but staring at Lee with the kind of besotted expression he was only too familiar with—except it usually came with two eyes and an entire head.

"They followed us?" Lee repeated.

"They did."

"The ghosts?"

"Yeah. They think the others are boring. They say there're lanterns and matches in the conservatory."

Stephen nodded and adjusted his head. "Graham found them one day when he was snooping around."

"Caretaking," Cassie corrected archly.

"Yes, well, he found them. He left them there."

"Then all we have to do is find the conservatory," Lee said before Tony could ask just what exactly Graham had been snooping around for, had he found it, and was it likely to now bite them on the ass.

"I'll take you!" Cassie wafted past.

"Only Tony can see you," Stephen muttered as he followed. "She thinks he's cute," he added as he drew even with Tony's ear. "She's the one who painted his butt."

"I figured. You okay with that?" A jealous brother would be such fun under the circumstances. Particularly given how close the siblings were—had been.

"Why should I care?"

Tony decided not to mention the whole lack of pants thing. He ran his hand down Lee's arm, found his hand—*I'm at the end of his arm? What else was I expecting to find?*—and tucked it into the crock of his elbow. "All I can see is the ghosts, but I'm assuming they can see the house, so I'll follow them and you stick with me."

Lee's fingers tightened, just for an instant, then loosened to minimal contact he no doubt felt was required when a straight man touched a gay man.

And that was minimal contact on the floor in the kitchen?

Shut up!

He didn't need the house to drive him crazy, he was doing a fine job all on his own. With any luck, mass murder wasn't next after inappropriate sexual fantasies and self-chastisement. Verbal self-chastisement. Not the physical kind.

If his sense of distance had seemed off before, it was totally screwed now as he followed the pair of pale forms through total darkness. His feet never entirely left the floor, the soles of his running shoes sliding over the hardwood with a series of soft squeaks as treads scraped urethane. Lee's dress shoes made an answering shush-shush that seemed to indicate he also intended to remain grounded. Given the total lack of light and their lack of planning in not being in contact with a wall when the light went out, the floor underfoot was all they had to be sure of.

Tony was beginning to think that they should have arrived *somewhere* and was beginning to worry that they hadn't when the hard/soft crash of body slamming into an opened door derailed his train of thought. The impact jerked Lee's hand off his arm.

"Son of a fucking . . ."

"Lee?" He grabbed for the other man. As his fingers closed around familiar fabric, he started breathing again.

"I seem to have found the kitchen." The wet velvet voice sounded rougher than usual. "Or at least the kitchen door."

"Is he hurt?" Cassie drifted in close and stared up at where Lee had to be.

Too bad they don't actually throw enough light to be useful.

Stephen shot his sister an exasperated eye roll. "Don't worry, he's fine."

Yeah, dead guys walking around were great judges of *fine.* "Are you okay?"

"I think so. Although if I've given myself a black eye, tomorrow's shoot will be interesting."

Tomorrow's shoot. *He thinks we'll get out of this.*

Of course he does, he's in the credits. The guys in the credits always survive.

Maintaining his grip on Lee's jacket, Tony reached out with his other hand and defined the rest of the kitchen door. "If we turn left here, the conservatory's about seven or eight meters straight ahead. If I keep my hand on the wall, we'll know when we arrive and avoid falling down those three steps."

"I'd have told you about the steps," Cassie murmured. "And we're sorry about the door."

"Why was that our fault?" Stephen demanded.

And that was the peanut gallery heard from. "Lee?"

The arm inside Lee's jacket had no give to it, the muscles tensed, the joints locked. "Tony, I don't hear the baby anymore."

Now it had been brought to his attention, he couldn't remember having heard Karl the entire time they'd been standing in the kitchen doorway.

The lights came up and Tony was all alone. He moved his hand before he thought to wonder if he was still in real-world contact with Lee. *Stupid, fucking . . .* "Lee, I know you can hear me—I'm in another replay. I've got lights now, so I'll walk to the conservatory and the cupboard and wait there until the replay stops. Stephen and Cassie are stuck in the bathroom for the duration and you can't see me to follow, so stay right where you are. Don't move. I'll come back with the lanterns as fast as I can." He tried to sound reassuring, but the scream from the conservatory distracted him a bit.

By the time he covered the seven meters, the gardener—he assumed it was the gardener given the location and the overalls—was lying on his back on an old wooden bench while an elderly woman in a dark brown dress and sensible shoes sawed off his right leg. From the way he was twitching, Tony didn't think he was dead. When she got through to the bone, she switched to a hatchet.

Good solid swing considering her age.

Right leg. Left leg. Left arm. Each piece—thankfully—removed much faster than in real time. As she hacked through each bone in turn, the sound was a lot less brittle than Tony had expected. He made a mental note to mention it to the sound guys. CB didn't want to pay for his own Foley studio, so they usually bought what they needed from independent artists. None of them had quite gotten the wet crunch right.

The extended dismemberment should have upset him more than it did. Maybe he'd become desensitized by the parade of axes and burning babies and antlers.

Maybe the past had lost its ability to affect him, given that in the present a person he actually knew was dead and he and another seventeen were in danger of dying. Maybe the whole old lady sawing and hacking thing was just so over the top, he found it difficult to believe it was real and, frankly, he'd seen blood done better. Spurting arteries were unfortunately forever tied to Monty Python marathons on Comedy Central. Whatever the reason, he found he was standing, arms crossed, drumming his fingers on his elbow and wishing she'd hurry the hell up.

He almost cheered as the head finally came off—but no, now she had to bury the pieces. One piece in each of the raised beds.

Damn. That extra *could* have felt fingers. Sure, there was no way that the actual hand remained buried in the dirt, but since metaphysical action was still going on . . .

And on.

He sighed and leaned against the cupboard.

Grunting a little with the effort, she dropped the gardener's head into the large urn in the middle of the room. Tony frowned at the muffled squelch. Hadn't he ended up with an extra background player when he'd done the final head count around that urn this morning? An extra head in the head count. Cute. A malevolent thing with a sense of humor—like that made it so much better.

Then the old woman was suddenly at the cupboard, reaching through him for the handle. He jerked to one side, far enough to get free of her arm but not so far he couldn't scan the shelves. No lanterns, not in this time, but that didn't matter as long as they were there when he got back to the present.

There was, however, a brand new box of rat poison.

She ripped open the little cardboard spout and tipped a generous portion into her mouth.

Modern rat poison contained warfarin—a blood thinner. The rats ate the bait, scuttled into the walls, and bled to death internally. It was a slow, painful, terrifying way to die. Emphasis on slow—which was why Tony even knew about it. The writers had wanted to use rat poison to deal with the crime *du jour* in episode eleven but had ditched the idea when they found out how long it would take. Pre-warfarin, the active ingredient depended on the brand of the rat poison but throughout most of rural Canada arsenic-of-lead predominated.

Eyes so wide bloodshot white showed all the way around pale brown irises, the old woman swallowed a second mouthful.

And then forced down a third.

Teeth clenched so tightly Tony could see a muscle jump in her jaw, she managed to keep all three down as she walked back to the bench and sat primly down on the blood-soaked wood, knees together, feet crossed at the ankles.

Tony had no way of telling how long after that the vomiting blood began, but once started, it continued for some time. Continued until the old lady was lying in a puddle of her blood and the gardener's combined, protruding tongue white, skin faintly blue. Her open eyes were staring directly at him and for a moment, just before she died, she frowned slightly—almost as if she could see him standing there.

And *that* was the most frightening thing he'd seen so far.

Then it was dark. Dark and completely silent. He couldn't hear the rain on the glass, but whether that was because it had stopped raining or the house prevented the sound from entering he had no idea. Half afraid he could still feel the old lady's eyes on him, he fumbled for the clasp of the cupboard as Karl started crying again.

How weird that the sound of a baby in a fire was comforting?

Pretty damned weird actually.

"Tony?"

Lee's voice much, much closer than the kitchen. He shrieked as fingers stubbed up against him.

"It was taking so long. I, uh . . . I got worried about you, so I followed the wall." And except for the desperate way he clutched at Tony's arm, he'd have sold it. "Did I startle you?"

"Startle me? I almost fucking pissed myself!"

"Way too much information." The chuckle was slightly strained but, still, an award-winning performance considering he was leaving bruises.

Tony was just as happy to have the contact maintained—and for a change the thought of Lee touching him in no way evoked a sexual response. Or at least not much of one. It was actually kind of encouraging that his dick was taking a mild interest since, mere moments before, terror had driven his balls up to sit on his shoulder.

Cupboard open, he found something that felt like he thought he remembered lanterns looked on the top shelf. Carefully holding the round middle section, he shook it gently. Liquid sloshed.

"Kerosene?" Lee asked.

"Let's hope so."

His other hand finger-walked along the shelf until he touched a greasy box. It rattled when he nudged it. "I think I found the matches."

He had a lantern in one hand. He had matches in the other. Time passed.

This chuckle sounded legitimate. "You have no idea of what to do, do you?"

"Yeah, well, lanterns—not so big in my life."

"Never a Boy Scout?"

"No." He tired to keep the disdain from sounding in his voice and didn't quite manage it. Back when he was on the street, he'd had a scoutmaster among his regulars. Every week, like clockwork, after his scout meeting . . .

"Lucky for you, I was. Don't move." The grip on Tony's arm moved down to his hand and then up the

board flaps. As he tucked it under his arm, three packets slid out and hit the floor. He bent to pick them up and froze. "Son of a bitch."

"What?"

The cables running out of the generator hadn't been packed up before the doors slammed closed. He was so used to spending his working day stepping over and around a web of cable that it hadn't even occurred to him to question their continuing presence or how impossible it would be to close a door on them. *Under the circumstances, maybe impossible isn't the right word.* The cables ran up to the door and stopped. Tony grabbed one and pulled to no effect. They hadn't been severed. They just stopped. "They're still going through the space," he muttered. "When is a door not a door . . . ?"

"When it's a jar?" Lee's tone had distinct hints of *let's humor the crazy man.*

"When it's a metaphysical construct."

"Say what?"

He sat back and glanced up at the actor. "This door was created by the house to lock us in. The actual door is still open."

"Can we get out it?" Lee frowned down at the point where the cables met the wood.

Good question. Eyes closed to keep perception out of the equation, Tony ran his fist along the top of the cables and punched it out the space they had to be using. "Ow." To give the house credit, that was one *solid* metaphysical construct.

"Tony! Lee!" Adam again. A little closer.

"We're on our way! We have to get back," Lee added, dropping his volume and nodding toward the salt. "If we can't get out the door . . ."

"Yeah." He rapped his knuckles against it again. Still felt solid. "I guess. Listen, why don't you light the other lantern, take the salt, and go back to the others. I'll catch up. There's something I want to try."

"I'll stay . . ."

Lee wanted to stay with him and he was sending him away. Maybe he should just tell him about the whole wizard thing. Which would lead to telling him about the whole shadow thing. Which would not be a good thing. "No. We've been gone so long they've got to be getting a little freaked."

"Uh-huh."

What the hell did that mean? Tony wondered as Lee set about lighting the other lantern. *If you want to know, dipshit—ask!*

Yeah, like that was going to happen.

Lee tucked the box of salt under his arm, much as Tony had done. "Don't take too long."

That was it?

Apparently.

As Lee left the kitchen, Tony turned his attention back to the cables and attempted to clear his mind of everything but his immediate surroundings.

He thinks I'm a freak.

And the longer they were stuck in this freak show of a house, the more evidence he'd have to support that theory.

So since this is our best way out, can we get on with it!

The door was only a physical seeming of a door. It made sense that he couldn't put his hand through something physical. Visualizing the back porch and the bucket of sand that had been left there for the smokers, he raised his right palm toward the space he couldn't see and snapped out the seven words.

Sixteen cigarette butts later, he stopped.

"That's not normal."

"Pot, kettle, black, dead people." He sat back on his heels and tried to flick a butt back outside. It bounced off the door and hit him in the forehead. Okay. He'd proved something here. Wasn't sure what, but it might be useful later. Brushing his experimental data off his jeans, he stood and faced his own personal Greek chorus. "What?"

"I think that's our question," Stephen snorted. "What *are* you?"

Why not. It wasn't like they could pass the information on.

"I'm a wizard."

Tony braced himself for the inevitable Harry Potter references.

Cassie frowned. "Like Merlin?"

And let's hear it for those who died before J. K. Rowling was born. "Yeah, sort of."

Stephen nodded down at the mess on the floor. "Is that all you can do?" he asked, realigning his head.

"So far." It wasn't all he'd attempted, but it was all he could do with any certainty of success.

"It doesn't look very useful."

"Bite me."

"Pardon?"

"Never mind." There were two unopened boxes of bottled water on the floor by the table. He set the lantern on top and carefully lifted them into his arms. It wouldn't hurt to bring back a bribe. "How many more of those replays to go?"

"Three. The ballroom, the drawing room, and the back stairs . . ."

"Let me guess." He could still hear a faint creaking sound over Karl's crying. "Someone got pushed and the someone who did the pushing hung themselves."

"Isn't it hanged?"

"Does it matter?" The lantern's flame flickered as he passed the basement door. Had his hands not been full, he didn't think he could have resisted trying to lift the latch. "Just as dead hanged or hung."

"You're getting just a little blasé about this, aren't you?" Cassie sounded almost insulted.

He shrugged and cut the motion short as the lantern

rocked. "They're just recordings of past events. They can't hurt me."

"Maybe not you."

"Maybe not yet," Stephen added.

Eight

"ALL RIGHT, let me just make sure I understand this. Tony, your daughters, and sixteen people from your show, including both your lead actors, are trapped inside a haunted house. This man . . ." Henry nodded toward Graham Brummel who lifted his beer in salute. ". . . says the house contains a malevolence that feeds on the trapped dead and is looking to add our people to its buffet table. We can't get in, they can't get out, the windows have been blanked, and all phones are nonfunctional. All they have to do is survive until dawn, but the house will spend the night working on their fears, attempting to drive at least one of them insane enough to kill the rest. Is that it?"

CB's attention remained directed out the window at the roof of the house. "Yes."

Henry sighed and ran both hands back up through his hair. "This isn't good."

"But you believe it?"

He turned to face the caretaker, one red-gold brow raised. "Of course."

"Oh, for cryin' out loud!" Graham jumped to his feet and began to pace back and forth over the minimal floor space in front of his recliner. "What is with you people? I mean, first the big guy, now you. How can you possibly buy into this kind of a cock-and-bull story?"

"Isn't it true?"

"Yeah, of course it's true, but what difference does that make? Haunted houses. Malevolent things. You should be in deep denial." He kicked at a yellowing stack of tabloids as he paced. "You should be making up something about how the doors all swelled in the rain and some weird air pressure thing is holding them closed and the rain is affecting the cell phone reception and you don't just calmly *believe* this kind of shit! I mean, if I tell you I'm a medium, you're supposed to tell me I'm a fake!"

"Are you?"

"No! But that's not the point. You two are really freaking me out!" The mouth of the beer bottle jabbed toward CB. "He was bad enough on his own." And back to point at Henry. "You are seriously upping the weird stakes here, and given my life just generally, that's saying something."

Henry stared at him for a long moment, contemplated dropping all masks just to see what would happen, and finally allowed his better nature to prevail. "I'm grateful you called me," he said at last, joining CB at the window, dismissing the other man entirely. "But I'm not sure what you expect me to do."

"Offer an experienced interpretation. Take advantage of any opening that lends itself to your . . . particular strengths. It also struck me that you're a little possessive and unlikely to allow the destruction of someone you consider to be yours."

"And if I find a way to get Tony out . . ."

"My daughters, and my employees, will be freed as well."

"You guys have done this kind of thing before!"

Vampire and producer turned together.

"You have!" Bloodshot eyes narrowed speculatively.

"You guys are like what? Some kind of otherworldly Starsky and Hutch?"

"How many of those has he had?" Henry asked nodding toward the bottle.

Graham snorted before CB could respond. "Oh, no, you can't blame the beer. I know how it is! Your show, the whole leading his people through the darkest night toward the dawn, it's based on real life."

CB blinked. Once. "The show is a work of fiction. Any resemblance to persons living or dead is purely coincidental." When Henry glanced up at him, he shrugged and added, "Usually."

Before Graham could continue—which he looked ready to do—a pair of feet in work boots pounded up the stairs and a heavy fist banged out a three-beat rhythm on the door.

"CB? Boss? You better get out here; something's happening!"

♥

"The cat tipped us off. It was sitting on the porch rail there and then it had a little freak-out."

"Cat?" Henry glanced down at the black cat being soothed in Graham's arms. There'd been a black cat up in the apartment, stretched out along the back of the sofa. He hadn't seen it leave . . .

"I got two." Graham's tone suggested he was bored with the explanation. "Same litter, eh." He shrugged, the cat riding the motion. "I named them both Shadow since they don't come when I call."

"*What* was the cat reacting to?" CB snarled as attention shifted to the cat.

"Sorry, Boss." And attention shifted around again within the crowded shelter of the back porch. "That." Ujjal pointed at the empty butt bucket. "There was a good pack and a half in there before, but one by one they just up and whooshed through the door."

"Whooshed?"

"Well, they didn't make the whoosh noise or anything, but yeah." The genny op shrugged, fully aware of how the story sounded. "It was iike something on the other side of the door was pulling them in."

When CB raised an eyebrow in Henry's direction, Henry nodded. Tony could call the butts from the bucket to his hand. Therefore, until another explanation presented itself, he was going to believe this had been Tony. But this was the first Henry'd ever heard of him moving them through a closed . . . "The cables." When all eyes turned to stare blankly at him, he pointed. "Look at the cables. The whole bundle is still running into the house."

A couple of heads nodded, but they were clearly continuing to miss the point. Cables were like background noise for this lot.

"The door is closed . . ." He frowned, thinking out loud. "The cables are running through a closed door, except that's impossible, so the space they were running through must remain regardless of how it appears."

"But you can't move them." Ujjal yanked at the bundle. "It's tight, no play at all. There's no hole—it's like it goes to the door and stops." He blinked. "You're right. That's not possible."

"So we just think the door's closed?" Karen asked, twirling a piece of red licorice as she squinted down at the porch.

"It doesn't matter." Chris cautiously poked a finger toward where the space should be. Ten centimeters out, a small red flare slapped his hand back. "We can't get to it."

"We can't," Henry agreed. "But power can go obviously go through it."

Ujjal snorted. "I'm shut down. There's no power in these cables." A pause just long enough to connect the dots. "Should I start the generator, Boss?"

"That kind of depends," Graham said before CB

could answer. "How big a mess will it make if it over-
loads and blows up?"

"My generator is not going to overload."

"I'm betting it will if you try and send power into that
house while it's locked down. You can bet against me if
you want to, though—that's why I asked about the
mess."

"The generator won't deliver the kind of power I
meant. You . . ." Henry whirled toward Graham, knew
he was moving at more than mortal speed by the way
the man's eyes opened, but he didn't care. They were
stalking a solution here. "When you talk to the
ghosts . . ."

"He talks to ghosts?" Chris repeated incredulously.

". . . you're using a type of metaphysical power . . ."

"Of what?"

". . . and that power can obviously go through the
door."

"Obviously?"

". . . because a metaphysical power moved the cigarette butts through the door."

"That's not exactly obvious."

"You call your cousins to the door and you tell them
to tell Tony . . ."

"Tony talks to ghosts?"

". . . what he has to do to defeat this thing."

"*What* thing?"

Henry turned just far enough to glare at Chris.

Who paled and took a step back. "Never mind."

"Look, I might be able to do that," Graham admitted
slowly. "But even if they can make some kind of contact
with this Tony person, I don't know what to tell them. I
don't *know* how to destroy this thing."

The cat in his arms yawned.

"I don't like that Tony was left on his own in the
kitchen." Kate ripped open another packet of salt and

glared across the circle at him as she passed it to Amy. "How do we know he was working on a way to get the back door open?" Her lip curled. "We only have his word for it."

"Why would he lie?" Amy asked as she added the salt to the circle.

"Same reason anyone lies. He wants to control the situation."

"Yeah, and he's sitting right here." Tony handed Amy another half dozen packets. The group had insisted she be the only one to draw the protective circle, but given that they actually wanted it finished before morning, there were no proscriptions on who could open the hundreds of tiny paper containers. "You want to know something, just ask me."

"Because you've been so open and forthcoming about stuff," Kate snorted.

"Hey, I told you about the ghosts." Who weren't back from their latest trip to the bathroom. When the lights came up and his coworkers disappeared, and someone sounded as though they were choking on glass in the drawing room—he'd stayed sitting right where he was until the lights went out again. The house, or more specifically the thing in the basement, could just do that whole not-at-all-instant replay without him from now on.

"He did tell us about the ghosts," Peter acknowledged, glancing up from his own pile of packets. "And at some risk to his reputation."

"What reputation?" Brenda demanded. "He's as strange as she is! Uh, no offense," she added hastily, lowering the arm pointing toward Amy.

"And yet, I'm offended."

"But I just . . ."

Lee tightened his arm around Brenda's shoulders. "Let it go," he told her quietly.

"Because you can't win," Amy added.

"Amy."

She rolled her eyes but allowed Peter to have the last word.

"So," Kate shuffled around on the floor until she was staring directly into Tony's face, "I'm asking. If you were just trying to get the back door open, why did you send Lee away?"

"I figured you could use the salt and the lantern."

"You didn't want him to see what you were doing."

Yeah, that, too. "I didn't think he needed to wait since you guys were waiting for the salt."

She waved a packet at him. "And this is *so* useful."

"Kosher salt." They were the first words Hartley had said since before Tom died. He paled as everyone turned toward him. "The salt on *The X-Files* ep . . . p . . . p . . . pisode," he stammered. "It was kosher."

And everyone turned to Zev. Who sighed. "How the hell should I know? I never watched *The X-Files.*"

"You swore," Brianna pointed out.

"Yes, I did. Don't eat the salt."

"I'm hungry!"

"You just ate . . ." Habit drew his gaze down to his watch. He sighed again. ". . . not that long ago. You're not hungry, you're bored."

"She's not the only one," Mason muttered.

Tony tuned out the overlapping litany of complaints and concentrated on opening salt packets. A circle large enough to enclose seventeen people required significant seasoning.

". . . there, see, everything's okay." The light of the second lantern lapped out of the library. The low murmur of sound became Adam's voice and broke up into words. "Just keep moving out into the hall and we'll be back with the others in no time."

After some discussion, Peter had sent Adam, Sorge, Saleen, and Mouse to bring the company's canvas chairs out into the hall. Amy had agreed they'd be safe enough to use inside the circle since they didn't actually belong to the house.

Mouse emerged first carrying four of the chairs, then Sorge with two, Adam with the lantern, and Saleen with the last two.

"Don't worry," Adam continued. "I'm right here and the light's not going anywhere. See, there's the other lantern right where we left it. Just go over to the edge of the circle and put the chairs down carefully."

It was clearly meant to be comforting. Comforting who, that was the question.

Mouse dropped the chairs, jumped back at the noise, bumped into Sorge, and leaped ahead. "Don't!" he snarled.

And that seemed to be the answer.

"Mouse got a little spooked in the library," Adam explained, splitting his attention between his audience and the cameraman. "Mouse, why don't you pass the chairs into the circle?"

"Pass the chairs?" His eyes were wild, his hands were visibly trembling, and damp circles spread out from the underarms of his faded *Once a Thief* crew shirt.

"Yeah, the chairs. Pass them to Hartley and . . . uh, Mason so they can set them up."

"I don't set up chairs," Mason muttered.

"I've got it." Tony pushed his pile of salt packages over in front of Tina and stood.

Mouse shook his head, graying ponytail making a swoosh, swoosh sound against his back. "Tony avoids me."

Tony didn't even bother to check and see if everyone was staring at him. *What's the point?* He just tugged the chair from Mouse's hand and opened it, fully conscious of people edging away. *Oh, yeah, the big guy's going crazy, but you'd rather displace onto the little guy.* Actually, he couldn't fault them for that. He'd faced Mouse under the influence of the metaphysical, and the evening had included a couple of cracked ribs, significant bruising, and some tongue he'd just as soon forget. Fortunately, the repetitive motion of passing over the chairs seemed to be calming the big guy down. Probably Adam's intent.

He shifted position slightly so he could overhear the 1AD's murmured conversation with Peter.

"... don't know what set him off. He said the library was full of dark and until I loaded him down with half the chairs, I was afraid he was going to bolt."

"The lantern didn't go out?"

"Hell, no, he was just freaky."

"High-strung is not a description I'd have ever applied to Mouse." Peter shoved his hands in his pockets.

"It's the house. The situation."

They turned to look at Tony who suddenly got very busy setting up the last chair. Mouse could hear the baby and Mouse had started to freak. Kate was not only talking a lot more than usual but was getting distinctly paranoid. Lee ...

He glanced over at Lee as he shoved the chairs into a tighter pattern.

Lee had Brenda plastered up against his side.

Those who'd been double shadow-held were starting to fall apart. Even Hartley, only a single, had picked up a stutter. Mason, however, seemed fine. He seemed no more obnoxious than he ever was—although he *was* voluntarily spending time with Ashley.

Bottom line, both actors had picked up distractions. And both of them were, well, actors.

♥

"I don't know about this ..."

"I do." Henry stayed hard on Graham's heels, herding him up the muddy lane toward the road. "You don't know how to defeat the evil in the basement."

"Yeah, I mean no, but ..."

"Neither do I. That doesn't change the fact that we need to defeat it." A gust of wind blew a scud of water off the firs. Henry avoided most of it. "Your research suggests that Creighton Caulfield interacted with the manifestation—that this was the purpose of the séances and the psychic investigators he had to the house."

Graham wiped water off his face, slicking thinning hair back over his skull. "Well, yeah, but . . ."

"So Caulfield could be the only person who ever put together the information we need. Information to defeat this thing and save the lives of those people trapped in the house."

"I guess so, but . . ."

"We're going to get that information." He gestured at his BMW. "Get in the car."

"Whoa! Hang on!" Graham stopped by the passenger door, both hands raised, brows drawn in. "I can't just call up Caulfield's ghost; it doesn't work that way. I mean, I could stand on his grave playing *Who Who* on a trumpet from now until doomsday, but if he's not hanging around, it won't do anybody any good. The dead have to want to talk to me."

"Good." Henry's eyes darkened as he stared across the roof at the caretaker. "Get in the car."

Graham did as instructed. Buckled his seat belt. Asked, "What are you?" as Henry pulled out onto Deer Lake Drive.

"Someone who plans to get what's *his* out of that house."

"Yeah. Okay. But what . . ."

Henry glanced over at his passenger.

". . . never mind." He sank down in his seat, head drawn into his shoulders, knees up, one thumb scraping mud off the side of his boots. "So, where are we going?"

"To talk to someone who knew Creighton Caulfield."

"What's this supposed to do?" Stephen asked, drifting back and forth across the curved line of salt.

"Lend a little peace of mind to the people inside the circle," Tony told him quietly. "Calm them, make it harder for the house to work on them."

"Oh." He blinked. "Good idea. How does it work?"

"Power of suggestion."

"I don't understand."

"You don't have to."

But it *was* working. The six chairs were clumped together in the center holding Mason, Ashley, Tina, Peter, Sorge, and Pavin—who had a bad back and couldn't sit on the floor. Around them in a loose circle, backs to the chairs, were Adam, Saleen, Zev, Brianna, Kate, Mouse, Lee, and Brenda. Amy was slowly walking the circumference, holding the largest blade of her Swiss army knife out over the salt and singing softly under her breath.

Tony, placed at her starting point so she'd know where to finish, couldn't hear the actual words but the tune sounded disturbingly like Painted Ponies. Disturbing because Amy and Joan Baez went together like reality TV and actual dramatic content. When she reached him, she drew what looked like an infinity sign in the air with the knife point.

"There. It's closed. Negative energy can't get in. We're safe." She snapped the knife blade shut. "If you want to leave the circle at any time, let me know and I'll open a door."

"Isn't this just a little tree-of-life tote bag for you?" Tony murmured under the rising sound of relieved conversation. Stephen drifted into and out of the circle again looking bored.

"Bite me. I'm a well rounded, multifaceted person."

"Uh-huh. You're making this up as you go along, aren't you?"

Her eyes narrowed. "Do you question my kung fu, Grasshopper?"

"I would if I knew what the hell you were talking . . ." He could hear music. But Karl was still crying.

"Tony?"

"What the fuck is happening now?" Kate. And Mouse didn't look happy. Tony could only see a bit of Hartley's hair on the other side of the chairs, but the boom operator never looked happy, so he wasn't sure actually seeing his face would help. Lee untangled himself from Brenda's arms and slowly stood.

"I hear music." Brianna launched herself to her feet, but Zev dragged her back.

"I think you all do," he said, looking around the circle and finally settling on Tony. "What is it?"

Tony, in turned, looked to Cassie who had backed into her brother's arms, her remaining eye wide and frightened.

"It's the ballroom."

"What's so bad about the ballroom?" he demanded.

"There's a lot of people in there," Stephen explained. "So it's strong. It pulls. Cassie got lured in there once, just after Graham brought us back." His arm around her waist pulled her closer still. "I almost didn't get her out. If it had been going, with the music and all, I think we'd still be there. When Cassie told Graham about it, he closed the doors and told us to stay away from it. Really helpful after the fact."

"Why can we hear it *and* Karl?" Tony waved a hand around the hall, still dark and full of his muttering coworkers. "The replay hasn't even started yet."

"I told you, it's powerful."

"But contained?"

"I guess. If the doors are closed. We're going up to the bathroom now, it's *our* place. We're safe there." The last sentence hung in empty air.

"Tony? Hey!" Amy grabbed his arm and jerked him around to face her. "You want to share with the living?"

So he told them.

Amy paled. "I left the ballroom doors open."

"Are you sure?"

She was.

"Is anyone *surprised*?" Mason snapped.

As it happened, no one was.

"I want to go dancing," Brianna whined.

"Tony . . ."

And the soundtrack of his life started playing the *Mighty Mouse* theme. "I'm on it."

He was almost to the edge of the lantern light when he realized voices were yelling about breaking the circle and that he hadn't brought a light of his own. He lifted his left foot, about to turn. The replay started before it hit the floor.

The music was suddenly a lot louder and vaguely familiar. People were talking and laughing, the clink of glassware suggesting expensive booze of some kind was flowing freely. Champagne, maybe. People who lived in houses like this weren't the type to open a few two-fours for friends. Faintly, he could hear the rhythmic pattern of dress shoes against a wooden floor. Step. Step. Slide.

No point in going back for a light, so he trotted out of the foyer and down the hall.

Turned out that the sound of dancing was muffled because the ballroom doors were closed.

He frowned.

Except Amy was sure she'd left the doors open.

All right, they were open in his time but not in the replay. And that was no help. In order for Graham's protections to work, they had to be closed in his time. Which he wasn't exactly in.

Great.

The music faltered. It was live, not recorded.

Someone in the ballroom banged on the closed doors. Which weren't only locked, they were barred.

On this side.

He reached for the bar but couldn't touch it.

The music stopped.

Muffled thuds. A lot of padded somethings hitting the floor.

Bodies?

You think? He could hear coughing, choking, what might be a little thrashing. And he could smell . . .

The lights in the hall were electric and they looked

new, the wires surface-mounted along the moldings. Henry had found him an apartment in Toronto with the same surface-mounted wires, surface mounted because the building had started out with gas lights. Apparently, so had this house. If the electric lights were new, then the gas lines were probably still in place.

Three guesses about what's killing the people in the ballroom, and the first two don't count.

Someone had opened the gas jets. Since all the murdering someones had, so far, stuck around for the actual deaths, Tony'd have been willing to bet that they'd barred these doors and gone back into the ballroom through the service door, locking it behind them with the key. Not that it really mattered.

A whole ballroom full of dead people. No wonder it was powerful.

And in his time, the doors were open.

The music started up again although the odds were good it wasn't exactly *live* anymore. Other replays had stopped with death. This one kept going.

Had it reset to begin again or were the dead dancing? Given the night so far, he'd bet on the latter.

He was standing in front of the doors in his time as well as in the replay—he'd established that movement was timeless beyond a doubt in the conservatory. Which was a good thing because right now doubt would be a bad thing. Eyes closed so as not to be distracted, he clung to an image of the open doors, held out his hand, said the seven words, and *reached*.

The doors are already closed, memory insisted.

Yeah, well, if it was easy, everyone would be doing it.

Once again, Tony could hear people talking and laughing, but it didn't sound like they were having a good time. Although he couldn't hear actual words, the voices had a nails-on-a-chalkboard kind of timbre and the laughter carried more than a hint of desperation. Step, step, slide had become shuffle, shuffle, drag.

He stepped forward.

Something brushed past his hip.

Something from his time because nothing in the re-play could touch him.

Oh, crap!

Hand. Words. *Reach!*

He opened his eyes just as the door slammed shut. Just in time to see a pale, corpse-gray hand snatched back from the front of Brianna's pinafore. An almost familiar pattern glowed gold against the wood.

CB's younger daughter turned and glared at him, squinting a little in the lantern light radiating out from behind him. "I wanted to go dancing!" she shrieked, and kicked him in the shin.

"Brianna!" Zev rushed past. "Are you all right?"

"I wanted to dance—and he closed the door!"

"Tony couldn't have closed the door, he's not close enough." He grabbed her wrist and pulled her hand away from the brass door pull. "And you don't want to go in there, it's all . . ." He glanced up at Tony. "Full of dead people?"

Tony nodded.

"I want to see dead people!"

"No, you don't."

"Do, too!"

"Tom . . ."

"Tom is boring, he's just lying there!" She folded her arms. "I want to see the gross dead baby, or I want to go in there and dance with dead people!"

"Why don't we . . ."

"No!"

"Cheese!" The odd acoustics in the house had no luck at all in muffling Ashley's voice. "You get your skinny butt back here, or I'm telling Mom you put those pictures of her in her underwear up on the Net!"

"Did not!"

"So?"

Brianna yanked herself free of Zev's grip and

charged past Tony back toward the entrance hall, the darkness between the lanterns of less concern than getting to her sister. "I'm gonna rip your tongue out, Ashes!"

"They're really very nice kids," Zev murmured as he passed.

"Sure." Tony turned to see Lee standing behind him with a lantern. "Zev thinks they're nice kids," he said, suddenly at a loss for words.

"That's because Zev likes kids. And Zev's never picked up a prop they've broken, then *fixed* with a tube and a half of Crazy Glue, and then gotten his picture in the tabloids brandishing a four-and-a-half foot cross in a hospital emergency room."

"It was a good picture."

"That's little comfort." Lee stared past Tony at the ballroom doors. "I can still hear the music."

"Yeah. Me, too." Although it was faint, distant. Distorted. "We should get back."

He didn't understand the moment of silence that followed his suggestion.

"Right." Lee turned as Tony came even with him and they fell into step. "Tony, why do you think I can hear the baby?"

He asked like he had a theory. Like he knew and he was just asking Tony to confirm his suspicions. Had he started to remember the shadows?

"Why me and Mouse and Kate and Hartley? Oh, and you . . . of course."

The pause was disconcerting.

Why "of course" me? None of the shadow-held remembered the experience and Arra had wiped the memories of everyone on the soundstage after the final battle. Lee was asking like he thought Tony knew the answer and just wasn't telling. If the shadow-held were more sensitive to the stuff the house was throwing at them, did that mean the house was restoring their memories?

"Why do you ask?"

"Last spring Mouse and Kate and Hartley all had lapses of memory, somewhat like mine. I had an . . . incident on the set. So did you. I thought it might be connected."

"I guess it might be." That seemed safe enough.

"I'm pretty sure Mason is hearing things, too. Remember that friend of his that showed up on the set just before the gas leak?"

They'd gone with the traditional explanation for a group of disoriented people whose memories had just been magically wiped. Had to have been a gas leak. Also the traditional explanation for a ballroom of dead people as it turned out.

"His name was Michael Swan," Lee continued, before Tony could answer. "I asked Mason about him, and he had no idea who I was talking about. Everyone else remembered him, though."

Mason had been shadow-held at the time. Of course he wouldn't remember.

Just like Lee didn't remember the actual weird shit— a shadow from another world in his body, the Shadowlord after his body—only the stuff around the weird. Unfortunately, he seemed to have gathered enough pieces to start trying to put two and two together. Fortunately, since two and two made five in this instance, it was unlikely he'd come up with the actual answer.

Suddenly realizing he was about to step out of the circle of lantern light, Tony stopped and turned. Lee was standing about five paces back, watching him. "What?"

"You changed since all that happened."

"Changed?"

"You're more confident. You're interacting with CB. And you don't . . ." He paused and brushed his hair back off his face, almost as though he wasn't sure he wanted to continue. ". . . you don't watch me like you used to."

"What?"

"You used to . . . there was this expression . . . I mean, every time I turned around you were . . ." He shrugged. "I guess I got used to it."

"Sorry." Tony had no idea what he was apologizing for, but it was all he could think of.

"Yeah. We should get back."

"Sure."

Four or five steps in an uncomfortable silence, then, "Did I mention everyone's a little pissed at you because you broke through the circle?"

"No."

"Well, they are."

A little pissed was a bit of an understatement. Kate was ready to throw him to the wolves and nothing said seemed to calm her down.

"He's putting us all in danger! We need to get rid of him!"

"And how do you suggest we do that, eh?"

Shut up, Sorge. You're not helping. Tony shot a whose-side-are-you-on glance at the DP, who answered with a Gallic and totally noncommittal shrug.

"We lock him away somewhere safe," Kate insisted. "Where he can't hurt us."

"He hasn't done anything to hurt us!" Amy snapped.

"Oh, yeah? How do you know? How do you know he didn't arrange all this? He sees things we don't. We only have his word for what's going on."

"She's right!"

Brenda. Big surprise. Tony shuffled a little closer to Lee. While Brenda hadn't been shadow-held, she was more than keeping up in the freaking-out department. Plus, lately, it seemed that she didn't much like him although he didn't . . . *Right. I'm an idiot.* He would have shuffled away again, but Lee grabbed his arm. Comfort? Restraint? Tony had no idea. *He misses the way I used to look at him? What the hell's up with that?*

"Maybe Tony woke the house! On purpose! Have

any of you morons even considered that?" Kate swept a narrowed gaze around the circle and Tony realized that more than one of their companions *was* thinking of it. Lee's grip tightened slightly. "Tony broke the circle," she continued, volume rising with every word. "He *wants* one of us to go crazy and kill the rest. That way we won't think it's his fault!" She lunged at him, but Adam caught her.

"I like Tony!" Brianna declared as Kate struggled to free herself from Adam's grip. She took two steps forward and pinched a fold of Kate's stomach.

"OW!"

"She pinches with her fingernails," Ashley commented from her place inside the curve of Mason's arm.

"You little bitch!" The fury of Kate's attack dragged one arm free of Adam's hold.

Brianna ducked under the swing and wrapped herself around Kate's lower leg.

"OW!"

"And she bites."

Zev took a blow that knocked his yarmulke half off his head, but he managed to get his hands under Brianna's arms and drag her away.

Eyes narrowed, managing to look dangerous in spite of age, size, a turn-of-the-century pinafore, and the fact she was essentially dangling from Zev's hands, Brianna jabbed a finger toward Kate and snarled, "You say one more mean thing about Tony and my dad will fire your ass!"

"He can't fire me if we're all dead!"

"Wanna bet! My dad fires dead people all the time!"

News to Tony but, given CB, not completely unbelievable.

"Does not!"

"Does, too!"

"Does not!"

"Does, too, infinity!"

"Does . . ."

"Hey!" Ashley moved away from Mason—who looked astonished at being left—to stand with her sister. "She said infinity!"

Kate glared at the two girls for a moment, then turned and growled, "You're hurting my arm."

Adam smiled tightly. "Seemed preferable to the alternative. Have you calmed down?"

"I'm *fine!*"

Oh, yeah. And we all believe you, too.

After a long moment, Peter nodded and Adam released her.

Okay, some of us believe you.

"We're in this together," Peter reminded them as Kate rubbed her arm and scowled. "Lynching Tony . . ."

Kate perked up.

". . . metaphorically speaking," Peter sighed, "just because he knows things strikes me as cutting off our noses to spite our face." He frowned. "Faces. I don't believe he's lying to us and I consider myself an excellent judge of character. Shut up Sorge."

The DP's mouth closed with an audible snap.

"But since you brought it up . . ." He turned to Kate. "The house, the thing in the house . . ."

"In the basement," Amy added.

"Right, the thing in the basement wants us dead so that it can feed off us . . ."

"According to Tony," Kate sneered.

"Granted. But why do you think Tony would want one of us to go crazy and kill the rest?"

Nostrils flared, she tossed her head. "Because."

"Oh, yeah, that's a good reason."

Mason's dust-dry delivery set off a wave of laughter. It sounded more relieved than amused, but Mason preened at the attention and it was almost back to business as usual.

"He's always going off on his own!" Kate insisted, trying to reclaim her audience.

"And he shouldn't be," Peter agreed. "None of us

should. If we leave the circle—once Amy has resealed the circle," he added pointedly, "we go in pairs. At least in pairs."

"Not going anywhere," Mouse muttered.

Kate ignored him, jerking her chin toward Tony. "Who's going to want to go with him?"

"I will."

"Oh, yeah." She curled her lip in Lee's direction. "Big surprise, *you've* been running around with him all night." Her observation dripped innuendo.

Heads turned. Eyebrows rose.

Tony—and, from the look on her face, Brenda—waited for Lee to release his arm and leap away but the actor only said, "Then he's hardly been going off on his own, has he?"

"That's not . . ."

Lee shook his head, a lock of dark hair sweeping across his forehead. "I can hear the baby, Kate, and the music—and so can you and . . ."

"So can I!" Mason announced.

Heads turned again.

Mason's chin rose and his face stiffened into what Amy had once referred to as his patently portentous expression. After Tony'd looked it up, he'd agreed with the description. "I've always heard the baby," he said, Raymond Dark's fangs adding a surreal touch. "But I felt I should remain as neutral in this situation as possible."

Amy snorted and asked what they were all wondering. "Why?"

"Because you thought we'd laugh at you!" Brianna kicked him in the shin.

"Don't you touch him!" Ashley launched herself at her sister just as Karl stopped crying.

Tony froze as the lights came up—gas this time, not electric—and he was standing alone in the entrance hall. He could feel a kind of pressure that had to be Lee's hand on his arm. What would happen if he pulled away? Would Lee hold on? Would he have to let go?

Tony didn't want to know the answer enough to try it. The house was absolutely silent and then, very faintly, he heard a series of thuds, some panicked profanity, and one final crash. Then, more silence.

Help, I've fallen and I'm not getting up again.

Educated guess, where educated meant "let's attach the sound to the worst case scenario": someone had been pushed down the kitchen stairs and had landed without Lee Nicholas to cushion the impact. Broken neck, temple slammed down on the corner of the kitchen table, impalement on a rack of salad forks—it didn't much matter; he was more concerned with what was going on with the live people in the house during his absence.

The replay continued to run, but death number two seemed to be happening quietly. And slowly. Tony ran through video production specs as he waited. *SD video is transmitted at SDI rates of 270, 360, or 540 Mbps; HD video is transmitted at the SDI rate of . . . of . . . crap.* He hadn't remembered on his final exam either. When reviewing Wizardry 101 got him no farther than: *In the manipulating of energies the price of intent is often greater than the price of manipulation*—which had made no sense the first time around either—he settled on counting backward from one hundred in French.

At *quarante-deux,* the lights went out. Lee was still beside him but standing now with his arms folded as he, and everyone else, listened to Peter who was clearly coming to the end of some lengthy direction. Kate was scowling, Brianna was sulking, Ashley looked triumphant, and every other face Tony could see wore the default expression common to those who worked in television production and spent most of their professional careers waiting for a thousand and one details to line up so they could do their jobs. No one seemed to have noticed he was gone.

"Does everyone understand me, then?" Peter raised a finger. "We're in this together. I don't want to hear accusations and no one wants to hear how certain people used to have a starring role in a network police drama."

Mason opened his mouth and closed it again as the finger jabbed toward him.

"Good." A second finger rose. "Most importantly, no one goes anywhere alone. Not Tony. Not me. No one." He looked around, gauging reaction, and frowned. "Where's Hartley?"

Nine

"LOOK, NO ONE'S more in favor of all this cultural crap than me, eh, but I thought you wanted to save your friend."

"The Lambert Theatre is haunted."

"No shit. Medium with an Internet connection, remember?" Graham slammed the car door and waited for Henry to join him on the sidewalk before he started walking toward the theater. "We got some poltergeist activity—you *don't* want to talk to those little shits—and repeat appearances of dark figure in a long coat suspected to be Alistair McCall, an actor who died during a performance of *Henry V*. The reviews said it wasn't the best death scene he'd ever done."

In spite of circumstances, Henry grinned. "Harsh."

"Yeah, well, we weren't there; they might've been right. So do you want me to try and talk to McCall, is that it?"

"If it *is* McCall, he was around at the same time as Creighton Caulfield, and they likely moved in the same social circles—Caulfield was nouveau riche and McCall was a local celebrity."

"Okay, sure, that's fine if it is McCall, but what if it isn't?"

"Then get what information you can."

"The dead don't usually like crowds." Graham nodded at the people milling about under the marquee. "And this lot doesn't look like they're leaving."

"They're not. There's a late show tonight."

"Yeah, so . . ."

"So you'll have to concentrate a little harder to ignore any distractions, won't you?" Henry wrapped his hand around the caretaker's elbow, the movement as much threat as restraint.

Graham glanced down at Henry's fingers, pale lines against the dark green fabric, and shrugged. "Okay. So we're what? Just going to walk right on in?"

"Yes."

"Because you got tickets?"

"Not exactly."

They slipped past two young women checking their watches as they discussed unlikely methods of revenge, pushed past a clump of slightly younger men who could only be first-year film students from the way they were pontificating, and went around the smokers desperately topping up their nicotine levels before they had to go inside. The clothes of all three groups were such an eclectic mix that neither Henry's white silk shirt and jeans nor Graham's workman's overalls looked out of place.

Muscles, tattoos, and a clipboard blocked the open door.

Henry smiled up at her, carefully keeping it charming. "Henry Fitzroy. Tony Foster."

The charm slid off without penetrating. She checked her list. Drew two lines. "Go in and sit down if you want. We'll be starting late—camera two's stuck in fucking traffic."

"Any idea how long it'll be?"

"If I fucking knew that, I'd be doing a fucking dance of joy," she snarled. "Sit, don't sit. It's all the same to me."

The Lambert had been built just before the turn of

the century when money poured into Vancouver from timber, mining, and fleecing unwary treasure seekers heading north to the Yukon gold rush. A group of the young city's most upstanding and wealthy citizens, stung by a federal study that said Vancouver led the Dominion in consumption of alcohol, vowed to bring culture to the frontier and, with their wallets behind the project, it took only five short months from breaking the ground to the first performance on the Lambert stage.

A hundred years later, a similar group ripped out screens, projection booths, and drop ceilings and restored the theatre to its original glory. In order to sell local wines in the lobby during intermissions, the restored Lambert had a liquor license.

Henry appreciated the irony.

"Jesus." Graham tipped his head back and stared up at the gilded Graces and cherubs dancing across lobby's ceiling. "That's a bit over the top, eh?"

"Well, when you're spending government money, why not go for Baroque."

"What?"

"Never mind." The lights on the stairs leading up to the balconies were off. It therefore seemed reasonable to assume that the balcony wouldn't be used during the performance and would offer them the privacy they'd need. Henry dragged Graham across the lobby. "Come on."

"We're not supposed to go up there."

"Then we'd better not get caught."

Graham didn't seem to find that comforting. Frowning, he stopped at the bottom step. "The lights are off."

"You talk to the dead and you're afraid of the dark?"

"That's not . . . Oh, never mind." He threw a nervous glance over his shoulder, pulled his arm from Henry's hand, and sprinted for the second floor, the muffled thud of work boots on carpet drowned out by Radiogram's new CD playing over the sound system.

Henry met him at the top of the stairs.

"Oh, sure . . . beat the old . . . man." He sagged against the flocked wallpaper and panted.

"You should exercise more."

"You should . . . mind your own . . . damned business." Pushing himself upright, Graham headed for the main balcony. "If we're going to . . . do this. I want . . . to sit down."

The balcony was deserted, but Henry noted the cables leading to the empty spot waiting for the delayed camera two. Down below, half a dozen crew members ran around attending to last minute details. On the stage, a pair of actors Henry didn't recognize—although Tony had assured him they'd been famous in their day—worked on blocking. The seats were about three quarters filled, the audience not yet restless but becoming loud.

Loud was good. Loud would cover the conversation Graham Brummel was about to have with the dead.

"Well?"

The replica turn-of-the-century red plush seat protested as Graham dropped into it. "Well, what?"

"Is he here?"

"Sure. But that's the wrong question. The right question is; does he want to talk. Actually . . ." Graham scratched thoughtfully at his comb-over. ". . . the real question is, will he say anything I can understand. The dead are not usually what you'd call articulate. Now these days I can't get them to shut up, but I still had to work on Cassandra and Stephen for a couple of weeks before I could get anything and I had a blood tie there."

"Here, you have me."

"That and thirty-two seventy-five'll buy you a two-four." He sighed. "I could use a beer."

"You've had plenty. Call. Or concentrate. Or do whatever you have to."

"You've got no friggin' idea how this works, do . . ." Twisting around, he looked up at Henry and froze. "Yeah. So like, I'll just, um . . ."

188 ♦ Tanya Huff

As little as he wanted to, Henry dialed it back.
Masked the Hunter. Destroying this annoying little man
would not help free Tony and the others. *More's the pity.*
Closing his fingers over the back of Graham's chair, he
waited.

"*I'd still like to know, why me?*"

"*Like attracts like. Look, there's a whole shitload of
myth about you. Okay, not you, specifically, but about
your kind. It's all around you . . .*" Tony spread his arms.
"*. . . like a metaphysical fog. I bet that's what the ghost's
attracted to. I bet that's what pulls him to you.*"

Tony's theory, expressed between visits from the last
ghost Henry'd had to deal with, had made a certain kind
of sense. Like was drawn to like. *Except, of course, when
opposites attract.*

That wasn't helping.

Fabric began to tear under Henry's fingers and he
snarled softly in frustration.

The temperature in the balcony plummeted.

"He's here." Graham's announcement plumed out
from his mouth.

"I figured."

A tall figure began to take shape in the place where
camera two would rest. The lack of light in the balcony
made it difficult to see defined edges, dark bleeding out
into dark. It almost seemed as though the pale, middle-
aged face cupped by the high formal collar of the early
part of the century floated, sneering and unsupported.

"He's complaining about the theater. I don't think he
means the building, I think he means . . ." Graham
waved toward the stage. "That stuff."

"Why couldn't I hear him?"

"Because you're not a medium." Graham snickered.
"You're short enough I bet you're barely a small. What?"

The ghost frowned.

"I think he thinks I'm brave talking to you like that
because you walk in darkness. Jesus, the lights are out.
Who doesn't?"

Alistair McCall, once given five curtain calls for his Faust, and Henry Fitzroy, once Duke of Richmond and Somerset, exchanged an essentially identical expression.

"Yeah, yeah, Nightwalker. What the hell is a . . ." Whites showed all the way around Graham's eyes as he slowly turned and gazed up into Henry's face. "Oh, boy, oh boy—I knew you were strange from the moment I laid eyes on you, but you're a *vampire?*"

Henry smiled, and this time he didn't bother being charming. "Ask him about Creighton Caulfield. We haven't got all night."

♠

"Hartley's gone?" Brenda's eyes were painfully wide and both her hands were wrapped around Lee's arm in a white-knuckled grip. "The house! It's the house!" she shrieked as Lee closed his hand over hers—not so much for comfort, Tony was just petty enough to observe, but to try and force her to loosen her hold. "It's eaten him!"

"No, it hasn't!" Amy snapped. Then she frowned and turned to Tony. "Has it?"

He shrugged and glanced over at Stephen and Cassie who'd finally rejoined them. Cassie still looked a little twitchy—which would have seemed reasonable given the dance music still playing a counterpoint to Karl's crying except that she was dead and therefore should, in Tony's opinion, be beyond twitchy.

"The house doesn't eat you, it uses the energy of your death," Cassie told him, smoothing down her bloodstained skirt and glaring at Brenda. The *you're an idiot* was clearly implied.

Tony repeated Cassie's statement, trying to keep the implication a little less obvious. "And since no one else is dead," he added, "Hartley can't be. It's been murder *then* suicide since the beginning."

"So he's probably just gone off looking for a drink," Peter sighed.

Arms folded, Kate shifted her weight from foot to foot. "Or he's gone off looking for someone to kill!"

"Who?" Amy demanded impatiently. "We're all here."

"So he wants us to go looking for him and when we're separated, then he kills one of us."

Heads nodded agreement.

"Yeah . . ." Amy pursed her lips, giving credit where credit was due. "That sounds reasonable."

"Tom wasn't a murder/suicide," Mouse muttered mournfully.

Tina shot him a flat, unfriendly look. "Stop saying murder/suicide around the children."

Safely out of the way beside Zev, Brianna rolled her eyes as Ashley pulled her ears out from between the script supervisor's hands. "First of all, not a child," the older girl snorted. "And second, it's not like we don't know the words. We watch *Law and Order*, you know."

"How can you avoid it?" Adam snorted.

Heads nodded again.

"Tom was kind of a metaphysical accident," Amy reminded them. "He didn't intend to kill himself, so his death is different."

Kate's lip curled. "If one death can be different, what's to say others can't be."

More nodding.

"Hartley wants a drink," she continued, "so the house, the thing . . ."

"In the basement," Amy interupted.

"Fine. The thing in the basement convinces him that a bottle of rubbing alcohol is just what he's looking for and the next thing you know, he's poisoned himself."

Amy spread her hands. "Come on, guys. This is Hartley we're talking about. He's perfectly capable of drinking a bottle of rubbing alcohol and poisoning himself without any help from a thing in the basement."

The nodding continued.

The circle was beginning to look as though it contained an assorted variety of bobblehead dolls.

"So do we go looking for him?" Tony asked.

"Oh, you'd like that, wouldn't you? Go off all alone. Come back and tell us stuff we're expected to believe. If all we have to do is survive until morning, then I think we stand a better chance if we use a little duct tape on Tony and keep him from wandering off." Kate patted the roll of tape hanging off her belt. "Who's with me?"

"No one is duct taping anyone," Peter told her. "Not unless I say so."

"Unless *you* say so?"

Stephen wafted closer to Tony as the shouting started. "It likes this. It likes anger. It likes any strong emotion," he added thoughtfully as Sorge shoved Pavin, Mouse shook Kate as she tried to lunge at Peter, and Amy, Adam, and Saleen were attempting to outshout each other—the three clumped together but yelling independently. Tina, Zev, Mason, Lee, Brenda, and the girls were being shoved toward the far edge of the circle. "Anger's easiest for it to use, though."

"Yeah?" Tony jerked back away from Kate's flailing arm. She wasn't flailing at him, but he still wanted to avoid impact. "How do you know?"

"How do I know what?"

He turned and glared at the ghosts. "How do you know what *it* likes?"

Cassie rolled her eye and stepped forward. "It feeds off our death, remember? We're its prisoners as much as you are. We've just been here longer, so we know more."

"Stockholm Syndrome."

"What?"

He frowned. "Helsinki Syndrome? Never mind. The point is; how do I know you haven't gone over to its side? How do I know I can trust you?"

"It's working on him now," Cassie muttered.

Stephen snorted. "You think?"

"It is not! It's more likely you two are working with it than with me against it because you and it are . . . OW!" Tony clutched his crotch with both hands and stumbled back through Stephen. Gripping her arms, Mouse had lifted Kate off the floor freeing her feet to swing. In spite of the pain—or maybe because of it—Tony felt more clearheaded than he had in a while. Clearheaded and cold. "Man, you are fucking freezing!"

"Heat is energy." Stephen adjusted his head. "We don't have energy to spare."

Heat . . . "You used the heat from the lights to look real this morning."

"The lights and the people. We . . ."

"Is that relevant?" Cassie interrupted, sounding remarkably like Amy. She waved a bloody hand at the rest of the crew. "I mean it was fun and all, but right now you need to do something about this!"

While Tony'd been distracted, the darkness had thickened around the circle of light cast by the lantern. It felt . . . anticipatory seemed the only—if clichéd—choice. Within the circle, the old arguments went on and new ones had started. Mason and Lee stood nearly nose to nose, yelling about fan sites. Brenda was on her knees between them—the tuxedo jackets covering just what exactly she was doing there—with Zev hauling at her shoulders trying to pull her away. Tina had left the circle and was banging on the front door demanding that Everett wake up. Her pinafore over her head, Ashley sat cross-legged on the floor singing "Danny Boy" at the top of her lungs.

That's a bizarre choice for an eleven-year-old . . .

It looked as though everyone had slipped over the edge, Tony realized as he slowly straightened. He had no idea how the hell he was supposed to haul everyone back.

"I HAVE TO PEE!"

Okay, not everyone.

Brianna stood in the center of the circle, hands on her hips, and as the echoes of her announcement died down, she glared at the suddenly quiet adults. "I have to pee, now!" Not quite as loud but just as penetrating. One bare foot lashed out . . . "Shut *up*, Ashes!" . . . and "Danny Boy" died. "Did you hear me? I have to PEE!"

"I think they heard you in Victoria," Amy winced.

"Do they have bathrooms in Victoria?" Brianna demanded. " 'Cause if they do, I want to go there! Right NOW!"

"Okay, okay . . ." Zev stepped up behind her and patted her shoulder. "I imagine there's a number of bathrooms in a place this size." He looked around expectantly at the others, and Tony remembered that the music director had only been at the location for about half an hour before the house closed down. "Right?"

"Yes and no," Peter admitted. "There're six bathrooms, but only the one in Mason's dressing room has been approved for use."

Amy opened her mouth to say something rude, but Zev stopped her with a raised hand and allowed his smile to say it for him. "Given the circumstances, trapped in a haunted house and all, I think we can ignore that rule."

"Sure, if we're planning on not getting out. But this was one of CB's directives, and I'm not leaping from the frying pan into the fire. I think I'd rather stay in the frying pan."

"She'll pee in the frying pan," Ashley warned ominously.

"Fine." With no time to argue, Zev surrendered. "We'll use the bathroom in Mason's dressing room."

"You won't," Tina told him, taking Brianna's hand from his. "*We* will. I think . . ." She swept her gaze around the circle, allowing it to momentarily alight on the other three women and Ashley. ". . . that we should all go. All us girls. Together."

"No!"

"Oh, for Christ's sake, Mason." As Amy lit the second lantern, Tina turned a withering glare on the star of *Darkest Night*. "Grow up and learn to share."

"Fuck you," Mason muttered. He pulled a battered

cigarette out of the inside pocket of his tuxedo jacket
and held out his hand for his lighter. "It's not about shar-
ing," he said as he lit up, staring at Tony over the flame.
"It's about shadows."

"She'll pee on the shadows," Ashley giggled.

"I'll pee on you, Zitface!"

"Try it, Cheese!"

Brianna lunged out to the end of Tina's arm.

"Enough!"

Everyone stared at Zev, impressed, as both girls qui-
eted.

Then all heads swiveled toward Tony.

He sighed. "There's something in that bathroom," he
began.

"Richard Caulfield," Cassie interrupted. "Creighton
Caufield's only son. He was retarded. We think he lived
in that room his whole life."

"We know he died in it," Stephen added.

"He's not like the rest of us. He doesn't . . . um . . ."
She frowned and sketched circles in the air.

"Replay?" Tony offered.

"Yes, he doesn't replay. He's just . . ." Unlike her
brother's, her head remained in place when she
shrugged. "He's just there."

"Tony?" Lee's voice had risen on the second syllable.
He closed his hand over Brenda's and moved it off his
arm, frowning at her while he did. "That hurt."

Her lips twisted into a bad approximation of an
apologetic smile. "Sorry."

Lee's smile was no more sincere. "Sure."

What the hell is up with those two? And then Tony realized that no one else had noticed as they were all—
like Lee—waiting for him to elaborate on Mason's
shouted no. "Uh, it's safe. It's . . ." He glanced at Mason
who sucked back half an inch of cigarette. ". . . shadowy,
but safe."

"Who cares!" Pulling Tina along behind her, Brianna
headed for the stairs.

"Wait!" Amy came forward with the lantern and swung it three times over the line of salt. "Okay, it's safe to step over now."

Stephen snickered and wafted back and forth over the line until Tony turned to glare at him. He knew Amy was spouting bullshit, but the section of salt the women were stepping over did look duller than the gleaming line that made up the rest of the circle. "Believing is seeing," he muttered thoughtfully.

"What?"

"Christmas movie, Walt Disney Pictures, 1999, John Pasquin directed and . . . never mind, long after your time."

"Brenda?" Amy paused on the outside of the circle. "You coming?"

"I'll stay with Lee."

"No, you won't," Tina said from the bottom step. "Get out here."

"But . . ."

"Now! He won't run off with someone else while you're gone."

"Why's the guy in the hat looking at you?" Stephen asked as Brenda reluctantly joined the others.

Guy in the what? Oh. Zev. Tony had no idea.

"Cassie?"

She smiled down at her brother from the stairs. "I'll be right back."

"What is it," Peter asked as, up on the second floor, the door to Mason's dressing room opened and closed, "about women going to the bathroom in groups?"

Every man in the circle shrugged.

Stephen adjusted his head.

As they reached the end of the lane, Henry could hear the three remaining crew talking inside the craft services truck, their hearts beating just a little more quickly than normal. He was impressed at how well they were continuing to react to some rather extraordinary circumstances. Was it because they were in television and used to thinking of the unusual as normal and the bizarre as something to get on tape? Was it because Arra's spell to erase their memories of the battle at the soundstage had a lingering, dampening effect? Was it because no stronger reaction would be permitted with CB on the scene?

Or because no stronger reaction was necessary with CB on the scene . . .

The executive producer of *Darkest Night* stood by the back porch, hands in the pockets of his trench coat, head sunk low between massive shoulders. If will alone could have forced the door open, his attention would have reduced it to a pile of kindling and a few bits of twisted metal.

He turned his head, and only his head, as Henry and the caretaker emerged into the light. "Well?"

"Graham spoke to an actor named Alistair McCall," Henry began.

"An *actor?*" CB snorted. "That's just what we need, another damned ego on legs."

"This one actually seems to *be* damned; at least by one of the looser definitions of the word." A quick gesture stopped Graham from speaking as Henry met CB's gaze Prince of Man to Prince of Man. "More importantly, he used to go to séances at this house while Creighton Caulfield was still alive."

The tense line of broad shoulders relaxed slightly. "Go on."

"He says Caulfield started out collecting grotesqueries— the finger of an alleged witch killed during the Inquisition, the skull of a cat that had supposedly been sacrificed in satanic rituals, a vial of dust and ash said to be the remains of one of the bloodsucking undead."

CB raised a single brow.

Henry shrugged. "Probably not."

Both men ignored the strangled choking sounds coming from Graham.

"Anyway, around 1892 Caulfield stopped collecting things and started collecting books. McCall said that some of those books made him very uneasy."

"He said some of them were warm," Graham added, shuddering.

CB's brow lifted again.

"It's possible," Henry told him. "Some books have the kind of contents that require a specific construction." He had, in his personal collection, a grimoire that recorded twenty-seven demonic names. The names were true—he had no desire to discover how the author had acquired them—and both the vellum pages and the thicker leather they were bound in maintained a constant body temperature. Blood temperature. Skin temperature. He'd taken it from a man who was using it to call demons into the world at about the same time as Caulfield had begun to collect the books that made McCall uneasy. He'd been told his was one of the last three true grimoires remaining. There was no reason Caulfield couldn't have gotten his hands on one of the other two.

"With the books," he continued, "came the séances. Séances and spiritualism in general were very popular at the time."

Graham snorted. "Yeah, well, you'd know."

Again, they ignored him.

"According to McCall, Caulfield was interested in contacting something he called Arogoth."

"Arogoth?" CB repeated, punctuating the name with a disdainful snort.

Henry shrugged. "Since the name seems to have no power, I suspect it's one that Caulfield made up. That whatever this thing was, it had no name—so he gave it one."

"Not a very original one. If one of my writers suggested such tripe, I'd take away their Lovecraft."

"So Caulfield was derivative. So what?" Graham demanded. "He was also more than dabbling in darkness."

Hands fisted on his hips, his gaze flicked between Henry and CB fast enough to dislodge his comb-over. "And stop ignoring me!"

"Sorry. Would *you* like to continue?"

"No." Defiance wilted under CB's attention. "It's okay." The toe of one scuffed work boot dug a trench in the damp gravel. "Henry here's doing good."

"Thank you. But Graham's right," Henry admitted. "Caulfield was more than dabbling. According to Mc-Call, the séances were often violent. The temperature in the drawing room would plummet, the darkness would thicken, and the spiritualists he used were never the same again. One of the more reputable died. The doctors called it a brain hemorrhage, but McCall—possessing a unique hindsight given his current condition—said he thought that something she'd contacted had overloaded the woman's brain. After a while, spiritualists refused to come to the house."

"And who can blame them, eh? If they were expected to talk to the thing in the basement." Graham frowned and scratched thoughtfully between the buttons on his overalls. "Except, it might not have been in the basement then."

"It makes no difference where it was, only where it is. How do we . . ." CB glanced back toward the house. ". . . they defeat it?"

"Caulfield kept a journal of his research. The séances, and the things he found out from books—he was determined to control the dark power found . . . acquired . . . stumbled over . . . who knows."

"And this journal is where?"

"Probably long gone."

"But there're ghosts in the house," Graham added, before Henry could continue, "who were alive when the journal was there. Servants."

"Servants." CB turned his attention back to the house, his expression dismissive. "What makes you think they knew anything about what their employer was up to?"

It was Henry's turn to raise a brow. If CB thought his housekeeper remained ignorant about any aspect of his life, he was being deliberately blind—which was, in Henry's long experience, the best way to deal with a good servant, the fiction of ignorance maintained by both halves of the relationship. "I think there's a very good chance they'd be curious about what their employer spent so much time and effort on, but we also have to consider that these ghosts died under . . ." He considered and discarded a number of words. ". . . familiar circumstances. One of the maids pushed one of the male servants down the kitchen stairs and then hanged herself from the third-floor landing. They were the first murder/suicide the house evoked and it may have been able to reach the maid because she'd read the journal. Tony has to talk to her."

"So now he's a medium, too."

Henry smiled at the weary lack of surprise in CB's voice. "No. But we know he saw Graham's cousins, so we stopped by his apartment and got this." He tugged at the strap hanging from his shoulder and swung Tony's laptop case into view.

"Is that . . . Arra's?"

"It is."

"And she left something on there that will help?"

"I have no idea, but there's eighty gig of magic instruction on here, so I'm hoping that there's something he can adapt."

"Adapt? Why does that not fill me with confidence?"

"He's a smart guy. He'll figure something out."

"Out. Yes. This may out his abilities to his companions. Have you considered that he may not want that to happen?"

It was Henry's turn to stare at the building. He could hear the five lives in the driveway—CB, Graham, the three crew—but nothing from the house. No life, no death—nothing. This house, this Arogoth, was attempting to poach lives on his territory. His lips curled back off his teeth. "Under the circumstances, what Tony does or doesn't want doesn't much matter. He'll do the right thing."

The silence pulled him around. Even with the Hunter masked, those who could meet his gaze were few. With the Hunter so close to the surface ... Henry could think of only two others who would even attempt it. After a long moment, CB nodded and looked away. "What happens now?"

"Graham will call his cousins to the door, then they'll go to Tony and tell him about the servants and the journal."

"I've pulled them pretty much into the here and now, you know? If this Tony can see them, they can get ..." Graham frowned. "Unless the house being awake is giving them trouble." He stepped back as both vampire and executive producer turned on him. "But probably not. You guys can just go back to ignoring me."

"Tony," Henry continued, emphatically doing just that, "will pull the laptop into the house, and use the information on it to find a way to talk to the maid. She'll tell him what was in Caulfield's journal, he'll use *that* information to either defeat the darkness in the basement or work around it and get the house open."

"There are a great many ifs in this plan."

"Got a better one?"

CB snorted. "I foresee one other problem," he said, not bothering to answer Henry's question. "Will the laptop work inside the house? According to my people, equipment batteries were draining rapidly all day."

Henry patted the laptop case. "Ah, but this doesn't run on batteries."

"Magic?"

"Apparently."

CB stepped away from the porch and indicated that Graham should approach. "Then let's begin."

As Graham sidled past him, he paused, and peered up into the taller man's face. "He's a vampire." The merest hint of a glance back at Henry. "Did you know he's a vampire?"

"Yes."

"And that doesn't bother you?"

"You speak to the dead."

"Yeah, but I don't suck blood."

"I have only your word for that."

♠

Brianna stepped past the lantern sitting on the threshold— the compromise between all of them crowding into the bathroom and privacy. "Okay, next. And don't worry, the boy's mostly scared about strange people coming in his room." She glanced around at the half circle of silent faces. "What?"

"What boy?" Ashley snapped.

"The boy whose room it is, Zitface." The younger girl rolled her eyes. "He's not even a little bit gross. I want to see the baby."

"Just hang on a minute." Tina cut off both Ashley's reply and any potential attack on her sister. "There's a boy in the bathroom?"

"Yeah, but you can see through him, so . . ." She pursed her lips and blew a disinterested raspberry.

"You can see the ghost of a boy in the bathroom?"

"Duh."

"Oh, my God! Oh, my God!"

Releasing her hold on Ashley, Tina grabbed the ward- robe assistant's arm, keeping her from bolting. "Brenda, calm down."

"Calm down? Calm down! How am I supposed to calm down! There's a dead person in the bathroom!"

"There's going to be another one right here if you don't shut the hell up," Kate growled.

Amy stepped forward and leaned over the threshold. "I don't see anything."

"Maybe that's because you're in on it, too." Kate

folded her arms as Amy leaned back to glare at her. "Well, you could be!"

Brianna shrugged. "She doesn't hear the baby neither." She cocked her head. "I don't hear the baby."

"Maybe you're too far away?"

"You can always hear the baby."

Kate's lip curled. "Unless Tony's playing ghosts again."

"Oh, for fuck's sake and for the last time!" Amy snapped. "Tony has nothing to do with this! You don't know him. Until tonight, you've hardly ever spoken two words to him. You're totally losing it."

"That's not helping," Tina warned as the two younger women moved closer together.

"You people are all nuts!" Whites showing all the way around her eyes, Brenda jerked her arm free and ran for the door of the suite.

Tina swore and raced after her.

The other four watched as the script supervisor crossed the dressing room and disappeared into the darkness of the bedroom. They winced in unison at the soft hard crash of flesh and furniture hitting the floor. After a moment, Tina limped back into the light, alone.

"I lost her in the dark, but I think she made it to the hall. I'm sure she'll be able to see the light of the other lantern coming up the stairs. She'll head right for it."

"She'll head right for Lee," Amy snorted.

Kate snickered an agreement.

"Do we go after her?"

"I'll go."

Tina grabbed Brianna's arm on her way by. "No, you won't."

Ashley pushed past Amy still standing by the bathroom door. "You guys can do what you want, but I'm going to pee. Any boy shows up and I'll slap him stupid."

"She will, too." Brianna tugged experimentally on Tina's grip, and relaxed against her side when it became obvious she was going nowhere. "She slapped Stewie so hard his nose bled. It was pretty gross."

"Brenda will be fine." Tina's tone suggested that the wardrobe assistant wouldn't dare not be.

Amy shoved her hands into the front pockets of her black cargo pants and rocked forward on her toes. "You know, that sounds a lot like famous last wo . . ." Tina's expression froze her in place. "Never mind."

She hadn't expected it to be so completely dark. Eyes open so wide they hurt, Brenda bounced off the side of the dressing room door and out into the hall. Arms outstretched, swaying in place, she tried to get her bearings.

There was someone with her in the hall.

Someone angry.

Too terrified to scream, she turned and ran.

Stumbled.

Found her balance.

Kept running.

Her left side slammed into something that moved and she grabbed at it as she fell. Wood. Smooth wood. And a handle. The door to the back stairs. It was open, swinging out into the hall. She'd run the wrong way, but she could get down the stairs to the kitchen and then find the others. Find Lee. Lee would make it right.

Eyes narrowed, Amy moved out to the edge of the lantern light. "Did you hear that?"

"It was the toilet." Tina folded her arms and glared at her companions. "I thought I told you no flushing until we were all done? With the power off, we only have the water in the lines."

"Toilets don't thud."

"Like someone chopping?" Brianna asked brightly. "Whack. Chunk."

"No . . ."

"It was the toilet," Tina repeated. "Keep the girls from running off while I use it."

"I'm not going anywhere," Ashley muttered as Amy took hold of Brianna's arm. "Don't touch me."

"It wasn't the toilet," Brianna insisted.

Kate nodded in agreement. "Sounded like an ax."

♠

The stairs were narrow enough she could touch both sides. She moved as quickly as she could on the steep uneven footing. Stumbled again at the bottom when suddenly there were no more steps. Groped for the table. Hand walked along the long side. Off the end. One hand still holding on, she reached for the wall.

Her fingers brushed something solid.

Something cold.

The basement door.

It was in the basement.

"Lee!"

♠

Tony shook off the sound of Stephen and Cassie's death in time to see Lee leap to his feet and cross to the edge of the circle, stumbling over Adam's legs and ignoring the 1AD's creative cursing.

"Brenda?"

Very faintly, from nowhere in particular, they heard a terrified, "Lee!"

"Brenda!" He paced the edge of the curve. "Where the hell is she?"

"She's not upstairs."

"No shit!"

Mason shrugged and lit another cigarette. "Fine. So you don't need my help."

Pivoting on one heel, Lee recrossed the circle. He looked, Tony thought, like he was trying to catch her scent. *Or I've just spent way too much time with Henry.*

"Brenda!" And across again. "I'm going after her."

"You don't even know where she is," Pavin muttered.

"And you're not taking the lantern." Mason hooked his foot around the base and slid it closer to his chair.

"Fine." Lee dropped to one knee by the box of candles. "I don't need the damned lantern, but I *am* going after her."

"No one's going anywhere," Peter began, his hands spread and his voice reasonable.

"She's in trouble."

"You don't know that." Reason began shading toward annoyance, but Peter managed to pull it back. "She just went off to use the bathroom."

"Yeah, and since she's calling for me, I suspect she's not using it now!" He snatched the lighter from Mason's hand and lit the candle. "I'm going to go ... uh ..." The candlelight threw his puzzled expression into sharp relief.

Tony understood his hesitation. The house had stretched and twisted Brenda's voice so that it could have come from anywhere.

Glass broke.

"Dining room!"

"Step over the salt! Over it! Ah, Jesus, right through it ..."

Snatching up a candle, Tony followed.

She thought the light was from the hall, but it was a candle, on the floor and shielded so that had she come out of the butler's pantry at any other angle she wouldn't have seen it.

Light glinted off glass.

"Hartley?"

Sitting on the floor by an open cabinet—one door hanging at a crazy angle—the boom operator straightened and lowered the now empty bottle.

The rush of relief was so great she had to grab the back of one of the dining room chairs. Trust Hartley to find the booze in an empty house. "I'm so glad to see you," she murmured as he stood, still holding the bottle loosely in one hand. "I thought I was following Lee's voice, but I guess I wasn't."

"Leesh not here." He staggered toward her and, although it was hard to tell for sure because his eyes were just at the edge of the small circle of light, he didn't seem to be focusing very well.

"Are you drunk? Because you know what CB said . . ."

The bottle smashing against the edge of the table cut off her comment.

"Brenda!"

"Lee?" She pivoted around her grip on the chair . . .

It was so dark in the dining room it looked as though Hartley had drawn a line of shadow across Brenda's throat. Tony didn't exactly find lines of shadow comforting, but they were infinitely preferable to the way the candlelight reflected off the liquid that flowed glistening down over the wardrobe assistant's chest.

Brenda's eyes widened. Her hand came up to clutch her throat. She gasped. Gurgled. Crumpled.

Lee surged forward, the movement blowing out his candle, and caught her before she hit the floor.

Tony stared past the two of them at Hartley who was turning the broken bottle so that the dark stain gleamed in the flickering flame of the candle melted onto the floor.

Murder.

Suicide . . .

Crap!

This wasn't a replay. This was real life. Real death. Really happening.

Lee was yelling. Voices out in the hall were answering.

Tony somehow managed to get to Hartley's side without his candle blowing out.

The boom operator looked over at him, blinked, and

stammered, "Hate that d . . . d . . . damned music." Then he tossed the broken glass aside and bent to pull another bottle from the cabinet.

Jamming his candle into one arm of the candelabra on the sideboard, Tony launched himself onto the older man's back. The rush of air blew both candles out.

♠

Graham sat back on his heels and swiped at the beads of sweat on his forehead. "They're not answering."

"Keep calling. They might just be distracted. We have no idea what's happening in there." Henry frowned down at the medium's expression. "Do we?"

"Know someone named Brenda Turpin?"

Old wood shuddered as CB stepped up on the small porch. "She works for me."

"*Worked* for you," Graham corrected matter-of-factly. "She's dead."

"Trapped?" Henry asked. "Like the others?"

"Well, I didn't feel her leave . . ."

"But you felt her die?"

He nodded. "And it wasn't pretty."

"It never is."

Ten

TONY WAS JUST as glad that Hartley's howling protests were drowning out most of the noises Lee was making. Unable to see anything in the pitch-black dining room, he fought to hold down the struggling boom operator.

"What is going *on* in here?"

As Tina's irritated question followed the light from the second lantern into the room, Tony shifted back and pinned Hartley's arms with his knees. The howling stopped and Lee's cries faded to pained gasping for breath. It might have been Lee . . .

It might have been Brenda.

"Holy crap." Amy's quiet observation held horror enough that Tony managed to twist around to see the women grouped in the doorway staring down at Lee holding Brenda crumpled across his lap. Tony could only see the curve of his back and Brenda's legs, but Lee looked broken and Brenda far too still.

"Lots of blood!" Brianna pushed between Amy's and Tina's hips. "Is she dead?"

"I don't . . . she isn't . . . I can't . . ." Lee shook his head, hair flicking back and forth with the violence of his denial, then he curled even more tightly around the body.

Not Brenda.

The body.

Amy stepped forward as Peter, Zev, and Adam pushed in from the hall. Zev took one look at the tableau and grabbed the girls, pulling them back out of the dining room.

"I already saw!" Brianna protested.

"Then you can get out of the way," Zev told her calmly. "Ashley, Mason stayed in the circle; maybe you should go sit with him so he's not alone."

"Her heart's not beating," Amy murmured over the sound of Ashley leaving. "It was fast, Lee, there was nothing you could do. The carotid artery was cut. Wound like this, you bleed out in less than three minutes."

"How do you know?"

Tony could hear hope in Lee's question and maybe, just maybe, a slight relaxing together of all the bits and pieces he'd become.

"I saw it on a television show." Amy sat back on her heels, and Tony could just see her face over the black line of Lee's shoulder. Somehow the magenta hair and heavily mascaraed eyes lent weight to her explanation. This was death. Goth girls knew about death. Right?

"It was the same situation," she continued solemnly, "except it was a gunshot and not a wardrobe assistant, but the same wound. Bled out in less than three. There was . . ." She gripped his shoulder, the black tips on magenta nails disappearing against his jacket. ". . . nothing you could do."

"Why was there nothing Tony could do, then?" Kate drawled. "He's supposed to be on top of all this."

She's right. I know what's happening. I'm the one talking to the ghosts. I'm the one with the metaphysical powers. I should have gone after Hartley.

"Hello." Amy ground out the word through clenched teeth. "He's sitting on the perp."

"Too little, too late. And I think . . ."

"No one gives a flying fuck what you think!" Without

rising or releasing her hold on Lee's shoulder, she swiveled around. "Peter!"

Given the director's reaction, Tony could imagine Amy's expression.

"Yeah. Right. Uh, Kate, be quiet, you're not helping. Lee, let Brenda go, and we'll carry her in and lay her beside Tom."

"What do we do with Hartley?"

And once again, Tony found himself at the center of attention.

Hartley, his right cheek flattened against the floor, glared up at him with one bloodshot eye.

"Duct tape."

"Kate, that's not . . ." Peter paused and Tony all but heard everyone considering it. "Actually, that's a good idea."

Once Mouse arrived in the dining room, Hartley stopped struggling. Given their relative sizes, there wasn't much point and Hartley was generally not an aggressive drunk. Tony slipped back and let the larger man flip Hartley over and effortlessly cocoon his arms to his sides.

"Why'd you do it? Why'd you do it?" Mouse moaned the words over and over as he moved down Hartley's body and began to tape his legs together. No longer needed, Tony stood and backed away. He didn't understand the look Mouse shot him. He wasn't sure he wanted to. The cameraman had been double shadow-held. *If Mouse snaps, we're fucking doomed.*

"Why did he do it?" Tina wiped tears off her cheeks with the flat of her hand, unaware she was repeating Mouse's quiet mantra. "I can't remember Brenda ever saying more than two words to him."

"It wasn't him," Tony reminded her wearily. He stepped back as Adam and Lee lifted Brenda—Amy covering her face and the ruin of her throat with Lee's tuxedo jacket. "It was the house. Nothing that's happened here tonight is anyone's fault. The thing in the basement is using us. Manipulating us."

"And there's nothing we can do?"

"Survive until morning." He wasn't aware he was clutching his throat until he saw the direction of Kate's scowl. Forced his hand back to his side. Put them both in his pockets just in case.

"You didn't cover his mouth," Peter observed as Mouse hauled Hartley upright and slung him over his shoulder, duct tape creaking ominously.

"Nose is plugged."

"And you're afraid he'll suffocate?"

"Let him," Kate muttered as Mouse grunted an assent.

"All right. That is it from you!" Tina blew her nose and turned on the younger woman, her words emerging with the kind of distinct enunciation achieved only by nuns and senior NCOs. "I am sick and tired of your attitude, young lady. From now on, you will either have something constructive to say or you will keep your mouth shut. Am I understood?"

Even the house seemed to be waiting for Kate's answer.

Tony had gone to a Catholic elementary school and lessons learned under the steely-eyed glare of the older nuns lingered. Apparently, Kate had also had involuntary responses installed by the Sister Mary Magdalenes of the world.

"Yes, ma'am." Strangely, she looked almost peaceful as she turned to follow Tina into the hall.

She knows who's in charge, Tony realized, stepping out of Mouse's way. He picked up the two candles, his and Hartley's, and waited for Peter, who held the lantern, to leave the room.

But the director stood staring down at the dark puddle on the floor, apparently unaware that the others had left. He moved the light back and forth, mesmerized by the reflection of the flame. After a long moment, he sighed. "That's way too much blood, people. Let's try and keep it realistic."

"Peter?"

"You may know what's happening, but you're not responsible for any of this, Tony." His voice was low, too low to be overheard by anyone more than an arm's length away. "I am. That's why I get the big bucks."

Peter, as much as Tina, was the voice of reason. She couldn't hold them in place alone. He couldn't slip.

Tony snorted. "CB pays big bucks?"

The older man started, stared at him for a moment, then he snorted in turn. "Relatively speaking. Come on, they'll need the light."

They left Hartley lying inside the circle of salt staring sullenly at the ceiling. The pair of candles lit so Peter could carry the lantern into the dining room were left burning, the second lantern blown out so as not to waste the kerosene, and everyone followed Brenda's body into the drawing room.

They set her down next to Tom. Lee's hands were visibly shaking as he released her shoulders and straightened. Although Adam moved to join the others, he remained standing over her, facing away from the group, the back of his dress shirt a brilliant white like a beacon reflecting the lantern light.

I should go to him. He needs . . . Except that Tony had no idea what he needed.

It was Mason who finally broke the tableau. Mason, who had made vested self-interest a cornerstone of his personality, stepped forward until he stood shoulder to shoulder with Lee and offered him a cigarette.

Lee looked down at Mason's hand, up at his face, and almost smiled. "No thanks, I don't smoke."

"Good." He slipped the cigarette back into his jacket pocket. "Because it's my last one."

Almost became actually and Lee's teeth flashed as he shook his head. "Jackass."

"And I thought you gay guys were supposed to be the sensitive ones," Amy muttered, so close to his ear her breath lapped warm against his skin.

He'd have suggested she bite him, but given the distance . . .

As Lee turned, he almost seemed to be searching for something. Someone. His eyes locked on Tony's face just for an instant and, for that instant, flashed . . . relief? Tony was too distracted by the dark stain dimming the brightness of his shirtfront to be sure. By the time he looked up again, Lee was moving away from the body and Amy was moving toward it and Zev's hand was around his arm. A quick squeeze. And gone.

"Is anyone going to say words over the body?" Amy asked as she worked off her two remaining rings.

"No one said anything over Tom," Adam pointed out.

"Yeah, well, Tom took us by surprise."

"And we expected *this*?"

Amy's arched brow was answer enough. She waited. "Fine. I'll do it." A deep breath. A glance down at the bodies, the rings jingling in one hand. "To the living, death sucks. But to the dead, it's just another stop on the journey. Have a nice trip."

"That was . . ." Tina began.

". . . stupid," Ashley finished. "Because they're not going anywhere, they're just trapped in the house like all the other dead people."

"You think you can do it better?"

"I never said that."

"Then shut up."

"You shut up."

"Girls . . ." Tina's voice held obvious warning. The phrase "clear and present danger" chased itself around Tony's head.

Amy rolled her eyes and dropped to one knee, lifting the edge of Lee's jacket off Brenda's face with one hand and dropping her rings on the dead woman's eyes with the other. "Anyone else goes," she murmured, "and we're going to have to hope silver plating works as well."

Foreshadowing, Tony thought. And he could see the

word on a couple of other faces. *Just what we need.*
Movement at the far end of the room caught his eye,
and he turned, expecting to see Cassie and Stephen but
instead seeing only the faint gray outline of the mirror.
He'd managed to be elsewhere when Peter had ordered
the hair spray cleaned off after finishing the cocktail
party scene. Given the length of the room, he was surprised that the lantern light reached that far. On second
thought, he wasn't sure that it did.

Movement in the mirror had nothing to do with movement in the room. Shapes offered other shapes something. Tea. Little cakes. Faces, made indistinct by distance,
formed and reformed as cups rose and fell and dropped
to the carpet when the convulsions started.

"Is that how we left him?"

Amy's question snapped his head back around so
quickly he nearly kinked his neck. Tom's left hand lay
by his side, the fingers curled up so that chewed fingernails pointed toward the ceiling. His right rested palm
down on his thigh. Under the tarp, his head flopped a
little to one side. Tony couldn't remember how they'd
left him.

"Who looked that closely?" Adam muttered, more or
less voicing Tony's thought.

"I think it would be cool if he walked around," Brianna sighed. "You guys never did zombies yet."

"Episode after next," Amy said without looking up.

"Seriously?" Mason didn't sound thrilled. Tony
couldn't blame him. The whole walking undead thing
was just too easy to parody. Once Sara Polley took up
arms against an army of animated corpses, zombies
were done to death—at least on the Canadian side of
the border.

"Writers were finishing the final draft when I left the
office."

"Peter . . ."

"Not now, Mason."

Amy nodded, having come to a decision. "Of course

that's how he was. I'm sure."

She almost sounded sure.

That would have to be good enough.

"You have a safe trip, too." She lightly touched Tom's shoulder before she stood, then tugged her Hello Kitty T-shirt down and headed for the door. "Let's get back into the circle and this time, let's *all* stay there."

"Brianna, Ashley, come on." Zev tugged the girls into motion and everyone else followed behind; walking slowly like mourners leaving a funeral. Which, Tony supposed, was what they were. Amy was right, Tom had taken them by surprise and they hadn't so much mourned him as feared for themselves. Brenda, they grieved for.

He watched Lee's bowed shoulders, found himself wondering just how much the other man grieved, and almost hated himself for it.

"Tony?"

"Right. Sorry." He hurried to catch up to Peter and Adam.

"Isn't this great," the 1AD muttered. "We have our own morgue. It's like we're being punished for inflicting yet another gumshoe with fangs on the viewing public."

"This seems a little extreme for bad television," Peter sighed.

"Episode nine."

"Even for that."

The silence waiting for them in the hall seemed weighted. The people waiting, numbed. Amy knelt by Hartley, everyone else stood around the outside edge of the circle.

Peter pushed past. "What is it?"

Amy's voice had lost most of its highs and lows. "He's dead. It looks like he puked and choked on it."

"You're sure?"

"I watched a lot of *Da Vinci's Inquest*." Her lip curled. "And besides, it's pretty obvious."

"Eww, puke." Even Brianna seemed to have lost her interest in the ghoulish.

"Right. All right." Peter visibly pulled fraying bits back together. "Saleen, Pavin, carry him into the drawing room beside the others. Don't even start with me," he continued as the sound tech opened his mouth to protest. "Half the time it's like you two aren't even here. Amy ..."

"Earrings." Her hands rose to the first of four silver hoops in her right ear. "I'm on it."

Sorge led the way with the lantern, then Amy, then the body. No one said anything. No one followed.

"At least it was his own vomit," Adam observed thoughtfully as the body passed.

Tony would have laughed, wouldn't have been able to stop himself from laughing, except that the lights came up and Karl started shrieking as he burned.

Some of the moisture beading Graham's forehead was rain. Most of it wasn't. Breathing heavily, he sat back on his heels and shook his head. "Still nothing. They're there. I can feel them, eh, but it's like they don't know where I am."

"The house." CB made it an accusation, not a question.

"Yeah, sure, probably. So what? There's nothing I can do. I need a beer." He started to stand but Henry's hand came down on his shoulder and held him in place.

"When we're done, you can drink yourself into a stupor if you need to." Henry reached past the medium with his other hand. "Try again while I'm in contact with the house."

"And that'll do what?"

"Like calls to like."

"Yeah. Okay." Graham watched the pale fingers approach the closest point the house allowed. "It'll just throw you off."

Hazel eyes darkened. "Let it try."

♣

"At least Karl doesn't take too long." Cassie rubbed her arms, hands ghosting over the rivulets of blood without disturbing them. "I need to get out of this bathroom."

Stephen snorted. "It's not Karl that takes the time, it's his mother. And what a way to go; poking her eyes out with knitting needles might not have even killed her."

"I think *it* made sure she was dead."

"Well, yeah." He sat down on the edge of the tub, the blood splatters from their deaths evident on porcelain and paint. "Did it seem faster this time?"

"Karl?"

"The time between us and Karl."

"I don't know." Cassie reached out and lightly touched her reflection in the mirror. Her face was whole and she never tired of looking at it.

"It seemed faster to me. I think *it's* speeding things up, putting more pressure on them now that they've started to crack. I mean, we barely pulled ourselves back together after dying when we were back in here again. And there's two more dead."

"I know." Her eyes were . . . were . . . "Stephen, what color were my eyes?"

Her brother shrugged and fixed his head in one practiced motion. "I don't know."

"Blue?"

"Sure."

"Gray?"

"If you want."

"Stephen!"

"Karl's stop . . ." Stephen didn't so much stand as he was suddenly on his feet. "Can you feel that?"

Cassie frowned and turned from the mirror. "It's Graham. He wants us."

"It's more than Graham!" Eyes wide, he reached for her and was still reaching an instant later in the kitchen. "How did we get here?"

A young man, his head lying in a spreading puddle of blood, appeared and disappeared by the corner of the table.

"Cassie, look! Colin's being pulled out of sequence!"

"Graham's never done that . . ." Only their lack of substance kept them from slamming into the wall by the back door. ". . . before." She spun around to face the door, parts of her moving faster than others, legs swirling unsubstantially in an effort to catch up. "All right, we're here. Stop shouting!"

♣

Power surged up his arm, locking his muscles into agonizing rigidity. The house fought to force him away. He fought to remain in contact. The flesh between suffered.

It burned.

And it froze.

And it melted off his bones.

"I've got them."

Henry heard the voice, couldn't quite comprehend the words. Knew they were important, couldn't remember why.

Then warm points of contact on each arm. Warm and painfully tight.

The slow and steady beating of a mortal heart beneath his cheek brought him back to himself. He could hear blood moving purposefully. Feel the gentle rhythm of mortal breathing. Feel solid muscle, below, beside, almost all the way around him. Smell expensive cologne over meat. He opened his eyes.

He was lying across CB's lap, cradled in the big man's arms. It was an unexpected position, but it felt surprisingly safe—which was a good thing since leaving it seemed to be temporarily out of the question. "What happened?"

CB smiled, dark eyes crinkling at the corners, but before he could speak, another voice broke in.

"You were kind of vibrating inside this red light, not

making any noise, but it looked like you were screaming. The boss grabbed your arms, and when the red light tossed him away, you came too."

Chris. Henry managed to turn his head and saw the three members of the production crew standing and staring down at him. Teeth clenched, feeling more like throwing up than he had in four-hundred-odd years—a remarkably effective way of keeping the Hunter at bay—he flopped his head back around until he could see CB again. "You knew the house would push you away."

"And I figured I'd take you with me." This close, his voice was a bass rumble in the depths of a broad chest.

"That explains why my arms hurt."

"Indeed."

"I wouldn't have been able to get loose on my own." No point in lying about it.

"So I surmised."

"Are *you* all right?"

"He put a dent in the side of the generator truck."

"I own the generator truck, Mr. Singh; I can dent it if I choose."

"Sure, Boss."

"Why are you three still here? There's nothing you can do."

After a long moment, Henry heard feet shuffling in damp gravel. Chris cleared his throat. "Well, there's weird shit going down and we wanted to see how it ends."

"Besides," Karen added, "those are our friends trapped inside that house. Just because we can't do anything now doesn't mean we can't do something later."

"Commendable. For now, I suggest you get out of the rain."

Ah. Right. Rain. After a while it became such a normal part of life on the West Coast it was easy to ignore. Henry rubbed a dribble of water off his cheek against the smooth fabric of CB's trench coat.

"We'll be in the craft services truck if you need us, Boss." And much more quietly as they moved away, voice barely touching innuendo, "You think they want to be alone?"

CB, Henry realized as the other man shifted beneath him, hadn't heard. Probably for the best. He was comfortable, recovering in this position that parodied passion, and had no wish to be tossed aside as smart-ass employees were summarily dealt with.

"Old Arogoth," he said after a moment, "is really starting to annoy me."

"You've felt its power. Can Tony defeat it?"

Henry could lie and make CB believe him, but they'd moved past that back in the spring. "I hope so."

"If he gets my daughters out . . ."

Carefully pulling himself up into a sitting position, Henry watched the other man's face as he stared up into the night sky, rain beading against mahogany skin. Conscious of the scrutiny, the ex-linebacker lowered his head and met the vampire's gaze. Henry could read no promises in his dark eyes, none of the futile bargains with death he'd heard made a thousand times.

"If he gets your daughters out?" he asked softly. Curious.

Broad shoulders shrugged. "I'll thank him."

"Okay . . ."

Both men turned toward the caretaker, the contact between them stretching to fill the new space.

". . . Cassie and Stephen'll tell your friend Tony to come to the door and get his laptop, but they won't be able to do it right away. They got dragged back to the bathroom and they'll have to wait until the replay is over."

"Replay?" Henry asked as he got carefully to his feet. When he swayed, a warm hand closed around his elbow and steadied him.

Graham shrugged. "Yeah, well, replay's what Tony

calls it. The deaths the house has collected are running over and over—they're powering the malevolence . . ."

"Arogoth."

"Yeah, whoever." Another shrug. "These replays, they're throwing off enough dark energy to drive even the most stable person nuts. It's how the malevolence does it; throws all kinds of dark and spooky crap at you until you break. Just, usually, it does it slower because it has more time."

"And my girls are in the midst of that?" CB's grip tightened. Had Henry been a mortal man, it would have done damage. "Of violent death replaying over and over?"

"Kind of. But not really. So far, only Tony is experiencing it."

"So far?"

Sitting splay-legged on the porch, sagging back against the lower part of the railing, Graham shrugged a third and final time.

♣

When Tony opened his eyes, he could still see Charles' broken body superimposed over Zev. He reached out and gently tugged the music director a little to the left.

"What?"

"You don't want to know."

Zev thought about it for a moment then nodded. "All right."

Things had settled after Hartley's body had been taken away. Tina had split up the basket of food she'd brought down from Mason's dressing room after the bathroom break and everyone sat quietly eating. With everyone holding tightly to the normalcy of food, Tony doubted they'd even noticed he'd been gone.

"Tony! You have to go to the back door!"

He jumped as Stephen and Cassie appeared directly in front of him. Jumped again as Cassie grabbed for his arm and the cold raised gooseflesh from the edge of his

T-shirt to his wrist. As they began to talk, overlapping each other's sentences, it spread.

"... and if Lucy read the journal, she might be able to tell you how to deal with the malevolence."

The lights came up with a scream, and from the conservatory came the wet crunch of limbs being hacked off.

Tony wrapped his arms around his torso, shivered, and waited. And waited.

As he recalled, the old woman did a thorough job. Dismembered. Buried. Was that the sound of a shovel? Finally, rat poison.

This time, when the entryway reappeared, lantern lit and smelling ever so faintly of sweat and vomit, Amy's hand came out of nowhere and impacted with his face.

"Ow!"

"Sorry." Except she didn't look sorry; she looked disturbingly disappointed that she wasn't going to be able to hit him again. At least the numbness she'd been wrapped in since Hartley's death had disappeared. "We thought you'd been possessed."

His cheek throbbed. "I was waiting out another replay!"

"Well, yeah. We know that now."

"I mentioned it at the time," Zev pointed out.

"I wanted to stick you with pins." Brianna smiled at him over the edge of her muffin. "But Zev said no. The poopy head."

Just Zev? Given the evening so far, stupid question.

"Well, what did they say?"

"Say?" If the second replay was identical to the first, the gardener had been quickly unconscious and the old woman had said nothing as she methodically hacked him to pieces.

Amy rolled her eyes and her arm twitched. "The ghosts you were obviously listening to before you went away."

"Oh, them!"

"Oh, them," she repeated ·sarcastically. "Messages from beyond the grave should never be taken lightly! Share!"

"I need to go to the back door."

Kate snorted. "The hell you do."

"A friend of mine—Henry," he added to Zev who nodded, "has my laptop there."

Kate snorted again, this time adding a sneer. "And this is exactly the situation that needs a game of spider solitaire."

Arra used to tell the future with spider solitaire. This didn't seem to be the time to bring that up.

Tony stepped to one side so that Amy no longer stood between him and the bulk of their companions. "Graham Brummel, the caretaker, is a medium." When everyone accepted that without throwing things, he continued. "He told Cassie and Stephen that one of the ghosts who died while Creighton Caulfield was still alive may know how we can deal with the thing in the basement. I need my laptop so I can figure out how to talk to that ghost."

"Why?" Peter asked, crossing his arms. "You've been talking to the brother and sister all along."

"Because the caretaker is their cousin and he redefined them as individuals, pulled them away from ... uh ..."

"Death?" Amy offered.

"Yeah, death."

"So your laptop came with software for talking to the dead." Peter used the tone he saved for dealing with unfinished sets, unlearned lines, and extras in general. "You got lucky, Tony. All I got on mine was a copy of Jukebox."

They were clearly not going to let him leave until he explained. No point in making a run for it since the light faded to total and complete darkness just past the curved line of salt. Granted, he could just wait for the next replay and move through the lit halls of that earlier time, but given the varying edges the group seemed balanced on, he couldn't guarantee he'd survive the experience. He really didn't want to be the headliner in the next murder/suicide.

On the other hand, the explanation wasn't likely to win him any friends.

"We're waiting, Tony."

While only Kate looked actively hostile, even Amy, Zev, and Lee—the three who'd been on his side throughout—looked impatient. Well, mostly Lee still looked shattered, but the impatience was there as well.

We know you're hiding something from us.

Spill.

He took a deep breath. Tom was dead and Brenda was dead and Hartley was dead, so in comparison . . . "Arra left me the laptop . . . her laptop. She left lessons on it. Lessons on how to be a wizard."

"Say what?" Amy spoke first, but they all wore nearly identical expressions of incredulous disbelief.

"Arra was a wizard." He had to take another deep breath before he could manage the corollary. "I'm a wizard."

"Harry Potter," Brianna announced.

"Gandalf," her sister added.

"Fiction," Mason snapped as Sorge muttered something in French that sounded distinctly uncomplimentary.

"That's not like some strange euphemism for gay, is it?" Adam demanded.

Tony's turn for incredulous disbelief. "For what?"

"Because we all *know* that."

"No. Wizard. Like Harry Potter." He gestured at Brianna. "And Gandalf." And at Ashley. Finally at Mason. Seven words. Mason's lighter lifted off his thigh and slapped into Tony's hand. "And it's nonfiction." He tossed the lighter back to Mason who instinctively caught it, then let it slide out of his hand onto the floor. *Yep, it's covered in wizard cooties.* "According to Arra, it's just a slightly left-of-center way to manipulate energies."

Brianna dove for the lighter. "I want to manipulate energy!"

"It's not something everyone can do."

"I'm not everyone!"

"Why doesn't Tony check you out later," Zev suggested, pulling the lighter from her hand.

Amy's hands were on her hips. "So Arra was a wizard?"

"Yeah."

"Did CB know?"

"Yeah."

"And you're a wizard?"

"Sort of."

"And does he know about you?"

"Yeah."

She smacked him hard on the arm. "So why the hell didn't you tell me?"

"CB didn't want any of this to get out." CB hadn't actually said Tony couldn't tell people. They'd been in full agreement on that. He glanced around the circle of staring faces. "You know how weird people can get about this kind of thing."

"What kind of thing?"

"You know, telling people you're a wizard."

"He has a point," Sorge murmured, nodding.

"His head points," Amy snapped. "Hello! Haunted house! People dying! I think at that point CB might have let you mention . . ."

Dance music drowned out her last words.

The lights came up.

Great. The ballroom.

Before he could decide what to do—should he put himself physically in front of the doors in case Brianna slipped the leash again—he heard laughing from the drawing room.

That couldn't be good.

Brenda and Hartley danced out into the hall. Like

Cassie and Stephen, Brenda remained drenched in blood. Hartley had lost the duct tape and was remarkably light on his feet. Tom shuffled gracelessly behind them; his broken bones an apparent handicap.

Who the hell is coming up with the rules for this shit?

Both men shot him somewhat sheepish looks as they passed.

"Come and dance with us," Brenda purred over Hartley's shoulder. "Just let the music pick you up and carry you along."

"I don't think so," Tony snarled.

"I'm not talking to you, asshole."

Oh, crap . . .

He turned and could just barely make out the translucent forms of Kate and Mouse and Lee and Mason. The shadow-held. And Brianna—whose youth made her susceptible to the other side. Currently, the side he was standing on.

"Don't let anyone leave the circle." Loud enough to be heard over the music. Loud enough to be heard over any shouting going on back in the real world. Loud enough to be heard across the divide. Loud enough they realized he was serious. "Sit on them if you have to!"

"Leeeeeee . . ." Brenda sang the vowels. "You want to be with me, don't you? You let me die. You owe me."

"Cheap shot," Tony growled, placing himself between her and the actor.

She smiled; her teeth red. "He's mine, not yours."

"You'll have to go through me to get him."

"Through you . . ."

He stood his ground as the ghosts danced closer.

". . . all right."

"Dancing. We should all go dancing!" Smiling broadly, Mason grabbed Ashley's hands and began to swing her around. "Everything will be fine if we just go dancing."

She tried to pull away. "Tony said . . ."

"Tony's a PA, what does he know?"

"Let go of me!"

"We're going, d . . . AMN it!"

♣

Stephen's hand passing through his arm had been cold. This was so much colder it was almost pain with temperature. Ice shards in his blood. Muscles tensed past stillness into trembling. The taste of copper in his mouth as he fought to breathe.

Tony's legs folded and his knees slammed hard against wood. He jackknifed forward, gasped in pain, managed to fill his lungs. Coughing, hands braced against the floor, he looked up to see Tom leaving the hall with Brenda and Hartley dancing behind.

"No! It's not fair!" The internal struggle to turn the dance was evident on Brenda's face. "I could have had him!"

The call of the ballroom was too strong. Cassie and Stephen were safe in the bathroom. Their place. Brenda and Hartley hadn't yet had a replay to anchor them in the dining room and Tom . . . who the hell knew.

He could hear Brenda protesting until the lights dimmed and he knelt, coughing and shivering at the edge of the lamplight.

"Tony?"

Amy. Beside him. Unable to straighten up, he got his head around. She'd dropped to one knee and was studying him like she was on the bomb squad and he was liable to explode at any moment. "Is everyone okay?" he coughed.

"Are *you* okay?"

"I asked first." It wasn't much of a smile, but she seemed to appreciate it.

"Well, Mason's a little bruised. Ashley got freaked by the whole 'take me dancing' number and kicked him in the nuts. Did you know she plays soccer?"

He didn't.

"Yeah, well, his Beckhams are a little bent, let me tell you. Mouse curled up in a ball. Zev stopped Brianna from running by lifting her off the floor, and the rest of us did what you suggested and sat on Lee and Kate. And by the way, it totally sucks that I seem to be without any psychic sensitivity."

His eyebrows may have risen. He was still so cold he couldn't tell for sure. "You have *no* kind of sensitivity."

"Bite me." Shuffling closer, she tucked her hands under his arm. "You're freezing. What happened?"

"Ghosts. Brenda and Hartley and Tom. The ballroom called them and Brenda and Hartley danced through me."

"Danced?"

"I think it was a two-step."

"How the hell do you know what a two-step looks like?"

"Square dance club." He tried to keep all his weight from sagging into her grip and almost succeeded.

"Gay square dance club?" she grunted heaving him back onto his heels.

"Duh. I went with an ex."

"I can't think of another reason . . . What's that on the floor?"

Exposed as he lifted his left hand, silver glinted against the wood.

She stopped him from bending forward. "You'll break your nose. I'll get it."

Four rings. Two earrings. The metal slightly frosted.

"I don't think they're working anymore."

"No shit. *I* think I'll just tuck them out of sight." Suiting action to words, she slipped them into the lower pocket on her cargo pants and stood. "Right. Let's get you on your feet."

"Actually, I'm fine down here."

"You going to crawl to the back door, then, Mr. Merlin?"

Right. The back door. Tony sighed and let her help him to his feet. He couldn't stop shivering, but other than the lingering chill, he seemed fine. He didn't want to turn and face the voices behind them—rising, falling, accusing, whimpering—but he knew he didn't have a choice.

"I won't need the other lantern."

Conversations stopped. Kate scowled at Saleen and Pavin until they let her go. Mouse remained curled in a fetal position on the floor—best possible reaction for a guy who once won a fistfight with a bear as far as Tony was concerned. Sure, the bear was handicapped by not actually having fists, but that was pretty much moot. Sorge stood next to Mouse. Face red, Mason still cradled his dignity; Zev had both girls now and was glaring protectively. Lee sat flanked by Peter and Adam, his lashes wet ebony triangles, his bloody dress shirt in a pile beside him on the floor. Unfortunately, Brenda's blood had soaked through to the white T-shirt he'd worn beneath it.

Shit! Where's Tina?

Then he saw her over by the door, tears glistening on her cheeks as she stared down at Everett.

"Is Everett . . . ?"

She shook her head without looking up. "He's still breathing."

Well, yay. Funny thing to cry about.

"You won't need the other lantern," Amy prodded, adding a sharp elbow to the ribs.

"Yeah, uh, the replays are coming faster, so I'll just move while the lights are up."

Peter shook his head. "You're not going alone."

"Peter . . ."

"Tony." His smile held no humor and very little patience. "Let me rephrase that in a way you'll understand. You're not going alone."

"Fine. Amy . . ."

"She stays here. Same reasons as before. Lee . . ."

"No way, he's . . ." . . . *falling apart.* But Tony couldn't actually say it.

As he stepped closer, Peter lowered his voice—not so low he couldn't be heard because right now secrets were the last thing they needed but low enough that an illusion of privacy could be created. "Lee needs something to do. He needs to not sit around . . ." Words were considered and discarded in the pause. ". . . thinking. Besides, he's gone out on all your other excursions and you've both always come back. Right now, that seems like a good omen to me."

"Yeah, sure, but . . ."

"You'll take the second lantern." Slightly better than normal volume now. Director's volume. "You'll get your laptop. And you'll come up with a way to get us all out of here."

Even Tom and Brenda and Hartley? Something else he couldn't actually say.

Maybe Peter read the thought off his face. "All of us," he repeated. "Get moving. Lee! You're going with Tony."

Propelled by Peter's voice, by the normalcy of Peter telling him what to do, Lee stood.

Tony surrendered. Even with the replays moving faster, they'd be back long before the ballroom started up again.

"You sure?" he asked quietly as Lee came to his side.

"Peter's right. I have to do something."

"Carry the lantern?"

"Sure."

They were at the door of the dining room before Tony realized they should have gone the other way. He stopped on the threshold, but Lee grabbed his arm and dragged him over.

"It's just a room with blood on the floor. That's all." And if his grip was tight enough to stop the blood from moving in Tony's arm . . .

Tony added that to the growing list of things he couldn't say.

"She'd be pissed about the blood."

She. Brenda. A quick glance down at the dark not-quite-puddle. "On the floor?"

"No. On the shirt."

"Oh. Right."

"She was always at us not to get the clothes dirty because CB never gave wardrobe enough money for them to buy more than one set."

"Technically, she made the mess."

The answering snicker sounded just on the edge of hysteria and Tony decided that maybe he'd better skip the manly banter for now. As they moved into the butler's pantry, he suddenly remembered his backpack, stored in the AD office back just after dawn and forgotten. "I've got a shirt with me if you want to change."

"Into what?"

"Out of . . ." He waved at Brenda's blood.

"Oh. Right. Thanks." Lee's movements had none of their usually fluidity as he set the lantern on the granite countertop. "I wish that damned baby would shut the fuck up!"

Karl had pretty much become background noise, tuned out the way they all tuned out traffic and elevator music and provincial politics. But he was a convenient excuse.

Reaching under the counter, Tony dragged out his pack and pulled out a black T-shirt. "It may be a little tight, but it's clean," he said as he straightened. And froze. Lee'd stripped off his shirt and was scrubbing at a fist-sized stain on his skin with the crumpled fabric. The lantern light painted the shadows in under muscles and gilded the upper curves. He kept his chest waxed for the show—body hair gave the networks palpitations—but Tony had no difficulty filling in the patch of dark curls he knew should be there.

He was having trouble breathing again.

Bright side, he wasn't cold.

"I was going to a play after work with Henry," he said

hurriedly, one arm stretched awkwardly out offering the change of clothes.

"Henry?" Lee raised his head. "Your *friend?*"

"*Just* my friend now."

Strange exchange. Weighted even.

What the hell is happening here?

He was still holding out the shirt. Lee was staring past it with a . . . Tony had no idea what to call the expression on the other man's face, but the green eyes locked onto his with an almost terrifying intensity.

Then his back was up against the counter, the edge of the granite digging in just over his kidneys. Lee's hands were holding his head almost too tightly, fingers wrapped around his skull like a heated vise, and Lee's mouth was on his devouring and desperate, and Lee's body was pressing against him, and there was a rather remarkable amount of smooth, heated skin under his hands and Jesus, people reacted to death in the weirdest damned ways! Tony knew that the worst possible thing he could do was respond, but he wasn't dead and he *was* responding . . .

And the lights came up.

Eleven

TECHNICALLY, since he hadn't moved, he had to be still kissing Lee. Except that he was also up against the counter in the butler's pantry with his mouth working and his elbow braced in a plate of insubstantial cakes. He could feel . . .

No, he couldn't.

Damn!

Lee'd probably jumped back. It didn't matter if it was an Oh-my-God-what-the-fuck-am-I-doing reaction or if he'd realized Karl wasn't crying or he'd sensed a different reaction when Tony'd turned his head to look at the cakes—the point was they were no longer in physical contact.

He stayed where he was for a moment, catching his breath—the other reaction would just have to take care of itself—then, in as steady a voice as he could manage: "I'm in a replay. It's happening in the . . ." Bathroom, nursery, stairs, conservatory, ballroom; he counted down the recent replays. ". . . drawing room. From the hall it sounded like someone convulsing, but I didn't go in, so it might, um . . ." He struggled to bring his brain back on-line, but talking made him think of his mouth, which made him think of Lee's mouth, which made him think of what Lee'd just been doing with his mouth, which made him wonder why he'd stopped and . . . *Jesus H. Christ! At the risk of betraying the side, getting some is not the issue right now!* "Look, it's not very long, so I'll head for the kitchen while I've got the light. You can wait here or you can follow."

As he finished talking, he started moving; pleased with the way he'd finally managed to sound almost as though nothing out of the ordinary had happened. Where nothing out of the ordinary *didn't* include convulsions by the long dead in the drawing room, of course. If Lee wanted to deny swapping spit, then Tony would give him that chance.

And if he doesn't?

Twenty-four hours earlier—no, twelve—Tony'd have given his right nut to have Lee Nicholas suddenly decide to change orientation. He even had a couple of scenarios all worked out where *he* was the reason. One of them involved kiwi-flavored lube and ended rather spectacularly in Raymond Dark's satin-lined coffin back at the studio. Right at this moment, however, it was a complication he didn't need. Unrequited lust was a situation he was used to dealing with—start requiting and God only knew where things would end up.

Actually, it was fairly obvious where things would end up. . . .

For chrissakes, Tony, get your mind out of your freakin' pants!

The moment the replay ended, he was going to beat his head against the wall a time or two. Not only a fine physical distraction, but this talking to himself in the third person had to be stopped.

Although a kettle steamed on the stove—had apparently been steaming while that killer tea was being served in the drawing room—the kitchen was deserted and the back door closed. Apparently closed. And apparently closed doors hadn't stopped him before. All he had to do was . . .

Problem.

Cassie had said that Henry would leave the laptop on the bucket the butts had been in, but that would mean he had to get a horizontal laptop through a vertical opening barely five centimeters wider than the laptop was deep. Someone had to hold the laptop up on its side, facing the opening.

Pity he hadn't thought of that while Cassie and Stephen were still around.

"Henry! Henry, can you hear me?"

If Graham could communicate with the ghosts of his cousins because of a blood tie, he should be able to communicate with Henry. Blood had tied them for years.

"Hen . . ."

Darkness.

And Karl.

". . . ry!"

No answer. Or not one he could hear anyway. After all, Henry was the metaphysical being—Vampire, Nightwalker, Bloodsucking Undead—he was just a production assistant helping to put together a second-rate show at a third-rate studio. Reaching out, he trailed his fingertips over the wall, touched the edge of the doorframe, and couldn't go any farther. He leaned his weight against the barrier and almost felt the power gathering to stop him. It felt substantial.

And the vaunted wizard power of copping a feel off the thing in the basement was no friggin' help at all. Fortunately, there was another way. An already proven way.

"Cassie! Stephen! I need you in the kitchen!"

"What's wrong?"

Not the ghosts. No mistaking that brushed velvet voice. Although the lantern light throwing Lee's shadow against the door pretty much made identification a gimmie.

"The door's only open this much." Tony held his hands about five centimeters apart as he turned. "Laptop's this wide." His hands separated. "It's got to be up on its side or I can't get it through the space."

"And why do you need the ghosts?"

"They can talk to the caretaker."

"You can't talk to Henry?"

"Can't seem to."

The borrowed T-shirt was tight. He'd seen Lee in tight T-shirts before but never in *his* tight T-shirt. It made an interesting difference where interesting referred to interest being taken independently by parts of Tony's anatomy. Dark strands of hair fell down in front of the actor's face, free of the product Everett had used to slick it back. Tony had a vague sensory memory of gripping a handful of hair as an invading tongue probed for his tonsils.

Lee's gaze bounced around the room like his eyes had been replaced by a pair of green-and-white super balls—stove, window, door, wall, cabinet, sink, floor, ceiling—alighting everywhere but on Tony's face. "Look, about what happened; I uh . . . I mean it was . . . There was just . . . Brenda . . ."

And then he stopped.

Man, actors suck at the articulate without writers behind them.

And by the way, Brenda? *Thanks for bringing her up. Nothing like being the substitute for a dead wardrobe assistant.*

Tony was half inclined to let Lee sweat. Fortunately, his better half won—but only because the part of his brain connected to his dick thought that a sweaty Lee Nicholas was a good idea and he was trying to discourage it. "You were freaked. I get it. It's cool." Rush to finish before Lee could protest. Or agree. Or say anything else at all. "But if we *have* to figure out what was going on . . ." With luck, his tone made his preference clear. The last thing he wanted to do was sit down with Lee and discuss *feelings.* ". . . can it wait until after we get out of this house?"

Maybe relief. "And until then what? Denial?"

"Hey, we're guys—we're all about denial."

Definitely relief. And most of a smile.

So Tony smiled back.

"I said; what do you want?"

Startled, he stepped back and brushed against Stephen's arm. The sudden cold took care of any residual "interest" and snapped his attention back to the problem at hand. "Sorry. I was . . . uh . . ."

Stephen rolled his eyes. "Don't tell me. I don't want to know." His voice rose. "Cassie, back off! We don't want it to know we're moving around!"

"It doesn't know?" Tony asked as Cassie reluctantly lowered her hand and drifted around to check Lee out from the rear. Cassie was distracted, but Stephen sounded nervous. No, more than nervous. Afraid.

"It doesn't seem to." He patted the front sweep of his hair with the heel of one hand. "As long as we do nothing to attract attention to ourselves, things should be okay. But it's safest in the bathroom."

"Safest?"

"That's our place. Until Graham came, that's where we stayed. But it was asleep when we started being us again, and now it isn't." The other hand patted down the other side of his hair. "And it's more awake now than it was. So . . ." He half shrugged, the motion not quite enough to dislodge his head. "It's already keeping us here—we can leave the bathroom, but we can't leave the house. And, you know, we keep dying. We don't want to know what else it can do."

Made sense. "So, what attracts its attention?"

Arms folded, Stephen nodded toward his sister. "Stuff that uses energy. Anything physical, like the paint, or making it so others can see us like we did this morning."

"Contacting your cousin?"

"No. That doesn't pull any energy from *it*," Cassie explained finally joining them at the door. "It pulls it from Graham."

From what Tony could remember of the caretaker, he didn't seem to have much energy to spare.

◆

Wiping sweat off his forehead, Graham sat back on his heels and sucked in long, slow lungfuls of humid air. "This Tony kid," he said after a moment, "he needs you to turn the laptop on its side or it won't fit through the door."

Henry flipped the computer up on one edge. "Like this?"

"Yeah and line it up like the door was open this much." He held his thumb and forefinger apart, both of them shaking.

"Like this."

"Like that. Okay . . ." Wrapping one hand around the porch rail, he hauled himself up onto his feet. Henry could hear his heart racing. "I need a beer."

"When we're done."

"Done what? Done this? Done the next thing? Guy could die of thirst around you," he muttered, then added quickly, his heart beating faster still. "Not that I want you to think about being thirsty."

"You're right. You don't."

"It's just you might be a little more sympathetic because you're still not looking a hundred percent after having been knocked on your ass and . . ."

"Shut up." Tony was just inside the door. Less than a body length away and he might as well have been on the other side of the world. So close, the song of his blood should have been an invitation. But Henry sensed nothing but the power keeping them apart.

The power that had, as the caretaker so elegantly put it, knocked him on his ass.

The computer case creaked in his grip. It took an effort to let go and a greater effort to stop the growl rising in his throat.

When the laptop quivered, he loosened his hold further so that it barely rested against his fingers. It inched forward, stopped on the edge of the bucket, and then disappeared. Mortal eyes couldn't have seen it move, and Henry barely made out a silver blur disappearing through what seemed a solid door. His fingertips were warm and so was the galvanized metal.

After a moment, Graham sagged against the rail and started to cough. "It's like yelling across the friggin' Strait of Juan de friggin' Fuca, but I think he's got it."

"You think?" Not quite a snarl.

"Okay, okay, he's got it."

"Good." Rising, Henry dusted off his knees and then moved down off the flagstone slab, moved in such a way it would be obvious to anyone watching that the power wrapped around the house gave him no trouble at all. Didn't make him want to tear through it and yank Tony free. Didn't remind him of pain.

"So." Arms folded, feet planted shoulder-width apart in the damp gravel, CB scowled at the door. "We have done all we can."

"You know," Graham snorted, pivoting shakily toward the driveway, "when you make pronouncements like that, there's bugger all anyone else can say."

"Good."

♦

"I can't find anything about talking to the dead."

"How about conversing with ghosts?" When Tony glanced up, Amy shrugged. "Hey, it's all about what you punch into the search engine. Also, try necromancy."

He frowned. "How do you spell that?"

He wasn't surprised she knew. Sitting cross-legged, the laptop on the floor in front of him, Amy on the other side of the laptop, he typed in the word.

No results.

Nothing for connecting with the dead.

Nor connecting with the spirit realm.

"I don't think there's anything in here."

"Try spirits all by itself. Broaden your search parameters," she added impatiently, reaching for the computer. "Give it to me, I'll do it."

"Don't . . ."

Too late. She jerked it out from under his hands and spun it around. "Tony! You're playing spider solitaire!"

"It's a glamour!" he snapped spinning it back. "It makes you believe . . ."

"I know what a glamour is," she told him, emphasis adding volume. "I have a complete set of *Charmed* on DVD!"

The silence that followed accompanied raised brows and general expressions of disbelief.

Amy flashed a sneer around the circle. "Hello. Vampire detective? It's not like we can claim the creative high ground here!"

Tony glanced up in time to see Mason open his mouth, but before any sound emerged, the lights came up and all he could hear was Stephen and Cassie dying while the band in the ballroom played a waltz.

"That was 'Night and Day'," Peter told him when the house returned to lamplight and Karl. "Cole Porter wrote it for Fred Astaire and Ginger Rogers in *The Gay Divorcee*. We all heard it this time. Well, all of us except Amy, Zev, and Ashley. Why not those three?"

"They're not Fred and Ginger fans?"

"Hey, Fred's brilliant during that number. 'Night And Day' is one of his choreographic peaks."

"Not the point, Zev." Arms folded, Peter glared down at Tony. "Try again. Why not those three?"

"How would I know?" Tony was afraid the question sounded more than a little defensive. Still, a little defensive was better than the can of worms he'd open with *"Because they were never shadow-held."*

"You'd know because you know lots of things, don't you, Tony?" Kate shoved Pavin away from her with enough force that he slammed into Sorge and the two of them nearly went over. "Lots of things you never thought to tell us before people started dying."

"I couldn't have stopped it. Any of it."

Her lip curled. "But you're a wizard." Bent fingers tapped out patterns in the air. "Ooooo!"

"At least *he's* more than a pain in the ass," Amy spat as she stood.

"Put another record on," Mason drawled, shaking free of Ashley's grip. "Bitch, bitch, bitch, yap, yap, yap. Who the hell cares what he knows as long as he gets us the hell out of here before I end up spending eternity doing an undead rumba!"

"I haven't heard a . . ." Tony began, but Mason cut him off.

"It doesn't have to be a fucking rumba. Just type, okay?"

Brianna poked Zev. "What's a record?"

"It's like a great big CD."

She snorted. "No one cool uses CDs anymore."

"They're like from another time," Ashley agreed with a disappointed look up through her lashes at Mason.

Tony let the argument about music downloads wash over him—on one level grateful the others were distracted. The less time they spent chewing at their situation the better, especially since they seemed to invariably end up chewing on him. Meanwhile, Ashley had given him an idea.

Time.

The replays were like pieces of time trapped by the malevolence. Mosquitoes in amber if *Jurassic Park* could be trusted. He had a certain amount of confidence about the science in one, very little in two, and none at all in three—even with the return of Sam Neil.

Time had its own folder on the laptop.

Time, Determining.

Look at watch, he snorted and scrolled down.

Time, Keeping Track of Passage.

If I tossed a couple of dozen Timexes through the gate, I could make a fortune.

Time, Finding More.

Time, Traveling Through.

That might do it. If he'd had a little more time, he could have learned more spells and been better prepared. *Ah, who am I kidding; if I'd had more time, I'd have gone clubbing.* He double-clicked and found himself staring at a single word on the screen.

Don't.

Oh, ha ha. Back a screen.

Time, in a Bottle.

Not going there.

Time, Speaking Through.

Possibly.

There were two subfolders. Speaking with the past. Speaking with the future.

He double clicked the first option.

"Warning: Speaking with the past can cause paradoxes and time splits. Changes made will never be for the better. Do not attempt to send a message to yourself to get yourself out of your current situation."

So much for that idea.

◆

"Okay, I found something under Elementals. Apparently, they're kind of spirits that are always around and there's a way to contact them." He felt like a total idiot talking about this, but they'd all insisted on knowing what he was about to do.

"Secrets get people killed," Kate had snarled.

Even Zev had nodded.

"So I have to go to the back stairs where Lucy Lewis is in order to cast the spell." There, he'd said it: *spell*. Could he sound any geekier? "Because I got her name from Cassie and Stephen, it should be easy enough to manage." Where easy was a distinctly relative term. Easier than trying it without her name, one hell of a lot harder than snatching illicit snack food from Mason. "At first I thought I was going to have to work with a banishing demons spell, but . . ." Oh, crap. Did he say that out loud? Apparently, yes. "What?"

"There is a spell to banish demons on that thing?" Sorge asked, nodding toward the laptop.

"Yeah."

"Then why haven't you banished it?"

"Banish Lucy's ghost?"

The DP rolled his eyes, hands curling into fists as he visibly searched for the English words. "Banish the thing in the basement!"

"Oh." Good question. He only wished his answer didn't sound so much like he was scared shitless. Which he was—but the actual reason was equally valid. "Because I don't know that the thing in the basement is a demon, and if I go down there and I try to banish it and the spell doesn't work, then it knows we're on to it and we've blown our one shot. I need more information before I face the big bad. I need to know what's in Caulfield's journal."

"Ghosts aren't elementals," Peter informed him.

Obvious much? "I know, but . . ."

"You're using a spell for an elemental on a ghost."

"Yeah, but I know her name, so if I slot that into the spell, it should take me to her, and if it doesn't work, there's nothing Lucy can do to me. She's just a captured image." Totally ignoring any indication Stephen or Cassie had given to the contrary because, well, why the hell not. "If I try something in the basement and it doesn't work, I've just poked the big bad with a stick."

"So?" Peter spread his hands like he'd be the one throwing magical energies around. "Worth trying. We're already up shit creek."

And, hey, heads were nodding again.

They just weren't getting it.

"All right . . ." Tony reached for an explanation from their world. ". . . let's say the thing in the basement is

CB in his office. His power extends through the soundstage and out onto location; he's sitting there quietly running our lives. Now, suppose someone who knows nothing about him goes into his office and pokes him with a big fucking stick! What happens to that person?"

"Is this a real stick or a metaphorical stick?" Adam asked before anyone could answer Tony's question.

"Pick one."

"I was just wondering because if it was a real stick, it'd likely end up shoved where the sun don't shine, and if it was a metaphorical stick . . . What?" Adam glared around the circle. "Okay, if it was a metaphorical stick, it'd have the same result, only metaphorically."

"I think he just likes saying the word," Tina sighed.

"So," Peter broke into the murmured round of agreement, "if you try this banishing thing on the thing in the basement and it doesn't work because you don't have the particulars, you could end up dead."

"Yes."

"For crying out loud, Tony, why didn't you just say so?"

He shrugged. "I didn't want to give Kate any ideas." It sounded stupid saying it out loud and he braced himself for Kate's reaction.

To his surprise, she merely scowled and stomped across the circle to sit on the floor by Mouse, snarling, "I hate ballroom dancing."

Under the circumstances, he couldn't blame her. "Because I've got to put myself on an elemental plane to do this . . ."

"Put yourself on a jet plane. Just stop talking about it and do it," Mason muttered.

". . . I need someone with me to anchor me and pull me back if I can't get back on my own."

"Yank physically or metaphorically?"

"Adam!"

"Both." He didn't look at Lee, but the rest of them did.

"No." Lee shook his head, dark line of hair arcing

across his face. "Not this time. I just ... I mean ..." Arms folded across the borrowed T-shirt, he stared down at the polished toes of his shoes. "Between the baby and the music, I can't ... That is, I might ..." The sound he made was far too dark to be called laughter. "I don't fucking know what I'm likely to do."

And he, in turn, was so very definitively *not* looking at Tony that every head swiveled around like they were forcing a tennis match between two players who refused to step onto the court.

"What happened in the kitchen?" Peter asked suspiciously.

"Nothing!"

Pavin rolled his eyes. "Tony probably put some kind of faggot whammy on him."

Zev handed Brianna over to Tina and stood. "Watch who you're calling a faggot."

"Trust you guys to stick together!" The sound tech rolled his eyes. "You know why faggots stick together? Not using enough lube."

It could have gone either way.

Tony could feel the darkness outside the circle of lamplight waiting. Waiting for anger. Waiting for pain.

Then Zev laughed. He glanced over at Tony, who had a sudden X-rated memory of a Sunday afternoon, a distinct lack of planning, and the less than adequate contents of his refrigerator.

It was fairly obvious what they were laughing about, at least in a general sense. First Amy, then Adam, then one after another the others joined in. Lee laughed last and when Tony caught a glimpse of his face, the word that came immediately to mind was, *"Actor."*

The laughter edged toward hysteria but never quite crossed the line.

"God, no wonder you two broke up," Amy gasped at last. "You're too warped to sustain a relationship."

"I don't get it," Brianna complained.

And that set everyone off again.

At least Tony thought it did. Right about then, the lights came up.

The music from the ballroom didn't seem as loud, but that might have been wishful thinking. Entirely too clichéd for laughter to be the solution.

When he got back, Peter had come to a decision.

"Amy's going with you this time. The girls don't want Zev to leave . . ."

Whole conversations Tony was just as glad he wasn't around for in *that* statement.

". . . and there's no one else . . ."

"Hey!"

". . . except for Ashley, who has any kind of resistance to this place. We don't want to lose you." One corner of Peter's mouth curled up as Kate growled the expected denial into the deliberate pause, then he continued, "Once you find out how we can fight the thing in the basement, get back here as quickly as you can. We're all getting just a little tired of this."

"And bored!" Brianna added, rocking from side to side, arms rolled up in her pinafore. "Bored. Bored. Bored. The walls don't even bleed."

"Hey," Mason glared down at her. "How about you don't give this place any ideas."

"Hey," Zev repeated, glaring up at the actor. "How about you don't give *her* the idea that she can give this place ideas!"

Amy took hold of Tony's arm with one hand and waggled the second lantern with the other. "Hey, how about we get out of here."

"Sounds good."

They'd gone about five meters when Adam yelled, "Follow the yellow brick road! Ow! What? They're off to see the wizard."

"They're off with the wizard, you moron."

"Don't turn around," Amy sighed as the girls began singing "Ding Dong the Witch Is Dead." "You'll only encourage them. Zev's got a good voice, though," she added thoughtfully a moment later when Zev joined the song.

"Yeah, *that* I knew."

"What?"

"Never mind." The emphasis had tied the comment to a previous conversation with Lee. He'd expected Lee to be at his side. Sure, they'd been thrown together in more than an actor/production assistant kind of way by a homicidal piece of architecture, but they'd been connecting. Amy was a friend, but he'd still rather have had Lee. . . .

Oh, crap.

Maybe all that wanting did put some kind of a fag whammy on him.

Wizards affect the energies around them. That was what Arra always said. Well, she'd said it once anyway. He was a wizard—since he was heading off to do wizardry, it seemed a little pointless to deny it—but he was untrained. Maybe he was affecting the energies around Lee without even realizing it. Warping reality to fit his own desires.

"You're thinking about Lee, aren't you?"

"You can tell?"

"Duh. You're wearing your patented 'thinking about Lee' expression. One part panic, two parts horny. It's totally obvious."

Great.

◆

"I don't want to leave the bathroom."

"What?" Cassie stared at her brother in disbelief. "One of the first things you said when Graham called us back to ourselves was that you hated this place."

"That was then, Cass. That was before it was awake. I don't want it to notice us."

"It can't . . ."

"It might." He took her hands and led her over to the tub, pushing her gently until she sat down on the edge.

Then he dropped to his knees and laid his head on her lap. "I know we're dead, but we're not like the rest—we're not just mindlessly haunting the place we died. We're aware. Of things. Of each other. If it found out, it could take that away. I don't want to risk that. I don't want to stop being."

"Oh, Stephen." She stroked his hair, could almost feel the silky strands under her fingers, could almost feel the heat of his cheek through the thin fabric of her skirt, could almost feel the desire that had gotten them into this mess in the first place. Almost. She thought of telling him that they weren't really *being*, but since she couldn't have told him what they were, she didn't bother.

Dead, yes. But also together. She didn't want to lose that either.

They'd done everything they could for Tony and his friends. Maybe it wouldn't hurt to stay in the bathroom for a while.

It was their turn to be murdered again anyway.

◆

"All right . . ." As the lights dimmed, and Karl started crying, Tony shook the sound of the ax impacting out of his head. "I have to get this done before we cycle around to her replay."

"Whose replay?"

"Lucy Lewis. The servant. The one who might know about the journal," he expanded when Amy continued to stare at him uncomprehendingly.

She leaned a little closer. "You know, it's totally weird when you do that."

Okay, not uncomprehending, lost in her own head-space. "Do what?"

"Walk in the ghost world." Apparently satisfied with what she saw, she leaned away again. "I mean, you're here, but you're so not. It's freaky. And not in a good way. It was like following a sleepwalker to the kitchen."

They were standing at the bottom of the back stairs.

"Sorry."

"Why? It's not like you're doing it on purpose." Artificially ebony brows dipped in. "You're not doing it on purpose, right?"

He opened his mouth.

"Good, I didn't think so, but you know. So why do you have to get this done before we hit Lucy's replay? And why her? Why not the dude she pushed down the stairs?"

"Since Lucy did the pushing, she was probably more corrupted by the thing in the basement."

Amy glanced over her shoulder toward the basement door.

"Come on. She's on the second floor. Be careful on the stairs."

"Can you do a wizard light?" Amy asked as they began to climb.

"It's called a Wizard's Lamp. And no."

Her snort held several layers of derision. "Why the hell not?"

"Okay, Arra said that the energy to control . . . things . . ."

"Things? Is that a technical wizard-type term?"

"Bite me. The energy comes from the wizard. Why would I suck power out of myself to do something a flashlight or a lantern could do just as well?"

"Batteries are dead in the flashlight and what if the lamp blew out?" She waved it just enough to make the shadows dance. "You just suck at being prepared, don't you?"

Yes. No. And second-guessing would get him nowhere. "I should have anticipated this?"

"Hey, you're the wizard. You're the one on speaking terms with the great unknown. Besides, a Wizard's Lamp would be enormously . . ."

Wasted. The lights came up—although they weren't as bright on the back stairs as they were in more public areas of the house. *I guess there's no point in wasting power on the servants.*

"Amy, this is 'old lady chops up the gardener' time. It takes her a while, so we'll just climb to the second floor and wait." He slowed down; hoping Amy would keep pace with him and not go charging on ahead. It might have been his imagination, but he thought he could hear the damp thunk crunch of the ax going through bone in time to the music from the ballroom.

Dah dah dah da-dah, da-dah, thunk crunch.

And then again, since he'd never imagined dismemberment in waltz time before, who knew?

The second floor landing consisted of a wall of linen cupboards and an even steeper set of stairs leading up to the third floor and the servants' rooms. The narrow window was as dark and unreflective as every other window in the house and the hanging bulb with the iron shade threw shadows very similar to the lantern.

Dah dah dah da-dah, da-dah, thunk crunch.

No, he wasn't imagining it.

"You know, Amy, I just had a thought." He gave her enough time to make a derogatory comment before continuing. "It's possible that the extra who went all hysterical this morning did feel fingers. I'm pretty sure I remember the old lady burying the gardener's right arm in that spot. Yeah, I know it's not still physically there—but maybe it was kind of a ghost grope. So it's also possible no one actually rabbited the claw. The gardener just reclaimed it."

Just.

As applied to not only dead but dismembered gardeners.

When did he start living such a weird, freakin' life? Oh, right, when Vicki "I know best" Nelson pulled him in off the street to donate blood to a wounded vampire.

He wasn't sure whether or not he should be deeply disturbed that CB had called Henry for help. Bright side, Henry wasn't alone at the theater plotting revenge for being stood up *and* he'd delivered the laptop *and* if they happened to finally need a member of the aristocratic bloodsucking undead to storm the barricades from the outside, they had one on hand. Not-so-bright side . . . well, it was hard to nail down anything resembling a decent reason, but Tony wasn't entirely happy with the thought of CB and Henry doing that buddy thing.

"Tony?"

The light levels hadn't changed significantly. Amy's sudden appearance right in his face was one of the more startling things he'd seen tonight.

"Why the frowny face?" she asked, clearly pleased with his reaction. "You worried someone hoofed it out of here with the gardener's actual hand?"

"No," he told her, opening a narrow drawer and balancing the laptop across it, while trying to reclaim a little dignity. "If they had, we'd be playing 'ghost rampages across city for missing body part' instead of the standard 'haunted house tries to eat the souls of trapped and eccentric group.' "

"Ghosts don't rampage."

"This one would."

"And if this plot is so standard, shouldn't we be doing a better job of getting the hell out?"

"Maybe we're not eccentric enough."

"Please, you're eccentric enough all on your own."

"Me?"

"Hey there, Mr. Wizard, you're the one with the magic lessons on a laptop that seems to show nothing but spider solitaire . . ." Reaching out, she tried, unsuccessfully, to move the cursor. "And eww . . . Why is your touch pad so sticky? Never mind." A raised hand cut him off cold. "I don't want to know. Just tell me how to haul your ass back out of the spell and . . . What's that noise?"

"The *er er* creak?" He glanced away from the screen just long enough to catch her nod. "When I heard it this afternoon, I thought it was the door to the stairs moving back and forth."

"The door isn't moving, Tony."

"I know."

"Is it . . ." Her voice dropped dramatically. ". . . one of the ghosts? And I can hear it? Why can I hear it? I mean, it's great, but why?"

"Maybe the house has finally worn down your natural cynicism."

"As if."

Contradictions wrapped in attitude, that was Amy. "Okay, maybe proximity. Take your boots off."

Amy set the lantern on the floor and took a handful of black parachute cloth in both hands, lifting the wide legs of her cargo pants to expose gleaming black ankle boots laced in glittering pink. "Off?"

"Off. According to this, I have to write runes on your bare feet to anchor you."

"Cool." She sat on the bottom step and began undoing the laces.

"It's July. Don't your feet get hot in there?"

"No. Besides, do I look like the little strappy sandal type?"

She really didn't. Her socks matched the laces. Her toenails matched her fingernails—magenta and black.

"That's a lot of work for something no one's ever going to see," he mentioned, dropping to one knee and taking her left foot in his hand. Her toes curled in anticipation as he pulled the top off the magic marker with his teeth.

"No one's asking you to do it," she told him. Squinted. "Tony, is that supposed to be an anchor?"

He leaned back and studied the black lines on her pale skin. "What's wrong with it?"

"I'm the anchor, so I have anchors? That's not magic."

"It's symbolism." He bent over her other foot.

"Big word. Do you have any idea of what you're doing?"

"Honestly?"

She leaned back on her elbows and tipped her head up toward the *er er* sound. Dark brows dipped in, and Tony could see her remembering Tom and Brenda and Hartley. After a long moment she sighed and met his eyes. "No. Lie to me."

He squeezed her foot gently before he released it. "I have complete confidence in my metaphysical ability to pull this off."

"Liar."

"Ow!" Blinking away the pain, he stood. "Why the hitting?"

"You lied to me."

"You told me to!" Tony was amazed to discover that when Amy stood up, she was considerably shorter than he was. And he wasn't exactly tall. A quick glance over at her boots explained the discrepancy. "How the hell do you walk in those?"

"None of your damned business. Now let's do this before you go ghost walking again."

The hand rubbing gave her away. Right over left, left over right—she looked like a goth punk Lady Macbeth. Since she didn't have anything to feel guilty about, it had to be fear. Since he didn't have anything to say she might find even remotely comforting, he kept his mouth shut and pulled off his T-shirt.

"It's a cheat note," he told her as he copied the symbol on the computer screen onto his chest. "Because I've never done this before."

"The line under your right nipple needs to curve up more." She stepped toward him, bare feet slapping against the linoleum. "Let me."

"No, I have to do it." Good thing he didn't have much chest hair. "Better?"

"Yeah." Half a step back. "You ever think of getting

your nipple pierced? You could go shirtless and wear a chain between it and your eyebrow."

It was a good thing he'd already moved the marker away from his skin. "Not exactly my style."

"You don't *have* a style."

He was about to disagree when he noticed Karl had stopped crying. "Amy, the ballroom's about to start. We'll just sit down . . ." He dragged her down beside him onto the step. ". . . and not go anywhere . . ." The fingers of his left hand linked with her right. ". . . and we'll be . . .

"Crap."

Eyes open, sight fought with sensation so he kept his eyes closed and concentrated on the feel of Amy's hand. Or more specifically on the pain of Amy's grip.

In spite of the greater distance from the ballroom, the dance music maintained the same volume it had in the front hall. Something humming along was new. It wasn't Amy. And it wasn't him. Certain Amy had no intention of releasing him, he risked a glance up the stairs. Nothing.

Probably Lucy.

Which meant the captured dead were beginning to overlap.

Which meant . . . actually, he didn't have a freakin' clue what that meant. Probably nothing good.

He swore as a sudden drop in temperature racheted Amy's grip tighter, the pain snapping his eyes open. In ballroom time, he was alone on the landing. "Whatever it is, breaking my fingers will not help!"

Amy apparently disagreed.

The music paused. Downstairs, the dead died again. The music restarted.

"It's almost over. I'll be back in a minute."

It felt like about five minutes. *Yeah, and if you think time is subjective trapped in a car with a vampire who likes boomer music, try being trapped in a haunted house without a working watch.*

Watching for him to focus, Amy started talking pretty

much the instant he could see her. "Tony, it was so cool! She was hanging right above us!"

"Who?"

"Well, I'm guessing it was Lucy Lewis . . . okay, her spirit—not actually her because of the whole translucent thing—but damn! I felt like Hayley Joel Osmond!"

"Osment."

"Whatever. Point is, I saw a ghost!"

"Trust me—after a while, less thrilling." He worked the feeling back into his fingers as he dropped off the step, back onto one knee, and pulled the top off the marker. "Let's do this."

"I wish I could talk to her."

"Well, you can't."

"Hang on. You just drew a circle on the floor in Magic Marker."

"Not much gets by you, does it?"

"CB is going to have your ass."

"If he can get it out of this house, he's welcome to it." As Amy made a series of totally grossed-out faces, he capped the marker and stood. "I need you to count slowly to a hundred and sixty, that's three minutes."

"Thanks for the math lesson, Einstein. A hundred and eighty is three minutes."

"Fine, count to a hundred and eighty. When you get there, grab the back of my jeans—don't touch skin— and haul me out of the circle."

"Me, I'm not the wizard, but that sounds a little dangerous."

"It is. A little." Arra's notes weren't specific on just how much. "But just to me, you'll be fine. It's the emergency exit procedure."

"Great. I'll be fine. What's the nonemergency exit procedure?"

"That'd be the second half of the spell."

"Then why not . . ."

"Because the laptop won't be coming with me, and I don't have time to memorize it."

"Tony . . ."

"Three people are dead, Amy."

"Yeah." She sighed and cuffed him on the back of the head. "Go on."

He stepped into the circle, bent, and set the laptop on the third step where he could see the screen. The first part of the spell was a string of seventeen polysyllabic words spaced to indicate the rhythm with room left to add the elemental's name if known. Arra had helpfully added a phonetic translation. The second part was also a string of seventeen polysyllabic words—not the same seventeen, not that it mattered since he was unlikely to remember the first seventeen. It was, essentially, hopefully, a more complex version of the Come to Me spell aiming for a totally different result. Trying not to think of exploding beer bottles, Tony began to read.

When he inserted "Lucy Lewis" between the dozen or so clashing consonants that made up most of the words, his lips twitched. It sounded like Jabba the Hut's dialogue.

Garble, garble, garble, Han Solo. Garble.

Concentrate, dipshit!

Lesson one: The spell guides the wizard. It is the wizard who manipulates the energies. With time and practice, the wizard will find such guides unnecessary.

Someday, he'd have to go back and read lesson two.

Garble. Garble. Garble.

Jesus, it's cold . . .

All except for the pattern drawn on his chest. *That* was almost uncomfortably warm.

Contact.

She'd have been cute when she was alive. Not very tall, brown hair, hazel eyes behind small round glasses—he thought there might have been a scattering of freckles but with all the swelling and discoloration, it was hard to tell. The *er er* sound was the creaking of the rope Lucy had hanged herself with.

Had PBS ever done a series on hanging? He didn't think so, but he knew he'd seen something about the way most suicides changed their minds when the rope started to tighten, that no matter how determined they started out, faced with slow strangulation they clawed trenches into their own skin trying to get free. Lucy hadn't.

Worst part, there was someone home behind the eyes. Trapped.

"Can you hear me?"

"Yes." Barely a word. The rope had destroyed her voice.

Great. If he wanted any hope of understanding her, he'd have to keep this to one-word answers. "My friends and I are trapped in the house and we need your help to get out. Did you read Creighton Caulfield's journal?"

"Some."

"Does it contain information about the thing in the basement?"

She shuddered violently enough to start her swinging. "Yes."

What makes the dead shudder?

"Can we use the information to defeat it?"

"Don't."

"Because you don't think it'll work?"

The laughing was worse than the shuddering.

This was taking too long and he didn't know what questions to ask. No way he could get the information one word at a time. "Do you know where the journal is?"

"Now?"

Of course now—no—wait, her now was a hundred years ago. No way the journal would still be there. Except during her replay, he was there, too. In the same time as the journal. His chest burned, his head started to ache, and he had a sudden insight about that Don't.

"Okay, now."

Even given distortions, the look she shot him quite clearly said, *I may be dead, but you're an idiot.* "Hidden."

"Caulfield hides it? Where?"

"Don't."

Very helpful. "Appreciate the warning but we don't have a choice. Where does . . . did Caulfield hide the journal?"

"Li . . .

Something grabbed his jeans.

". . . bra . . ."

Pain blocked out the last syllable. When it faded enough for him to speak, he was propped up against the wall of shelves with the taste of copper in his mouth and a splitting headache. "Ow."

"Ow my ass." Boots back on, Amy squatted in front of him. "You had convulsions."

"Didn't plan to."

"You bit through your lip."

Talking hurt. "I know."

"You scared me half to death."

She flicked him just above the naval. His skin felt tight, sunburned. "Ow."

"Suck it up. Did you find out what you needed to know?"

"I think so."

"If your head wasn't so damned hard, you'd have a cracked skull, so be sure."

"I'm sure."

"Let's hear an amen from the choir!" She reached out to help him up. "Come on, get dressed and we'll tell the others."

♦

The others had moved into the butler's pantry. Amy flatly denied panicking when they returned to the hall and found a scattering of salt and two disks of warm candle wax.

"We needed a better way to keep people from wandering during when Fred and Ginger take center stage," Peter told them, beckoning them through the dining room. "This room is small, we can block both doors, and no one's died in it."

"What about Everett?" Tony asked as everyone shuffled closer together to make space for two more. With fifteen people crammed into the butler's pantry, small was an understatement.

"I convinced Tina that Everett wasn't going anywhere."

"What about the circle of salt?" Amy demanded.

"Keeping evil spirits out is going to have to take a back seat to keeping actors in," Peter snorted. "I can work with the possessed, the dead are a little beyond my skill. What the hell happened to Tony?"

Amy rolled her eyes. "He didn't stick the dismount."

"I don't really care what that means." Turning back to Tony, Peter folded his arms. "What did you find out?"

"Well, she wasn't a big talker . . ." Head to one side, he lifted an imaginary rope.

"The dead can dance, but they can't talk?"

"I'm not making up the rules. I'm not even sure there are rules. Back when Lucy killed herself, the journal was hidden in the library. I'll have to find it and read it during her replays."

Crammed in between Kate and Saleen, Mouse began to shake, eyes wide and cheeks pale. "You can't go into the library," he moaned, twisting both hands in his T-shirt. "The library is haunted!"

Her head pillowed on Zev's backpack, Brianna managed to combine a yawn with an expression of complete disdain. "The whole house is haunted, you big baby!"

Twelve

"ALL RIGHT, that's it for me," RCMP Constable Danvers rolled her chair away from the desk and stretched. "Bad guys caught, paperwork filed electronically and redundantly, government satisfied—I'm heading home for a shower and four blissful hours of shut-eye before I have to get up and get my darling children off to day camp." She balled up a scrap of paper and tossed it at her partner. "Jack! Hello, Earth to Jack! You planning on staying here all night?"

"I'm just checking into something that Tony kid said."

"What, this afternoon out at the house?" When Jack grunted an affirmative, she ran over everything she could remember of the conversation. "He asked about that murder/suicide from the fifties."

"Uh-huh."

"So you looked it up?"

"I looked it up."

"You don't have enough to do?"

"He got me curious."

"Uh-huh." Like all good cops, Jack could get a little obsessive and over the last few months she'd gotten used to dropping in on CB Productions—studio or location shoots—when the mood took him. She had no idea what he thought he was doing, but she trusted his instincts and Lee Nicholas was easy enough on the eyes she didn't begrudge Jack the time.

"It went down pretty much the way Tony told it. Father went crazy, axed his two kids and then himself."

"And . . . ?" They'd been working together long enough that she knew when the story wasn't over.

"And then he asked if we'd heard about anything more recent."

"And you gave him grief about ghosts. So?" Jack looked up from his computer and Geetha stifled a sigh. He was wearing his bulldog expression, the one he wore when he was hard on the heels of a hot tip. The one that said RCMP Constable Jack Elson always got his man. *If he doesn't make detective in the fall, I'm asking for a transfer to Nunavut.* "I know I'm probably going to regret this, but what did you find?"

"November 17, 1969, Gerald Kranby bought the house."

"Kranby of Kranby Groceries? The largest independent chain west of Winnipeg? Best in the west? Fresh or frozen, Kranby keeps costs do . . ." His new expression cut short her commercial moment. "Sorry. It's late, I'm a little punchy. That Kranby?"

"Yeah, that Kranby. In the early seventies, his ten-month-old son, Karl, was killed."

"Murdered?"

"Set onto a roaring fire like a Yule log."

"A Yule log being something you Christian folk burn at Christmas?"

"That would be it."

"Hey, I'm all about context." She stacked her fists on her desk and rested her chin on top. "Did they nail the perp?" When he winced, she grinned. "Just trying to sound hip, dude."

"Don't. And they didn't have to look far. His mother was lying beside the fire with burned hands and knitting needles in her eyes."

"Knitting needles? Plural? She put her baby on the fire and killed herself with knitting needles?" The shudder was only half faked. "That's very twisted."

"Or she tried to get the baby off the fire and was killed by whoever had put it on."

"That's a theory." One her partner clearly didn't believe. "Official line?"

"Murder/suicide. The nanny found the bodies when she came back from the kitchen with snacks. The cook and gardener were both in the kitchen at the time. Kranby had a rock-solid alibi and no one had a motive."

"Please, Kranby was a successful businessman. They always have enemies."

"And that's what Kranby said. But here's the odd bit . . ."

"Odder than Yule logs and knitting kneedles?"

". . . Kranby said that someone was piping ballroom dance music into his house."

"So he suspected Baz Lurman. *Strictly Ballroom* . . . it's a movie," she continued when Jack stared at her blankly. "You have got to start watching something besides crappy science fiction. Let me guess; the dance music drove his wife mad."

"That's what he said. In her statement, the nanny agreed that Mrs. Kranby had been getting increasingly nervous of late and had mentioned that she was afraid of the man with the ax."

"The man with the ax?"

"Chris Mills killed his teenage children with an ax."

Geetha blinked and sat up. "And Chris Mills would be the father who went crazy?"

Jack nodded.

"That happened a little over a decade before Kranby bought the house." She knew what he was implying. And she was staying as far away from it as she could.

"That's not all."

"Oh, joy."

"I went down to records and I pulled everything we

had on the house. March 8, 1942, Captain Charles Bannet killed his wife Audrey and then took a dive over the second-floor railing onto his head."

"Well, that's . . ."

"Not all." Jack ran one hand back over his scalp, brushing his hair up into pale yellow spikes, and fanned the papers on his desk with the other. "Constable Luitan, the officer who wrote up the report about the Bannets, did some research of his own. January 12, 1922, Mrs. Patricia Haltz, a wealthy timber widow, hacked her gardener into pieces and then swallowed a fatal amount of rat poison. February 15, 1937, thirty-nine people—hosts, guests, and band—died at a Valentine's Ball. Official verdict was a gas leak, but Luitan's notes mention that two of the entrances were barred from the outside and the third was locked. The host had the key in his pocket."

Habit replayed the scene. "That ballroom's got glass all down one wall. Okay, it's February so the windows are closed, but you'd think someone would have tried tossing a music stand or something."

"Yeah. You'd think." Then he waited.

Cops learned two things early on. The first was that, occasionally, coincidences were just that. No more and no less than the laws of probability winning out. A suspect with both motive and opportunity wasn't automatically guilty. The second was that while a suspect with both motive and opportunity wasn't *automatically* guilty, the odds were good. Coincidence be damned.

"You're seeing a link between what happened to the Kranbys and the earlier deaths, aren't you?"

"Man with an ax. Ballroom music. Weird piling on weird."

"You need some sleep."

The corners of his mouth twisted up into a fair approximation of a smile. "Not arguing. There's people who say that Caulfield House is haunted."

"There's people who say the moon landings never

happened." She shoved her chair out and stood. "There's people who swear to all kinds of strange shit. Some of them are even straight at the time. Come on, let's get out of here."

"I . . ." Jack stared at his monitor a moment then he shrugged and shut down. "Yeah, you're right."

"I often am." Waving good night to the team processing a very stoned hooker, Geetha herded her partner out of the squad room. "Mind you, I'm not arguing that it's weird, all those deaths in the one house."

"That wasn't all of them. In the twenties, Creighton Caulfield's aunt, who inherited the house, died, along with a visitor, after drinking cyanide-laced tea." A pause to sign out with the desk sergeant, then Jack continued as they headed out the door and across the street to the lot for personal vehicles. "In 1906, one of Caulfield's maids, a Lucy Lewis, shoved a male servant down the stairs and then hung herself."

"Hanged."

"What?"

"I think that when people do it to each other or themselves, it's hanged."

"Okay, hanged herself."

She grinned, hearing his eyes roll in the tone of his voice. "That's a lot of dead people. Why isn't this better known?"

Standing by his truck, Jack rubbed a thumb and forefinger together. "Money talks. Money also tells you to shut the fuck up."

"Yeah, I guess." Geetha unlocked her driver's door—probably the only car on the lot without an electronic key—and paused, one foot up on the running board. "What happened in the teens?"

Jack leaned out and stared at her over the top of the driver's side door, hair and skin the same pale gold under the security light. "When?"

"The nineteen-teens. Death every decade up to the seventies except for in the teens."

"Right. Well, according to Constable Luitan's notes, in 1917, a year after his only son died—of natural causes," he added quickly before Geetha could ask, "Creighton Caulfield disappeared."

"Disappeared?"

Jack nodded.

She snorted. "Well, that's clichéd." When he clearly had no idea of why, she rolled her eyes. "For a haunted house."

"Who said the house was haunted?"

"You . . ." Her brows dipped as she ran over the conversation. "Okay. Fine. Get some sleep, Jack."

"And you."

But she sat in her car for a moment, watched him drive away, and remembered the expression on Tony Foster's face when Jack had jokingly asked if he thought the house was haunted.

Knew that Jack remembered that expression too.

Tony hadn't liked the library when he'd gone into it earlier and he liked it less now. There were shadows lingering in corners and on empty shelves that had nothing to do with the light thrown by his open laptop sitting on the hearth. After last spring's adventure, lingering shadows were not on his list of favorite things. These weren't the same kind of shadows. And that didn't help. Hell, if even Mouse could sense bad shit in the library, where did that leave him?

Sweat ran down his sides and the pattern burned into his chest itched under the onslaught of damp salt.

"I am Oz, the great and powerful!"

The library seemed unimpressed.

"Right. And don't look at the man behind the curtain." He had no idea of just what exactly he was doing, but at least, this time, he was only risking himself.

"Look, Peter, the replays are happening so close together now that anyone who goes with me—Amy or . . . you know . . ."

To give Peter credit, he didn't pretend not to know.

"*. . . is going to be on their own. I mean, I'll be there, but I won't . . .*"

A raised hand had cut him off. "*I get it.*"

"*If the thing in the basement figures out I'm looking for Caulfield's journal, it could try to stop me.*"

"*How?*"

"*No idea, but if it's got half a brain, it'll go after the . . . the um . . .*"

"*The nonwizard.*" Peter nodded. "*Very likely.*"

"*So I think I should do this by myself.*"

"*I agree.*"

"*Come on, Peter, you can't . . .*" Tony went back over the conversation. "*Wait; no argument?*"

"*No. And Tina wants you to check on Everett while you're out there.*"

The lights came up—midafternoon by the lines of sunlight not pouring through the matte-black window glass—and Tony could hear convulsing and china shattering next door in the drawing room. There were books on the shelves, but the room looked dusty, unused. Felt unwelcoming. Not to the Amityville "*Get out!*" level, but it wasn't a room he'd linger in by choice.

With *A True and Faithful Relation of What Passed for Many Years between John Dee and Some Spirits* snuggled up next to *The Confessions of St. Augustine,* he suspected the shelving would give an actual librarian heart failure. He wouldn't have minded taking a look at a scuffed copy of *Letters on Natural Magic,* but his fingers passed through the spine as though it wasn't there. Or more specifically, he wasn't there.

During the previous replay, while dance music had filled the house and he'd had to force himself to stop moving to the beat—"Night and Day" was back at the top of the play list—the shelves had been filled with leather-bound books on law and business. Anything that might have belonged to Creighton Caulfield was long gone. Anything except the huge mahogany desk that continued to dominate the far end of the room.

People had clearly died in the drawing room years earlier than they'd died dancing since these books were obviously Caulfield's. There were as many in French and German as in English and a depressing number of them looked like journals. Who'd notice one more? The perfect hiding place. Tony was up on the ladder peering at the badly worn titles on a set of three dark-red volumes when the lights went out.

Fade out the past. Fade in the present.

"Ready camera one," he sighed as he climbed carefully to the floor. "Take two."

It seemed a safe assumption that the darkness lingered where the really nasty books had been. Most of them were clumped around Caulfield's desk—which emanated a distinct nasty all of its own. Retrieving his laptop and setting it down on the seat of the desk chair, Tony told himself he'd best make the most of the ten minutes or so he had until Lucy's replay and his one chance to find the journal during its own time.

The top of the desk and the drawer fronts had all been refinished to a high gloss and as he reached for the center drawer's ornate brass pull, his reflection shot him a look that clearly asked if he was sure he wanted to do that.

"I'm sure I don't."

The drawer was locked. Using the cheap pocket knife attached to his key ring, he applied lessons learned a lifetime ago at juvie and jimmied it open. There may have been a spell on the laptop that wouldn't scratch the finish, but he didn't have the time.

Didn't care much about the scratches either.

The drawer was empty.

All the drawers were empty.

No secret compartments. Nothing taped to the bottoms.

He stuck his head into the empty right side. Nothing.

Left side. Something gleamed. Fingertips identified it as a square of glossy paper. It had probably fallen from a higher drawer and moisture or time or both had stuck it to the side wall. Edge of the knife behind it . . .

He caught it as it fell and held it by the monitor.

Photograph. A smiling woman sitting on the front step of the house, one hand raised to push dark hair off her face, the other holding a laughing baby on her lap. Most of the writing on the back had been lost against the side of the desk. The only word Tony could read clearly was Karl.

Up in the nursery, Karl stopped crying.

"Crap."

He shoved the picture in his pocket as the lights came up.

"Son of a . . ."

Eyes closed, stomach heaving, he scrambled backward away from the desk, bouncing off discarded drawers and the chair. He didn't stop until his shoulder blades slammed into the lower edge of the nearest bookshelf.

During all of the other replays the house had apparently been empty of everyone but the dying. Not this time.

Tony opened his eyes.

There was no one at the desk.

Except that he'd seen Creighton Caulfield sitting there. His head had practically been in the man's lap. Tony's left shoulder and Caulfield's left leg had been occupying the same space.

Vomiting was still an option as he stood.

Caulfield *had* been at the desk. He'd been . . .

"Fuck!"

He'd been writing.

In the journal?

No way of knowing. *Sure, now I want to see him, where is he? This is worse than Stephen and . . .*

He ran for the hearth and the mirror.

In his present, a light film of dust covered the glass. Here, in a memory of 1906, it gleamed. It was about a third the size of the gilt-framed mirror in the drawing room and appeared no more metaphysically revealing.

Raise your hand everyone who thinks that's relevant . . .

Deep breath. One foot up on the hearth. Left hand flat against the stone just to one side of the inset mantle. Tony arranged himself so that he wouldn't be staring at his own reflection, and looked into the glass.

Creighton Caulfield sat at his desk writing in what could be a journal. The distance and the angle made it difficult to tell for sure. Frowning in concentration, Tony leaned a little closer.

And Creighton Caulfield looked up.

Fuck!

Tony jerked back instinctively and glanced toward the other end of the room. No one. Heart pounding, positive Caulfield had been staring right at him, Tony took another cautious look in the mirror.

Nothing had changed.

Caulfield continued to sit, pen motionless over the page, staring toward the hearth.

Calm down, he's just thinking.

His head cocked at a sound Tony couldn't hear— actually, he couldn't hear much of anything over the damned dance music—Caulfield smiled and placed his pen back in what looked remarkably like the inkwell that had gone missing from Raymond Dark's desk. He closed his journal and stood. Tony adjusted his angle. Picked up the journal, still smiling, and headed . . .

Right for me.

Tony backed up as far as he could and still maintain the reflection.

Not for me.

For the hearth. His face filled the mirror. His eyes

were a pale, pale blue with the same edge-of-insanity
stare a husky had. Tony was not a big fan of crazy-
looking dogs. Liked crazy-looking people a lot less,
though. Even ones who'd been dead for decades.

Yeah, like that matters.

The sudden vertigo was unexpected. The library
twisted and pitched, slid several degrees sideways, and
the floor came up to slam Tony in the knees.

Where he already had bruises from his visit with
Lucy.

The actual vomiting was new, though.

Fortunately, his last meal had been some time ago
and the puddle of warm bile barely covered a square
foot of floor. He was still kneeling, back arched, dry
heaving like a cat horking a hairball when the lights
went out.

Suddenly, forcing his stomach up his esophagus became less important.

His laptop was at the far end of the room.

There was a limit to how far the light from even a
magical laptop could travel.

He was alone, in a haunted library, in the dark.

Except it didn't seem to be as dark as it should be.

"Amy?"

No answer, just the almost echo of a nearly empty
room.

"Stephen? Cassie?"

Nada. Just Karl crying and the band playing on.

Since he was still fairly certain he was alone, prece-
dent suggested that the extra light making it possible for
him to see his surroundings wasn't a good thing. *Okay,
so maybe I shouldn't have skipped over that protection
spell . . .*

It was the mirror.

It was glowing. It was glowing like a computer monitor. The mirror was picking up the light of the monitor
aimed at it from the far end of the room and reflecting
it back. Which was impossible.

Vampires, wizards, ghosts . . . Your life is a freak show and this *you find impossible?*

So what had just happened? He'd been staring into the mirror and suddenly, with Caulfield all up close and personal with the glass, the world went wonky. Odds were good it had something to do with the mirror. Like the mirror had . . .

. . . moved.

"I'm an idiot."

And the benefit of an empty room was that no one agreed with him.

The mirror had moved. Specifically, Caulfield had moved the mirror. Why would a man carrying a journal he kept hidden in the library move a mirror?

Making a wide circle around the desk, still a little weirded out by the whole Caulfield experience, Tony retrieved his laptop and with it balanced in the curve of his left arm examined the mirror frame. And if he was more than a little careful about not looking in the glass, who was going to know?

There had to be a hidden latch.

If he could get it open and expose the hinges, he had complete faith in his demolition ability. If he could get the mirror off the wall, next time Lucy went swinging he could stand behind the desk and use it to read the reflection of the journal entries. In spite of what Henry seemed to think, the odds were good that the exposed pages wouldn't contain detailed instructions on thing-in-the-basement removal, but any information was more than he had now.

About to run his finger along the edge of the frame, he had a sudden memory of one of the gaming geeks at film school yelling at the screen during *Name of the Rose.*

"Check for traps!"

Everyone had roared with laughter when Sean Connery'd fallen through the floor a second later. Best part of a long and boring movie as far as Tony was concerned, given the distinct lack of Connery and some skinny kid actor doing the nasty.

"Homoerotic subtext, my ass." Setting the laptop down, he pulled his keys from his pocket and opened his knife. "Where was the action?"

The blade caught about an inch from the bottom on the left side, but no amount of wiggling it made anything happen. The light was so low and the wooden frame so dark he couldn't see exactly what was stopping the knife.

"Stephen! Cassie!"

The dark didn't seem to matter to them. Maybe they could spot what he was missing.

"He's calling us."

"I know." Stephen turned away from the mirror and smiled. He almost looked relieved. "But so's Dad."

"He's not . . ."

Stephen raised an eyebrow.

Just on the edge of hearing. More a feeling than a sound. Their father calling them back to the past. Back to the ax. Their wounds disappeared as they faded and the two voices became one.

"I guess death's a decent excuse." Tony winced as the impact of ax against door seemed to shake the whole house. On the bright side, he had the afternoon sunlight back and could actually see what he was doing. Could see cracks too regular to be actual cracks in the side of the frame.

The mirror was the same in his time as it was now. Same mirror in the exact same place on the stone. So although he couldn't touch this mirror, he could touch the mirror in his time. The same way he could reach out for the door to the ballroom. Right?

Who the hell do I think I'm asking?

Only one way to find out.

From the sound of the screaming, Cassie and Stephen had reached the bathroom.

He pressed his thumb down on the wood between the cracks.

Oh, right. Traps . . .

Didn't seem to be any.

Well, that's . . . good.

The piece of frame under his thumb depressed slightly, then swiveled away. At least that's what he thought it did. He closed his eyes quickly as sight and touch veered off in different directions.

His fingertips found a finger-sized hole in the midst of metal parts.

Put your finger in the hole and pull the latch back.

And I'll never play the piano again.

But a knife blade fumbled in by touch didn't work. Neither did a key.

Put your finger in the hole and pull the latch back.

Would you shut the fuck up, I heard you the first time.

A final thud from the second floor. He cracked an eye to determine that yes, the lights had gone out. Karl and the band started up almost instantly.

In the light of his laptop held up to the frame, he could see that a two-inch veneer of wood had opened to expose the latch works. Mechanism. Thing. He squinted and tried for a slightly different angle. There seemed to be something *in* the finger-sized hole. Something pointy.

Something pointy that glistened.

"Oh, give me a fucking break," he muttered as he maneuvered his knife blade back into the hole and scraped a little of the glistening away. In the slightly blue light from the monitor, the drop of liquid on the edge of the steel looked purple.

Apparently, it took a blood sacrifice to open the mirror.

This blood was fresh.

Creighton Caulfield had just opened the mirror.

Yeah, about a hundred years ago!

With Karl ready to hit the fire, if he was going to do this, he didn't have time to dither. Not that fear of having his soul sucked out his finger was exactly dithering.

It hurt precisely as much as he thought it would. And, oh great, he'd just exchanged bodily fluids with a crazy dead guy from the beginning of the last century. *Kind of makes all those condoms seem a bit redundant.*

And closely following that thought: *Henry's going to be pissed.*

But the mirror swung open, exposing a shallow hole in the stone about a foot square and maybe four inches deep.

No problem to get the mirror off the wall now. I just ream on the hinges and . . .

In the hole was a book.

Or maybe I should just grab Caulfield's journal while I'm here.

Out of replay or not, Tony half expected his fingers to pass through the book, but they closed around the worn, red leather. It should have smelled of mold or mildew, but it didn't, it smelled like smoke—made sense he supposed, it *was* in a chimney. The leather felt greasy and a little warm. And it was heavy. Heavier than it looked anyway. A quick flip of thick, cream-colored pages showed notes and diagrams written and drawn in thick black ink.

Nowhere inside or outside the book did it say that this was Creighton Caulfield's journal.

But then, it didn't have to.

Tucking the book under his arm, Tony closed the mirror just as the lights came up and Karl started to scream.

Tony almost joined him. Creighton Caulfield's reflection stared at him from just behind his right shoulder. Heart pounding, he spun around, but there was no one in the library, no one standing behind him close enough to touch, and, when he turned again, no one in the mirror.

It wouldn't have been so bad, but the son of a bitch had been smiling.

♥

"Brianna's gone!"

"What?"

Zev yanked Tony the rest of the way into the butler's pantry, cast and crew scattering back from their entrance. "The girls were sleeping over there under the counter. I went to check on them and she was gone. So's the second lantern."

Tony glanced at Ashley still curled up on a pile of discarded clothes and then stared at Zev in disbelief. "You had got fourteen people in a six-by-ten room. How the hell could she just grab a lantern and leave?"

"Look, it's late. People are tired and that damned music is distracting."

Wait.

"You can hear the music now?"

"Yeah." He winced. "The trumpet's off a semitone."

"She probably went to the bathroom." Tina lit another two candles and handed them to Kate. "There. This room is lit. I'm going after her."

"I'm going with you," Zev declared.

"Maybe she went to look at the burning baby," Ashley offered sleepily. "She's always boring yack yack yacking about it."

"She's your sister." Tina frowned down at her. "You should be worried."

Ashley snorted. "As if. She once rode a polar bear at the zoo."

No one in the room assumed it was a scheduled ride.

"How did she get into the polar bear enclosure?"

"No one knows."

Mason did a fast soft shoe, his white shirt gleaming almost as much as his smile. "Maybe she went dancing." He started humming along with the band.

"Stop it!" Eyes wild, Mouse grabbed his shoulders

and shoved him into one of the canvas chairs which rocked and creaked with the force of the landing. "Stay there! Don't move! Nobody move. They can't find us if we don't move!"

From the total lack of reaction, Tony realized that this was just more of the same. Mouse was dealing with Mason, having apparently worked the no-longer-entirely-stable actor into the scary movie playing out in his head. Kind of the inmates running the asylum, but if it worked . . .

The situation had clearly deteriorated while he was in the library. The thing in the basement had made significant inroads into the minds of the shadow-held. So far, no one seemed about to do its evil bidding—unless its evil bidding involved dancing in an enclosed space—but things didn't look good. Pavin and Saleen sat one on either side of Kate, who was scowling—no big surprise there—and the sound tech held a prominently displayed roll of duct tape. Lee stood by the far wall, arms wrapped around his torso, head down, eyes closed. He seemed to be muttering under his breath but didn't look likely to either make a run for the ballroom or commit mass murder. Or commit mass murder and *then* make a run for the ballroom.

"Tony!" Peter pulled him around. "What about your ghost buddies? Can they find her?"

"I haven't seen them since they told me about the laptop. I called, but they didn't answer."

Hope faded, but he rallied quickly. "All right, we'll do it without them. Tina, Zev; take the lantern and check the bathroom. While you're up there, check the burning baby room."

"I believe it's called a nursery," Tina snorted.

"Fine. Call it what you want. Then Adam, Sorge, and I will take the candles and . . ." As Peter opened the door, the candles blew out. "Shit."

"Anyone want to bet that's going to keep happening?" Amy muttered.

No one did.

Tony set his laptop on the counter, opened it and powered up. "This doesn't throw a lot of light, but it's a small room. If Tina and Zev check upstairs, I can make it to the ballroom on the replay light."

Shooting a disdainful glare at Mason as he passed, Lee moved out of the shadows in the back of the room. And Tony really hated that imagery. "*I'll* go with you."

"No. You can't. It's too dangerous. The ballroom already wants you."

"I'll be fine."

"You'll stay right here," Peter told him, one hand against the borrowed black T-shirt.

Lee sneered at the director's hand but moved back against the wall.

"I'll go . . ."

"No." Tony threw Amy the book. "Go through this, see if there's anything useful."

"You found Caulfield's journal?"

"Duh."

"I don't see where it says it's Caulfield's journal. How do you know?"

How did he know? "When I hold it . . ." He frowned. "There's power there. When I hold it, it feels like my laptop."

Lip curled, Amy rubbed her hand against her pants. "It feels like it needs a facial."

A couple of Henry's oldest books, the dark ones, the one the demon had wanted way back when, were made of human skin. "Don't go there," he advised as she flipped pages. "Tina." He stopped the script supervisor on her way to the door. "Do you have a mirror in your purse?"

Running full out, Tony made it to the ballroom before Charles impaled his wife. One of the double doors hung open just far enough to allow an eight-year-old access.

"Brianna!" But he doubted she could hear him over the yelling in the front hall and the now constant music. Tina's compact ready in one hand, Tony sidled sideways into the ballroom. No point in opening the door any farther. No point in asking for trouble.

And speaking of trouble . . .

He thought he could hear Brianna's voice, but the music was louder now, even though it wasn't the ballroom's turn. He couldn't see her; there were too many boxes stacked in the way. Apparently while Charles and the missus were in the house—*living* in the house, since they hadn't actually gone anywhere after they died—the ballroom had been used for storage.

Movement to the left.

More boxes.

To the right, a glint of gaslight on expensive jewelry and the rhythmic patter of hard-soled shoes against the floor.

Except, of course, there was nothing there but more boxes.

The replays were beginning to bleed into each other more and more.

So. He'd ignore any distractions, grab the kid, and haul ass back to the butler's pantry. It was *good* to have a plan. Of course, it would help if he knew where in the room the kid was because this replay wasn't one of the longer ones and the last thing he wanted was to be stuck in here in the dark. Brianna's voice rose, and the string section very obviously screwed up a few bars.

It seemed she was with the band.

Logically—as much as logic could be applied to this fun house—the bandstand would be at the far end of the room.

The boxes were stacked in no particular order and it seemed to take forever to race through the maze. *I can't believe mice fucking enjoy this!*

Certain he heard a familiar protest . . .

"My father will do you!"

. . . he opened his mouth to call her again and remembered just in time there was power in a name. Henry'd taught him that years before Arra'd further complicated his life. Sure, he'd yelled it once, but that had been in the hall and okay, maybe they'd been using each other's names all night but there was still no point in gifting it to the ballroom. Fortunately, there was an option.

"Cheese!"

The indignant, high-pitched descant shut off. He might have been reading too much into it, but a certain bounce as the music carried on suggested relief.

"Tony?"

Clearly, no one had taught Brianna the name thing.

She didn't sound close. Had he gotten turned around?

A heartbeat later that was the least of his problems as the lights went out.

But Brianna had one of the lanterns!

And in a room the size of the ballroom, that meant bugger all. She was standing maybe three meters away in the center of a small circle of orange-red light, the lantern on the floor at her feet, both hands balled into fists and planted firmly on her hips. "What did you call me?" Her eyes had orange-red highlights.

"That's not important," he said as he trotted toward her, "we've got to get out of here."

"No. I'm not going nowhere until they do what I say!"

"They?" He grabbed for her arm, but she scooped up the lantern and skipped back out of his way.

"Them!" A determined finger jabbed toward the wall. "I want to hear something good!"

Flipping open the compact with one hand, Tony grabbed and missed with the other. In the minimal light, he could just barely make out the band.

Brianna stomped into the reflection, took up a position directly in front of the band leader, and screamed, "I want something good NOW!"

Holy shit! Was that Creighton Caulfield at the piano?
No.

Great. I'm losing my mind.

Another grab. Another miss. It was like chasing a
pigeon.

"*Tony . . .*"

He jerked back, away from the voice. It sounded a little like Hartley. Right, he didn't have to worry about the
house discovering his name. The house knew his name.
Hell, with Brenda on board the house knew what size
jeans he wore.

"*Tony . . .*"

Too far away now to see the reflection of the band.
But there was definitely something there. Something
between him and Brianna. A couple of somethings.
They might have been waltzing.

"Cheese, we've got to go."

"Don't call me that!"

"You're right. I shouldn't. You should come here
and kick me."

"I'm not stupid!"

"I never said you were."

"*Tony . . .*"

Crap.

Mrs. White with the ax in the conservatory. Just after
he'd arrived in Vancouver with Henry, Tony'd bought a
box of cereal that came with a free CD-ROM of Clue. In
the current situation, it wasn't at all comforting that he totally sucked at the game.

Now that he had light, he could see the reflections of
the couples dancing between him and Brianna. Couples
he didn't know.

"*Tony . . .*"

"Fuck!"

Hartley was behind him, grinning his fool head off at
the reaction he'd evoked. Behind Hartley; more dancers.
They all turned to look at him as they drifted by. It wasn't

the ballroom's turn, but with him and Brianna standing in the midst of things, that didn't seem to matter.

"No! The way I want or I'll tell my dad!" Lantern on the floor, arms in the air, Brianna was dancing.

Her reflection was dancing with Brenda.

Sure, warn your kids about strange men and never say a thing about dead wardrobe assistants.

"Bri, come on!"

"I'm dancing."

She said it like she thought he was an idiot. Brenda laughed.

Two steps toward her seemed to put him four steps back. Eyes closed, eyes open, it didn't help. Brianna kept dancing—one little girl alone in a big room—and no matter how much it seemed like he was running forward, he kept moving toward the door.

"Tony . . ." Hartley. Pulling him by his name. He didn't remember Hartley's eyes being such a pale, pale blue.

The mirror showed more ghosts now between him and Brianna than between him and the door. The ballroom's replay was next. If he didn't get Brianna out before it started, she wouldn't be leaving alive. He didn't know how he knew that, but he'd never been more certain.

Great. Why can't I be certain of things like lottery numbers?

He stretched out his hand.

Were little girls more fragile than glass? The beer bottle had shattered into a hundred pieces.

Don't think about the beer bottle, you idiot.

Seven words. Shouted. Demanding.

Brianna screamed as she flew across the ballroom into his hand. Not fear. Not pain. Rage.

Little girls weighed a lot more than beer bottles. They both went down. Tony grunted as a bony elbow drove into his stomach, got an arm around her waist, and started dragging her backward toward the door. They were close. He could feel the edge of the ballroom behind him.

"*Tony . . .*"

Hartley had moved out in front of him.

"Oh, sure, *now* you don't want me to leave."

Brianna kicked and bit, but he hung on. He had no idea where the mirror was, but he didn't need to see what was going on.

"*Tony . . .*"

Brenda joined the chorus.

"*Tony . . .*"

And that was Tom finally heard from.

"**Tony . . .**"

Fucking great. The whole room.

What's next, chanting in waltz time?

Yes.

He fought the pull of his name. He wasn't going farther in. He was leaving and he was taking CB's youngest with him. He just had to break their concentration for a moment . . .

"My father is going to fire your ASS!"

There should've been a light bulb, the idea was that good.

"Look, ballroom people, I know you're dead but just think for a minute." He jerked his head to one side as a flailing fist tried to connect with his nose. "Sure she's young, full of potential power you can use, but do you honestly want to spend an eternity of trapped torment with a tired, obnoxious eight-year-old!"

"I am NOT noxious! You're noxious! And you SUCK!"

The last word echoed and there was good chance, given proximity, that his ears were bleeding.

On the bright side, as the echoes died there was a stunned pause in the chanting.

Tony scrambled backward, dragging Brianna with him. The instant he felt his butt cross the threshold—so not questioning how his butt knew the difference, but hey, go butt!—he rolled back, cleared his legs, cleared Brianna, and slammed the door.

Things thumped against the other side.

"Yeah, yeah, give it a break." Maintaining his hold on the girl, he got to his feet, dragging her upright with him. "Are you okay? Nothing broken?"

"I wanted to DANCE!"

Over the years with Henry, biting had become a sexual thing for Tony. That changed.

"OW!"

Brianna dove for the doors. He caught her again, favoring his bleeding hand.

"Hey, bigger, stronger, smarter here! You're coming with me, so you might as well make it easy on both of us. OW!"

So much for reason. However, actually carrying a fighting eight-year-old was the next thing to impossible. One option left.

"If you come quietly, I'll take you to see the burning baby."

"Liar!"

"Cross my heart."

"And hope to die?"

"Not in this house."

She thought about that for a moment. "Deal."

"Good. Now let's get back to the butler's pantry before we lose ..."

The light.

And the lantern was in the ballroom.

"I can't see anything." She sounded more than a little put out.

"Nope. Me neither."

"Wait, turn this way." Small hands tugged him around. "What's that gray thing coming down the hall?"

Didn't seem to be a lot of point in making something up. "I think it's the gardener's right arm."

The snort sounded remarkably like her father. "Is it supposed to be scary?"

"I have no idea. If we hold hands and I keep my other hand on the wall to guide us . . ." He pressed his fingertips against the paneling. ". . . we can't get lost."

"Yeah, right."

"Just walk."

He felt her twist around. "It's following us."

"Of course it is."

Zev met them in the entry hall with the other lantern. A quick glance showed the arm remaining beyond the edge of the light, scuttling back and forth and not looking at all frightening. Still, points for the attempt.

Passing the lantern to Tony, Zev dropped to his knees and gathered Brianna into his arms. "You're safe!"

"I was dancing." *And this bozo dragged me away!* was clearly audible in her tone. *My father is going to fire his ass* was evident in her body language.

"You can dance later. When we're out of here," Zev amended hastily, tightening his hold. "The important thing right now is that you're safe!"

"I'm safe, too."

He looked up and smiled, and Tony couldn't remember a good reason why they broke up.

"Were you looking for us?"

"No."

The pause as he straightened and took Brianna's hand went on just a little too long.

"What?"

"Lee's missing."

Frankly, Tony didn't have the words.

Brianna did.

"What's he missing? Because if you started doing something without me, I'm telling!"

Thirteen

"HOW THE HELL could you just let him walk out?" Tony demanded of the room at large. "You knew the thing in the basement was getting to him!"

"We didn't *let* him do anything!" Peter snapped, dabbing at a bit of blood running from the corner of his mouth. "Kate managed to grab a brass candlestick out of that lower cabinet, coldcocked Saleen—he probably has a concussion, thank you for asking—kicked Pavin in the nuts, and charged the door. Thank God, Mouse wrapped himself around her leg screaming *Don't go!,* or we wouldn't have been able to subdue her."

Gray, duct tape shackles wrapped around Kate's wrists and ankles, and she glared up at him over the linen napkin they'd used as a gag. From the way her jaw kept working, Tony suspected she was chewing her way free.

"So what you're saying is, you traded Lee for Kate."

"What?"

Good question. While his brain wondered if he wanted to get fired, his mouth rephrased and repeated. "You saved Kate and just let Lee waltz out of here."

"Wasn't a waltz," Mason said thoughtfully while Peter looked stunned. "I could show you a waltz that would make you weep. I'm exceptionally graceful. I could have been a professional dancer."

Ah the hell with it; he'd survived without a job before. His head snapped around and he glared at Mason. "No one cares."

"Tony . . ."

"Shut up, Zev."

Tony had shoved Brianna at Zev and raced back to the ballroom the moment he'd heard Lee was missing. He'd run on instinct through the pitch-black mess, bounced off at least one wall, may have kicked through something numbingly cold. Arriving seconds before the ballroom's replay, he'd placed himself in front of the barred doors. He wouldn't be able to see Lee, but he'd be able to grab him if he tried to push by.

He hadn't. Although Tony could feel the dead brushing up against the door at his back . . . Heard his name whispered, called, caroled, sung, and rapped with a painful lack of skill. Rap that bad *had* to have been Tom. Heard nothing that gave any indication things in the ballroom had changed during the replay. That Lee had reached the doors before him.

Or used one of the other two.

Damn!

The door into the garden required leaving the house, so it was off limits. Obviously. The door the servants used that led into a hall off the kitchen, however . . .

When the replay'd ended, Zev had been there with the lantern and a worried frown—the worry obviously for him, the immediate cause of the frown a little less obvious. He'd followed as Tony raced around to the servants' door. Padlocked.

The replay was over and Lee wasn't in the ballroom.

Which was of dubious comfort since he wasn't in the butler's pantry either.

Mouse cowering, Mason dancing, Kate taped—no Lee.

"Did you just tell me to shut up?" Zev.

"Who the hell do you think you are?" Adam.

"Jesus, Tony, chill." Amy.

"Me, I never trust him." Sorge.

"Now, let's all just calm down." Tina.

All five simultaneously.

Pavin was moaning about his balls. Saleen sat quietly, holding his head. He could hear Ashley and Brianna talking but lost content in the mix.

Peter held up a hand and the babble dimmed. Ginger brows dipped as he fixed Tony with a basilisk stare. "I'll make some allowance for the situation, Mr. Foster . . ." Mr. Foster. CB talk. Peter used it when he was emphasizing he was the boss under the boss. ". . . but I will not be accused of trading my costar for a number two camera. And *you* should try to remember you're a *production assistant*." Emphasis suggested he might not be for much longer.

"No."

"Excuse me?"

Tony stretched out his hand, said the incantation, and the Caulfield journal slipped out of Amy's fingers, across five feet of crowded pantry, and slapped into his palm. "Until we're out of this house, I'm the wizard who's trying to save everyone's ass."

Silence. Even Kate stopped gnawing and muttering.

Peter glanced from Amy's hands to Tony's, his eyes tracking the trajectory of the book. Everyone else merely stared. Sure, he'd moved Mason's lighter way back when, but that was small stuff. A book looked impressive. It was the most impressive magic any of them had seen him do. Even Amy had only seen him talking to empty air and then convulsing. Hell, back when he'd been shooting up, he used to do that all the time.

"And after?" Peter asked at last.

"After?" Tony's shoulder's sagged; he was tired and Lee was gone. "Fuck, can we just worry about during?"

The director nodded. Once. "Sure."

He'd probably never work in this town again. Hard to get worked up about it at the moment, but he had a strong feeling he'd regret that whole mouth first, brain second thing later. "All right. Lee. If he didn't answer the call to the ballroom, where did he go?"

"He didn't go in to see Brenda. I stuck my head in the drawing room before I met up with you," Zev expanded when the mention of Brenda brought puzzled frowns.

Amy wiped the hand that had been holding the journal on her pants and folded her arms. "He's not in the kitchen. He went out the door that leads that way, so I used the monitor and just kind of looked without leaving the pantry. I leaned." She tilted a little, illustrating. "If he's been, you know, possessed, I don't want to end up dead. Like Brenda."

If he's been possessed . . .

Tony couldn't think of another reason why Lee'd leave the others and go wandering around in the dark. Especially when he considered the way he'd been acting. What with the kissing and all.

"So he could be in the conservatory, the library, or up on the second floor." In a house this size that was a lot of territory to cover. "We've got one lantern, a computer monitor, and candles that blow out the moment we open the pantry doors."

"Why not while they're lit in the pantry?" Tina wondered.

Amy shrugged. "Maybe the thing in the basement is hoping we'll burn ourselves down."

"Nice," Zev snorted, smacking her shoulder.

Amy smacked him back. "She asked." And to Tony. "Bet you're wishing you'd learned that Wizard's Lamp now."

"He can make light?" Tina folded her arms. "Then why isn't he?"

"Because I can't," Tony told her, wondering just who exactly she'd been asking. "There's a spell in the computer, but . . ."

"You learned the talk-to-Lucy spell," Amy reminded him.

"No, I didn't learn it, I just performed it. Half of it." He held up his shirt, so the others could see the burn.

Tina's expression softened. "Does it hurt?"

Only when I slam an eight-year-old into it. "Yes."

Zev acknowledged the burn and moved on. "But what harm could making light do?"

"Well . . ." Stretching the fabric out a careful distance from blistered skin, he pulled down his T-shirt. ". . . the first attempt at a spell's always tricky, so I could blind myself." Okay, that received more in the way of thoughtful consideration than sympathy. "Or I could blind everyone still alive in the house."

"The amount of light may be moot," Peter announced suddenly, hands shoved deep in his pockets, weight back on his heels. "I'm not sure we should go looking for Lee. Remember what happened when Brenda found Hartley," he continued when all eyes turned to him. "Lee's safer if no one finds him. Remember, it's murder and then suicide." He stressed the second word. "No murder; no suicide. And we're *all* still alive." Met Tony's gaze. "Oh, wait, you have powers that will protect us from Lee, don't you?"

He could lie. He wanted to lie. He was a *good* liar.

"No. But there's safety in numbers. We'll search for him in groups."

Peter nodded toward the lantern. "Group. Except you probably have a plan to retrieve the lantern you left behind."

Because he was the wizard who was going to save their asses. He sighed. That had to have been the world's shortest coup. "Look, I'm sorry. You know, Lee . . . Brianna . . ." Except he *had* saved Brianna; that should count for something. "Anyway . . ." He punctuated the truncated apology with a shrug.

Peter's eyes narrowed. "So you don't have a plan."

Oh, for . . .

"No, I don't have a freakin' plan, all right? The lantern's in the ballroom and at the speed the replays are happening, I don't want to open the ballroom door and risk being caught with it still open when its turn comes around again."

"I think I have a solution to that." Amy crossed the room and pointedly took the journal back. Tony suspected there'd be an apology in her future as well. "There are these symbols that keep the thing in the basement's power contained. They're all over the house, probably all that's kept it from murder/suiciding its way across the lower mainland." She flipped the book open to a page of what looked like random squiggles she'd marked with a doubled-over piece of tape. "If you copy this symbol here from wall to wall across the threshold of the ballroom like a barricade, then those dead dancing fools—since they're part of the thing's power—they won't be able to cross."

"Are you sure?"

"Yes, absolutely. Mostly. Caulfield's notes are a little . . . undetailed."

Brianna pulled a water bottle away from her mouth with a pop of releasing suction. "Why don't you draw the symbol thingie in front of the hand?"

"What hand?"

She pointed with the bottle. "That one."

It had come through the door as far as the wrist, gray and translucent fingers combing the air.

"It's come to take me dancing," Mason announced over the perfectly understandable screaming. He jumped to his feet and would have run to meet it except Mouse's sudden hysterics knocked him over backward, slamming them both onto the chair he'd been sitting on and crushing it. Kicking himself free of the wreckage, he dove onto the wildly thrashing cameraman, fists and feet flailing into flesh as he accused the other man of never taking him dancing.

"Well, that settles that," Zev muttered. "Mason's reality has left the building."

The arm was through the door to the elbow. Barely

an inch or two of hacked bicep remained outside the room.

As the others dove to break up the battle—Mouse having found a direction for his hysteria in violence—Tony grabbed Amy's arm. "What symbol exactly?"

A black-tipped nail tapped what looked like a three-dimensional sketch of a croissant. "This one."

Given her previous answer, it seemed pointless to ask again if she was sure. Besides, it looked a lot like the mark the basement door had left on his hand. And like the mark he thought he'd seen as he closed the ballroom doors. Maybe all the doors had them.

All the doors but the two leading into the butler's pantry.

Great choice of room, guys.

He didn't have a pen.

The arm scuttled toward Ashley, who drew her bare feet up under the edge of her pinafore and screamed. The sound was piercing, echoing around the enclosed space like shards of glass. Even the arm paused.

He didn't have time to find a pen. Using the tip of his tongue, he licked the pattern onto the palm of his left hand and made a grab for the stump end of the arm.

The cold burned, but he could feel resistance under his fingers, so he tightened his grip and whipped it back out through the door.

"Here!" Amy shoved a small plastic tube into his other hand. "Mark the threshold before it comes back."

"And that'll help how?" he demanded, staring down at the lipstick. "It's a ghost hand; it can go through the wall!"

"No, it can't or the ballroom doors wouldn't keep the dead contained!"

That actually made sense. Mostly.

Dropping to his knees, he twisted up half an inch of magenta cream. "Hold the book where I can see it."

"Why don't you . . ." She whistled softly as he raised his left hand. Fingers and thumb were curled in toward his palm—touching neither palm nor each other. Tendons stood out across the back in sharp relief. "Ow."

"Yeah."

It wasn't a particularly difficult symbol compared to some Arra had loaded onto the computer. Although as far as he knew, none of Arra's lessons involved precision copying while racing the return of a disembodied ghost arm. Trying to balance speed and accuracy, Tony laid out the pattern end to end on the floor in a slight curve from one side of the door to the other.

"So," Amy murmured by his ear, voice pitched to carry over the roaring and swearing and shrieking behind them. "This is the arm the little old lady chopped off the gardener?"

"One of." A sharp impact against his shoulder spun him around in time to see Amy shove Adam back into the battle. She apologized and adjusted the angle of the book.

"Kind of makes you wonder who the Addams family chopped Thing off of," she mused as he continued drawing.

"Hadn't occurred to me."

"Oh, please. You see a hand chugging around and you don't think Thing? I loved those movies."

"First one didn't suck. The second . . ."

"The second was brilliant. I mean it so speaks to all us outsiders who were told by brutal authority that sleeping in a cabin with gum chewers and gigglers was for our own good." When Tony shot her a look of blank incomprehension, she sighed. "You must've had some kind of a camp experience when you were a kid."

The lipstick left a ridge of color on the floor as he pressed just a little too hard. "I had a couple of friends who were drag queens."

"That's not what I meant."

"I know." He finished the last line of the last symbol, rocked back on his heels and up onto his feet. "I guess we'll know this works if the arm doesn't come back."

"What if it's heading for the other door?"

"Uh . . ."

Between them and the other door was a roiling mass of bodies. Brianna appeared momentarily above the mix of arms and legs and torsos wrapped around what—given the size and the work boot—could only be Mouse's foot. Tony half expected her to yell "Yee ha!" as she disappeared back into the fray.

". . . it doesn't move very fast."

"Good thing," Amy acknowledged philosophically. "What about your hand?" She lightly touched the pale skin. "It's freezing!"

"No shit."

"Ghosts need energy to manifest, so the cold is indicative of them sucking power."

"Yeah, Stephen said something like that earlier."

"Stick it down the front of your pants."

"What?"

"Your hand—stick it down the front of your pants. It's the warmest place on your body."

Footwork Mason would have been proud of kept him from scuffing the pattern as he backed away. "Yeah, and I'd like it to stay that way."

"Well, you're not sticking it down the front of my pants."

"Damn right, I'm not." He stuck it into his right armpit, sucked air through his teeth at the cold and watched as Amy darted forward and dragged Kate out from under Mouse's descending ass just in the nick of time. Kate's snarl was incomprehensible, but the attempted kick in the head with her bound legs was fairly easy to understand.

Amy patted her shoulder. "You're wel . . ."

He lost the end of the word in the next replay. The good news: this time there'd been a little more time between the ballroom and the drawing room. The arm had to be using energy now that it was out of its piece of history so that could be why the replays were spreading out again. The bad news: well, actually that was more of a disturbing question. The gardener had been cut into six pieces. What else was out there moving around?

The plate of little cakes was back on the pantry counter. Last time he'd been here . . .

He couldn't believe he was just standing here when all he wanted to do was tear the house apart looking for Lee.

The good of the many outweighs the need of the one.

And thank you, Mr. Spock, for your two cents' worth. Stupid, goddamned, sanctimonious Vulcan . . .

The familiar sound of duct tape being ripped from the roll accompanied his return to the present pantry and seemed to indicate that the battle was nearly over. The slightly less familiar sound of duct tape being ripped from Mouse's legs—with accompanying bellow— suggested there were still a few loose ends to tie up. And a lot less hair on Mouse's legs.

"Reste alongé!"

Light glinted off the ornate, brass candlestick as Sorge raised it above his head. It was on the way down before Tony realized where it was headed and it was close enough to part Mason's hair when he called it to his hand.

"Sorge! Sorge!"

The DP's eyes were wild as he glared first at Peter's hand on his arm and then up at Peter.

"Beating Mason to death is not the answer! Trust me, if it was, I'd have done it months ago!"

"Il reste toujours alongé de won't!"

"In English. Please."

"I say, he won't lie still!" He smacked his palm against Mason's chest. "I make him lie still!" He scanned the room and his eyes locked on the candlestick still in Tony's hand. "Give me that!"

"Sorge, look, the guys have got him taped."

"Taped?" His brows drew in and he shook his head. "No, we can't tape. The light, she is all wrong."

"No, no, *duct* tape."

His focus moved to the bands of gray around the cuffs of tuxedo pants and dress shirt. "Ah."

Mason craned his head up and stared at the tape as though he was seeing it for the first time. "You can't do this to me! Don't you know who I am? It's all about me! I'm Raymond Dark! You have no show without me!"

"We have no show if you go for a wander and get killed," Peter told him, shaking out a match to the linen napkin gagging Kate.

"My agent is going to hear about this!"

He was sounding remarkably lucid. Apparently Peter thought so, too, because he paused and peered into Mason's face, napkin ready. "If you lie quietly, I won't gag you."

"And the tape?"

"The tape stays."

"Because I've been captured by vampire hunters and I'm lying quietly, listening to their plans."

Okay, so much for lucid.

"Why not." Peter pocketed the napkin and patted Mason's shoulder. "Please don't mention that to the writers," he muttered as he stood. Turned. Frowned down at both techs, Brianna, Zev, and Adam who were sitting on Mouse. "Why isn't *he* taped?"

Saleen held up the empty cardboard roll. "We've got electrical, but it won't hold long enough for us to get enough around him."

"Wonderful. You couldn't have taped him first?"

"Oh, sure, criticize." His lower lip went out.

Brianna bounced on Mouse's wrist. "I have to pee!"

"Big surprise the way you sucked back that bottle of water," Ashley sniffed from within the circle of Tina's arms.

"I have to pee NOW!"

"Fine." Shoulders squared, a man facing the inevitable, Peter pointed at Tina. "Tina, take the lantern and . . ."

"No!" Ashley tightened her grip. "Mason's gone mental, so Tina stays with me!"

"Whatever, Zev . . ."

But when Zev shifted his weight, Mouse got an arm free. Tears streaming down his face, the big man grabbed the back of Saleen's shorts and very nearly started the whole fight again before Zev wrestled his arm back to the floor.

"All right, Amy, you take Brianna upstairs. Zev, move *carefully* around to hold down both arms. Adam, once Zev's in place, you go with her. Check the bathroom for Lee—maybe he's just taking a piss. Tony, do the lipstick writing in front of the other door."

"I want Tony to go with me!" Brianna opened her mouth to shriek, but Tony clamped his good hand over it.

"Bite me," he warned, "and I'll pull your brains out your nose. No more shrieking, the room's too small and everyone's on edge."

Her nostrils flared dangerously over the edge of his hand, but she nodded. "My father would fire you if you pulled my brains out my nose," she growled when he uncovered her mouth.

"Yeah? Well, right now, on a scale of one to ten, that's about a minus two. I'll go with you . . ." *Because the needs of little girls trump the needs of possessed actors. I'm sorry, Lee.* ". . . but first I'm securing this room."

"No, *me* first."

"You want your sister to be safe, don't you?"

Brianna shot him a look that suggested he was out of his mind, but after a moment reluctantly nodded. "Yeah, whatever."

He stepped over Mason, and crouched by the other door. The door that led to the kitchen. The door that Lee had gone through when he left. The door he was not charging through, racing off to the rescue. *You can't go after him right now, so try concentrating on the immediate problem.* How long would it take an arm to get around the first floor? Hopefully, a few minutes longer. "Amy . . ."

And she was there with the book.

No longer distracted by a battle behind him, the copying went a little faster. When he finished, he handed Amy the flattened lipstick. She sighed, capped it, and handed it back.

"Hel-lo! I still gotta pee!"

"Fine." One hand clamped on her shoulder, Peter gestured toward the supine cameraman with the other. "Tony, take Zev's spot on Mouse. I'll keep Sorge from braining Mason . . ."

"And I do the same for you," Sorge muttered staring down at Mason who smiled and said, "What the vampire hunters don't know is that it's my show, so it's all about me. It's always all about me."

Peter nodded at his DP. "Thank you. Zev, go upstairs with Amy and Brianna and Adam."

Hang on. Tony stepped forward and bumped up against Mason's leg. "I thought I . . ."

"No. You're staying here. I'm not having the boss' youngest daughter escorted through a haunted house by a PA who keeps zoning out. Unless you can protect them with your magic power."

Man, he just wasn't going to let that go. Tony sighed and surrendered, moving around to where Zev had Mouse's arms laid out over his head with a knee on each forearm and a good grip above the elbow. The moment they got back from the can, he was heading out for the other lantern and the moment after that, they were going to find Lee.

Brianna stomped one bare foot. "I want Tony!"

Peter smiled down at her. "Tough."

"My father . . . !"

"Isn't here."

Her brow furrowed and she glanced around the room, gaze finally lighting on her sister.

Ashley's shrug got lost in the depths of Mason's jacket. "He's right. And there's like arms walking around, so stop being such a pissant, Cheese."

"But Tony said he'd show me the burning baby." Volume dialed down to a whine. "He promised."

"You promised?" Tina's head snapped around like a bad horror effect. "You promised to show an eight-year-old a burning baby?"

Although they were a good four feet apart, Tony leaned away from the force of the script supervisor's affronted gaze. "It got her out of the ballroom," he muttered defensively, then turned his attention to the girl. "Look, Bri, Peter's right." Probably too late, but it never hurt to suck up. "I can't protect you if I zone out, but I can still be dead weight here."

"You're not dead!"

"It's a . . . never mind. Zev can show you the baby."

"No, he cannot!" Tina snarled.

"If I don't see the baby . . ." Volume ratcheted back up again. ". . . you'll all be sorry!"

No one doubted it.

"Show her," Peter said, eyes rolling.

"You won't be able to see it," Tony reassured Zev as he choked, "but I'm pretty sure she will." Given that everyone had seen the hand, it was possible that Zev would also see the baby. Since that hadn't occurred to Zev, Tony wasn't going to bring it up. "Just open the nursery door, give her a three count to look, and then close it. Don't let her go in and don't keep the door open any longer."

"Do I want to know why?" Zev asked taking Brianna's hand.

"No." He popped the top off Amy's lipstick with his teeth, and beckoned Brianna closer with his nearly useless left hand. "Pull your apron thing out tight." He carefully drew the symbol on the fabric. "There, that might help."

She peered down her nose at it. "With what?"

"I have no idea."

"Brenda is going to have a fit!" Mason giggled. As all eyes turned on him, he sighed dramatically. "Yes, I know, an out-of-character comment. Unless, of course, one of the vampire hunters' name is Brenda, in which case it's a perfectly valid . . . Hey! Don't stop looking at me! I'm acting here! I'm the star!"

Tony had assumed that the killers were always the ones the house had driven over the edge. If the common urge to brain Mason was any indication, apparently not.

"The kitchen sink's closer than the bathroom," Amy sighed, taking Brianna's other hand. "Why can't she just pee in that?"

Even Mouse stopped weeping long enough to look appalled.

"What? You've never done it? You're guys; you pee in corners for chrissake!"

"*I* am not a guy," Tina reminded her, "and this child is not peeing in the sink."

"But . . ."

"No."

"What is it with people and bodily fluids?" Amy demanded. "Healthy urine is safe to drink."

"Why do you know that?" Zev asked as Adam picked up the lantern. He shook his head when it looked like she was about to answer. "Never mind. I don't actually want to know."

Lantern high, Adam paused, his hand almost to the doorknob. "What if the arm didn't go around to the other door? What if it's waiting in the dining room for this door to open?"

"It's an arm," Tony said after a moment. "I don't think it's that smart."

"It's an arm," Zev repeated. "We shouldn't even be having this conversation."

"Just stay inside the pattern. That's what's stopping it, not the door."

"What if Lee's waiting in the dining room?"

Where Hartley killed Brenda.

"Then slam the door and Brianna can pee on someone's foot."

Hanging between Zev and Amy, Brianna looked intrigued.

Door open.

No arm.

No Lee.

"If Lee goes after them, do you think they can stop him?" Tina asked as footsteps started up the stairs.

"Zev and Adam can handle him," Peter told her leaning against the counter. "He's an actor, for crying out loud."

"He's a costar," Mason muttered.

"What happened to lying quietly and listening to the vampire hunters' plans?"

"Right."

Tina tightened her grip on Ashley. "I can't believe you're allowing that child to look at a burning baby."

"It's not a real baby," Tony offered. "It's a ghost baby."

"She'll be traumatized."

"Perhaps," Peter allowed. "But better a supervised visit than have her go charging off on her own again. I think CB'd rather get her back traumatized than not at all."

"The Cheese doesn't have nightmares, if that's what you're worried about. Mom says she's like Dad; sensitivity of a post." Ashley pulled out of Tina's arms and stuffed her hands in the pockets of Mason's tuxedo jacket. "Me, I'm like Mom. I'll have screaming nightmares about that arm coming right at me for years. And years. It'll probably stunt my growth." She shot Mason a challenging look through her lashes. "I'm very sensitive."

Mason nodded. "So am I. But then, I'm a star. I thought we were going dancing; why am I tied up?"

"Captured by vampire hunters," Peter sighed, fondling the napkin.

"Right."

Tony shifted position to give a different set of bruises a chance to ache and saw that Mouse, who'd been lying quietly under the weight of three men, was staring up at him, his eyelashes clumped into damp triangles. "You okay?"

"You've been avoiding me."

So not the time to go into this. "No, I haven't."

"Yeah."

"I'm right here."

The big man sighed. "Not now, before."

"I haven't." He looked up to see he was once again the center of attention. "Really. I haven't."

"Ever since I kissed you."

Crap.

"He's not himself."

Peter leaned back, folded his arms and crossed one ankle over the other. "Sounds like he's having a lucid moment to me."

"He's not."

"Did I hurt you?" Mouse's lower lip trembled.

"No," Tony reassured him hurriedly. "No, you didn't hurt me." And just to reassure everyone else. "He didn't kiss me either."

"Kissed you in the bus shelter."

Sorge snickered. "Bus shelter? That one of those gay euphemisms?"

"Kissed you when the Shadowlord controlled me."

And crap again.

"Okay, he's definitely delusional," Tony sighed. And given the condition Mouse had been in for most of the evening—the irrational terror, the weeping—it would have been believable except . . .

"Oh, sure, acting like you're the only one to remember the Shadowlord! You're just a cameraman. He liked me best."

Mason's current condition made him less than reliable as backup except . . .

"The Shadowlord?" Kate spat out the last of shred of damp napkin. "I remember that son of a bitch!"

And Tina—who spent fourteen-hour days keeping track of dialogue changes and shot numbers and continuity while half a dozen people clambored for her attention and a dozen more built and brought to life Raymond Dark's world around her—put the pieces together. "I wonder," she said softly, "if Hartley and Lee would remember this Shadowlord. What else aren't you telling us, Tony?"

"What else?" Best defense—good offense. "What do you mean what else?"

"You didn't tell us you were a wizard."

"I told you!"

"Somewhat after the fact. And since this is apparently a new thing," she added, folding her arms, "I find myself wondering about the circumstances of your discovery and just where these particular people and the Shadowlord fit in."

"The Shadowlord made me kiss Tony," Mouse sniffed.

Saleen finally looked interested. "Kinky."

"If the Shadowlord wanted to kiss someone, he should have kissed me," Mason muttered indignantly.

"The Shadowlord can kiss my ass!" Kate barked.

"Tony?"

"I'm sure both Mason and Kate are very kissable." Great. Humor; not working. Tina was clearly not going to let it go. "Look, it happened way back in the spring. It's not important now." He waved his still not entirely usable left hand around the room—both a gesture and a reminder. "We've got other stuff to worry about."

Right on cue, a door slammed in the distance and multiple pairs of feet pounded down the stairs. Adam yelled for Amy. Then they were in the dining room. Then the pantry door opened. The three adults charged in, Brianna riding Zev's hip.

"We didn't see Lee," Adam began, setting the lantern

on the counter. "Although this one . . ." He jerked his head at Amy. ". . . went for a bit of a wander."

"I went to the front door," Amy snorted. "I checked on Everett. And the good news is he's still breathing. We skipped across the hall to Lee's dressing room *together*." She threw the emphasis at Adam. "He's not there." Suddenly realizing her audience wasn't paying full attention, she frowned. "What's wrong?"

"Seems that Tony only came partway out of the wizard closet."

Amy glanced over at him and he shrugged, hoping he looked like the rational one in the room.

"Does the term *Shadowlord* mean anything to you?" Tina asked her.

"Not to me." She glanced over at her companions. Adam and Zev shook their heads. Brianna yawned.

"Mason, Mouse, and Kate all remember a Shadowlord."

"Yeah, and they're loopy."

Go, Amy. Point out the obvious.

Tina shook her head, denying that was the end of the matter. "Tony as much as admitted there was something to it."

He had? Why the hell had he done that?

"It happened last spring," Sorge put in.

"Last spring?" Amy rolled her eyes. "Please, a lot of strange shit happened last spring. Just before Arra left, everyone was having those weird memory lapses."

"Not everyone," Tina said slowly, thoughtfully. "Lee lost about eight hours. Kate lost nearly forty-eight. Mouse got into that fight that broke his jaw but doesn't remember it. Hartley fell off the wagon. And Tony had that little fit in the soundstage."

"Tony?"

And that little fit gave him the perfect excuse. He just had to convince them that he'd lost his memory, too. Unfortunately, the lights came up and Lucy Lewis pushed a nameless fellow servant down the back stairs before he could begin.

♠

Tony didn't know why Saleen thought the electrical tape wouldn't hold Mouse; it seemed to be holding him just fine. A quick glance to the right showed that Mouse was weeping again, Saleen and Pavin were looking bruised, and Mason had a rising goose egg on his forehead. He thought about apologizing, but since he had no idea if he'd been responsible, he decided to let it go.

"The boy in the bathroom didn't even notice the thing you drew. He's hiding 'cause he's scared of his daddy." Crouched by his head, Brianna fingered her apron as she murmured into his left ear. "Karl's mommy didn't like it. 'Cept she couldn't see it because she had sticks in her eyes. The baby was way gross. I saw a movie just like it once."

"This isn't a movie."

"I know. If it was, there'd be popcorn and I wouldn't be ..." She yawned. "... bored."

"So you're back." Peter took Brianna by the shoulder and pulled her away.

Since he'd obviously been talking, there didn't seem to be much point in denying it. "What's with the tape?"

"Just don't want any surprises."

"Surprises? What kind of surprises?"

"You tell us, Tony. Last spring, two people died."

"I had nothing to do with that!" How could they possibly connect that to him? "Amy? Zev?"

"A man who cheats on his wife will cheat on his mistress," Amy muttered unhappily.

"What the hell is that supposed to mean?"

"It means you lied to us," Zev told him, looking betrayed. "And if you can lie about one thing ..."

"You mean about being a wizard?" Neck aching, he let his head bounce back on the floor. "I didn't exactly lie. I mean, you never asked if I was a wizard."

"I asked how you got a hunk of beer bottle embedded in your arm. You said you were just goofing around."

"I was."

"With a spell?"

"Yeah, but I didn't exactly *lie*."

Before Zev could respond—although his opinion of Tony's answer was pretty clear from his expression, Peter stepped between them. "We want the truth about what happened last spring, Tony."

"Because nothing says trust us like electrical tape," Tony muttered, struggled a moment, and glared up at them. "What about Lee? Lee's still out there!"

"Before we go after Lee, we want the whole story."

"Why? The shit that went down last spring has nothing to do with the shit that's happening tonight."

"If the Shadowlord was here, he'd take me dancing," Mason muttered.

Tony winced. "Okay, some people are more . . . uh, *open* to the house because of it, but that's all."

"You don't think it might have been helpful to know that?"

"No." Maybe. "Lee . . ."

"You want to go after him? Talk fast."

Seemed like he didn't have an option.

♠

"You messed with our memories!" Tina clutched at the front of her blouse with one hand and balled the other up into a fist. Appalled or angry—it looked like it could go either way. Tony knew what he was voting for.

"I didn't. Arra did."

Amy snorted. "Oh, that's so much better."

"Your memory didn't even get messed with," he reminded her. "You and Zev had already left the studio."

"Yeah, and that's another thing; how come I got left out!"

"You weren't left out. You'd just gone home."

She tossed her head. "Oh, sure, you say that now."

"How do we know he's not still lying?" Peter asked Sorge as Tony tried to figure out Amy's damage. "Gates

306 ♦ Tanya Huff

to another world, invading armies of shadows . . . this is the kind of crap our writers keep coming up with."

"No, it's crappier."

"Not as clichéd as that story about the gas leak, though. I can think of half a dozen shows that've used it to explain away stuff with no explanation."

"True."

Tina leaned between them. "He messed with our memories!"

And he left out the part about Tina providing snackies for the bastard son of Henry VIII, too. In fact, he'd left Henry out entirely. He and Arra and CB had saved the world all on their own.

Backhanding both Peter's and Sorge's chests to ensure she had their attention, Tina added, "What's to say he won't mess with our memories again?"

"Hey! I had nothing to do with that decision. It was all CB and Arra!"

Her eyes narrowed and her upper lip curled. "We only have your word for that."

"So we keep him tied?"

Peter shrugged. "I'd feel safer."

Oh, for . . . Tony bounced his head on the floor a couple of times.

"What about the second lantern?" Peter asked. Sweat beaded the five o'clock shadow on his upper lip. He wasn't as calm as he sounded.

"We could go get it," Adam suggested. "We only have his word that the ballroom's dangerous."

Oh, man. Tony lifted his head again. "Brianna, what's in the ballroom?"

"Dancing dead people. And a really gross band." She thoughtfully scratched the back of her right leg with the toes of her left foot. "And Brenda. She danced with me."

"That's it. Untie me immediately. What kind of place is this where a wardrobe assistant can go dancing but not a star!"

Peter hurriedly shifted over so that he was in the

actor's line of sight. "Mason, we just need to work out a few parts of the shot with the vampire hunters."

"But . . ."

"You know how your fan mail increases when we tie you up."

"Right."

It did, too. Tony couldn't see why. Mason tied up did nothing for *him*, but forty-year-old straight women were into the damnedest things. Shifting position, he discovered that the tape around his wrists might have stretched just a little. Rolling his wrists together, he kept working at it.

"All right." Peter squared his shoulders. "I think we should leave the lantern in the ballroom and go looking for Lee." He didn't sound completely convinced, but it was a start.

"It's a big house," Tony reminded him. "You'll need . . ."

"You'll need to be quiet." The director waved a napkin at him. Kate had recently been regagged with another in the set. The abusive profanity had nearly drowned out Tony's story. "Adam, Zev, you're with me. Amy, light a couple of candles after we're gone and work on the journal."

"What about the gardener's arm?"

"I think we can handle one ghostly arm."

"Tony had to handle it the last time."

"And we haven't seen it since, have we?"

"Peter . . ."

"No, Mr. Foster." Peter's smile was tight and uncompromising. "I think we'll manage to save our own. . . ."

Asses, Tony finished silently as the lights came up and Cassie and Stephen's father started swinging his ax.

When the lights went out, Zev was cutting the tape around his ankles with the knife attached to his key chain.

"Lee's in the basement."

"How do you know?"

"The door was open."

"Open!"

"It's all right, it's closed now. The gardener's hand closed it. But not before we heard Lee calling for you."

"For me?" Why was Zev rolling his eyes?

"He sounded . . ." Adam paused to search for a description clearly not in his vocabulary. "Well, he didn't sound happy," he finished at last.

"I told him he was no hero," Mason sniffed.

"When?" One question, multiple voices.

"Just before he left. He said he was going off to be a hero. I said he was only a costar. He told me to fuck myself. And then he left. Rude bastard."

Peter ran both hands back through his hair, exhaling as he brought them down, and clasped them together. "Why didn't you mention that before?" he asked wearily.

Mason rolled his eyes. "Well, it's not about me, is it?"

Fourteen

"WHY WOULD LEE go down in the basement?" Tony demanded, ripping the severed pieces of electrical tape off his wrists.

Amy snorted. "Because he's possessed by an evil house?"

"Yeah, that was a gimme." Throwing the tape aside, he stood. Now he knew where Lee was, he wanted nothing more than to go charging off to the rescue. Challenge the thing in the basement to single combat for the hand of the fair ... okay, not fair ... and not a maiden either, but the challenge to single combat stuff still stood. Except, he wasn't the hero. Hell, he wasn't even the costar. He'd survived on the streets by brokering information, and— although he hated taking the time because of the whole Lee-very-likely-in-mortal-danger thing—there was just too much information here he didn't have. "What does the *house* want Lee to do down in the basement?"

"To get beer out of the fridge?" Adam shrugged as attention turned to him. "What? It's why I go to the basement."

"And very not relevant in this case," Peter snapped.

"Well, excuse me for trying to help."

Tony wanted to pace, but there wasn't enough room.

"It can't want his energy, that's what the ballroom's for."

Brianna looked up from searching through Zev's backpack and blew a raspberry. "The ballroom's stupid."

"If the thing in the basement set up the ballroom as the big bad, it's not that impressive," Zev agreed, taking his earphones out of her hand before she could completely unspool them. "You two got out really easy."

"It wasn't *that* easy," Tony protested.

"You're a production assistant who knows one spell; you're not exactly . . ."

"Raymond Dark," Mason muttered.

Mason had a point. Raymond Dark always won through no matter how great the odds stacked against him because if he lost, there wouldn't be a show. But no one was writing a script filled with coincidence and handy FX for Tony.

"Who told you the ballroom was the big bad?" Amy asked, her brow furrowed.

"Stephen and Cassie."

"The dead-as-doorknobs duo."

"Yeah, so?"

"Ignoring the whole dead-people-maybe-not-a-reliable-source, maybe the ballroom is bad for them *because* they're dead. Brianna says it sucked in Brenda . . ."

"And Tom and Hartley," Tony added, remembering. "And Stephen said something about it almost getting Cassie once."

"It's like the ballroom is a big tornado." She sketched spiraling visual aids in the air. "And all the replays are little tornados and the big tornado, just because of its size, keeps trying to suck the little ones into it. Although not actively *trying* as such."

"That makes sense." And that was almost the scariest thing Tony'd run into all night.

"So it's bad for the ghosts, not so bad for the living."

"And if the door is open?"

"Tornado spreads throughout the house and again, all

the little ones are sucked in. But it only works one way because Brenda and Hartley and Tom got in through a closed door. It wants the energy of the living—that's why it's calling—but it can't suck it up unless it can keep them in there dancing until they die."

"Please tell me you're not working on a script," Peter muttered.

Amy ignored him. "So it's not the ballroom we should be worrying about. It's the basement. It always was."

"So you could have stopped him if you'd gone to the basement door instead of the ballroom."

Tony glared over at Mason, still taped but now propped up against the lower cupboards.

The actor shrugged. "I'm just saying."

"We need the other lantern back," Tina announced in a tone that offered no room for argument. "Tony can't go down in the basement with our only reliable source of light."

"Because he might not be coming back," Peter agreed.

"Because the thing in the basement wants Tony specifically."

"Say what?"

Zev sighed. "Lee was calling for you, remember. It's just using Lee as bait. As soon as it had full possession of him, it took him away. It didn't use him to strangle Tina."

"Why me?" Tina wondered, fixing him with a worried stare as she leaned away.

"Nothing personal. You were just closest."

"If you're having a problem with me, Zev, we should talk about it."

"There's no problem." He made soothing gestures with his hands. "It didn't use Lee to strangle Peter or Sorge either."

Or Mason, who, in Tony's opinion, had to be the odds-on favorite. Although, since Mason was also at least partially possessed, he was probably safe. "But why would the thing in the basement want me?"

"I don't know," the music director sighed. "Could it be because you're a wizard?" *You moron* rang out so clearly it was more text than subtext. "If it can take you out, we're sitting ducks."

"There's three dead with his help," Adam muttered. "How much worse can it get without him?"

"Look around. You do the math."

"Doesn't matter." Tony had all the information he needed. Lee as bait was a different matter than Lee possessed. As long as no one made themselves available as the murder half of the murder/suicide, a possessed Lee was safe. As bait, the danger he was in would escalate until Tony arrived to save the day. Night. Whatever. Point was, Lee needed him.

Amy grabbed his arm and hauled him away from the door into the kitchen. "And what'll you do when you get to the basement?" she demanded.

"Call Lee into my hand and get the hell out. It'll work!" he added as her brows disappeared under the fringe of magenta hair. "It's how I got Brianna out of the ballroom."

"Point one . . ." The first finger of her free hand flicked into the air. ". . . does this spell have a weight limit? Because Brianna's eight and Lee, as you very well know, is not."

"What's that supposed to mean?"

"It means Lee isn't eight," Zev snapped. "Lay off the defensive crap—we all know how you feel . . ."

Heads nodded. "You should, like, get a room," Ashley muttered.

". . . even the thing in the basement knows how you feel."

"You're like a puppy when he so much as talks to you," Tina told him.

Sorge nodded. "If you have a tail, you wag it."

Puppy feelings? "I do not."

Zev rolled his eyes. "Yeah, you do. Now answer the question."

Question?

Oh, yeah; weight limit.

"I don't know. Brianna was the heaviest I've ever moved."

"Cool." Brianna bent Zev's sunglasses case open until the hinges started to crack.

"And was it easy?" Amy demanded.

"Sure."

She smacked him hard on the back of the head.

"No. Not really."

"So you don't know that you could move Lee." Zev pried his case out of Brianna's fingers.

"And I'm not going to find out standing here." He was bigger than Amy, not by a lot but bigger. Adam stepped between him and the door. Okay, not bigger than Adam. "Get out of my way. Lee needs me!"

"He needs you thinking with your head," Amy told him hauling him away from the door. "Not your . . ."

"Amy!" Tina's gesture took in both girls.

"Weiner," Brianna offered calmly.

"It's called a penis." Ashley sneered at her sister. "Only babies say . . ."

The lights came up and Karl started to scream.

"I'm going for the other lantern," Tony told the now empty pantry. There was resistance as he started to turn. "Amy, let go of me. You're right, it won't help Lee if I go charging to the rescue unprepared, but I can't be a part of any plans right now and it'd be stupid to waste the light." After a moment, the resistance disappeared. "This isn't a long replay," he said as he walked to the other door, sliding his feet along the floor lest he step on someone. "I promise I'll come right back with the lantern."

And the moment we're out of this, he promised himself silently as he closed the pantry door behind him and started to run. *I'm learning shield spells and lightning bolts. Maybe fireballs. Don't wizards always use fireballs?*

He couldn't believe his feelings for Lee were that obvious.

Had Lee noticed?

Learning the mess-with-the-memory spell was looking better and better.

He didn't need both of the ballroom doors open, so he whipped out Amy's lipstick and began to block the right side. Fortunately, he could open his left hand almost all the way; a raised ridge of skin gave him the necessary symbol etched in white across the flesh of his palm. Finishing the last curve and dot required the final bit of color gouged out of the tube on his little finger. Although his left hand continued to ache, he found he could hold the lipstick against the pressure and the return of manual dexterity banished a fear he hadn't acknowledged.

Karl stopped screaming just as he opened the blocked half of the ballroom door.

His experience with this sort of thing was limited, but the tiny orange speck of light over by the bandstand probably meant the lamp was nearly out of fuel.

"*Tony . . .*"

He had a feeling he should be a little more distracted by ghosts of workmates calling his name while "Night and Day" played in the background. Hand outstretched. First three words of the incantation . . .

"Tony!"

Lee's voice. Distant. Desperate. Afraid. It wrapped around Tony's heart and squeezed.

Now that was a definite distraction.

Brenda slamming up against an invisible barrier and screaming jealous curses no more than four inches from his face—that was almost expected.

"I had him!" she shrieked, the wound gaping in the translucent ruin of her throat.

"I know."

"He likes girls."

"Yeah, *live* girls."

"Tony!"

Save me.

The good of the many, he reminded himself and fought his way back to focus. The lantern slapped into his hand and he almost dropped it. "Son of a . . . !"

"Was it hot?" For a dead wardrobe assistant, all Brenda's sarcasm facilities seemed intact. "Did you burn yourself?"

Strange; still a third full. "Nearly. Thanks for asking."

Hard to tell for sure, given that she was a gray sketch against the darkness, but she looked confused by his response. "I win in the end, you know. Me."

"You're dead. Not my definition of winning."

"He'll be dead with me. Dancing. Forever."

"What? Lee dies after the thing's destroyed me? Not so easy as that."

"Easier. You'd let Lee slit your throat or cave in your skull or rip out your heart and never lift a hand to defend yourself because it's him."

The third option, maybe.

"But that's not what it waaaaaaaaaaaaaaaaaaaaaaaaaa aaaaaaaaaa . . ."

Hartley spun her away from the door. Danced her howling across the ballroom until she faded in the darkness, the ballroom door slamming shut in Tony's face. Slamming shut. He hadn't shut it. Maybe Brenda'd been about to tell him the secret weakness of the thing in the basement. Maybe she'd been about to taunt him with Lee's breakfast preferences. Either was as likely in Tony's opinion. Dead or not, Lee was still between them.

The same way Brenda would always be between him and Lee.

Except that there *was* no him and Lee, for fuck's sake, because Lee was straight—random kissage aside—and possessed by the thing in the basement. There'd be no Lee at all if he didn't get the lantern back to the butler's pantry and figure out a way to get him back.

Glaring down at the lantern—responsible for the delayed rescue—he realized the wick was almost burned

away. Two turns of the wheel on the side and he was re-
warded by a sudden increase in light. Eyes watering, he
made his way back to the pantry.

Kissage.

Lee possessed by the thing in the basement.

Oh, crap, not again . . .

Aspects of this were becoming frighteningly familiar.

As he entered the dining room, he caught a glimpse
of something moving by the bottom of the door leading
to the butler's pantry door.

Gray. Translucent. And rolling!

The gardener's head came out from under the table
into the circle of light and rolled, wobbling, toward the
entrance hall.

Eyes and ears for the thing in the basement. The only
possible reason for it to be there—where the word reason was stretched to the limit. The head had been eavesdropping on the plan to free Lee .

Tony got between it and the door.

It smiled and kept coming.

It? He? Did a ghost head have gender?

Not important right now . . .

I really don't want to do this.

Not that he had a choice.

He relicked the pattern onto his left palm and
grabbed the head as it went to roll through his legs.

"Zev! Dump your backpack and bring it to me!" Yelling
helped the pain. "Amy! Quick, another lipstick!" Although
not significantly.

The pantry door slammed open.

"Tony? What the . . ."

"Your backpack . . ." Fingers pressing into the gardener's skull, he set the lantern on the dining room
table and ran toward Zev. ". . . is it empty?"

Zev glanced down at the pack dangling from one
hand. "Yeah, I ditched . . ."

"Tony, here!" Amy shoved Zev farther into the dining
room and thrust another tube into Tony's free hand.

"It's Tina's!"

"Zip the backpack shut and hold it up!" This lipstick was pale pink—easy to see the symbol against the black fabric and over the black plastic zipper. Easy to tell why Amy had disavowed it. With both Amy and Zev holding the pack steady, he finished the last curve. "Open it!" Slam-dunked the head into the pack. "Close it!"

The sides of the pack bulged, but the symbol held.

"More of the gardener?" Amy asked, breathing a little heavily.

"Yeah." Tendrils of pain extended from his hand to his shoulder. "I think . . . I think it was spying on you."

"On us?"

Peter's question drew Tony's attention to the doorway. It seemed that everyone but Mason, Mouse, and Kate were crammed into the narrow space, watching.

"Yeah, on you." When expressions remained mostly skeptical, he added, "Can you think of another reason a head would be hanging around outside the door?"

No one could.

No surprise.

"Me, I seen better heads," Sorge remarked thoughtfully. "More realistic."

Tony stared at him in astonishment. "This head *is* real!"

The DP shrugged as he turned to go back into the pantry. "Maybe it's the lighting."

"Weird that there's no weight," Zev murmured as he held the backpack out an arm's length from his body.

"It's captured energy, not substance," Amy snorted. She poked the bag with one finger. "You know, if people weren't dying, this would be so cool."

"You'd think so. Can I put it down?"

Curled around his left arm, Tony nodded more or less toward the table. "Sure. Whatever."

"Are you all right?"

"Uh . . ."

"Let me look." Zev gently pushed Tony up into a

more vertical position. His eyes narrowed. "That can't be good."

Tony's hand had curled back in on itself and his lower arm was tight against his upper, tight in turn against his torso.

"How does it feel?" Amy asked.

"Like frozen flames are lapping at my skin."

"Ow. Mixed metaphors. That's gotta hurt."

Zev laid two fingers against Tony's forearm and snatched them back again almost immediately. Two red marks remained behind for a heartbeat. "This is just a suggestion, but I don't think you should grab anything else. This kind of cold is going to do some serious nerve damage if it hasn't already."

"Just tell me it was worth it and that you have a plan."

Amy picked up the lantern and led the way to the pantry. "We have a plan."

"Really?"

"No. We've got nothing. But," she continued as they stepped over the lipstick line and closed the door behind them, "I did find out that the thing in the basement has a name. It's A . . ."

Tony slapped his good hand over her mouth. "Don't! Names have power. We don't want to . . ."

"Attract its attention?" she snarled, dragging his hand away. "Because I think it knows we're here. I mean, ignoring the story thus far with us locked in and three people dead, it's sending body parts to spy on us!"

"Speaking of body parts; where's the head?" Peter asked.

"In the dining room."

"Is that safe?"

How the hell should I know? "Sure. It's contained. Look, you don't have a plan to save Lee, so we're going with mine."

"Which is?"

"I'm charging to the rescue."

"With a useless wing?" Amy snorted. "Good plan."

His mouth twisted into something he suspected looked nothing like a smile. "Only one we seem to have."

"Tony?"

It took him a moment to place the voice—he was getting just a little too used to ignoring people calling his name—and a moment after that to notice Tina holding out a pair of caplets on the palm of her hand.

"For your arm."

"Thanks." He swallowed them dry then drank half a bottle of water after, just because. Odds were good, they'd do nothing for the pain in his arm but what the hell, they couldn't hurt.

"There's what?" Adam wondered, frowning. "A crapload of ghosts in this building, right?"

"Given that crapload isn't an exact number, yeah."

"So why is the thing in the basement sending the gardener to mess with us? He's in friggin' pieces."

"Well, it's obvious." Mason looked superior as attention turned to him. "He's a servant."

Tony shook his head. "Lucy Lewis is a servant."

"Yes, but she's all tied up."

"The guy she pushed down the stairs . . ."

"Maybe the pieces take less energy to control than the whole body," Amy suggested, her eyes gleaming in the lantern light. "If the thing in the basement is feeding off the energy of the dead, it's going to want to give as little back as possible."

"I was just about to say that." Mason's lip curled. He was still wearing Raymond Dark's teeth and Tony felt a rush of longing at the sight. If only Henry were here. Inside. Independence be damned, he'd give up control to Henry in a minute.

The heels of Mason's shoes thudded against the floor as he lifted his legs and let them drop. "Why am I tied up again?"

"You're not," Peter sighed. "You're taped."

"And I find I'm getting just a little annoyed about it."

He sounded annoyed. He sounded, for the first time in a while, like Mason Reed.

Her hands shoved deep into the pockets of his tuxedo jacket, Ashley padded across the room and crouched beside him, peering into his face.

"Your father is going to hear about this," he muttered, struggling with the tape around his wrists.

Ashley's smile lit up the room. "He's back!"

"You're sure?"

"She knows," Brianna sighed before her sister could answer. "She's in love. Makes me want to . . ."

Probably puke, Tony thought as Charles started yelling at the top of the stairs. Hurl, upchuck, and ralph also contenders. He slid down the cupboards and sat cross-legged on the floor trying to work some feeling that wasn't pain into his left arm. He had to believe Lee wasn't in any immediate danger. He had to believe it because Amy was right—in a way. It wasn't that he couldn't use his arm; it was more that until it stopped hurting quite so damned much, he couldn't think of anything else. No way could he maintain enough concentration to pull Lee into his hand.

Inadvertent imagery very nearly made him forget the agony in his arm.

The lights dimmed and the present crowded back into the butler's pantry, just in time for him to see Mason get to his feet.

"There's tape debris on my cuff links."

"I'll help." Ashley began picking happily at one sleeve, Mason watching her with an *it's the least I'm entitled to* expression.

A little more disconcerting, considering, was seeing Mouse on his feet, staring through a . . .

"What the hell is Mouse looking through?"

"It's the viewfinder off his camera," Amy told him dropping down on the floor beside him. "Zev detached it when we were upstairs taking Bri to the can. Isn't it brilliant?"

"Isn't what brilliant?"

"Zev's idea. You know how cameramen are always walking into war zones with this weird idea that nothing they see through the camera can hurt them?"

"Yeah, and then they get shot."

"Sometimes, but that's not the point. The point is, Mouse is a cameraman and now he has a camera to look through, he's completely stabilized."

"He has a viewfinder."

Amy shrugged. "Seems to be enough."

Since Mouse was coming his way, Tony sure as hell hoped so. Large, bare, hairy knees poked out to either side of him as Mouse squatted.

"We have to talk."

"Now?"

"No. When we get out."

"About."

The big man chewed on a scarred lip. "Shadows," he said at last.

"Yeah. Sure." He watched Mouse rise and move away. *And if I'm really lucky, I'll have to sacrifice myself to free everyone else.*

"I'm not sure it's just the viewfinder," Amy murmured. "I think the thing in the basement is pulling back, depossessing. I mean, Mouse seems fine and Mason's his usual arrogant nondancing self."

"What about Kate?"

Kate was still taped and gagged.

"Well, we tried releasing Kate, but since there seemed to be a good chance she'd try to kill someone, we gave it up as a bad idea."

"Funny that the thing in the basement's still holding on to her."

"Yeah . . ." Amy picked at a bit of chipped nail polish. "I'm not so sure we can blame the thing. She's always been a bit . . . prickly."

"Prickly is hardly homicidal."

"Yeah, true, but now she's motivated."

"Tony . . ."

He pushed himself up onto his feet as Peter approached. Had a feeling he needed to be standing.

". . . we talked it over while you were ghost walking and decided that if you want to go charging down to rescue Lee, we'll charge after you." Peter's gaze flickered over to Tony's arm and away.

Okay. Hadn't expected that. Apparently, all he needed to have done to be taken seriously from the beginning was cripple himself. A near concussion and a couple of magical brands were apparently no more than par for the course.

"You look all sappy," Amy sniggered in his ear as Peter continued.

"Not all of us, of course. Tina will stay here to look after the girls . . ."

"And I'll be . . ." Mason trailed off, cleared his throat, and started again. Shoulders squared. Declarative. "I'll be helping her."

"With these girls, she'll need the help."

The almost gratitude in Mason's eyes was almost enough to make up for the kick Brianna landed on his shins. Almost.

"And if you phase off again . . ." Peter shrugged. "Well, we can still hear you, so just keep talking."

"I don't think that'll be a problem. The conservatory's up next and we have the gardener's head in a backpack. Part of the program's missing. It can't reboot."

"Computer metaphor?" Zev asked him, grinning.

Tony grinned back. "Best I could do on short notice." Fuck, maybe it *was* all about Mason because with him up and about, the mood certainly had changed. They were all working together again. The "us" defined against Mason's "them." If the basement had taken Mason instead of Lee, they'd be out of here by now. He managed to move his lower arm about two inches from his upper. His fingernails still looked kind of opalescent, but he could feel his fingers. He kind of wished he couldn't, but the pain breaking up into specific areas was probably a good thing. "Okay, then. Let's . . ."

The door leading to the kitchen began to swing open.

Everyone crowded to the far end of the room. Behind Tony.

And given the size of the room and the numbers in the crowd, having everyone behind him pushed Tony to within about three feet of the door.

Sure. Now *you're all fine with the wizard thing.*

The lantern light extended just far enough to illuminate Lee's smiling face.

No one moved.

Tony's heart beat so hard the burn on his chest ached in time.

"Lee?"

Might have been Peter. Might have been Adam. Tony wasn't sure.

Green eyes gleamed. As Lee opened his mouth, Tony answered for him.

"No. That's not Lee."

His smile had too many angles. Tony knew Lee's smile and this wasn't it.

"The thing in the basement," Lee said mockingly, "wants to talk to you."

No need to be more specific. They all knew who he was referring to.

"Why?" Tony demanded.

"I don't know."

"Give it up. For all intents and purposes, you *are* the thing in the basement."

"Why, so I am." One long-fingered hand brushed back through the fall of dark hair. "But I don't want to talk to you in front of an audience—talk about a tough room. Unfortunately, you refused to be lured, so I had to go with the direct approach. Come downstairs and face me."

"And if I don't?"

Lee's hands started to tremble and the velvet voice roughened. "I think you know the answer to that."

"If you don't go with him, the thing in the basement will hurt Lee!"

Tony sighed. "Yeah, Tina, I got it."

"Well, pardon me for wanting to be clear about things," the script supervisor muttered.

This time the smile was almost Lee's.

Tony looked past him, into the darkness of the kitchen, at the edge of the ceiling over the door, down toward the floor at his feet—anywhere but at the smile that almost *wasn't* Lee's. "Let me talk it over with the others."

"Why? You know you're going to come with me."

"Let's pretend I have a choice."

"All right." Dark amusement flashed in the depths of the green eyes. "Let's pretend. You talk. I'll wait."

Tony turned, stepped back toward the pack, and motioned for the others to huddle around him.

"If you go down there and the thing in the basement destroys you, what the hell are we supposed to do?" Amy demanded.

"Thanks for caring."

"You know what I mean!"

"If it destroys me, you stay in here and do anything you have to in order to survive until sunrise."

Adam shook his head. "How do you know it'll let us go at sunrise?"

"It's traditional."

"In order for a thing to become a tradition, it has to happen more than once," Zev pointed out, dragging Brianna back into the huddle and away from Lee.

"In every movie . . ."

"This isn't a movie!"

Tony closed his eyes and counted to three. "Look, you'll just have to trust me on the sunrise thing. Besides, I think I'll be okay. Brenda implied it didn't want me destroyed."

"Why not?"

"She didn't say." Technically, she'd only said that the

thing in the basement didn't want Lee to destroy him. It could still want to do the nasty itself. Since he was going into the basement regardless, Tony didn't see a lot of point in mentioning that. "Does anyone have a mirror? I left Tina's in the ballroom."

"Honestly, Tony, you should be more careful when you borrow something!"

"I'm sorry."

"I'd had that compact for years."

"It's still there; you can get it in the morning."

"Oh, sure." Her nostrils flared. "*If* I survive. Well, even if I were willing to lend you another mirror, I don't have one."

"Amy?"

"Please." She tucked a strand of black-tipped magenta hair behind her ear. "I look this good when I leave the house and it lasts all day."

After a long moment, Mason sighed and pulled a small silver compact out of his pants pocket. "I like to check my touch-ups," he explained as he passed it over.

"You always look wonderful!" Ashley gushed up at him.

He nodded. "True."

All eyes tracked Tony as he slid the compact into his front pocket. He leaned farther into the huddle and murmured, "Let the gardener's head out while I'm gone. I want to see how the thing in the . . ." Screw it, life was too short. ". . . the *thing* reacts to a replay."

"Mouse and Mason?" Zev asked.

Glancing over at the actor and the cameraman, he didn't immediately understand Zev's point. Mason ignored him—business as usual—Mouse peered at him through his viewfinder. Oh. Right. The possible return of the crazies. If the replays began again, would the house then feel it could expend the power to repossess? If Mouse and Mason didn't remember how far they'd fallen apart, could they make the decision to risk it again?

Did he have the right to risk them—all of them; a crazy Mouse was a dangerous roommate—for the sake of information that might not be relevant?

Might be, though.

No way of telling.

"Tony?"

"Ask them first." The good of the many. *Yeah, like that'll apply to Mason.* He touched the hard ridge of the compact, and straightened.

"So you going, then?" Sorge asked.

"Of course he's going," Peter answered. The director reached across the huddle and clasped Tony's forearm. "Bring Lee back to us. We can't lose him now; he's pulling in as much fan mail as Mason is."

"More."

As Mason sputtered, everyone else craned their heads to stare at the thing that was Lee.

He shrugged. "Small room, and Peter's voice tends to carry. Are you coming, Tony?"

No," Tony muttered under his breath as he turned, "just breathing hard. Ow!" He scowled at Amy as he rubbed his bad arm. "What the hell was that for?"

"So not the time to make jokes!"

"Can't think of a better time." Picking one of the lanterns up off the counter, he waved it toward the kitchen. "Let's go."

"Don't want to be alone in the dark with me?" Lee asked as the pantry door closed behind them.

"Stop it."

"You don't think your attraction to me might have caused me to ask myself a few questions about the way I'm living my life?"

"Yeah, right," Tony snorted. "With one bound, he was up and a gay? I don't think so."

"Perhaps you're selling yourself short."

"Perhaps you should shut the fuck up."

He could hear the creaking of Lucy's rope up on the third floor. Karl crying. The band playing on. Aware of each sound momentarily before it faded to background again.

The basement door was open. The memory of touching the doorknob spasmed though Tony's left hand and the new pain burned a little of the rigidity out of his arm. Eyes watering, he realized that *no pain, no gain* was quite probably the stupidest mantra he'd ever heard. And that whole wizard being able to feel power thing truly sucked.

As he followed Lee down the basement stairs, the lantern light seemed to close around him, as though the darkness was too thick for it to make much of an impression. Old boards creaked under his weight as he hurried to keep up, not wanting to lose sight of the other man.

The splash as he stepped off onto the concrete floor came as a bit of a surprise. So did the cold water seeping in through his shoes. Apparently Graham Brummel hadn't been kidding about the basement flooding. *Great. And the thing knows, because Lee knows, about tossing live wires into the water and making soup.*

He'd half turned back toward the stairs before he realized he'd moved. He didn't want to be soup. But then, who did? A rustling from above caught his attention and he lifted the lantern. The light just barely made it to the top of the stairs. The gardener's hand rose up on its wrist and flipped him the finger.

Looked like they hadn't released the head.

On the bright side, he could hear neither Karl nor the band. The silence was glorious. Muscles he hadn't realized were tense relaxed.

"Cold feet, Tony?"

"Yeah. Cold and wet."

"You're perfectly safe. I don't want to hurt you."

Not Lee, he reminded himself. *Also, big fat creepy evil liar.* Wrapping his left hand carefully around the handle of the lantern, he slid Mason's compact out of his pocket and quietly thumbed it open. He almost pissed himself as Lee's hand closed around his elbow.

"Come closer."

"I was *going* to."

"You're still standing at the foot of the stairs."

"I know! I said I was going to." He took a deep breath, hated the way it shuddered on the exhale, and allowed Lee to pull him forward. The basement smelled of mold and old wood and wet rock.

He stumbled once on a bit of cracked concrete, but Lee's grip kept him on his feet. Hurt like hell, since he was gripping the left arm but better than falling when falling would have extinguished his light. "Thanks."

"Like I said, I don't want you hurt."

"I wasn't thanking you."

Amused. "Yes, you were."

Not amused. "Bite me."

At least the reflection of the lantern light off the water pushed the darkness back a little farther. Enough to see Lee if not the actual basement. Under the circumstances, it didn't exactly help to see Lee, but it was nice to know he wasn't alone. Of course, Lee all by himself wasn't alone. He suppressed most of a totally inappropriate snicker.

"Care to share the joke?"

"It's not really very funny."

The sound of them splashing forward bounced off hard surfaces, nearly but not quite an echo. Made sense; big house, big basement. Tony was pretty sure he could hear water . . . not so much running as dribbling . . . somewhere close.

"So, is there a laundry room down here?"

"Yes."

"Wine cellar?"

"There is."

"Bathroom?"

"No."

"That's too bad because all this wet is reminding me that I could really use a chance to piss."

"Too bad."

He snorted. "Yeah, well I've walked through worse, so how are you going to stop me if I just whip out and let 'er rip?"

Lee's grip tightened way past the point of pain. Tony's hand spasmed. The lantern fell. Without releasing his hold, Lee bent and gracefully scooped it out of the air just before it hit the water, straightened, and hung it back over Tony's fingers.

Teeth so tightly clenched he thought he could hear enamel crack, Tony held the lantern as securely as possible and yanked his arm free. He staggered, would have fallen but slammed up against a stone pillar instead, forgave it for new bruises, and collapsed against its support. *Right. Taunting the thing in the basement—bad idea.*

Gaining a little more movement in his left hand—bad trade.

"I don't *want* to hurt you."

"Yeah, I get the emphasis." His voice sounded almost normal, which was good because he hadn't totally ruled out screaming as an option. "You don't want to, but you will."

Lee continued walking to where the edge of the light lapped up against a section of the fieldstone foundations then he turned and spread his hands. "I have a proposition for you."

Déjà vu all over again. "What is it about evil," he wondered aloud, "that makes it so damned attracted to my ass?"

The thing raised Lee's eyebrows into a painfully familiar expression. "Excuse me?"

"You, the Shadowlord . . . Is it something I'm doing? Because if it is, I'll stop."

"What?"

"My ass," Tony sighed. "Your interest."

Understanding. Then disgust. "My interest in you has nothing to do with your body or your perverse and deviant behavior."

"Oh." Wait a minute. "You shove people off the sanity cliff and then pull a *Matrix* battery thing on them and I'm a deviant?"

"What are you babbling about?"

"Little trouble keeping up with contemporary culture? Here, I'll translate. You drive people crazy and then you feed off their deaths. You have no business calling me a deviant."

"Homosexuality is against the law of nature."

Tony felt his lip curl. "You're one to talk; you're a thing in a basement!"

"I am a power!"

"Yeah, big power. So you've killed a few . . . dozen people." He kicked at the water. "You're still stuck in a flooded fucking basement."

Lee shuddered and his nose started to bleed.

"Okay, I'm sorry." Jerking away from the pillar, Tony took a step toward Lee. "I'm sure it's a very nice basement."

"Enough."

"Right."

"Or I may just kill him now." The shudders grew more violent.

Would another step closer make it better or worse? "I said I was sorry."

"You'll consider my offer?"

"So *make* an offer."

"I want you to join me."

"Say what?"

"With your power added to ours, we could be free."

Ours? Thing*s* in the basement? Plural? Listening for a second presence, Tony remembered the mirror. He glanced down, adjusted it to pick up Lee's reflection, saw movement to the actor's left—looked up at a blank fieldstone wall—looked down, made another adjustment, and saw something looking back.

Sort of.

The wall was in constant movement. Roiling. A description he honestly thought he'd never use. Features appeared and disappeared, pushing out from the stone and reabsorbing a moment later. Eyes. Nose. Mouth. It was as if someone with a scary sense of proportion had animated one of those abstract paintings Henry liked so much—where the proportions were already a little frightening.

"You're very quiet."

"Just a little surprised," Tony admitted. When it spoke, the features appeared in the standard arrangement. The mouth even moved although Lee still did the actual talking. Tony couldn't shake the feeling he'd seen the face before.

"Why surprised? I've been helping you. The journal was a tad . . . convenient, wasn't it? I left it there in the library for you."

He *had* seen the face before. He'd seen it every day they'd been on location hanging against the red-flocked wallpaper over the main stairs.

"Creighton Caulfield?" Seemed Graham Brummel's theory that Caulfield was the template for the thing's personality came up just a bit short.

On the wall, brows connected to nothing in particular drew in as Lee said, "You've only just figured that out?"

"Excuse me for being distracted by being trapped in a haunted house with dead people—including," he added, "a few that weren't dead when the doors closed!" He waved the lantern for emphasis since if he moved his other hand, he'd lose the reflection in the mirror.

Caulfield looked a little confused. "Well, yes, but . . ."

"So I'm thinking that if you want me to join you, you'd better assume I know nothing and make with the backstory."

The face on the wall couldn't sigh, but Lee could. "Did you even *read* the journal?"

Tony actually felt his ears grow warm and the water lapped a little higher on his calves as he shuffled his feet. "A friend's reading it."

"A friend?"

"I'll get to it! I just haven't had time."

"I left it for you."

"So you said." Best defense, good offense. "I'm finding that hard to believe since you stuffed it behind that mirror almost a hundred years ago."

"Fine." Lee and the reflection of Caulfield in the tiny mirror snorted—although only Lee made the actual noise. "I left it there for someone *like* you. Someone like me."

"I'm nothing like you!"

"You thought you were the first?"

"The first what?"

"Heir to ancient power."

And the anvil dropped.

Fifteen

"SO YOU'RE a wizard?"

Lee drew himself up to his full height, the movement echoed by an upward surge of the features roiling on the wall. "I am nothing so tawdry!"

"But you said . . ."

"I did not."

A quick glance down into the mirror showed that Caulfield's reflection looked as offended as Lee did. Tony, who'd been forced to embrace his inner wizard in a big way over the last few hours, tried not to feel insulted. "Whatever. My bad." Although he didn't try too hard.

"Your what?"

"Just forget it." Tony's left hand ached, the weight of the lantern pulling his fingers away from his palm and, in turn, his lower arm away from his upper. Probably a good thing in both cases, but the pain was distracting. Unfortunately, if he wanted to keep an eye on the thing Caulfield had become, he couldn't switch the lantern to his other hand as he very much doubted his left hand had recovered enough to manipulate anything as small as Mason's touch-up mirror. "So if you're not a wizard, what are you?"

"We are Arogoth!"

Tony closed his teeth on his initial reaction to the pompous declaration—*Dude, you sound like an alt-rock cover band*—but the snicker slipped out before he could stop it, before he could remind himself of what the consequences would likely be. And who'd suffer them.

Lee went to his knees in the water, features twisted in pain, mouth open in a silent scream.

"I'm sorry!" He surged forward and, as the collection of powers trapped in the wall surged out toward him, realized that touching the darkness would be a really bad idea. Only one step away from the pillar, he jerked to a stop. Lee remained on his knees, writhing. In the mirror, Caulfield's face had disappeared from the roiling darkness leaving nothing but threat. "I said I was sorry, damn it! Leave him alone!"

"Do not mock me!"

Bright side; if Caulfield wanted to use Lee's voice, he had to ease up on the punishment. Ease up. Not stop. It was pretty fucking amazing how much punishment the human body could take and still keep talking.

"I wasn't!" Growing frantic, Tony searched for something he could use to reach the other man without putting himself in danger of being absorbed. "I'm tired, that's all!" There was nothing near him but the stone pillar. And nothing on the stone pillar but a nail about head height. *Yes.* Twisting around, he looped the lantern's wire handle over the nail, spun back, and *reached* for Lee.

With his left hand. Nerves shrieked as he spread his fingers. Tony just barely stopped himself from shrieking along with them.

Fortunately, there wasn't much distance to cover. Fortunate, because although there wasn't exactly a weight limit the heavier the item the more it took out of him and Tony was running near empty. Also fortunate because Lee wasn't an eight-year-old girl and the less time he had to accelerate before impact, the better. Tony hit the water, sucking back a scream as the other man slammed into the burn on his chest. As they fell, his left arm wrapped around Lee holding the actor close.

So close he could feel Lee's heart pounding within the cage of his ribs.

So close he could smell the faint sweet iron scent of the blood dribbling from Lee's nose.

Was this what Henry felt? So intimately aware of another's life?

So desperately needing to protect it.

He lost his grip on the mirror but somehow managed to keep both their heads above water. Up close and personal, it was numbingly cold. Under the circumstances though, numbing was good. He finally folded his legs and settled Lee on his lap. Snarled, "If you kill him, you've lost your leverage."

Lee went rigid. And not in a good way.

"If you kill him, I'll destroy you," he continued. "I don't care who else you throw in my way. I don't care if I have to die to do it. I will take this house apart, brick by brick, and I will wipe you off the face of this Earth."

A shudder. Then the dark head tipped back against his shoulder and green eyes focused on his face. "You mean that."

"I do." And he did. At that moment, he'd have thrown the world away to keep Lee safe. *How will Lee live with no world?* the more rational part of his brain wondered.

Shut up.

"Then it seems we may be able to come to an arrangement." And just like that, with a second shudder, all evidence of pain disappeared from Lee's face. "Release me."

There didn't seem to be any point in holding on, although it took Tony a moment to convince his arm of that. Or maybe it just hurt too much to move it. Who knew? Eventually freed, Lee bent forward and splashed a handful of water against his face, rinsing the red streaks from his mouth and chin.

"Me, I'd have left the blood." Tony braced himself as the other man moved against his lap. "You don't know what's pissed in this water." His bladder was giving him some definite ideas in that direction himself.

No real surprise when Lee . . . or specifically, Caulfield . . . ignored the comment. He probably knew exactly what was in the water and didn't care. It wasn't his body after all. And the bastard had borrowed it without permission.

Tony pulled his legs back out of the way as Lee stood. As Caulfield walked the body back to stand by the wall, he groped around the floor for the mirror.

"Were you planning on remaining down there?"

His fingers closed around metal and glass. "Just need a moment to catch my breath."

"You're weakening."

"Still got enough going to kick your ass," he muttered as he crawled back to the pillar and used it to get to his feet. "So, what kind of an arrangement did you have in mind? You know, with the joining you and all."

"Simple. You join me and I will release your coworkers and the object of your unnatural lust."

"He has a name."

"So?"

Yeah, okay. Probably didn't matter much. "I join you in the wall?" An eternity of roiling. Hard to resist.

"With you as a part of us, I will be free."

"You said that earlier. Free how?"

"Free of this place. Free to go where we will. Free to do as I will."

"Will some of that *doing* involve unnatural acts?" He flipped the compact open again, and rubbed the glass against his jeans. Wet denim didn't exactly help clean up the reflection.

Lee's brows drew in disapprovingly. "Not the kind you enjoy."

"Duh. I meant that whole murder/suicide thing you've got going upstairs."

"The whole murder/suicide thing, as you put it . . ." His lip curled. ". . . will be unnecessary. As we will be free to move from this house, I will not need to contain the dead as nourishment."

"But there'll be dead? Dying?"

"Of course. I will gain power and we will make a place for myself."

Caulfield seemed to be having a bit of an identity problem. Seemed like he wasn't completely merged with the original darkness. Or after being stuck in a damp basement for almost a hundred years, he'd gone completely bugfuck. Oh, wait. Odds were good that being bugfuck was what had brought Creighton Caulfield to the basement in the first place.

"Okay, if ∴ ." Tony stopped as Lee's face went blank. He looked down at the mirror and saw that the roiling had progressed to writhing. The darkness had become thicker, nearly obscuring the fieldstone wall completely, and Creighton Caulfield was very nearly defined as a separate presence. It almost seemed as though he'd been pushed out of the darkness by its more aggressive movement. His features actually held together as a face on a head over a body, cheeks and shoulders held a faint tint of color and . . . oh man, the old guy was naked. Obviously naked.

A quick glance over at Lee showed a similar response—although less blatant given the generous coverage of a pair of wet tuxedo pants.

Response to?

A replay. Had to be. Replays fed the thing in the basement and since it was definitely reacting positively to whatever was going on, Amy and Zev must've released the head and let the cycle start up again. The memory of pain tried to force Tony's arm back up against his body, but he fought it and won.

Breathing heavily, sweat burning in the broken blisters on his chest, he studied the image in the mirror. Caulfield arched out from the wall, spine bowed, only hands and feet a part of the darkness. The position looked painful. Given Caulfield's reaction, it either wasn't, or that was part of the attraction.

It's like porn for elderly masochists. And it would *be the gardener's replay; it's one of the long ones.*

Eyes narrowed, head cocked to one side, Tony could nearly see Caulfield without the mirror. The faintest translucent image of a man bowed out from the wall; easy enough for those who didn't know—who didn't believe—to dismiss it as a trick of the light.

He returned to the reflection, hoping Caulfield wasn't heading for a big finish because that would put a distinct bend in his sex life for some time to come.

Unfortunately . . .

Great. Something to look forward to. Tony sighed silently as Caulfield snapped back into the darkness and began to roil again within it. He could hear that future conversation now.

Damn, there it goes again. Is it me?

No, I was just thinking of this evil old guy I saw once . . .

Of course, if he wanted Lee to survive this, that particular problem was unlikely. A very minor bright side.

"So." Lee's arms made a pale band across the black T-shirt as he folded them. "Have you made up your mind?"

Seemed that Caulfield—both on the wall and in Lee—planned to ignore what had just happened. Worked for Tony. Forgetting would be harder, but ignoring he could do. "If I join you, then Lee and the others walk away?"

"Yes."

He snorted. "Like I can trust you."

"As a gesture of good faith, I no longer possess the other actor or the two who use the camera. And besides . . ." Lee spread his hands and mirrored the smile that appeared briefly at the surface of the darkness. ". . . when you become a part of us, there is a chance you will be able to influence our actions." And his hands crossed over his chest. "It is the only way for you to save him."

"Yeah. I got that a while ago." Tony fought the urge to scratch at his blisters. "So why does freedom ring after I join in? What difference will I make?"

"Unfortunately, I made a slight miscalculation and did not have substance enough on my own to give Arogoth existence independent of this house. Together, we will."

"You're sure of that? Because a hundred years stuck to a basement wall—not appealing."

Lee's smile twisted into a darker curve. "It had its moments. The taste of death is sweet as you will learn. If you'd die to preserve this man, think how much better to live forever."

"Forever?"

"Yes. As Arogoth, immortal devourer of death!" Not even the use of Lee's talent could pull that line back from the brink, and Caulfield seemed to realize it. His eyes closed briefly before disappearing into the churning mix of features. Obviously trying to save face, Lee scowled and pointed. "Choose."

"What choice?" The pain in his arm was constant enough to almost ignore as he reached for the lantern. "I have to tell the others what I'm doing or they'll be down here trying to pull off some half-assed rescue attempt."

"That is . . ." Lee paused and Tony got the impression that Caulfield was shuffling through what he knew about the people who put together *Darkest Night*. Without perspective, they seemed like an insane bunch—twelve-to-seventeen-hour days making a vampire detective believable . . . at least for forty-three minutes at a time. "Fine. Tell them."

"They'll try and talk me out of it." He carefully bent his fingers around the handle and then more carefully still lifted the lantern from the nail. "They'll try and convince me there's a way we can beat you."

"Convince them there isn't."

"Easy for you to say." His gesture with the lantern made shadows dance, made it seem as though the whole basement was roiling. Roiling. He just couldn't get enough of that word. "Well, come on, then."

"Come . . . ? Ah." Lee leaned back against the wall. Not the piece of wall where Arogoth was contained and Caulfield's features continued to surface but a section of fieldstone empty of everything but a little mold and mildew. "I don't think so. This one stays with us while you are gone."

Tony froze. "No," he snarled. "He goes with me."

"He stays."

"The hell he does."

"Exactly."

Bugger. "If he stays, how can I be sure you aren't hurting him?"

"You can't. And I can hurt him while he is with you—or have you forgotten already?"

Not something he was likely to forget in a hurry. "But if he's with me, I'll know you're hurting him and I'll know you're a lying sack of shit. I want him with me."

"You don't always get what you want." There was nothing of Lee in that smile at all. "Best hurry back."

"I don't . . ."

"Have much time." No mistaking the threat.

"Lee, if you can hear me, I'll be back for you." Without waiting for a response, Tony spun on one heel and splashed toward the stairs. Although he hated leaving Lee in Caulfield's control, hated leaving him in the dark, his protests had more to do with convincing Caulfield to keep his hostage in the basement. Had he not protested, the—well, *thing* still seemed to apply—the thing would have grown suspicious about why he didn't want Lee upstairs. Didn't want Lee in a position to be Caulfield's eyes and ears.

When the splashing wasn't quite enough, Tony matched his breathing to the rhythm of the other man's lungs so that he couldn't hear him receding farther and farther away. Shoes and socks squelching, he climbed to the kitchen just in time for Karl to stop crying and the ballroom's replay to begin.

Just for a moment, he missed the quiet of the basement. If he never heard "Night and Day" again, it would be way too soon.

"Tony . . ."

"Give me a break." Spinning on his heel, spraying dirty water as he turned, he stuck his head back into the stairwell. "Hey, you want to tell your ghostly minions that the plan's changed. Because the name calling is really fucking annoying!"

"Tony . . ."

"Oh, right. I forgot." Caulfield was just a little too distracted during replays to respond. Where distracted meant getting his metaphysical rocks off. Pot, kettle, black on that whole unnatural lust thing. Eyes rolling, Tony headed for the kitchen sink. He couldn't connect with anyone alive during the replay anyhow and he *really* had to take a leak.

The door to the butler's pantry opened as Tony reached for it. They'd clearly been waiting for him. All eyes were locked on his face as they shuffled back to give him room to enter.

"You're wet," Mason pointed out, moving fastidiously farther away.

"Basement's flooded."

"Chest high?"

"There was a bit of sitting," he admitted, sagged against the counter and twisted the top off a bottle of water.

"Where's Lee?" Peter demanded.

"In the basement, still possessed." A long swallow. "Creighton Caulfield is a part of the thing."

"So it worked."

He turned to stare at Amy in confusion. "What worked?"

Mouse shuffled back against the far wall as Amy waved the open journal. "The last entry." She glanced down and read: "*I go to become great. I go to become immortal. I go to become* . . . the name you won't let me say."

"Well, he hasn't quite *become*," Tony snorted. "Not yet anyway. He wants me to join him—them—and finish the project, or he'll kill Lee. If I join him, you all go free."

"Including Lee?"

"So says the thing in the basement." He waited while everyone in the room thought about how easy production assistants were to replace.

"What are you going to do?" Tina asked at last.

Tony took another mouthful of water, swallowed, and shrugged. "Save Lee. Save you guys. Save the day."

Zev's hand closed around his arm. "You're going to join him?"

"Not if I can help it."

"You have a plan."

He smiled wearily at the music director. "I got nothing. Amy, he implied that the journal would explain all. What have you got?"

"Um, okay . . ." She turned a couple of pages. "He started out as a collector of the weird. Grave dirt, cat skulls, mummy bits . . . not really unusual for a man of his time."

"How are you knowing that?" Sorge asked, his tone more intrigued than suspicious.

"Amy knows her mummy bits," Tony told him. "Go on, Amy."

"Anyway, later . . . Why are you squirming?"

Fabric squelched as he flexed his butt muscles against the edge of the counter. "Wet underwear."

"Okay, didn't really want to know. The stuff Caulfield collected led to books to look the stuff up in, to verify it, and then he started collecting the books. *Then* he found a book that convinced him that . . ." She bent her head to read again. *"That there is a world beyond what fools admit. There is power for those who dare take it. There is power here."*

"What an idiot," Mason muttered.

"Except he was right," Tony said thoughtfully. "All that nasty shit he collected . . ."

"I'm guessing waxy buildup of evil," Amy agreed. "And that's when he started calling in the mediums, trying to contact this power. You know he had a developmentally handicapped son, right?"

"He's in the bathroom," Brianna added, crawling backward out of one of the lower cabinets clutching a silver salad fork.

"Well, one of the mediums—one of the ones who survived—thought that spirits were attracted to those kind of brain waves, so Caulfield started using his son."

"Using?"

"That's all it says."

"I think we can fill in the blanks," Zev growled.

"He never hit him." Brianna patted Zev on the arm. "But he was scary. Really, really scary. Except I wouldn't have been scared."

"I don't doubt that for a moment," Zev muttered, taking the salad fork away.

Tony frowned. "It likes fear, strong emotions." There had to be a way he could use that.

"Looks like the fear was enough," Amy continued, "because contact was made. Meanwhile, Caulfield had been using his books to research how to hold the power when he found it. Thus the pages of mystic symbols."

Tony held up his left hand. His palm throbbed and

the skin under the pattern itched like crazy. "This was what he used to hold the power here in the house."

"Yeah, kind of like a roach motel. Nasty energy checks in, but it doesn't check out. He used a bunch of the other symbols to get it all gathered up in one place. He's not writing for the ages here, so he's kind of obscure, but I think he believed that the more of it he gathered in one place, the more real it would be."

"Half an inch of water spread over an entire room is harmless," Saleen announced unexpectedly. "Put that water in a bucket and you can drown someone."

"Exactly!" Amy shot Saleen an approving smile. "Caulfield used his own blood to gather this thing up. *My heart pounding with anticipation, I opened a vein and dipped in the brush made to the specification in the ancient text. Chanting and breathing the fumes of . . .*"

"*Reader's Digest* version," Tony interrupted. "I don't have a lot of time and there'll be another replay blowing through in a minute."

"Okay, he burned some herbs, lifted some bad poetry out of an old book, painted on the basement wall in blood and all the power scooted there and what was abstract gained enough substance to become . . . stract. Defined. Sort of like catching a demon in a pentagram. Then his son died . . ."

"Of what." It might be important.

"It doesn't say."

"He was scared," Brianna offered. "Really, really scared. He's still scared."

"He died of fright?"

She shrugged, dismissing the concept. "He was too scared to go away. That's why he's there."

"Without his son, Caulfield couldn't access the power he'd trapped in the basement, so he went looking for a way to draw it into himself. He figured he found one. And then . . ." Amy held the journal up again. "We're back at the last page. *I go to become . . .*"

"Except the stuff he wrote on the wall held him as

well as the power and probably that's what kept them from completely merging as well. He thinks that with me added to the mix, we'll be strong enough to break the spell, merge and emerge, and become that name."

Sorge rolled his eyes. "If it isn't that name yet, why can't we say it?"

"We don't want to lend it definition."

"What the hell does that mean when it's home?" Adam demanded. Then he raised a hand as all eyes turned to him. "Never mind. Don't really care."

"With you in the mix, what makes Caulfield think he'll be in charge?" Peter wondered.

"He's read the right books and he's had a hundred-odd years to work out what he'll do. I'm winging it. And I've used a lot of energy tonight already."

Brianna poked him in the leg, then held out her other hand. "Sugar?" Her fingers peeled away from a damp, crumpled paper package.

"Where did you get that?" Zev asked plucking the package off her palm and examining it. Tony wondered what he thought it might be. What dangers it might contain.

"From the box with the salt."

"You haven't been eating it, have you?"

"Duh."

"Maybe that explains why Ashley's asleep . . ."

Covered with Mason's coat, her head on Tina's lap, Ashley murmured at the sound of her name but didn't rouse.

". . . and this one's still bouncing off the walls." He handed the sugar to Tony. "Will this help?"

"Can't hurt." He ripped it open and poured the sugar into his water bottle. "Bri? Can you get the rest of the sugar out of the box?"

She drew herself up and saluted. "I'm on it!"

The box was by the other door. *Sugar rush*, he thought as she raced toward it. *Use it wisely.*

"So he's like physically stuck to the wall?" Amy wondered as Brianna raced back with a double handful of packages.

"No. It's more like he took himself down to his component atoms and mixed them with the power he'd already trapped on the wall."

"Component atoms?" Peter looked hopeful. "So there's a scientific explanation for all this?"

Pouring more sugar into the water, Tony wondered what explanation Peter had been listening to. "Not a chance. Caulfield was a wizard, although he doesn't like the word. Instead of an Arra, he found the wrong book."

"If there's a book, then there must have been other wizards."

"Yeah, I'm not unique. It sucks to be me." He took a swallow of the sugar water, made a face, and took another. "The way I see it, I have two options. I join with Caulfield to save you all, hoping that something outside the house will be able to stop our combined power before it destroys the mainland and kills everyone living on it." And everyone unliving on it. Caulfield didn't know about Henry now, but he would the moment Tony joined up. "Everyone means you lot as well," he added.

"So if you go join up now," Tina said thoughtfully, "you're not really saving us, just delaying the inevitable."

"Yeah." He took another swallow. "Sucks to be you, too."

"And the second option?" Zev prodded.

"We destroy Caulfield. We remove the writing on the wall. We disperse the power."

Amy closed the journal. "You mean destroy the power."

"I mean disperse. You can't destroy energy, you can only change it." He glanced around the room. There were half a dozen degrees in here; one of them had to have been in something useful. "Right?"

"He's right," Saleen answered. Pavin nodded agreement.

Let's hear it for tech support.

"Great. So how do you destroy Caulfield?" Amy asked. "Snatch him away from the power?"

"He's not in this reality anymore. I can't touch him."

"Use the flypaper on your hand to grab him."

"Flypaper?"

She shrugged. "Roach motel, flypaper; amounts to the same thing."

Tony glanced down at the mark and thought of how much it would hurt to snatch up a handful of Creighton Caulfield. Good thing his pants were already wet. "I can't. If I get too close, he'll pull me in."

"So you need something out of this reality that can destroy him from a distance?" When he nodded, Amy snorted. "Good luck."

"You have an idea," Zev said softly, eyes locked on Tony's face. "But you don't like it much."

Flexing his left hand, Tony grinned at his ex. "I don't like it at all. But I think it'll work."

"All right." Peter's tone suggested he was bringing up a point that they'd all missed. "How do you destroy Caulfield without him hurting Lee?"

"I'm going to need a little help with that."

"We're here for you," Amy declared. Most heads nodded.

"Not from you guys," he said as the drawing room replay began and he was alone in the pantry with that damned plate of tea cakes. "I'm playing a wild card." Because they could still hear him, he explained.

". . . the paint's buried in our gear in the library," he finished as the lantern light came up again. "So it's going to have to be dug out."

"Saleen, Pavin . . ." Peter jerked his head toward the door. "Take the other lantern, get the paint."

"On it!"

"They'll need to pull energy from something," Tony said as the door closed. "Someone."

Amy raised her hand and waved it. "I volunteer!"

No one looked surprised.

"It might be dangerous."

"Please." Her grin widened. "Danger is my middle name."

"I thought your middle name was . . ."

"And unless you want your e-mail address written on the wall of every virtual truck stop on the Web, you'll hold that thought."

"What's your plan for removing the writing on the wall?" Tina asked before Tony'd entirely decided that would be a bad thing.

"Don't have one exactly." He shrugged. "But there's a lot of water down there."

"No." Tina shook her head. "Water won't work. Not on ancient bloodstains. Trust me on this; I have two sons who grew up playing rugby."

"The cleaner." All eyes turned to Sorge. "The cleaner we use to clean off the blood on the walls in the upstairs bathroom. During the scenes the girls do!" he expanded when no one seemed to get it. "We splash the walls with the fake blood, but we have to clean it off again. The cleaner, she is guarantee to cut through anything. Old. New. Fake. Real. There are six different warning on the label about the contents."

"And you sprayed that around the girls?" Zev asked him, visibly appalled.

Sorge looked affronted. "Not me. I don't clean locations, I design fantastic scenes that are ignored during award times. But there is a spray bottle also with the gear in the library."

"Sounds like it'll work. Thanks, Bri." Tony accepted another bottle of sugared water from the girl and frowned. "Crap. I won't be able to spray the wall."

Peter rolled his eyes. "And why not?"

"He's not sure he'll survive destroying Caulfield."

Attention flicked from Zev—who stood arms folded—to Tony, who was looking pretty much anywhere but at Zev.

"Is that true?" Peter asked him.

"I should survive." Another long swallow helped him ignore Zev's expression. "I just won't be in any condition to do much else, so someone needs to be available to haul my ass out of the water."

"Me."

Surprised, Tony glanced over at Mouse. Thought of the last time the big man's hands had been on him. Banished the thought. "You sure you're okay?"

The cameraman shot a wary glance at the journal and nodded. "And Lee?"

"Yeah, he'll likely need to be hauled as well."

Adam stepped forward. "That'll be me, then."

"Good. Okay, now for the spray . . ."

"Hello!" Amy waved her hand.

"No. Mouse and Adam can charge in after the fact, but whoever is spraying is going to have to be with me. Close to the thing. If we don't do this at the same time, I'm not positive that one half of that thing can't heal the other. Besides, you've already got something to do."

Her lower lip went out. "Well, yeah, but I'll be done by then."

"You might also be unconscious."

She perked up at the thought. "There is that."

"Me."

"You're . . ."

Peter folded his arms. "In charge. I'm there to see that the thing keeps its half of the bargain and lets my costar go."

"I don't know . . ."

"I do." Zev moved closer to Tony. "It should be me."

"Zev, Peter's plan might . . ."

"We have history. I've come with you to say good-bye. Caulfield's a product of his time as well as his ambition; first of all, two men are going to throw him off and second, he's not going to consider another fag to be a danger to him. You're going to need all the edge you can get."

"Actually, yeah." He sighed. Did it make him a bad person if he'd rather have Peter in danger than Zev or just a good friend? "We could throw Caulfield a bit off his game. But the bottle . . ."

"Will be duct taped to his back." Mason included them all in his smile. "Episode eight. That asshole who tried to stake me in my own office had the stake duct taped to his back."

"Oh, for the love of God, Mason . . ." Peter paused, reconsidered, and started again. "Mason, that didn't work."

"Because I saw the reflection of the stake in the mirror. There are no mirrors in the basement and that thing sure as hell isn't Raymond Dark."

All Zev would have to do was walk across the basement by his side. He wouldn't have to turn. He wouldn't ever expose his back. Tony swallowed more sugar water. "Damn. That might just work."

"Don't tell the writers," Peter muttered. Tina snickered, then stroked Ashley's hair as she stirred.

"One problem." Mouse scowled at no one in particular. "No duct tape."

No duct tape? Well, that was practically unCanadian. "The electrical . . ."

"No." Sorge shook his head. "If we wrap electrical tape so it holds a bottle, Zev won't be able to get it off."

"You need duct tape? Why don't you use some of mine?"

Positions shifted until everyone could stare down at Kate sitting propped and taped against a lower cabinet.

"You chewed through another gag?" Amy sounded impressed.

"Please." She spit a bit of damp fabric to one side. "My boyfriend is a terrible cook; I've eaten worse and smiled while I did it."

Two napkins down, Tony had no doubt that she'd

eaten anything set in front of her. The smiling part was giving him a little trouble, though. "Used duct tape . . ."

Kate snorted. "Will work fine. It'll peel off itself just like it does off the roll. You'll lose the layer that's against me, but that's all. And stop bloody worrying," she snapped as no one stepped forward. "Sitting around with our thumbs up our collective butts while people get possessed and other people die makes me kind of cranky, but I'm fine now. We have a plan."

"You still sound cranky," Tina pointed out.

"Always sounds cranky," Mouse grunted.

"Yeah, yeah," she muttered as he pulled open his pocketknife and knelt by her feet. "Bite me, you big rodent. One more thing, though. The tape's not going to stick to fabric. It'll have to be attached to . . ."

Mouse pulled the final layer of tape off skin.

". . . son of a fucking bitch! . . . Zev."

Zev looked understandably less than thrilled. "If it's under my shirt, how will I reach it?"

"We'll have to cut the back of your shirt away. Tina . . ."

Tina pulled a pair of nail scissors out of her purse and handed them up to Amy who advanced on the music director's shirt with a gleam in her eyes.

"And then we'll tape down the edges of your shirt so it doesn't flap and then we tape the bottle to you."

"Is a big bottle," Sorge observed with a grin. "Why don't you just stuff the bottom down the back of his pants?"

Amy paused in her advance, glared at the DP, and handed Tina back the scissors. "Well, aren't you just a big bunch of no fun at all."

The door leading to the dining room opened. Saleen came in first carrying the paint followed by Pavin with the lantern. "We got it."

"Great." Peter smiled approvingly at them. "Set it down and go back for a spray bottle of cleaner."

"We didn't see any spray bottles."

"It's in there." Sorge walked the length of the butler's pantry and paused with his hand on the door. "Come. I'll go with you."

Pavin held out the lantern. "Why don't you go by yourself?"

"I don't want to. Come on. Varamous."

"That's not French," Saleen muttered as he set the can of paint on the counter and turned to follow Sorge and the sound tech out of the room.

"Me, I'm a man of many talents," the DP said as the door closed.

Tony drained the last of the sugar water and slid off the counter. "Okay. Open the paint can and then put it outside the door in the kitchen. Amy, wait by the can. When the guys get back with the cleaner, Zev and Adam and Mouse get ready to meet me by the basement door. Wait until you hear me coming down the back stairs and then move. Delays will be . . ." He could feel sweat dribbling down his sides. ". . . not good. Make sure the spray bottle is on a tight, hard spray—all we have to do is cut through the blood pattern, break it up. We don't have to completely erase it. The rest of you . . . If this goes completely to hell, the pattern on the floor will keep anything from coming in; you'll have the laptop and the candles for light and all you have to do is stick it out until morning."

"What if Caulfield sucks you in?" Amy asked.

"You die and I spend eternity as part of a three for one that even our writers would consider over the top, where the other two parts are a hundred-year-old naked homophobe and evil waxy buildup."

Amy's smile came nowhere near her eyes. "Dead sounds better."

"Yeah, no shit."

♦

Tony went upstairs while Lucy Lewis killed her coworker and waited by the second-floor bathroom while she hanged herself. When the only light on the floor came from the lantern in his hand and Karl started crying again, he went into the room.

"Cassie? Stephen?"

He didn't know where they'd been for the last— impossible to tell exactly how long since he'd seen them, without a watch and only the very subjective replays to determine the passage of time, but it had been a while.

"Guys? I need to talk to you. It's important."

Nothing. Big white empty bathroom.

He sighed and crossed to the mirror. Not so empty anymore. Not so white. The mirror showed Cassie and Stephen sitting on the edge of the tub and the walls covered in splashes and sprays and dribbles of blood. Too much blood for a double murder? Even considering that head wounds bled like crazy? Maybe every replay left its mark. And wasn't that depressing.

"Guys, I can see your reflection. I know you're there."

They were looking at him. But only in the mirror. Cassie looked sad. Stephen stubborn.

Fine.

"The thing in the basement wants me to join it, and it's holding Lee hostage to make me. I think we can beat it if one of you two helps me to save Lee."

Cassie glanced away. Stephen lifted his sister's hand off his leg and wound their fingers together. He couldn't have said *"Mine."* more obviously if he'd said it out loud.

Tony counted time by his heartbeat. He had to convince them before the next replay started. Before their replay started.

"If I can't save Lee . . ." Try again. "If Lee dies, I die with him. You guys are dead. You have to admit that alive is better. Together and alive. Because, him and me, we won't be together if we're dead." Yeah. That was articulate—not! Entirely possible all that sugar water had been a bad idea as he couldn't seem to maintain a coherent thought. Time to pull the big guns. Time to use the magic word . . .

"Please."

"If we help you, it'll know we have more than the existence it allows us."

He turned. Cassie sat alone on the tub, the fingers of her right hand, the fingers wrapped around her brother's hand, fading into nothing. Her single eye locked on his face, willing him to understand.

"If it knows we're awake and aware ..."

"It'll kill us again." Stephen was there now. "It'll take away the little bit of life we have. Is that what you want? Because we're dead, we don't count for as much as the living?"

Yes.

No.

Damn.

"If you're dead, then what you have isn't life, is it?"

Stephen's eyes narrowed and when he rose, he looked menacing for the first time that night. "Get out."

Remembering what a glancing touch against his shoulder had felt like, Tony backed toward the door both hands raised. "I'm sorry!"

"Not good enough." Then he jerked to a stop, his head dislodging.

Cassie stood, still holding her brother's hand, his arm stretched tautly between them. "He's right, Stephen. What we have isn't life."

"All right, not life." He settled his head. "But we have each other and we can't risk losing that. *I* can't risk losing that! Can you?"

"We don't know that we will. But if we don't help, we know that Lee will die?"

She'd made it a question. Tony answered with a nod. "It hasn't noticed you yet, right?"

"Because we've been staying in our place." Stephen spat the words at him. "Here. Together."

"You were walking around earlier and it didn't notice you."

"Before it was awake!"

"And after."

"We were lucky. We can feel it. We can tell that it's awake. It has to be able to do the same."

"Why?"

Stephen frowned. "What?"

"Why does it have to be able to do what you can do? It can't move around, you can. It can't communicate without possessing someone's ass, you can."

"How does it communicate with someone's ass?"

Tony's turn to frown. "That's not what I meant, I meant . . ."

"What do you want us to do?" Cassie interrupted.

Free hand holding his head in place, Stephen whirled to face her. "Cassie!"

She shrugged, broken sundress strap swaying with the motion. "I'm just asking."

"I need you to draw this symbol . . ." Tony held up his left hand, palm out, and both ghosts leaned away. "Oh, shit, you can't, can you?"

"I don't think . . ." Her single brow drew in. "It pushes at us. What is it?"

"It's complicated. It's kind of a protection. A protection against the thing's power, but you're a part of that power."

"Only while we're dying." She studied the symbol. "But *this* it would definitely notice. And if we had anything to do with it, it would notice us."

"Told you," Stephen grunted.

Cassie glanced over at him, her expression unreadable, then turned back to Tony. "The symbol would protect Lee from the thing? Keep it from hurting him?"

"It should."

"Should?"

"Should. No chance of a rehearsal. We have to go live and hope it works, but that doesn't matter because you can't." He slammed his fist into his thigh. "Shit! Fuck! Damn it!"

"You want this done with the paint, like before?

Right?" When Tony nodded, the sudden rush of hope making it impossible to speak, Cassie nodded with him. "I like Lee. He's cute."

"It's dangerous." Stephen almost wailed the word, and the skin on Tony's arms pebbled into goose bumps.

"It's a little paint," Cassie argued. "It's no more than what I did this morning. Where is Lee?"

"In the basement."

"Are you insane!"

"The door will be open," he told them quickly before Stephen could continue. "So you'll be able to go downstairs. There's an open can of paint in the kitchen and you can suck energy out of Amy to use it. You don't need much right? Just for a little symbol like this. She says it's okay. Actually, she's looking forward to it." He was almost babbling but couldn't seem to stop. "And the shit won't hit the fan until the next replay after yours, so first you get the paint then you wait until Karl stops crying then you flick the symbol onto Lee just before Karl starts screaming and then, as Karl's replay starts, you get sucked back here . . ." He tapped the wall. ". . . to safety."

"No." Releasing Cassie's hand, Stephen folded his arms. "Not in the basement. No way."

"But . . ."

"I said, no!"

"Tony . . ."

He looked past Stephen to Cassie.

". . . go away. I need to talk to my brother."

Yeah. That would work. Cassie wanted to help, he could see that, and Cassie was the only person, living or dead, Stephen would be willing to listen to. Except . . . He paused in the doorway. "How will I know?"

Her expression said, *trust me.* The shrug that went with it, not so confident.

◆

"Stephen . . ."

"No."

"If we don't help, Lee will die."

"And if we do help, what happens to us?"

"If we each stroke on half of the symbol, maybe nothing. But maybe something. And that's good because nothing has happened to us since we died. We're as trapped now as we were before Graham woke us. Except now we know it."

"But . . ." He started to shake his head, remembered, and caught her hands in his instead. "I can't lose you. I can't." When she sat back on the edge of the tub, he sank to the floor and buried his face in her skirt. "I can't. I won't. And there's more!"

She freed a hand and stroked his cheek. "More?"

"Have you thought of what happens to us if Tony destroys it? What happens to us if we're not trapped here anymore?"

"We move on."

He lifted his head then. "Where? Because, you know, there was sinning."

The corners of her mouth trembled up into a smile. "I remember."

"So, I'm thinking we're better off here." His smile suggested he'd found definitive reasoning.

"Maybe if we save Lee, the sinning won't count for as much. And if we don't save him . . ." Her fingers remembered the soft silk of Stephen's hair. "If we don't save him and Tony still destroys the malevolence, well, that won't look good for us if we move on. Given the sinning and all."

"No."

She sighed. Or she thought she sighed; her fingers, it seemed, had a better memory than her lungs. "I'm going to help Tony. So if we do move on . . ."

"No."

But that "no" was less definite. And he'd stopped smiling.

◆

Waiting outside the bathroom door, Tony flicked open his pocketknife. His left hand had only just regained enough strength to grip it while he poked the point of the blade into the tip of his right index finger.

Here's irony for you . . .

Caulfield seemed to think the answers Tony needed in order to understand the metaphysics of the situation were in the journal. The journal told them that Caulfield had used his own blood to trap the accumulated power against the basement wall. After folding the knife and slipping it back into his pocket, Tony pressed his thumb against the ball of his finger, just under the cut, and squeezed out a steady supply of blood as he painted over the symbol on his left palm.

He'd only just finished, cut finger in his mouth, when Karl stopped crying.

Quiet on the set.

Action . . .

Sixteen

MR. MILLS STAGGERED back as the ax came free and screamed, "You can't hide from me!"

Tony didn't watch as Cassie and Stephen came out into the hall and then ran, hand in hand, for the bathroom. He knew he wasn't seeing them alive, that their reality was a nearly severed neck and three-quarters of a head, but to see them appear alive, to see their last few moments and to know they'd be trapped replaying those moments over and over—well, it was fucking tragic, that's what it was.

It was supposed to stop with death. Maybe there was a judgment, maybe there wasn't—Tony had seen enough weird shit he was unwilling to commit—but the point was: end of something, start of something else. Cassie and Stephen didn't end, didn't start, didn't do anything but sort of exist. And maybe that *sort of* was better than risking the alternative, but Tony didn't think so.

Maybe he should just stop thinking about it. He'd had his chance to convince them.

He winced. Twice. Ax into flesh. Ax into bone. Funny that the impact of the ax—an impact that wasn't particularly loud—made more of an impression than the screaming. Actually, Karl had pretty much desensitized him to screaming. Karl, and before Karl, Aerosmith.

Splattered with the blood of his children, Mr. Mills turned and walked out of the bathroom. Once in the hall, he looked down at the bloody ax as though he'd never seen it before, as though he had no idea whose brains and hair were stuck along its length, then he adjusted his grip and slammed the blade down between his own eyes.

Tony took a step forward as the body fell, held out his left hand, his own blood glistening on his palm, and he reached. Energy never went away and bottom line, the ghosts were captured energy.

Line below the bottom line, this was really going to hurt.

But he couldn't think of another way.

It was all a matter of manipulating energy. Any and all types of energy if Arra's notes could be trusted. It was, in the end, what separated the wizards from the boys. Or maybe, more accurately, those who were willing to risk losing the use of an arm from those who'd come up with a less debilitating solution. And, man, he'd sure like to talk to that other guy . . .

The ax slapped against his hand as the lights dimmed. His fingers didn't so much close as spasm around the handle. *Well, whatever works.* When the replay ended, he couldn't see the ax, but he sure as hell could feel it.

The pain was . . .

Definitively pain.

The kind of pain that, should he actually survive this, he'd compare to every other pain for the rest of his life.

You think that *hurts? I once pulled a ghost ax out of its time and walked through a haunted house with it.*

Except he wasn't exactly walking. Or doing anything but trying to suck enough air into his lungs to stay conscious.

Come on, feet, move!

A deeper breath. And then another.

A guy can get used to anything in time.

Yeah, but he didn't have time. Or not much of it anyway. He had to be in place in the basement before the next replay started.

Okay, don't think about the basement. Think about one step. Just one.

One step didn't hurt any more than standing still. Neither did two or three.

Now just get to the back stairs. Straight hall. Easy trip.

He could do that. Hell, he'd once walked to Wellesley Hospital in February with two broken ribs, a fat lip, and only one shoe. To this day, he had no idea where his other shoe'd gone.

Now down the stairs. This should be easy, gravity's on your side.

Wait.

He needed a test. Some way of making sure that the energy he held continued to act like an ax. It'd be piss useless if it didn't.

Instead of down, he went up. And gravity was a bitch.

Lucy's rope had crossed the lower edge of the third floor just slightly off center. The stairs were so steep he could reach the lower edge of the third floor from four steps up. If he could reach it from four, he wasn't going for five. No point being stupid about this. Sucking in a lungful of air, he willed his arm to work and swung the ax.

He felt the blade cut into the wood.

Felt the burn of a severed rope whistle past his cheek.

Felt dead weight just for an instant roll against his legs.

Staggered back down the four steps, panting; small quick breaths that didn't hurt quite so much.

Heard a voice destroyed by a noose murmur, "Thank you."

And felt a lot better.

For just a moment, he had the strong feeling it was 1906 and he was a chambermaid, but since that was a huge improvement on what he had been feeling—pain, pain, and, well, pain—he could cope. He still felt as though his left arm had been dipped in acid and then rolled in hot sand, but whatever Lucy was doing—Lucy being the only chambermaid he knew from 1906—it gave him a little distance from the feeling. It got him down the stairs and across the kitchen to where Mouse and Adam and Zev waited with the second lantern.

When he joined them, the double circle of light expanded to include Amy sitting cross-legged just outside the butler's pantry by an open can of white paint. She shook her head at his silent question.

It took them a while to recover from their own murder.

There was still time.

"Come on, Zev."

As the music director came forward, Tony grinned. "Is that a bottle of cleaner in your pants or are you just happy to see me?"

Adam rolled his eyes and handed Mouse five bucks as Zev reached back and touched the bottle crammed into the top of his jeans. "What about us?" the 1AD asked. "When do we charge to the rescue?"

"You'll know," Tony told him.

"You sure?"

"It'll be obvious."

"Obvious how?"

"I'm thinking, screaming."

"Yeah." Adam forced a hand back through thick hair, standing it up in sweaty spikes. "Listen, if this thing's been around for so long, what makes you think we can beat it?"

Time for the big, last minute motivational speech.

"Duh. We're the good guys. Zev, can you get the door? My hands are full."

Lantern in one hand. Ax in the other. Of course, no one could see the ax. Zev made a clear decision not to ask and opened the basement door. He frowned as Tony stepped over the threshold. "What's that on your cheek?"

"Rope burn."

"Do I want to know?"

"I doubt it." He shifted over as Zev joined him on the top step. "Stay to my right, by the lantern. And remember," he added as they began to descend, "anything Lee can hear, it can . . . Fuck!"

Lee's face appeared in the darkness at the bottom of the stairs looking for an instant like it was on its own, floating unattached. "I was beginning to think you weren't coming back to us."

Tony shrugged and tried to pretend he wasn't carrying an invisible ghost ax. Lucky break that Lee—Caulfield—couldn't see it either. He hadn't been one hundred percent certain about that, but given the total lack of reaction, it seemed *no one* could see it. "I told you it would take a while to convince them."

"But convince them of what; that's the question. Hello, Zev."

"Lee."

"Not Lee," Tony growled.

"Close enough." The green eyes narrowed, pupils dark pinpricks in the direct glare of the lantern. "Why are you here, Zev?"

"The odds are good that you . . . your body . . . will need a little help leaving after Tony does his thing." He waved a hand, the gesture managing to encompass all the possibilities inherent in the word *thing*. "And besides . . ." His eyes narrowed in turn. "I had no intention of allowing Tony to go through this alone."

"So you're here to hold his hand?"

"I'm here to hold anything that might make it easier for him."

Lee fastidiously brushed a bit of muck off his dress pants. "The depth to which moral rot has penetrated this age astounds me. Perversions accepted as normal behavior."

Tony turned just enough to grin at Zev. "You never said anything about perversions."

"I didn't want to get your hopes up." He shrugged philosophically. "There may not be time."

"Fair enough."

"Stay with him, then, if you must," Lee snarled. *And be the first to fall!*

That had to be some of the loudest subtext Tony'd ever heard and, given the volume of the subtext over the course of the night, that was saying something. "You go first." He motioned with the lantern. "I want you out where I can see you so that I know you're not mucking about with Lee's body."

"I do not muck about!"

"Muck about, torture. Potato, potahto. Move."

Lee pointedly turned and began wading across the basement.

"Since when do you quote Gershwin?" Zev murmured as they descended into the water.

"Sometimes I like to embrace the stereotype." The water felt warmer than it had. Tony really hoped that was because his legs were already wet.

"Gilbert and Sullivan?"

"Not in a million years."

"That's a pretty halfhearted embrace, then."

"I gotta be me."

The thing seemed closer to the stairs than it had been, but, as it was a part of the foundation, Tony was fairly certain it hadn't moved. As Lee took up his old place by the wall, Tony realized that with both hands full, the mirror in his pocket was about as useful as last week's *TV Guide*.

"Hand the lantern to your friend . . ." The final word dripped with distaste. ". . . then come forward and merge with us."

"Dude, you make it sound so dirty." He motioned for Zev to step back, splashed closer to the pillar and hung the lantern on the nail. "Less likely to take damage if I leave it here."

"Dude?" Lee's lip curled. "Your speech patterns are strange."

"You'll have time to get used to them." He never thought he'd miss the sound of Karl's crying. Or rather the sound of Karl not crying to mark the beginning of the next replay. They had to fill the time and they had to fill it in such a way that they didn't seem to be stalling. He stepped in front of Zev and leaned in. "So, I guess this is good-bye."

A faint smile within the bracket of the dark beard as Zev silently agreed to take one for the team.

Give one?

Whatever . . .

Physical incompatibility had *not* been the reason they'd broken up. Tony finally had to pull back from the kiss lest he miss the next replay entirely. Also, he needed to leave a few brain cells functioning.

Lee's lip had been curled before, but it had enough lift in it now to give Raymond Dark a run for his money. "Perversions!"

"Protesting too much?" Zev looked smug.

"He doesn't want you." Lee's voice, Caulfield's disgust.

"I think *he* means me," Zev murmured.

"Yeah, I got that."

Caulfield spread Lee's arms. "He wants this!"

Zev snorted. "Who doesn't?"

That seemed to throw him for a moment. "He settled for you!"

"Duh."

"Hey!" Tony palmed the mirror under the cover of his protest. "I didn't settle! I didn't!" he repeated as neither Caulfield nor Zev seemed to believe him. He could only hope Lee wouldn't remember any part of being possessed. "Wanting something does not keep you from

being content with something else. I like hot dogs, but
I'm happy with . . ."

"Blintzes?"

"Don't start."

He had the mirror now. Was that a flicker of gray on
the edge of the lamplight? Two translucent figures waiting for their cue? Or was it hope and nothing more?
"I want Lee standing over here with Zev before I come
to you."

"Fine." The actor took a step forward, away from the
wall. Room enough behind him for a ghost to do a little
finger painting.

Or a pair of ghosts.

Lee took another step, shuddered, and stopped.

Good luck. Rough rasp of a voice in his head and the
sudden return of pain as Lucy Lewis snapped back to
the stairwell, to her place during the replay.

Tony checked the reflection in the mirror . . .

Eyes in the roiling black bulged out toward him.

Then formed a face. And a head. And a body.
Caulfield defined.

And without the mirror?

The faintest hint of a pink and naked shape arcing out
from the wall.

No way of knowing if Lee was protected.

No way of knowing if Lee was about to die.

Even if they managed to delay Caulfield until the
next replay, he'd never be able to hold onto the ax.

Now or never.

Never.

Now.

Teeth clenched, Tony stumbled closer to the wall,
somehow got his arm raised over his head, and put
everything he had left into snapping the ax forward,
not so much releasing it at the right moment as forcing his fingers to straighten and hoping momentum
would do the rest. The ax became visible as it embedded itself in Creighton Caulfield's head.

Lee screamed.

They hadn't . . . He wasn't . . .

Tony splashed toward him. Didn't seem to be getting anywhere. Streams of cleanser were going by awfully high.

Oh, wait, I'm on my knees.

He didn't remember falling.

His left hand hurt up his arm, across his shoulders and chest, and all the way down to his right hip. Waves. Of. Burning. Pain. The gardener's arm and head had both been smaller and he'd held them for a lot less time. Lucy's presence had masked the damage, allowed him to get this far, but hadn't stopped it from happening. Water was cool. Water would help. He started to topple forward.

Wait.

That wasn't Lee screaming. Tony forced his eyes to focus. Lee was also on his knees, staring into the water like he couldn't believe what he saw, lower lip caught between his teeth and dripping blood. But he wasn't screaming.

So who was?

Right. Naked writhing guy with ax in head. Eyes wide in the streams of darkness running down his face Caulfield pulled an arm free and grabbed for the ax handle. His fingers passed through the shaft.

His other arm came free on its own. Spat free.

Then his feet.

Seemed that the accumulated power wasn't too happy about having been trapped.

Tony scrambled backward as a decomposing body dropped face first into the water. Bobbed up. Rolled over. Head split open, no sign of the ax.

He screamed as hands grabbed his shoulders.

"It's me." No mistaking Mouse's voice or size.

Right, the cavalry.

"Let's move it, people, I think that wall's going to blow!"

Adam's voice.

"Lee?" Tony twisted as Mouse lifted him out of the water.

Mouse shifted his grip, the pressure making a strong nonverbal argument that squirming would not be tolerated. "Puking."

Puking was good. At least he *thought* puking was good. "Alive?"

They were climbing the stairs. The big guy could really motor when he had to.

"The dead don't puke."

"Didn't some freelancer pitch that title for episode nine?"

"No."

Tony was fairly certain that he'd been kidding, but when he started to explain that to Mouse, he found himself passing out instead.

♥

"Something just happened." Henry stepped out onto the front path and frowned at the front of the house.

Graham joined him, rubbing at the rain running down his neck and under the collar of his overalls. "Yeah, I felt it, too."

"Felt what?" CB demanded. His tolerance for obscurity had never been high and what little there was had clearly already been used. "Is it over?"

Vampire and medium exchanged a glance. Finally, Graham shrugged. "Unfortunately, there's only the one way to find out and you're still fucked up from the last time."

Henry's eyes narrowed. "I'm fine."

"You usually got those big purple bruises around your eyes? Nope. Thought not. And you keep rubbing your temples when you think no one's looking. Bet it's been a while since you had a headache."

Henry snarled softly.

"Long while. So it's up to me." He scrubbed his palms

against his thighs, walked up the path, reached out, and touched the edge of the porch.

Flash of red light.

And he was lying at Henry's feet. "Are you all right?"

"I'm fine," he muttered as he put his hand in Henry's and was set upright again. "It's not over."

"What's not over?"

The three men turned slowly.

Jack Elson stood in the driveway at the edge of the light.

"Cop?" Graham asked quietly.

"Cop," Henry replied at the same volume.

CB drew in a deep obvious breath and let it out slowly before meeting the advancing RCMP officer halfway. "My night shoot is not over. Can I help you with something, Constable Elson?"

"No, not really. I was just driving by and I saw some cars were still parked out on the road, so I thought I'd come in and find out if there was a problem."

"I see." And included in those two words, was the certain knowledge, shared by everyone who heard them, that Deer Lake Drive didn't actually go anywhere, which made just driving by . . . unlikely.

"Not as many cars as there were."

"We don't need as large a crew at night."

Elson smiled in a hail-fellow-well-met kind of way that set Henry's teeth on edge. His father used to smile like that. "I assume your permits for a night shoot are in order?"

"We've been shooting at this location all week," CB told him.

"But not at night."

"No, not at night."

"So your permits?"

"Are inside."

There was an undercurrent of warning in the producer's voice that Elson ignored.

"All right." His smile broadened. "Let's go take a look."

"The doors have swollen shut in the damp."

Blinking rain off pale lashes, Elson shot Graham an incredulous glare before turning his attention back to CB. "Damp?"

"Yes. Damp. My people are working on getting out."

"There're no lights."

"Constable Danvers." CB nodded as a second figure appeared in the driveway—nodded politely enough but with an edge of impatience in the movement.

Elson turned to scowl at his partner. "What are you doing here?"

"I could ask you the same question." She shrugged and stepped up beside him. "But I won't. After all that research you did, I had a feeling you weren't heading home."

"So you followed me?"

"I didn't have to follow you, Jack. I knew where you were going. There're too many unanswered questions here for you to stay away."

"Research?"

Both constables turned to face the producer.

"There've been a number of unusual occurrences in this house over the years," Danvers told him, ignoring the signals her partner was shooting her. "After speaking with Tony Foster this afternoon, Constable Elson took a look at our records and found a list of murder/suicides as long as your arm." She paused, dropped her gaze to the arm in question, and amended, "Well, as long as my arm anyway. Funny how these sorts of things start piling up in one place."

"Yes. Funny." CB didn't sound particularly amused. "So you're not here to check our permits."

It wasn't a question, but Elson answered it anyway, lips curved into a tight smile. "Might as well look since we're here."

"I get the strong impression you're here off duty."

"The Horsemen are never off duty." Danvers glanced over at Henry as though somehow aware he was the only one of the four who knew about the blood rising in her cheeks. "Heard the line in an old movie once; I've always wanted to say it."

"Yeah, now you've said it," Elson sighed. "What do you mean there're no lights?"

"What?"

"When you arrived, dogging my heels, having not followed me, anticipating my interest . . ."

A raised brow cut off the list.

". . . you said there were no lights."

"Oh. Right. There're no lights on in the house." One hand gestured gracefully toward the building. "If they're in there, shooting, why is it so dark?"

"Because we've been shooting day for night and the windows are covered in blackout curtains." CB's words emerged clipped of everything but bare fact. If Henry had to guess, he'd say that at the end of a long night of waiting and worrying about his daughters, CB was beginning to get angry. Too practical to lose his temper at the house, fate had just given him a pair of targets. Given that the last time Henry'd seen CB angry he'd lifted a grown man by the throat and thrown him across a soundstage, it might be a good idea to intervene.

"Blackout curtains? Okay. And you've probably got an explanation for that flash of red light that knocked . . ." Elson paused, the question in his stare unmistakable.

"Graham Brummel," the caretaker muttered.

". . . Mr. Brummel here five feet back onto his ass?"

The fabric of CB's trench coat rippled as he settled his shoulders. "You saw that?"

" 'Fraid so."

The faintest growl and Henry was there, left hand wrapped around CB's right wrist, holding the big man's arm to his side.

"I saw it, too. From the driveway." Danvers' eyes locked on the muscles straining under CB's coat, the movement obvious even in the darkness.

"What the hell is going on here?" Elson demanded, his attention having snapped instinctively to the greater threat. "You were there. Now you're here. No one can move that fast."

Henry kept his smile just to the safe side of dangerous. "Obviously, since I did, someone can. I'm very fit." Feeling the pressure against his grip ease, he let his fingers slide off CB's heated skin. Holding Constable Elson's suspicious gaze, his eyes darkened. "I suspect what happened to Mr. Brummell was a result of weather. We've had a fair bit of lightning and old houses like this can acquire quite the buildup of static electricity."

"Static electricity?" The suspicion began to fade slightly. "Yeah, I guess that could . . ."

"What a load." Danvers' attention flicked from CB to Henry and back to CB again. "I'm thinking that either one of these cables you guys are running in from your truck here isn't properly grounded and you've created a hazardous environment—in direct violation of any number of workplace safety regulations—and that's what's screwed up the doors, or the house is haunted, has grabbed your people . . ." One slim finger jabbed toward a broad chest. ". . . including your daughters—who we saw entering the house this afternoon—which is why you've lost your vaunted cool, and that red flash was the house keeping you—all of you—the hell out. Were you not listening when I said we've done the research? Why don't you tell us what's really going on?"

"Vaunted cool?" Elson muttered.

"Not now, Jack."

"I think you're confused, Constable Danvers." CB's voice had returned to its usual masterful tones. "My studio is shooting a haunted house episode in this building. The house, therefore, is haunted because I choose it to be."

"Uh-huh." She rocked back on her heels, eyes narrowed. "And the murder/suicides?"

"Not in this episode."

"Not in *any* episode." Emphasis dared him to deny he knew about the incident she referred to.

"Ah. You're referring to the unfortunate deaths of Mrs. Kranby and her infant son?"

"And the others. In the thirties, a number of people were killed during a dance. During her time in the house, Mrs. Kranby heard dance music. In the fifties, Christopher Mills killed his two children and himself with an ax. Mrs. Kranby was terrified of a man with an ax that no one else ever saw."

"So you're saying that during her postpartum depression, Mrs. Kranby thought the house was haunted because of its unfortunate past?"

"No, that's not what she's saying." Elson, who'd been staring at his partner in disbelief, moved to stand beside her, shoulder to shoulder. "She's saying we're going to stick around until those doors open."

"Hauntings aren't against the law," Graham pointed out, folding his arms and moving up the path to fall in at Henry's right.

"No one said they were. But, since we're here and since it's our job to know what the hell is going on, I think we'll stay."

"You're wasting your time."

"It's our time." Eyes narrowed, Elson's expression dared all three men to try and run them off. When no one took the dare, he flashed them a triumphant grin. "Now, if you don't mind, just so we're dotting the i's and crossing the t's, I'm going to go try to open that door."

"You saw what happened to Mr. Brummell."

"I did."

CB stepped out of the way. "Then be my guest."

Graham tried and failed to hide a smirk as the pair of RCMP constables walked past.

A moment later, he tried and failed to hide a snicker

as light flared red and Constable Elson swore, stumbled back, sat, and squashed an overgrown plant by the side of the path.

"Didn't go far," he murmured as Henry moved up beside him.

"I suspect that paranormal ability affects the amount of force used—got a lot, go far. None at all . . ." He nodded at the constable. ". . . don't."

"Yeah, but CB made some distance when he got zapped earlier."

"CB is a law unto himself."

Graham glanced back at the producer still standing by the end of the path somehow managing to dominate a scene that involved a haunted house, a shocked police officer, a medium, and a vampire and nodded. "I hear you. Satisfied?" he asked as the two constables passed again going the other way.

Elson glared at him but turned a less readable expression on Henry. "Static electricity, eh?"

"It's an explanation."

"Not a good one." He took Constable Danvers' arm and headed for the driveway. "We'll be waiting over here if you need us for . . . anything."

"Go ahead. Say it. Tell me I've lost my mind."

Rubbing the back of his neck in the hope of getting the hair to lie down, Jack stared up at the dark silhouette of the house. "I wish I could."

Geetha ignored the house and watched him. "You're glad I said it because you couldn't."

"Not glad." His mouth twisted into and out of half a smile. "I *know* there's something going on with these people. There was something going on last spring and there's something going on now. Something that isn't . . ." His hands sketched words in the air.

"Normal?"

"Close enough. And, although I'd rather you'd spoken to me before you info dumped on them, I'll hold my opinion on your mental state—and my own—until after those doors open." Folding his arms, Jack nodded toward the cluster of men on the front path. "Or until they tell us what's really going on."

"Is that why we're over here? So they can talk among themselves?"

They were close enough to the edge of the light she could see the glint of a pale eyebrow rising. "Yeah. That's one of the reasons."

And he wanted her away from them before she said anything else that might make it look like RCMP Constable Jack Elson believed in something other than crime and punishment, but she was too tired to take the bait. "The greasy one's right, though. If the house *is* haunted, that's not a crime."

"Granted."

"So why are we here?"

"We? Why are *you* here?"

"Because you are."

"Right." He rubbed the hand that had been in contact with the house against his sleeve. "I like to . . . I mean, I need to . . . We're supposed to . . ."

"Know?"

"I'm betting that Tony Foster is in the thick of it."

"Of what, Jack?"

"Yeah, that's the question." He sighed, unfolded his arms, and folded them again the other way. "I hate it when I know there's *something* and I don't know what it is."

She turned and stared at the three silhouettes on the path. "Bet you we could find something if we ran Graham Brummel."

"Sucker bet."

♥

"A few misdemeanors, that's all. Nothing big. Oh, and a fraud charge down in Seattle that got tossed." Graham exhaled loudly. "Never take financial tips from a dead guy." A quick glance at Henry. "No offense."

"As, technically, I'm not dead; none taken."

"What? You're not dead? I thought you guys, you know . . ." He stuck out his tongue and let his head fall to one side. Before Henry could respond to an image unlike that of any unanimated death he'd ever seen, Graham jerked his head upright and said, "Wait, I should've tried this before. I just look at you on the spirit level . . ." His eyes unfocused. "Holy shit." Skin blanched gray, he snapped back to the here and now. "You're . . ."

Henry smiled.

"Mr. Fitzroy is not our problem," CB growled. Graham started at the sound and stuffed trembling hands deep into his overall pockets. "Our two overly diligent police officers are." His attention landed on Henry. "Can you take their memories?"

"Wipe them out like Arra did?" Henry shook his head. "No. Even . . ." He shot a glance at the caretaker. ". . . fucked up as I am, I could make them forget me, but they'd remember terror and darkness and the night and given that they're police officers and trained to both notice and investigate things like that and because they're already looking beyond the obvious—which is rare even for the police—I can't guarantee it would hold. Unless I took them both to bed—which I suspect would cause Constable Elson more trouble than anything else he might discover."

"Together or separately?"

A slow pivot on one heel. "Pardon?"

Graham shrugged, clearly wishing he'd kept his mouth shut and just as clearly unable to stop himself. "Would you take them to bed . . . you know, together or separately."

"Now, I'm offended."

"Sorry."

"When that door opens," CB said pointedly, "there

will be at least one body, maybe more. There will be an investigation. Can Tony use Arra's information to erase the memories of the people inside the house?"

"I very much doubt it." Since, as far as Henry knew, Tony's one sure spell involved retrieving snack food without rising from the couch, erasing multiple memories would very likely be beyond him.

"So they'll know about his abilities and during the investigation . . ."

Henry nodded. "It'll come up. Especially if it's his abilities that get them out of the house."

"He'll either be the next amazing fucking Kreskin," Graham sighed, "and his life'll be hell, or he'll be stuffed in a loony bin. Trust me on this," he added when Henry and CB turned, frowning. "The world's not kind to the psychically abled. They tend to read the psychic as psycho, if you know what I mean."

"Unfortunately, yes."

"Fortunately, yes," Henry corrected deliberately. "I think we're looking at this the wrong way." He waved the other two quiet and began to build the ending as though he were building the final chapter in one of his books. "When the doors open—at sunrise, if not before—your people will come out of the house claiming it's haunted. That they saw ghosts. That they were under an attack by a malevolent thing in the basement. They won't be able to prove any of it, though, and the general public will think they're nuts. And given that they're television people, they won't get the benefit of the doubt. Everyone knows television people are slightly crazy."

"Is this true?" CB wondered.

Graham nodded. "Common knowledge around Hollywood North, that's for damned sure."

"Now then, put hallucinating television people in a house with a history of gas leaks and what do you have?"

"Probable cause of crazy. What?" Graham demanded as eyebrows raised. "I watch a lot of *Law and Order*."

"Who doesn't?" CB wearily asked the night. "Suppose my people say nothing at all about hauntings or ghosts or things in the basement? Suppose they collectively agree on a more plausible story?"

"It won't matter; even if they could agree on a story— and most groups that size can't agree on where to have lunch—there's no way they'll all be able to maintain it throughout a police investigation."

"The truth will out?"

"And not be believed."

His next question was less rhetorical. "Did we not use a gas leak to explain what happened at the studio last spring?"

"There's a reason it's a classic," Henry reminded him. "And I'm guessing—given that the police know the other deaths in this house were murder/suicides—that the actual cause of your wardrobe assistant's death will be obvious. People were trapped in a house. They all went a little crazy. Someone went a lot crazy and killed someone else."

"And that someone is probably dead, too," Graham added. "If the house stays to the same MO."

"So the actual crime committed becomes an open and shut case. Why did they go crazy?" Henry spread his hands. "Not our problem. What exactly caused the doors to jam shut? Also not our problem. One of the people trapped did amazing magical things? But we've already established that they all went a little crazy, so no one can be considered a reliable witness."

"But these two . . ." Graham nodded toward the driveway. ". . . think something is up."

"And it's one thing to tell us what they think is going on and another thing entirely to put it in an official document. They're not stupid, they've proven that already. If they find out what actually happened, who can they tell? Not only is there no empirical proof, there's no way to get it."

"Whoa. What about you? You're walking, talking, empirical proof, eh?"

"They don't know about me."

Graham snorted. "You're standing right there." As Henry's eyes darkened again, he backed up a step. "Oh. Right. They don't *know* about you. And no one who does is going to say anything. Not a word. Lips are sealed. Hey, I talk to the dead; who am I to point fingers, right?"

"Right." The masks were back in place. The smile held only the faintest hint of warning. "Given that there's been a death, the sooner the police are involved, the better our people . . ." CB's people except for Tony. ". . . your people . . . look. And given that these particular police are already somewhat sympathetic to the situation . . ."

"Sympathetic?" CB growled.

"To the situation," Henry repeated. "And if they do mention anything about hauntings, well, there's no faster way for anything else they say to lose credibility with the powers that be." A quick glance at the house. "The judicial powers that be."

"Yeah and what about the press?" Graham demanded. "Friggin' tabloids'll be all over something like this."

Henry glanced up at CB, one eyebrow cocked.

After a moment, CB smiled. "Of course. Given the right slant, this may even provide *Darkest Night* with a bonanza of free publicity. May even jump our ratings. If there's a chance that ghosts are real, why not vampires?"

"You might want to go easy with that."

"Of course."

Seventeen

TONY REGAINED consciousness slowly, pulled out of a comforting darkness by the suspicion that while he was gone, people had been sticking red hot needles into the left side of his body. When he forced his eyes open, Brianna's face swam into focus.

"He's awake!" she yelled without turning her head.

Amy's face appeared almost immediately behind her. "You okay?"

"Maybe. You?"

"I didn't even go out." She sounded disappointed. "I just got woozy. Define maybe."

"Define okay."

"Not about to kick it."

Fair enough. "Not sure," he told her in turn. "Help me sit up."

Relying on Amy and Brianna's help, he ended up slumped against familiar lower cabinets. Still in the butler's pantry, then. Not good. Expressions on the half circle of faces staring down at him seemed to support that conclusion.

"The doors are still locked." The voice of doom from above.

He blinked up at Peter. "It didn't work?"

"Worked," Mouse told him before Peter could say anything more. "Caulfield's rotting. The wall's clean. Cleaner," he amended, clearly remembering he was speaking of a fieldstone foundation.

Peter's lips were thin, white lines. "But the doors are still locked."

"Okay." Tony managed to raise his right hand. "Let me think about this. Caulfield's gone . . ."

Mouse shot a hard look at Peter and nodded.

". . . the symbols that held the accumulated power to that specific spot on the basement wall are gone . . . Lee!"

"Lee's fine," Zev told him, handing him a bottle of water. "All right, he's not exactly fine, but he's back. He's himself. Tina and Mason and Ashley are . . . dealing with him."

Comforting. Zev had been going to say comforting, but changed it to dealing at the last moment. Tony could see another pair of legs in dark trousers tucked in behind Mason, but he couldn't see Lee. He wasn't sure he wanted to see Lee as long as he knew Lee was fine. Back. Himself.

"Lee is not your concern," Peter interrupted his train of thought, looking thoroughly pissed. "Your job is to figure out why the hell the doors are still locked!"

"Right." He could do that. It would keep him from thinking about Lee. Stalling for time while he got things straight in his head, he took a swallow of water and almost spat it out. Zev had dumped sugar into it. "Okay," he muttered, shooting his ex a *thanks for the warning* glare. "The power was cohesive down there for a long time. Maybe it stayed together even without the symbols—maybe it chose to stay together. It was definitely a separate thing from Caulfield, so maybe it had a kind of consciousness. It could go wandering off through the city, but it's choosing to stay as a part of this house."

"Why?"

The lights came up. The band played "Night and Day." In the ballroom, the dead danced.

"Because the house is feeding it," Tony sighed, knowing that although they couldn't see him, they could still hear him. "The ghosts are still trapped."

♠

"If it's not trying to add us to the collection anymore, then we just sit tight and wait it out." Peter glared at Mason and Mouse who did their best to look sane. Kate glared back. "It can't be that long until sunrise."

"Probably not." Not knowing was making Tony a little edgy. Edgier. Was Henry still outside?

"They're not our responsibility; they've been dead for years."

It took Tony a moment to realize just who *they* were and switch back over to the problems inside the house. After four-hundred-and-fifty-odd years—some of these later ones, very odd—Henry knew enough to get out of the sun. "Brenda and Hartley and Tom are trapped, too."

"You know, we only have your word for that."

"And mine." Brianna folded her arms, every line of her body daring Peter to argue. "I danced with her."

"Fine." He sighed impatiently. "Brenda, Hartley, and Tom are trapped, too."

"And Karl's still crying. I can hear him."

As Brianna pressed up against Tony's side, he felt something crumple in his pocket. The photograph of Karl and his mother. "I can hear him, too." He pulled the photo out and handed it to Amy. Multiple dunkings in icy water hadn't improved its condition any, but it was still painfully obvious who it . . . they were.

"So we have to free the ghosts." Amy left the *duh* silent but obvious as she passed the picture to Peter.

He studied it for a moment, looked up, realized everyone was waiting on his word, and sighed again.

"Fine. We free the ghosts." His gaze locked on Tony's. "What do we do?"

"I don't know."

"You don't know?" Peter repeated and threw up his hands. "Great. Does *anyone* know?"

No one seemed to.

Tony glanced down at the top of Brianna's head, and frowned. "According to the journal, Caulfield used his son, Richard, to connect with the power and Richard is haunting the master suite bathroom."

"Are you going somewhere with this, Tony," Amy asked, peering into his face, "or are you just reiterating random bits of information?"

"He doesn't replay. All the other ghosts replay," he continued as the expressions he could see ranged the short distance from puzzled to confused. "Even Stephen and Cassie keep getting sucked back into the loop of their death although they're aware the rest of the time. Richard doesn't. And he's always there. Even Mason was aware of him."

"Hey." The qualifier got the actor's attention. "What do you mean, *even* Mason?"

"He means you're generally considered too smart to get mixed up in any supernatural nonsense," Peter interjected smoothly.

"Oh."

Amy reached out and poked him in the leg. "Get to the point, Tony."

"Richard Caulfield is the key."

A moment of contemplative silence.

Then Adam asked what they were all wondering. "The key to what?"

"To freeing the ghosts, starving the thing, and getting us the hell out of Dodge."

Peter took the photograph from Amy. The way he was staring at it made Tony realize he probably had kids of his own. For a long moment, the distant sobs of a dead baby were the only sounds in the butler's pantry. Finally, Peter shoved the photograph into Tony's hand and jerked his head toward the door. "So, what are you waiting for? Go turn your key."

Right. Because, of course, it was his job to be the hero. They'd already established that. His left hand and everything attached to it was pretty much unusable with only minimal movement in the fingers *and* his entire arm felt as though someone had peeled all the skin off before seasoning it liberally with chopped jalapeños, but, wizard or not, he was just a PA and crap jobs landed like sediment down there at the bottom of the totem pole. Standing hurt. Hell, breathing hurt. He was working his way up to feeling really remarkably sorry for himself when a high-pitched voice slammed the door on his pity party.

"I'm coming with you."

"Bri."

She looked up at him and said very slowly and very pointedly, "He's not scared of *me*."

But he'd been terrified of his father and Tony was a man. Younger, thinner, and with more piercings, but still . . .

"Okay. Sure." He expected Tina to protest, but she was still too busy mothering Lee to even notice. "Can you carry the lantern?"

"She can, but she probably shouldn't." Zev picked the lantern up off the counter just before Brianna's hand connected. "I'll come along, too."

"So will I."

"No." Peter physically put himself in Amy's path. "Caulfield might be gone, but this house remains dangerous. The fewer people we have wandering around, the better."

Amy jabbed a finger toward Brianna. "No fair! She's the boss' daughter and you're letting her wander around!" Her mouth closed with a sudden snap. "That sounded about six, didn't it?"

Tony and Zev nodded in unison.

"Brianna's going because the boy isn't afraid of her. Tony's going because this is his show . . ."

·Oh. Well, that sounded significantly better than *Tony's going because we don't want to endanger anyone more significant.*

Stop being such a whiny ass, he told himself.

But my arm hurts.

Deal with it. You're still the only one who can do this.

". . . and Zev's going because Tony looks like shit and I'm not sure he can make it up the stairs without help," Peter continued. "You . . ." He jabbed a finger toward Amy. ". . . are not going. We're all going to sit here and stay out of Tony's way. The last thing he needs on his plate right now is another rescue."

Shoulders slumped, Amy shoved her hands into her pants pockets. "Fine. Whatever."

"So, go!" Peter waved at the door and Tony, who'd been staring at him in astonishment, shuffled forward, feeling good about being appreciated. Feeling good being a relative term and nothing twelve hours of sleep and a kilo of painkillers couldn't fix.

Cassie and Stephen were waiting in the dining room, held out of the butler's pantry by the line of lipstick symbols on the floor. As Zev pulled the door closed, they rushed forward looking . . . looking as happy as Tony'd ever seen dead people look. Well, except for Henry who was really more undead than dead.

"It worked!" Stephen spun around them faster than mortally possible. "I wrote half and Cassie wrote half. We put it up between his shoulders and it worked!"

Tony hid a smile. Stephen sounded as though the plan had been his idea from the start. *Teenagers.* He thanked them after he explained to Zev and Brianna that they were there. No more talking to empty air. "You saved Lee. I'm sure of it."

"No problem. And the thing is gone. There's a whole different feeling in the house now. Different even from when it was asleep. It's still ... I mean there's still *something,* but it isn't aware anymore. We're more aware than it is. And we're still us." He took hold of his sister's hands and spun her around. Stopped, settled his head, and grinned. At her. As though she was the only person in his world—which, technically, Tony supposed she was. "We're still here. Together. Only the bad stuff has changed. And you look awful."

"Yeah. You should see it from this side."

Cassie seemed happy, laughed with her brother, allowed him to spin her around, but, for the first time, seemed the more reserved of the two.

"You're still replaying," Tony reminded him as they left the dining room.

"True. But we're used to that." Stephen dismissed his reoccurring death with a jaunty smack on his sister's ass. She shot him a look Tony couldn't translate. "Once you're gone and there's no people in the house, it'll happen less and less and then what remains of the thing will probably go to sleep again and we'll be left alone. Not completely alone, because Graham will be here, but left alone. No one bothering us."

"You don't mind being dead?"

"Hey, I guess I'm used to that, too."

"Where are you three going?" Cassie asked as they reached the stairs. And the way she asked told Tony why she hadn't joined her brother's slightly manic celebration. She knew it wasn't over.

"To talk to Creighton Caulfield's son. Cassie wants to know where we're going," he explained to Zev, grabbing the back of Brianna's pinafore with his good hand. "We're staying together," he told her as she glared up at him. "That means no running off."

"So walk faster!"

The ghosts floated backward in front of them, up the stairs.

Stephen snorted. "Why do you want to talk to Richard? He's not exactly a sparkling conversationalist."

"Creighton Caulfield was a part of the thing in the basement." Tony's arm hurt all the way down to his legs. Both legs. And his feet. And all ten toes. "Caulfield's dead."

"Yeah, we know. We helped, remember. So you're what, off to offer Richard your condolences?"

The stairs were killing him. "No."

"Then why?" Stephen demanded, impatient with anything getting in the way of his good mood.

Cassie smoothed down her skirt, her fingers carefully arranging each gather. "He's why we're here." She seemed to be confirming something she'd known for a while even if she'd only just realized she'd known it.

One hand holding his head in place, Stephen spun around toward her. "What are you talking about?"

"Creighton Caulfield's son, Richard, is why we're still here. They . . ." A chill breeze as she gestured. ". . . are going to talk to him about us—about all of us— moving on."

"NO!"

Tony froze. Zev and Brianna went up one more step, half turned, and stopped as well. They might have started back toward him, Tony wasn't sure. His eyes were locked on the ghost. "Stephen . . ."

"We helped you!"

It was like the scene in Scrooge's rooms in *A Christmas Carol* when Marley's ghost shrieked, and suddenly the slightly comical dead guy looked a lot more dangerous.

"We risked everything to help you and now you're doing this? I knew it! You're trying to destroy us!" Hands outstretched, fingers crooking into translucent claws, Stephen dove toward him.

Tony didn't know if he was going for his throat or about to drive his hands into his chest and squeeze his heart—both classic ghost-goes-in-for-the-kill possibilities— but he did discover that under the right conditions—

like, oh, threat of imminent death by severely pissed ghost—his left arm moved. Hurt like hell, but it moved. He smacked his branded palm into the side of Stephen's head, flinging him across the entrance hall. Tried to blink away the fireworks exploding inside his own skull, then positioned himself in front of the other two as Stephen came shrieking back.

Cassie was there first.

"It's over," she said softly. "We had each other for so much longer than we should have, but it's over."

"NO!" When he tried to go around, she blocked him again.

She glanced back at Tony over her shoulder, her face at such an angle that she looked whole and beautiful. "Go on. I won't let him stop you."

"What's happening?" Brianna demanded.

"Stephen's pissed. Cassie's keeping him from hurting us." Tony grabbed Brianna's free hand and motioned for Zev to start moving again. "We have to get there before the next replay," he explained as they half dragged her up the stairs between them. "The sooner we finish this the better."

"But it's you and me against everyone else!" Stephen's protests followed them up to the second floor—lost, disbelieving, and painfully young. "You and me, Cass! It *can't* be over! We did what he wanted! Why is he doing this to us?"

"He's doing this for us. It's time to move on to someplace better."

"You don't know what you're talking about! Get out of my way, I have to stop . . ."

As the door to Mason's dressing room closed and cut off the argument, Tony hoped Cassie was right. He could be sending them to hell for all he knew. Did he have the right to choose for them?

"They chose when they agreed to help in the basement," Zev said quietly. "They decided to risk moving on no matter what might happen to them."

"How did you . . ."

He smiled and shook his head. "When you feel something strongly—like, say, guilt—it's all over your face."

Brianna nodded agreement.

"Not just when I'm thinking about Lee?"

"All the time."

"Well, that's . . . embarrassing."

Zev nodded. "Most of the time, yeah. Come on." He held the lantern up and led the way to the bathroom, pausing on the threshold to let Brianna push past.

Tony stopped beside him and peered into the small room. "Where is he?" He squinted along the line of Brianna's pointing finger. There was something . . . something too big for the space between the toilet and the corner shower unit. A shape. A shadow. No. Gone.

"You really can't see him?" Zev murmured.

"I really can't." Then, "Can you see him?"

"No. It's just that Brianna can and you can see everything else, so . . ." The music director shrugged. "Seems strange."

"As compared to what?"

"Good point."

He could hear a snuffling sound, but he couldn't see . . .

"Stop seeing the bathroom."

"What?"

Squatting by the shower in the boneless way of small children and elderly Asian men, Brianna rolled her eyes. "Stop seeing the bathroom," she repeated.

He took a step into the room. "How do I do that?"

The look she shot him suggested he was stupider than she'd ever suspected. "Pretend it's not there."

Right. Sure. He could play let's pretend. Let's pretend he didn't still wake up aching for the feel of teeth meeting through his skin. Let's pretend Lee had kissed him in the butler's pantry because he'd wanted to, not because of some weird mix of guilt and being possessed. Let's pretend that the something between the toilet and the tub had plenty of room because neither toilet nor tub were there.

Actually, he sucked at let's pretend.

"Tony?"

And he didn't want to know what was showing on his face. A raised hand to answer Zev's question and another step into the room. No toilet. No shower. Focus on the something between them. Just the something.

He might suck at let's pretend, but he aced obsession.

Brianna was talking to Caulfield's son, so Caulfield's son was obviously there . . .

. . . sitting on the floor, leaning against the side of a big old wardrobe that filled the corner where the shower . . .

The scene wavered.

. . . that filled the far corner of the dingy room. The walls were gray, the floor some kind of early industrial tile, and if he'd had a cigarette, the smell would have reminded him of nights spent crouched in doorways on the Yonge Street strip. Hard to forget the smell of old urine walked on by expensive shoes.

Blond, blue-eyed, and somewhere between twelve and twenty, Richard Caulfield had Down's syndrome. Tony was no expert, but he'd known people with Down's syndrome and this didn't look like it was that severe a case. Certainly not lock-the-kid-in-a-room severe. Still, in a hundred years he supposed the definition of severe changed and, not to forget, he'd already determined that Creighton Caulfield was bugfuck. Evil and bugfuck.

Bare feet peeking out from under a white-and-blue-striped nightshirt, Richard hugged his knees, rocked, and cried. Every now and then, he wiped his nose on the fabric stretched over his knees. That explained the snuffling sound.

Brianna, crouched in front of him, was telling him about what had been happening down in the butler's pantry. ". . . and like Ashes keeps falling asleep because she's a total loser until Mason, he's the actor I told you about, he stopped being a spaz and they untied him and then she was all over him again and the real creepy bit is that he seems to like it now."

Ashley's adoration would act like an anchor, redefining Mason's unpossessed self. Mouse had his viewfinder. Mason had a fan. Kate had her temper. And Lee, who'd been through so much more, Lee probably had a whole lot of therapy to look forward to.

"Get down." Brianna's voice cut through his reflections. "You're too tall and you scare him."

So Tony crouched. "Hey, Richard."

Richard tried to push back farther into the space.

"It's okay." He held out his hand, expecting Richard to cringe away, not expecting a grab that flipped stubby fingers through his with no contact. The wail of despair brought tears to his own eyes.

"What's wrong?" Brianna demanded.

Tony wasn't sure if she was asking him or Richard, but he answered anyway. "He's lonely. He's been alone up here for a long time." Resting one knee on the floor, he glanced down at the throbbing pattern on his left palm, cupped his left elbow with his right hand, and lifted. The fingers of his left hand brushed the warm, damp skin of Richard's cheek, trailed down, and were suddenly clutched so tightly that he literally saw stars.

"Easy," he gasped. Richard seemed to understand. The pressure eased off a bit. Most of the stars faded. "Good. Thank you."

"Ank ou."

"Hey, you can talk!"

"Risherd Cawfud."

"That's your name!" Brianna punched Tony. "That's his name!"

"No hit!"

To Tony's surprise she looked abashed at Richard's protest. "Sorry."

"S'okay. Richard . . ."

"Risherd Cawfud."

"Right. Richard . . ."

"Risherd Cawfud."

Okay. Rewrite and try again. "You don't need to be afraid anymore."

New tears. And a tighter grip.

"OW!"

Richard cringed back but continued to cling to Tony's hand. "Shurry. Shurry! No hit!"

Brianna understood immediately. "Tony's not going to hit you!" Her voice lowered to a near growl, and Tony was, once again, reminded of her father. "No one is ever going to hit you again!"

And like her father, it was impossible not to believe her.

"Not hit?"

"Never again! Tony . . ."

"No hit," Tony agreed as reassuringly as the pain allowed. "Come on." He started to stand and thanked any gods that might be listening when Richard scrambled up onto his feet with him. "It's time to go."

"Go where?" Brianna asked as Richard wiped his nose on the back of Tony's hand and stared trustingly at them both.

Good question.

Where did the dead go? Questions of religion aside.

A snail trail of snot glistened on the back of Tony's hand.

Glistened.

I'm an idiot.

Where did the dead always go?

"Go into the light."

"Cliché much," Brianna muttered.

Richard looked worried. "No leave room."

"You don't have to." When Tony smiled, Richard smiled with him. "All you have to do is walk into the light. It's right here. It's been here all along." He stepped closer to Brianna so that Richard could look past him.

His eyes widened and his smile with it. "Light."

"Yeah."

The one thing all the replays had in common was light. He'd thought, while it was happening, that it was just the difference between the small circle of light thrown by the lantern or the candles or his monitor and the gas or electric lights of the past. In his own defense, while it was happening, he'd had other things on his mind. But the light had been exactly the same for all the replays. Richard didn't replay, but the light was exactly the same in his room.

Wiping his nose one more time, Richard shuffled forward. Tony moved with him, teeth clenched, trying not to scream as the movement pulled his arm out away from his body. As he turned, pivoting to follow, the light grew until there was only light and Richard Caulfield silhouetted in front of it.

It was like the world's cheesiest special effect. All it needed was that Czechoslovakian women's choir that seemed to be wailing in harmony on every soundtrack recorded in the last twenty years.

The extended dance version of "Night and Day" just didn't have the same effect.

Tony could only see Richard, but he could feel the crowd passing by. As they brushed against his injured arm, falling to his knees and screaming was starting to feel more and more like a good idea. Richard held him in place.

There might have been voices and some of the touching might have gotten a bit personal, but he couldn't be sure over the distraction of his arm.

Distraction.

Yeah. When distraction meant constant bone-grinding, blood-boiling agony. He wanted to snatch his hand away, but he couldn't. After so many years alone in this room, it had to be Richard's choice.

The outside edges of the light started to close in. A gentle tug.

"Come with."

"I can't." A harder tug that should have hurt more than it did. "It's all right. You won't be alone. You won't ever be alone again unless you want to be. But you have to go into the light."

"Risherd Cawfud."

Tony managed a smile. "I'll remember."

The band stopped playing and the light condensed into a brilliant globe that lingered for a moment with the touch of Richard's fingers against Tony's palm.

Then it was gone.

♠

"Do you see that?"

"See what?" CB asked as the two RCMP constables rejoined them on the path.

"The um . . ." Elson gestured with one hand and then stopped, fully aware that no one—not the three guys they'd joined, nor the three people who'd just come out of one of the trucks, nor his partner, nor, hell, himself— was looking at anything other than the brilliant white light rising up from the house. "The that."

"Yes, Constable, we see it."

"Okay. Good. What is it?"

"If pressed, I'd have to say it's a shocking absence of originality."

Something hummed.

Something sparked.

And the lights came on.

♠

They were standing in the bathroom of the master suite. The light over the sink was on.

"What the hell just happened?" Zev demanded. "Are you two all right?"

Tony glanced at Brianna who shrugged. "Yeah, we're fine." And then added, surprised. "Really." His left arm no longer hurt. The symbol was still there on his palm, etched into his skin like a scar, but everything worked. Muscles, ligaments, bones, joints, those stringy things that attached stuff . . . tendons, that was it. Everything. No pain. The absence left him a little light-headed.

Light-headed.

The light.

It had to have been the light. Or some kind of freaky coincidence, but Tony preferred to think he'd sent Cassie and Stephen and Richard and Tom and Hartley and, hell, even Brenda to a place where good things happened.

They could hear shouting downstairs.

"We should join the rest of them." Zev gestured with the lantern. Brianna took his other hand and led the way out to the hall.

As Zev flicked the hall light on, Tony paused.

He could hear . . .

"You guys go on, I'll be down in a minute."

"I don't think . . ."

Then they all heard: "Ashley! Brianna!"

"DADDY!"

Zev shook his head as Brianna yanked her hands free and raced for the stairs. "I should go with her, so he knows we weren't letting her wander around alone."

"Go on. I'll be fine." Tony could see that the other man didn't entirely believe him—or more specifically didn't believe him at all but decided to give him the benefit of the doubt. He watched until Zev disappeared down the stairs then turned and headed the other way.

Paused at the door to the bathroom, flicked on the light, glanced in. White walls. A scuff on the floor from where the camera had been set up. Not where the noise was coming from. He left the light on.

At the door to the back stairs, he recognized the sound.

Er er. Er er.

When he opened the door, Lucy Lewis was sitting on the lowest step leading to the third floor, the noose around her neck, the end of the rope—the rope he'd cut with the ax he couldn't see—hanging against the upper bib of her apron.

He frowned. Thought about it for a moment. "You died before Richard did."

She nodded, toying with the end of her rope.

The light levels hadn't been the same in all the replays. They'd always been different at the back stairs. Not as bright. "You weren't under the control of the thing when you pushed that guy, were you?"

"No." Her voice sounded a little better now the pressure on her throat had been relieved. More like the engine on an old truck and less like a working cement mixer. "He said he loved me and then he met this girl from town . . ."

Oldest story in the book. "You gave the thing the murder/suicide template. Two dead for the price of one."

She shrugged.

A glance down the back stairs showed nothing but a patch of kitchen floor. And a black cat. "So *he's* gone?"

A nod and an adjustment that reminded him of Stephen. They'd barely been gone for ten minutes and he was missing them already. And they *had* gone into the light with the rest. Of course they had. They hadn't been responsible for what they'd done that last afternoon of their lives and if they were, well, they'd certainly paid. He asked, but Lucy shrugged.

"Not part of my story."

Yeah. That was helpful. "Okay, your story's still . . . uh . . . in progress because . . . ?"

Her hand closed around the dangling rope. "I need to make amends."

"You saved my ass. I don't think I'd have made it to the basement if you hadn't come in and diverted the pain. And if I hadn't made it to the basement, we'd all still be stuck here. That's amends where I come from."

"You're not enough."

"Way to pander to the old ego."

"What?"

"Never mind. You think God . . ."

"Not God. Me. *I* need to make amends."

Ah. That was different.

She waved the cut end of the rope at him. "This will help, thank you. I can do much more now than if I was just hanging around."

Joke? He wasn't sure. She looked perfectly serious. "If the rope's cut, how come I can still hear it creaking?"

"The house remembers."

Before he could decide if that was something he should seriously freak out about, the stairs were empty. "So, um, maybe I'll see you again?"

"You know where to find me."

Fair enough.

The night caught up to him as he started down the stairs. By the time he staggered past the cat, events were sitting on his shoulders and bouncing, trying to drive him to his knees. He grabbed the edge of the kitchen table. Heard shouting. May have heard his name although his ears didn't seem to be working properly. Or they weren't connecting to his brain properly. There seemed to be a lot of high-pitched howling going on. He stumbled toward the back door. It was open about four inches to allow the bundles of cable access to the house.

"Ha!" he said to no one in particular as he grabbed the edge and yanked it open.

A step out into fresh air.

Another step.

More voices.

Another step and he was falling.

Either I'm walking crooked or the porch is.

Funny thing, he didn't hit the ground.

"I've got you."

Not the voice he was expecting. He blinked and, like he was suddenly Samantha Stevens and that whole blinking thing actually meant something, the world came rushing back. The man holding him was blonder than Henry. Bigger, too. Smelled like stale pizza and . . . law enforcement.

"Constable Elson."

"So you can talk."

"For years now." He was oddly comfortable cradled across the lap of an RCMP officer. *Not going to think about* that *too hard.*

"You know, since I busted my butt to keep you from landing chin first in gravel, you think you could lay off the smart-ass for a minute?"

Seemed fair. "Sure."

"What the hell happened here?"

Best to stick to the basics. "The doors wouldn't open."

"That door *was* open."

Tony turned his head just far enough to see the cables running up over the porch and into the kitchen. Then he turned it back. Jack Elson had very blue eyes and they were locked on his. Not at all hard to tell what he wanted. "You want the truth." Given his current state of exhaustion, Tony found it impossible to stop his lips from twitching.

"Do *not* tell me I can't handle the truth!" Elson snapped.

Fortunately, he didn't have the energy to laugh for long. Even more fortunate that he didn't have the energy for hysterics because he sure as hell was due. He half expected the constable to dump him onto the driveway but he didn't. Finally he managed a long, shuddering breath, and said, "*I* can't handle the truth right now. Can I tell you later?"

The blue eyes narrowed and examined his face.

Tony tried to look trustworthy but gave it up after a second or two as a lost cause.

"That depends on when later is."

"Not now?"

After a long moment, narrow lips curved, pale stubble glinting in the porch light.

Something growled.

No. Tony knew that sound. Some*one* growled. "Henry."

"Your partner is calling for you, Constable Elson."

A familiar pale hand reached down, took hold of Tony, and lifted him to his feet. Then the arm attached to the hand went around his waist and effortlessly kept him standing. Constable Elson rose under his own power, eyes locked on Henry's face. Given his reaction, Tony could tell without looking that Henry had the Prince of Man thing going full blast and would, in a heartbeat or two, slide into Prince of Darkness. Not a good idea. Not tonight. Not here. Not now. He just wasn't up to it. So he said, "Call me. You have my number."

A long look, and a nod, and Elson trotted off to where Constable Danvers was directing a crowd of police and EMTs. Ah. Not howling. Sirens.

Glad to have that explained, he turned in Henry's grip. "So you're still here."

"Obviously."

"It must be nearly dawn."

"Nearly. I have forty minutes."

Tony actually felt his heart lurch. "You can't . . ."

"It's all right. I'll wrap up in the blackout curtain in my trunk."

"In your trunk?"

"It's a big trunk, it's lightproof, and once I'm in it, it can only be opened from the inside. I've made some modifications."

"You were prepared for this?" Relief made his knees weak. Well, relief on top of everything else.

"This? Not likely. But I was prepared." Henry pulled his keys out of his pocket and offered them discreetly on his palm. "Can you drive me back to the condo's garage?"

"Sure."

"Think about it for a moment, Tony. Can you?"

If he didn't . . . "Of course I can."

"You look terrible."

That didn't exactly come as a surprise. "You look kind of off peak yourself."

"It was an interesting night."

His tone suggested Tony let it go. Reluctantly, Tony did.

The keys were cool and heavier than they looked. Which reminded him. He moved so that Henry's body blocked him from the milling crowds out front and he stretched out his left hand toward the house. Caulfield's journal slapped against the pattern on his palm.

"Impressive."

"Thanks." He hadn't doubted for a moment he'd be able to do it. Had known where the journal was, touched the shape of its power, and had called it to him. It hadn't even hurt. Much. He'd come a long way in a short time from bagels and honey. "You need to take charge of this. I don't trust anyone else with it."

Henry's lip curled at the touch of the leather. "It feels familiar."

"I think Caulfield found what was intended to be another grimoire like the one you have, but it hadn't been written in yet, so he made it his own." He frowned at Henry's expression. "I think!"

The expression changed; quickly enough that Tony knew he'd called it close to right. "Of course you do. I have to go."

"I know."

"You're all right?"

"I'm fine."

The hug drove the breath out of his lungs and gave him some indication of how much Henry had worried. Then he was gone, moving up the driveway in such a way that it was hard to watch him. Even with practice. Another man would have seen only shadows. Tony knew the difference.

He frowned as Henry was suddenly very visibly standing at CB's side. The big man put his hand on Henry's shoulder for a moment, nodded, smiled, and then Henry was gone.

Henry and CB?

Tony didn't like the look of that. His hand tightened around the keys.

Sure Henry came to the set on occasion and maybe he'd helped defeat the shadows last spring, but CB was his. CB Productions was his. Not Henry's.

What the hell had been going on out here?

"So the spirits have done it all in one night."

He grinned and met Amy halfway.

"I brought your laptop out."

"Thanks." Tucking it under his arm he fell into step beside her.

"I think he likes you."

"Who?"

"RCMP Special Constable Jack Elson. You guys going to get together?"

"I don't date straight boys."

"Right. They're taking Everett to the hospital," she said, breaking the chaos swirling around them into chunks. "Tina made some calls and she's going with him."

"Good."

"You should maybe think about a trip yourself. You look like crap."

"Maybe later. And thank you."

"There're cops swarming all over the bodies. They seem to get what happened with Brenda and Hartley, but Tom's giving them palpitations. Good thing there's a full body print of him on that window."

"Word."

"Brianna won't let go of Zev's hand, and Mason's actually being kind of sweet to Ashley. Although I think he's using her as a distraction, so he doesn't grab a smoke in front of witnesses. He's a star, you know, got to keep up appearances."

Mason was still wearing Raymond Dark's fangs. Ashley was still wearing Mason's jacket.

"Whatever works."

She snorted. "You're feeling mellow."

"It's not mellow, it's exhaustion. You know, that moment of clarity just before you puke?"

"And wouldn't that be the perfect end. Speaking of perfect ends, what have you got on your ass? And don't get too excited about the perfect bit," she added through a yawn. "It was just a convenient segue."

Between twisting and dragging his jeans around, he managed to see a small heart. Two pieces. Drawn in white paint, each line thick at the top and then trailing off at the end.

"I wrote half and Cassie wrote half . . ."

"So what is it?"

"I'm pretty sure it's a happy ending."

She bumped her shoulder with his. About as sucky as Amy got. Four-hundred-year-old vampires hugged. Amy bumped. "Speaking of, I think someone wants to talk to you."

He turned instinctively toward where Zev and Brianna stood by CB.

"Idiot." Amy took hold of his shoulders and turned him toward Lee sitting in the open back of an ambulance, a blanket draped over his slumped shoulders.

"He doesn't . . ."

She shoved him forward. "Yes, he does."

Yes, he did. That was obvious when Tony came closer.

"You okay?" Stupid question. The man was sitting in an ambulance.

"I guess. I don't know. They want to check me out. Thanks for . . . uh . . ."

"The T-shirt?" Tony offered hurriedly. He had no idea of how much Lee remembered of the basement, but he wasn't going to be the one to bring it up.

Lee stared at him for a long moment, then he smiled. There was nothing of Caulfield in it. Tony felt his heart start beating again as a fear he hadn't been willing to admit was banished. Since leaving the house, his heart had been having a rough time of it.

"Yeah. For the T-shirt."

"All right, Mr. Nicholas, let's go." The EMT began to step up into the ambulance, got a good look at Tony, and paused. "Has someone seen you?"

"Seen me?"

"Have you received attention from emergency personnel?"

Tony wondered if she always talked like that or if Lee's presence was making her self-conscious. "No."

"Wait right there." She pointed to a spot about a meter from the back of the ambulance. "There'll be another team along shortly. Now, Mr. Nicholas . . ."

Lee raised his head. "Could you give us a minute?"

She hesitated.

"Please."

And melted.

"But no more than a minute," she warned as she moved just out of eavesdropping range.

Lee took a deep breath. Hesitated. Visibly remembered their time limit and said quietly, "When I kissed you. I wasn't kissing Brenda's ghost."

Tony blinked, but it was still Lee. "Good," he managed. "And, you know, eww."

"Yeah."

That howling was back in his ears again. Not a siren

this time. "So what happens now?" he asked as the EMT tapped her watch and pointedly climbed on board.

Lee shrugged. "The show goes on."

"I meant . . ."

His smile held regret and something a little lost as the doors closed. "I know."

Tanya Huff

The Finest in Fantasy

SING THE FOUR QUARTERS	0-88677-628-7
FIFTH QUARTER	0-88677-651-1
NO QUARTER	0-88677-698-8
THE QUARTERED SEA	0-88677-839-5

The Keeper's Chronicles

SUMMON THE KEEPER	0-88677-784-4
THE SECOND SUMMONING	0-88677-975-8
LONG HOT SUMMONING	0-7564-0136-4

Omnibus Editions:

WIZARD OF THE GROVE   0-88677-819-0
(Child of the Grove & The Last Wizard)
OF DARKNESS, LIGHT & FIRE   0-7564-0038-4
(Gate of Darkness, Circle of Light & The Fire's Stone)

To Order Call: 1-800-788-6262

Tanya Huff

Victory Nelson, Investigator:
Otherworldly Crimes a Specialty

"Smashing entertainment for a wide audience"
—*Romantic Times*

"One series that deserves to continue"
—*Science Fiction Chronicle*

BLOOD PRICE
0-88677-471-3
BLOOD TRAIL
0-88677-502-7
BLOOD LINES
0-88677-530-2
BLOOD PACT
0-88677-582-5

To Order Call: 1-800-788-6262

DAW 20

Tanya Huff

The Confederation Novels

"As a heroine, Kerr shines. She is cut from the same mold as Ellen Ripley of the *Aliens* films. Like her heroine, Huff delivers the goods." *--SF Weekly*

VALOR'S CHOICE
0-88677-896-4

When a diplomatic mission becomes a battle for survival, the price of failure will be far worse than death...

THE BETTER PART OF VALOR
0-7564-0062-7

Could Torin Kerr keep disaster from striking while escorting a scientific expedition to an enormous spacecraft of unknown origin?

To Order Call: 1-800-788-6262

Kristen Britain

GREEN RIDER

As Karigan G'ladheon, on the run from school, makes her way through the deep forest, a galloping horse plunges out of the brush, its rider impaled by two black arrows. With his dying breath, he tells her he is a Green Rider, one of the king's special messengers. Giving her his green coat with its symbolic brooch of office, he makes Karigan swear to deliver the message he was carrying. Pursued by unknown assassins, following a path only the horse seems to know, Karigan finds herself thrust into in a world of danger and complex magic....   0-88677-858-1

FIRST RIDER'S CALL

With evil forces once again at large in the kingdom and with the messenger service depleted and weakened, can Karigan reach through the walls of time to get help from the First Rider, a woman dead for a millennium?   0-7564-0209-3

To Order Call: 1-800-788-6262

DAW 7

C.S. Friedman

The Coldfire Trilogy

"A feast for those who like their fantasies dark, and as
emotionally heady as a rich red wine." —*Locus*

Centuries after being stranded on the planet
Erna, humans have achieved an uneasy stale-
mate with the fae, a terrifying natural force with
the power to prey upon people's minds. Damien
Vryce, the warrior priest, and Gerald Tarrant, the
undead sorcerer must join together in an uneasy
alliance confront a power that threatens the very
essence of the human spirit, in a battle which
could cost them not only their lives, but the soul
of all mankind.

BLACK SUN RISING   0-88677-527-2
WHEN TRUE NIGHT FALLS   0-88677-615-5
CROWN OF SHADOWS   0-88677-717-8

To Order Call: 1-800-788-6262